# REBORN
## VOLUME III POWER OF THE BLOOD

### NANCY KILPATRICK

**PUMPKIN BOOKS**
**NOTTINGHAM**

Published in Great Britain by Pumpkin Books

An imprint of MeG Enterprises Limited
PO Box 297, Nottingham NG2 4GW, ENGLAND.
Also at http://www.netcentral.co.uk/~pumpkin

First edition, October, 1998

Trade paperback edition ISBN 1 901914 20 8

A CIP catalogue record for this book is available from the British
Library.

Printed in Great Britain by Cox & Wyman Ltd, Reading,
Berkshire

# *Acknowledgements*

Thanks for the love and other help to: Philippe Bourque; Christine Christolakis; Seph Giron; Alison Graham; Stephen Jones; Eric Kauppinen; Mike Kilpatrick; Mitch Krol; Hugues Leblanc; Eric Paradise; Michael Rowe; Mandy Slater; Caro Soles; Mari Anne Werier.

Thanks to these good folk for help with research: Sonja Barbe and Enrique Novella; Ezio Biasi; Daniel Dvorkin (aka Medic); Peter Kenter; Cathy Krusberg; Julie Leblanc and the researchers at St. Luc's: Marc, Pierre Pannumzio, Allan Hazeth, Julie L. Hildebrand; Caro Soles; Lois Tilton.

Special thanks to Rob Brautigam, without whose support I would never have visited Germany. To Fab Dulac for his wonderfully evocative poem. And I'm especially grateful to Hugues Leblanc for graciously reading over the manuscript and for keeping me sane throughout. The subscribers on Genie who read my topic gave me plenty of emotional support and encouragement during the writing of this book. And David Marshall of Pumpkin Books went the distance — he provided me with the opportunity to actualise what has been gestating in my mind for a decade.

Nancy Kilpatrick

"Hope is a waking dream."
Aristotle

# EVENING PRIMROSE

You who walk with shadows
Bruised flower heart
Here I am
Waiting for cold kisses
Hungry for the death
Can you feel my soul
I am afraid of you, of me
Into the dusk I hasten
Rain upon my face
Then you are against my neck
Hungry fingers at my breasts
My nipples bloodied petals
Shroud me within your wings
Inhale me, devour me
Leave me floating as your ghost
You who walk with shadows
Let my heart be the bruised flower in your arms
My nails the thorns upon your back
Here I am
Eager for your lips
Thirsty for your love
Here I am
Can you feel me?

Fabrice Dulac


"He lives not long who battles with the immortals..."

Homer

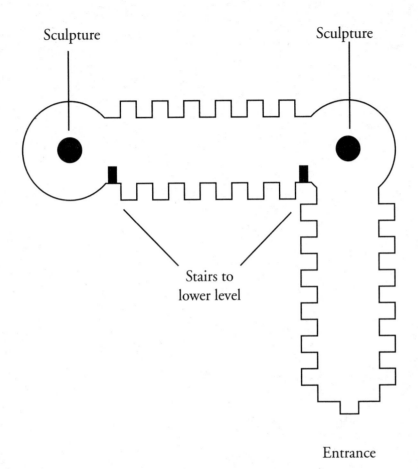

Sculpture

Sculpture

Stairs to
lower level

Entrance

## The Columbarium

This plan shows the overall shape of the Columbarium. The first
section of corridor by the entrance is single storey. The remainder
is built on two levels. The Exit is found at the left hand end of
the lower level corridor next to the stairs. The inner dentilations
all have windows. The roof and outer sections are terraced into
the hillside.

# Part 1

"For every complex problem, there is a solution that is simple, neat, and wrong."

H. L. Mencken

# CHAPTER ONE

D OMED AMBER STREET LIGHTS CREATED A turn-of-the-last-century feel, or at least that was how Michel imagined things had appeared one hundred years ago. He'd seen the look in period-piece movies. And sepia photographs. But he had existed on this earth less than two decades, not the century plus his Aunt Chloe had been walking the planet.

Michel and Chloe climbed the winding streets of the mountainside in silence. Eventually, the street reached a fork, right or left; straight ahead stood the wrought-iron gates of the small Jewish cemetery. This isolated graveyard lay protected from the other cemeteries on the mountain.

As they passed the locked gates, Michel stared in at the modern, crisp stones, so white, so low to the ground; a graveyard almost free of monuments. And no crypts. He'd been here several times, inside the gates, and although some of the inscriptions touched him, this cemetery as a whole did not inspire him in any way.

They turned right and slightly further up the hill approached the dead end, the arched stone gates of the Mount Royal Cemetery. From here, he did not see the enormous lighted cross that could be viewed from just about everywhere else in the city of Montréal. Crosses didn't bother his kind, although mortal legends said they should. But so much of the literature on vampires was false. And funny. He guessed it made good reading for somebody. Somebody he probably wouldn't find too interesting.

The large Gothic gates of stone and iron closed to vehicles at sunset, but conveniently, a small pedestrian gate stayed open. They entered there, by the guardhouse; Michel sensed the guard busily reading, not too interested in the two beings illegally entering the cemetery after hours.

1

This, the 'English' cemetery — although French were buried here as well — appeared relatively ordered. Grass mowed. Tombstones spaced well apart. No hidden sections. Few unusual stones. Oh, there was the monument just past the lawns, when the tombstones started. He and Chloe stopped to read it:

**THOS. LETT HACKETT, L.O.A.**
*who was barbarously murdered on Victoria Square*
*when quietly returning from Divine Services*
*12th July 1877.*
*This monument was erected by Orangemen and Protestants*
*of the Dominion as a tribute to his memory and to mark*
*their detestation of his murderers.*

"Think it was a political murder?" Michel asked.

"It could have been," Chloe said. "From the date."

"Could have been a bar brawl, too," Michel laughed. "But they sure are trying to convince everybody he was some kind of martyr."

"Mortals need to give death meaning. We are not so unlike them."

They walked up the wide path, up and up the hill. On the left in the distance against the trees he saw the enormous Molson crypt — the family that owned the brewery. It occupied a big area, and he'd come up through the woods around the other side a couple of times.

Further on stood the McArthur monument, white, pink and beige stonework, a mini temple with four pillars supporting its peaked roof and high reliefs. Three small-human-size angels leaned against the pillars — one had been stolen or broken years before. A century of pollution determined their colour, black; the colour was cool. Yes, there were definite attractions here. Once, when he was alone, he had stood at that fourth, empty pillar, pretending to be the missing angel. "The angel of death!" he cried in a macabre voice, raised his arms, palms to the sky. Then he let himself fall forward, face-down, onto the soft grass.

As they walked on, he saw the odd monument that resembled the rectangular boxes in European cathedrals where Popes and Cardinals and other high-religious types were buried. These blocks of marble were usually elaborate. He'd seen a few made of iron, now rusted. Often the graves were cordoned off with linked iron chain.

Michel and Chloe had chosen the eastern entrance, not because of its proximity to their home in Westmount, but because they had wandered all over the city that night and ended up circling the mountain. It didn't matter. There were hours yet till sunrise. Sunrise was sleep time for Chloe, but Michel could still bear the solar rays, although not as well as when he had been a kid.

A new moon hung high in the clear fall sky, washing the grounds with white light, illuminating the stones enough to make them appear to be whitewashed. They continued in sympatico silence, intuitively moving along the main path, turning up one of the side paths and not another at a crossroad, at the same moment synchronised by instinct, as if they knew where they were headed.

"I read there are more people alive now than have ever died. I did the calculations. I think it's true," Michel said.

Out of the corner of his eye, he saw movement. A red fox darted between the graves. The animal's sinuous muscles slid beneath it's furry skin. The eyes glinted red as it froze and stared at them, aware that it was in the vicinity of predators. Michel wouldn't harm it, and neither would Chloe, but they could, and the fox knew that. Good intentions only go so far with animals, Chloe once said, and he believed that was true.

Michel sensed mortals, an odd energy that changed the air, visually and intangibly, making it feel more solid yet electrical. With his sharp night vision, he scanned the hill beyond the fox. There! On a tombstone, surrounded on three sides by trees, sat a couple. No, the female sat, or more, reclined on top of the tombstone. The male stood between her open legs. They were naked. He realised what was happening, something that filled

3

him with endless curiosity. His sensitive ears picked up their rapid breathing, the slippery sound of their bodies connecting in wild passion. The man moved rhythmically. The woman moaned softly. And then the scent hit Michel, startling him: blood. The woman's menstrual blood. Released with each stroke, gushing down the stone face of the grave marker, turning the stone a brilliant red!

Suddenly, the fox bolted. It raced through the night. Michel heard a clack as its claws snapped a branch, desperate to create distance and therefore safety for itself, not from the fornicating mortals, but from Michel and Chloe.

Chloe had turned her head slightly to watch the animal, and the couple. "Sex and death," she said softly. "Mortals love the combination. I suspect we are not so different in this regard either."

The mortals were oblivious to the fox, and to the beings walking on the path who might make them permanent residents of this place they had chosen for intimacy.

A smile played on Chloe's full lips, so reminiscent of his own. Michel stared at his aunt's profile. Her white hair glinted silver in the moonglow. She was a striking woman. All of the females of his kind were attractive — it was their nature, he guessed, to look seductive, no matter at what age they had transformed — it was probably a survival thing. Not only were they seductive to mortals, they mesmerised one another. It was both defensive and offensive he knew, for his kind were a threat to each other, although he didn't have a really clear idea of that yet.

Chloe had the same Gallic features as his dad, features he had inherited — a strong chin, long nose, expressive almond eyes. Gerlinde said they all looked like models in a Renaissance painting, and he'd seen enough artwork to know it was true.

"The poor earth supports more life than it ever has," Chloe finally said, startling him, because he'd forgotten he'd even said anything. "That always amazes me. It's a fine gesture of the Great

Mother, the mother of us all, to nurture us, every one. But I wonder that her milk hasn't dried up by now."

They moved up the low hill, past the children's graveyard on the left, the ground dotted with little stones for small occupants six feet below. Simple markers — names, dates, sometimes a biblical quote — often adorned with a stone image. Baby lambs and fat cherubs were favoured. Someone had put a toy unicorn against one of the stones.

Michel wondered what it would be like to die. He would never die. He knew that now. He had made his decision, or at least most of the time he felt he had, although he had yet to believe that a mental choice could change anything. It wasn't much of a decision anyway, for what were the options? Grow old and expire, and alienate himself from his parents, and all the others in his community? Or be part of their world forever and continue to embrace its riches. Forever, or for at least as long as their kind could survive. No-one had yet figured out the scope of their longevity, but the oldest they knew about was over seven hundred years. He could barely imagine such a time frame. He'd only been breathing for fifteen.

But things were changing. He was changing, and that felt disconcerting. He could still tolerate the world of daylight, although clearly not for much longer. His skin had become far more sensitive as he consumed less and less solid food and relied only on blood. He would not envision a life where he could never again look up at the blue sky and stare at the brilliant sun, and yet everyone he was close to had existed without sunlight for a long time. He wondered if he would miss it. The others did, because sometimes he heard them talk about the sun in the same reverent tones he'd heard priests and rabbis discuss God, or Buddhists mention the Buddha, or the way Moslems referred to Allah. The sun became to his kind a holiest of holies, something always out of reach and yet eminently desirable. He had a hard time imagining feeling that way, and yet how else would he feel once he was deprived of sunlight permanently?

But his days were still filled with mortals, all around him, sometimes suffocating him with their smells that became almost tangible, as if he could taste the air wafting scent from their bodies, or the breath emitted from their nostrils. Already he felt their heartbeats within him like the vibrations of eternal drums. He watched and heard air passing through their porous lungs, listened to the digestive juices squishing in their stomachs and intestines. At times, the stimulus was nearly unbearable. His mother told him he'd get used to such sensory overload and learn to block it out, except when he hunted, which he had yet to do. Maybe that was so. Maybe not. At the moment, it felt that he would be this way forever. Even now, though he and Chloe had moved away, he could still hear the panting, the wet sounds of the two on the hill as they approached mutual orgasm, and that both aroused and terrified him, for the feelings were so strong. And then he heard them laughing together, kissing...

He had to admit that he found mortals fascinating. They lived as though they would live forever, and yet that was not so. He wondered how their minds worked, how they could disregard death until they were boxed in, forced to open that door with trembling hands. They were so mysterious to him. And a few — around his age — he found incredibly appealing, although most youth he thought appalling. They acted stupidly, and had developed coarse, false mannerisms that offended him. Their concerns were banal, and only peripherally jelled with his own. His wider scope had been expanding and developing since his birth. He couldn't help being the way he was. The world of his kind was one these blood-bearers hardly dared dream about, and yet he lived it. All the time. It was his reality. And none of the books and movies on what they called 'vampires' came anywhere near to capturing his experience, so how could these mortals relate to him?

The worst part of being around mortals was his changing attitudes. Now he felt attracted for new reasons. More and more, he was aware of their sexual energy, and equally aware of the *vitae* pumping through their veins. He saw them as fresh, succulent food, which both excited and disturbed him. He had yet to get a handle on these conflicting appetites which rocked him to a greater and greater extent every second of his life. His father said to relax. He was an adolescent. He would have his passions under his control, in time, and when he began to take blood from human veins, that would help. Michel didn't feel all that convinced. After all, his parents, nobody in his community had gone through what he was going through. None of them had been born to this existence, they had all been created. His feelings vacillated in such an extreme way that a lot of the time he just wanted to run and hide. From everything. And everyone. Especially from himself.

They reached the low fence separating the two main cemeteries — someone had left open the narrow gate again. Just on both sides of the fence were the military graves, standardised whiter-than-white thin curved stones with crosses etched into them, and little maple leaf flags stuck into the ground marking a tribute to each soldier.

Farther up the hill, the chapel that held the urns with ashes came into view. The building contained drawers, with dying flowers tied to the handles, and colourful funereal lamps lining the floor. Sometimes there were photographs of the dead one. He didn't like this building much, but far preferred it to the underground vaults. Those, so modern, airless, so hideously medical that it was like being in a sterile laboratory beneath ground where the dead were not truly dead, just packed away until some unsuspecting being walked through... Maybe he'd seen too many horror movies, but that place gave him the creeps. If he were to die, he certainly hoped his remains would never be stored in a such a gruesome location.

They were now in *le cimetière Notre-Dame-des-Neiges*, commonly called the Côte des Neiges Cemetery, the French cemetery. Stones dating back to the early 1800s congested the sloped land. Maybe it was cellular, but instantly he relaxed and felt 'home', part of a community. His cultural ancestors lay here, and he found that comforting and reassuring.

Lights from candles and lanterns dotted the crowded hills and valleys, glowing spectral guideposts, beckoning night visitors this way, or that. A variety of designs and materials had been used over nearly two centuries and this view of graves surrounding the trees felt chaotically familiar to Michel, as if he belonged here.

"Do you think I'm morbid?" he suddenly asked his aunt.

Chloe gave him a quick hug. "No more morbid than I am. This cemetery is so lovely and peaceful. Why would you say that?"

"Well, they're all dead. But I like it here. Are you afraid of death?"

Chloe looked a little wistful. "Michel, I did die. We all did."

"I didn't."

"No, but you are exceptional."

He hated it when they said this. Just because he was the only one who had been born of mortal woman and one of their kind — well his mother had been mortal then, but his dad brought her over —

"We all went through death, Michel. It's a miraculous process. To be born, to live, to die, and then to be reborn."

He had been born, and was living a life. But he wouldn't die. Something about that seemed so strange. So wrong. Most of the time it was okay, but sometimes it made him feel a bit... cheated. And lonely. Was he the only being in existence who would never die? How could that be? "But, when you died... were you afraid?"

"Yes. I suppose everyone is. And in my case, it came so suddenly, the attack..."

She'd never really talked about it, although he had the overview. His aunt, David, Karl and some of the others had been taken by one of their kind they called Antoine. He was, they said, insane. Michel had seen him once, in action. He'd been ten years old but, like some terrifying nightmare in his memory, it had an impact that stayed with him. He didn't like thinking about those days he'd been kidnapped.

"Would you tell me about what happened? When... Antoine changed you? What it was like?"

Chloe just stared straight ahead for a moment. "Let me think about it."

They climbed another hill, and took a narrower path, towards the giant crypts buried in the earth. Only the doors and front walls lay exposed. Michel stopped before a particularly ornate door of curved metal grillwork. Inside, dusty wooden coffins had been piled on top of coffins, in turn resting on heavy iron bars, half a dozen in all. In one corner near the air vent at the roof three baby coffins had been haphazardly stacked, tiny things, black wood, chevron-shaped, each unique, with ornate metal handles... They had all died. Every one of them. Yet he would not...

Michel liked looking into the crypts. The iron-earth odour appealed to him. It reminded him a bit of the taste of blood. There was also the scent of decomposition, since embalming hadn't been invented back when most of these people died. Time travel must be like this, he thought, catching the scent of another era, of time compressed into a small space.

The next crypt had a heavy iron door, with a few small holes in it, like bullet holes. With his acute vision, he could see clearly through the holes into the gloom. An old broken kneeling chair, the back with it's armrest high, the seat low to the ground, the fabric mouldy and the straw stuffing long ago rotted... A lovely glass and brass lantern sat on top of a coffin. From what year? he wondered. Who had put it there? Who knelt on that chair, and who did they grieve for? How many years had those dried flowers lain on top of that now rusted metal coffin? How long had the tarnished silver crucifix hung on the back wall collecting the dust of the ages? Etched in the stone above the door was the name Leblanc. Who had come to mourn the Leblanc's? Did anyone still come? What was it like to mourn the loss of someone you loved who died?

9

He had mourned for no-one, for no-one he'd been close to had died. And he'd only known one who died — one of his captors — but he felt nothing about that although he had been a witness to the death. He felt nothing yet all the others of his kind experienced that demise in a personal way, a physical way, something he could not comprehend. His world felt small, and he longed to break out and explore the larger realms of physical and emotional reality. He sensed that something lay beyond what he knew and he heard a call, like a siren luring him. He did not care whether it was to life or to death — the fact that he could not be certain of the outcome made it all the more exciting. He just wanted to, needed to go and follow that song, as if it were the call of his own heart and to ignore it would spell doom.

They had wandered along the main paths, back down, further down. So many graves. So many dead.

"This way," Chloe said, and he knew where she was leading him. A slight diversion. Towards the Cotroni monument, a large white sculpture of an angel kissing the head of the reclining figure. It was incredibly lovely, and Chloe's favourite in the cemetery.

They stood before the monument, the lines of the marble so fluid, the sweetness of the gesture very touching.

"I was alone, of course," Chloe said suddenly.

Michel wondered what she was talking about, but then it became clear — her encounter with Antoine.

"He came to me one night, in my bedroom. Why me, why that small village near Bordeaux, why that time?... I've asked myself what twisted Karma I had had to live out, but there are no answers to such questions. I didn't know him. He did not know me. As far as I can determine, there seemed no reason for him choosing me."

She said nothing more for moments, and Michel wondered how to get her to continue. "I know our kind often seduce mortals —"

"This was no seduction! It was an attack!" She cut him short with a tone unmistakable.

"I'm sorry. I didn't mean to upset —"

"I'm not upset with you, Michel. The incident upsets me, although it was almost two hundred years ago. The sheer violence... the malevolence of what occurred is something that will always be with me. He tore at my body like a rabid animal. Half my throat was ripped away. One breast was gouged. The flesh of my arms and legs and particularly my genitals... as though he had a special hatred for females. Although now, of course, after speaking with Karl and David, I see this was not the case. There are others who were turned by him centuries ago, and Antoine must have been different then. Less barbaric, although still vicious."

Michel could feel Chloe's terror and fury. He slipped an arm around his aunt's shoulder, and the vibrations from her body made him feel very protective. He could hardly imagine the violence she had suffered. Antoine, from his brief encounter with him, had seemed deranged. Still, he had had no direct dealings with him after he had been kidnapped in the park. The ride in the van. Then the train station. Then David. During all that, Antoine had been a silent figure in the background. He said little, but his energy felt malignant, and Michel steered clear of him.

And then there was the night on Fire Island. Antoine had been there, challenging with his soldiers, and Julien had led Michel's parents and the others like an army, and Michel had to go along because they couldn't leave him alone. It seemed so long ago, and the details had faded in his memory. He only knew that all of this had centred around him, and some power Antoine wanted from him. A power Michel could not understand, because he couldn't sense it within himself, although his mother and father and the others seemed to agree he possessed it.

Chloe started to relax a bit. She reached up and patted his hand and laid her head against his shoulder. "The experience of being taken so brutally was nothing compared to my awakening. I was alone. In my coffin. Six feet beneath the earth. Of course, no-one could have known, since strictly speaking I was not alive by normal standards. But clearly, I was not dead."

Michel felt horrified. "I didn't know you were buried alive!"

"Yes."

A chill ran through him. He could only imagine what that must have been like.

"In those days in that region it was fashionable for a bell to be hung over the grave, with a chain stretching down through the dirt into the coffin — in case the deceased was not really dead, they could ring the bell and be exhumed."

"Did you ring the bell?"

"My body was so mutilated there was no question in the minds of my loved ones that I was gone. They did not bother with a bell."

"How did you escape your grave?"

"In a very traditional manner." She shifted slightly, and moved a few steps, breaking the contact. Chloe placed her hand on the head of the angel. "I clawed my way out."

"Wow!"

"Coffins were still made of wood then. And the earth was shovelled in, not ploughed as today. And, of course, bodies were not embalmed. Fortunately, it had rained and while it is not easy to dig through mud, it was easier than if the soil had been dry and hard-packed. It took me the better part of two nights, and then when I neared the surface, half crazed, starving, not yet knowing what I was, I had to rebury myself as the sunlight struck me, and wait for a veil of darkness before I could emerge."

"But you love cemeteries!" Michel blurted. He could not see why.

"I suppose one is always attracted to the place where trauma struck. As Carl Jung said, our greatest wound is our greatest blessing, and the place where healing can occur. Come," she said, and, much to his dismay, they headed down the hill.

"Once I'd surfaced, I returned home, naturally. Where does one go when one returns from the dead? Most of my children were adults, and married, and they took me in, of course, rejoicing that a mistake had been made. Still, they were clearly troubled.

The severe wounds Antoine had made healed very quickly — the thought was that I had been attacked by a wolf, since wolves were still prevalent in Europe then. Those wolves, not like the ones we see today, were larger, more feral. They are the basis of the werewolf legends.

"My eldest daughter and her husband gave me a room. They thought I was exhausted, and let me sleep several days. Surreptitiously, I awoke at night and made my way through the house, watching them and their children — my grandchildren — sleeping. Plagued by hungers which I could not identify yet instinctively knew were a threat to my family.

"You know how we see mortals. How we feel the blood, can hear it pulsing through veins, can smell its coppery fragrance even before the skin is pierced. All this and more I experienced acutely. I had not as yet fed. I was weak, yet the hunger became obsessive and it took all my strength to not indulge. Finally, after a week passed, I had to flee. There was no other way. I did not know what I was but I knew I was a danger to the ones I loved."

"Where are we going?" Michel asked, although he felt he knew. They were headed towards the Columbarium, the modern underground vaults. The place gave him the creeps. For some reason, Chloe always wanted to walk through there. He didn't know why, didn't want to know, but as the entrance came into view, he steeled himself for what would be an unpleasant experience.

"I just want to check on the new burials," she said. "I want to make sure there is still burial space."

"But why?" he asked.

"You never know when you might need to find an eternal home for a loved one."

"How can you stand this place?" he asked. "I find it scary, like something in a horror movie."

She looked at him and laughed. "I'm so much older than you. I suppose that the intensity of the compressed space beneath ground compels me in some way. And it reminds me of my burial."

"Then why go in there?"

"Maybe I'm trying to relive it all. Find a way to purge myself of the memories."

That made sense to him mentally but not emotionally. The last thing he wanted to do was relive anything painful. Maybe when people got older they changed. Maybe they wanted to face frightening things. He didn't know for sure. What he did know was that it wasn't in his plan.

"Michel, why don't you walk around and meet me at the exit."

He felt relieved that she suggested it.

The Columbarium felt a little like a space station to him, but not one he liked to visit without a lot of mental preparation. Karl had turned him on to science and he'd been a Trek fan for years. He no longer played with it of course, but he still treasured the phaser Karl had bought him when he was a kid. He'd given it to his mother when everybody was giving her gifts, but later she told him she wanted to loan it to him — an extended loan — and he kept it on his wall.

He thought of the Columbarium as L2 — Legrange Point 2 where a space station might be placed — and also a structure of two different levels. It was built into the hillside, to make the most effective use of the land, Chloe said. Overall, it was a crude design, two rectangles of equal length joined to form an 'L' shape. There was a circular area where the two rectangles met, and another one at the exit end. He'd seen a diagram of the interior, and thought the whole thing looked like two keys, at right angles. The image of two keys worked for him because each of the corridors had six short passages on both sides. He wondered whether the architect was making a joke — keys to open the Pearly Gates!

The Columbarium ran the length of a couple of city blocks, embedded in a giant mound of grassy earth. All you really saw from outside were the entrance and exit doors, twelve small windows on the one side, and two skylights let into the top of the hill where the circular areas were. At night, the space station effect was accentuated because the cemetery was so dark, and they left the dim yellow lights of the Columbarium on. A space station floating in hell, he thought, hating this place.

Chloe could stay in there for quite a while, and usually did. If he went with her he would be uncomfortable the whole time.

"Okay," he said quickly. "I'll meet you at the other end."

"Fine," she kissed him on the cheek.

Chloe turned and continued on to the door. It was locked, of course, but she used the keys she had made so that she could go there whenever she wanted. He turned away and headed for the line of crypts along the path, old structures, up a little rise.

The old crypts here were as fascinating as the ones they had just visited. He could walk across to the next one without going down and up the steps, like a mailman who just steps over the fence to the next house without descending and ascending. Most of the doors were solid, but a few had openings. Within were all types of caskets. The mouldy smell was intriguing. One crypt held two coffins, and a plaque outside said they were married, Natasha-Louise and Jacques-François, and had both died young. He wondered what it would be like to have sex in there. Likely that couple he saw had sex in a crypt. Kinky. Of course, he wondered what it would be like to have sex at all! Except with himself, which he knew about.

There was one girl he'd met recently, outside a movie. He went with Gerlinde and Karl, and the girl was with three of her girlfriends. She had short, spiky hair, dyed a pale shade of blue. And she had long extensions in black that made her head look like a spider, which he thought cool. He found the ring in her lower lip particularly sexy and wondered what it would be like to kiss someone with a pierced lip.

She gazed up at him with shiny almond-shaped eyes lined in black make-up, and smiled. He felt embarrassed. Mortal females were always embarrassing him, although he knew they found him attractive. It was his nature, of course.

He didn't know what to do, but smiled back.

"Looks like a good movie," she said.

He felt stupid and nodded, still smiling, wondering why he was so stunned.

Gerlinde turned at that moment, opened her mouth to say something, then closed her mouth and turned away, for which he was grateful. Gerlinde was pretty funny, but now was not the time for one of her clever remarks.

"I... I saw the first one," he said.

"Me too."

Now what?

"The leather coats were great."

"Oh yeah! *De la belle confection. C'est sûr!*" She spoke franglais, like so many people in Montréal, a blend of French and English.

"*J'aimerais en avoir un.*"

"*Moi aussi!*"

Well, they'd both like to own a coat from the movie. They had something in common. But then the line started moving, and she turned back to her friends, and he moved ahead with Karl and Gerlinde. They sat about half way down, Karl's choice, and the girl sat with her friends near the front. At one point, she turned in her seat and scanned the crowd, as if searching for familiar faces. Their eyes locked, and she smiled again and waved. He'd just lifted his hand to wave back when she turned away.

And then the movie played, and he spent most of it watching the back of her head. She laughed a lot with her friends. Ate popcorn. Drank Coke through a straw. Scratched her nose. He liked the way she leaned over to whisper in her friend's ear, and how the hair extensions flipped like the tails of snakes. In fact, all of these actions, so simple, so ordinary, he found compelling.

And by the time the movie ended — and he missed most of it going through mental machinations about what to do or not do — he vowed to go and ask for her phone number.

He left Gerlinde and Karl, saying he'd meet them out front, and chased the four girls who were leaving through a side exit. He caught up with them as they emerged laughing on the street.

Suddenly, he felt nervous. This was such a stupid idea! How could he just ask her for her phone number? She didn't even know him, so she wouldn't give it to him, of course. She'd think he was some sleaze or something.

He walked past them, but not far, stopped, and looked up the street, wishing he smoked, or at least had a cigarette and he could pretend he smoked.

He was afraid to turn back. Afraid she wouldn't notice him. Or remember him. Or worse, that she would see him and turn away, ignoring him, revealing the truth that he had entertained for the last hour and a half — that she was just being nice, as she would be to anyone. There was no special interest. He was deluding himself, seeing attraction where there was none. How humiliating that rejection would be. And embarrassing.

But now she was walking past him with her friends. And then her head turned, and she smiled and said, "Like the movie?"

"Yeah, it was cool."

"It wasn't as good as the first one."

"No, I guess not."

Her girlfriends had stopped and were chatting to each other, giggling a bit, tossing secret looks his way. He felt awkward, silly. How could he just blurt out that he wanted her phone number?

"We're going for coffee. Want to come?"

He did want to go. But he'd left Karl and Gerlinde at the other side of the theatre. And he hadn't eaten yet, and maybe that would put an edge on things that shouldn't be there, and... "Uh, sure. I just have to tell my friends. Where are you going, and I'll meet you?"

17

"Bring them."

The last thing he wanted to do was bring Karl and Gerlinde on a date, if this was a date, which it wasn't. "Uh, I think they have to get home. They're older..."

"OK. We don't know where we're going, so we'll wait for you here."

"OK," he said, backing away quickly. "I'll be right back."

He saw her friends circle her, as if probing for information. He ducked back into the theatre.

"Can't come in here," an usher said.

"Uh, I was here. I just saw the movie. I have to get to the main entrance to meet friends —"

"Go around," the usher said, a pimply-faced youth on a power trip.

Michel hated to do it, but he used his hypnotising abilities to plant a seed of compliance in the usher's mind and, within seconds, he was rushing through the empty theatre, past the other ushers clearing away empty popcorn boxes, soft drink cups and candy wrappers.

Karl and Gerlinde were engaged in an embrace, kissing in public. He didn't care about that, but they weren't young, even though they looked in their twenties. And they'd been together for so long and he couldn't figure out why they couldn't save it for the bedroom. Even as he thought that, he chided himself. Most of the time he thought it was cute. Sweet. He hoped if he ever found anybody to love that they would be that affectionate and in love after so long a time. Still, there were so many attractive people, he found it hard to envision being with the same person for decades...

"Hi, guys," he said, breaking up their *tête-à-tête*.

"Hey! Where's the girl?" Gerlinde said, cutting right to the point, as usual.

"She's on the other side. Wants to go for coffee."

"Great! It will be nice to eat some new people," Gerlinde said. "Oh, did I say 'eat'? I meant 'meet'."

"Uh, well, I was thinking you two might like to be alone."

"Not really," Gerlinde said. "We've been alone together for three nights in a row. Karl's ready to drive a stake through my heart."

"Hardly," Karl laughed. "But I think Michel might like to be alone with her."

"Oh." Gerlinde suddenly twigged. "Well, make sure you're home by midnight."

"It's twelve thirty now," Michel reminded the woman who had acted as his mother when his own mother had been missing.

"I meant tomorrow midnight. As the bat flies. Ta, sweetie." She kissed his cheek, and Karl patted his arm, and they left.

Michel tried to get through the theatre again, but there were too many people at the entrance and he couldn't manage it. He rushed around the long block in time to see the girl and her friends at the corner in a crowd of people. They were crossing the street when he caught up with them.

"We thought you weren't coming," she said.

"I told you I'd be right back." He didn't mean to sound harsh, but it had scared him that she was already leaving, and he'd only been gone a few minutes. Suddenly, he realised that things were different. The four females were with four males. The girl he had pursued, who he thought was interested in him, took the arm of one of the guys. Now he was really confused. He just wanted to escape.

"Uh, listen," he said, trying to get her attention. She turned and smiled at him, that brilliant smile again, but not letting go of the arm she held. "I came back to say I can't make it. Maybe some other time, okay?"

"Sure. Another time. See you." And she turned away.

He left them at the other side of the street, watching them walk away. Clearly they all knew one another. If she had a boyfriend, why was she flirting with him? Or had she been? Maybe he was wrong. Maybe it was just being friendly. Maybe the guy was her brother or something. Or just a friend.

Whatever, he felt his heart sink. He didn't know what to think about all this, where to go with it. He spent hours walking the streets through the rain, and still, nothing was clear to him. He waited to return home until the sun broke the horizon. That night, the last thing he had wanted to face was Karl and Gerlinde, or his mother and father, and have any of them probe him for details about this girl.

The last crypt came into view, just around a corner, separate from the others, and he looked through the grate. This was a crypt devoted to nuns. Inside were simple dark coffins, quietly resting one on top of another. Nothing spectacular.

He'd taken his time, to give Chloe the time she needed to soak up the morbid environment she longed to be in. He walked a little until he could see the exit, but she hadn't emerged yet. Above, the sky was beginning to lose some of its darkness, and his Swatch said it was an hour till sunrise. They were fairly close to home. Plenty of time to get there.

He walked to the exit and waited outside. Even peering through the glass doors upset him. It was as though some malevolent presence existed in this modern, surgically clean tunnel. How was it he could look into crypts, even into open graves and see the bones spilling out of shattered coffins and not be repulsed, and yet walking through those corridors filled him with dread?

He climbed up the mound. In the darkness, the dim light coming from the skylights drew him. He looked down into the skylight nearest the exit. Nothing to see. He moved along the mound to the second skylight and walked all round it, peering down. He could see both the upper and lower levels, the railings on each, and the hideous metal sculpture that extended from the ground almost to the skylight. He also saw a bird flying around near the skylight, stopping just short of the glass, looking for an exit it would not find. On second glance, he realised it was not a bird but a small bat. He felt an instinct to rescue it, but then he'd have to go inside to do that, and he didn't want to be inside.

Finally, he went to the exit to wait. Chloe had said there was a reason this place was called a Columbarium, which meant a storage house for homing pigeons. There were small boxes inside for ashes, but most of the building was a mausoleum for bodies. Officially, the place was a mausoleum and a columbarium, but why everybody called the whole thing a Columbarium he didn't know. Chloe, who had a kind of spiritual outlook about everything, said it was like the souls were being stored till the resurrection, then they would fly home like birds, which was all the Christian belief system.

He examined the younger trees in this more open area, to see what shape they were in from last winter's ice storms. He carved pictures in the dirt with a stick, pretending to draw in hieroglyphics, imagining that somebody would spot it tomorrow and wonder. But finally, when he checked his watch again, he realised another half hour had gone by — Chloe had been in there for ninety minutes. She'd probably lost track of time. She could stand being outdoors right before dawn, but still, it would leave her exhausted for days, and he didn't imagine she wanted that. He felt he had to rescue her and unfortunately, that meant going in.

With a frustrated sigh, he used a skeleton key from the ring each of them carried to open the door. The second he pulled on the handle, he felt something was very wrong, but he couldn't identify what. All he could focus on was the intense smell of embalming fluid. It was the smell in this building that always got to him, and it was worse than ever.

"Chloe?" His voice sounded hesitant to his own ears. He called a few more times, but there was no response. There was no way around it. Reluctantly, he stepped into this underground house of the immaculate dead.

# CHAPTER TWO

T HE MOMENT THE INNER DOORS SHUT BEHIND
Michel, the air closed around him. It was like being inside
a giant plastic bag in a freezer. Every molecule froze, turning
from gas or liquid to solid, or so it felt. He could not breathe. Yet
he did. And what he inhaled made him retch: an overwhelming
stink of embalming fluid, crushing the odour of rotting flesh.

"Chloe?" he called. Silence. His mind, locked in panic,
moved aside to give autonomic responses full sway. Let the body
do what it was doing anyway, don't make it harder, he thought.
Then, this is crazy! It's just a place for remains. Get a grip!

By will alone, he moved forward ten paces to the long
corridor, although the elements seemed to be working against
him, trying to hold him back.

He glanced left. It was no more than forty feet to the end of
the corridor. There, it opened out into a circle, and that was it.
To his right he could see the length of the corridor, with six side
passages or branches on each side, the whole thing leading to
another circle at the far end.

He had been here before — too often, it seemed to him at
the moment — and knew the second corridor which he was in
was composed of two levels. He turned right and forced himself
to move through the lower level, but it was like walking in slow
motion, or through a heavy, thick substance that would not allow
his limbs free rein.

On each side of him were high walls composed of big marble
squares, like drawers, large enough to hold a coffin within, which
they did. Each square of white marble had been 'decorated' with
a horrible green marble cone with a round low-watt light in it.
Most were lit. The lights are on, he thought, somebody's home.
And that gave him the creeps.

As he walked, the 'drawers' as he thought of them —
although there were no handles — held names, dates and

sometimes pictures. Glassy two-dimensional eyes stared at him. The ones that bothered him most were the hazy photos in black and white, where the grain was large, and the image poor, making the person look like a ghost.

The lighting went beyond subdued. He had never been to a funeral home, but assumed this was what would best create a mood of bereavement. And, in his case, terror. He had no idea why he feared the Columbarium, but he did, and that was good enough for him. Or bad enough.

As Michel came to each pair of branches he looked left, then right. The branches were about ten feet in length. Those going to windows were straightforward enough. But the ones leading into the hillside had indentations right and left, where the branch met the back wall. Someone could hide there, he thought, then wondered what was wrong with him. *He* was the supernatural being. The one with inordinate strength. The one mortals were afraid of. He had the edge, so why was he shivering?

As if to steady his nerves, he moved a bit faster, and soon approached the connecting circular area. The stairs leading to the upper level were to his right, set into the corridor wall just before the circle. With the whole of the upper level still to check, he had to go up at this point. Just before he entered the stairwell, he walked into the circle and glanced up the two floors to the skylight. The bat was still there, trapped. Thank god for sonar, he thought. The poor thing flitted back and forth hysterically, stopping short of one pane, then heading toward the one opposite in the octagonal skylight, stopping short again, reversing direction, desperate to escape. Michel knew how it felt. He thought when he reached the upper level he might try to rescue it, although the skylight was pretty high up.

It suddenly occurred to him as if lightning had zapped his brain that Chloe must be outside. He couldn't sense her inside the building, and she didn't answer him, so she must have gone out the entrance as he came in the exit. That made sense, and he thought he was an idiot to not think of that sooner.

He went back to the exit door and outside. Fresh, crisp air rained over him like a shower of sanity, and he realised just how frightened he'd been. And how oppressed. The odour of embalming fluid still clung to his nostrils — how disgusting that he could still smell it outdoors! He took a second to enjoy the freedom of the graveyard, and to clear out his nose, but then realised he did not sense Chloe out here. "Chloe?" he called. He could almost feel the sound on the air.

For a fraction of a moment he had a feeling that there was someone, somewhere... But no, now that he focused, there was nothing, just a now faint scent of embalming fluid. Given how unsettled he felt, that didn't seem odd at all. Why was he so nervous? He could only wonder at his extreme reaction to this mass grave, for that's what it was. Canals of marble, and that horrible smell, and just beneath it, struggling to get through, the stink of rotting flesh. On top of that were all the things Chloe had said, her macabre attitude toward the Columbarium. No doubt that contributed to what he already felt.

Light filtered through the eastern sky. He could survive the daylight well enough. At least soon he could go home and forget it. He wouldn't have to lie in bed wondering if his aunt was trapped somewhere. Chloe could not survive outdoors in daylight, although she could resist sleep if in total darkness. She must have just left. Yet, that was so unlike her. But what other explanation could there be? He couldn't sense her. He was wasting his time. He'd find her at home. Asleep. Maybe she had something to do she forgot about and didn't have time to find him. That had to be it.

No matter how he tried to rationalise it, though, he knew he was too driven a personality just to give up the search until he'd walked every inch of this hideous place. Besides, it was now a point of honour to get through the damned Columbarium, and to know he could do it. It was too easy to look for an excuse to avoid finishing.

He ducked his head back inside the exit doors. No, she wasn't in here either. Still, he called her name, just in case.

Reluctantly, he stepped in and the doors shut behind him. He paused. Nothing in the building either, just the bat, probably a fruit bat. And yet the feeling of... how could he put it?... ethereal intangibility?... yeah, that would sum it up nicely, he thought — if you were talking to a psycho!

All right, bury it!, he told himself, and a nervous, staccato laugh burst out of him — bury it! What sick humour!

Chloe *could* have gone home. But she was not like that. She wouldn't have left without telling him, and she'd said she would meet him at the exit and it wasn't like her not to meet him if she said she would. Even with the impending sunrise. At the very least, she would have left him a note. Well, not a note, but some communication he would see and understand. And he didn't linger at the crypts that long. And he would have felt her presence if she'd exited. And she would have felt his and found him — he wasn't that far from the exit...

But more than from all his tormented thoughts, he knew something was not right. Intuition told him that, and both of his parents had been careful to teach him to respect his intuition, since it could save his life.

Okay, he thought, she isn't outside, she isn't inside. But he would need to investigate the entire edifice beneath the earth and then tour around the outside of the structure before he could go home. And then there was the older, smaller mausoleum across the path, which was like the Columbarium... He didn't want to think about that. He hated this compulsion to be so thorough, but it seemed to be in his nature, and he just had to make sure.

Again, the scent of embalming fluid nearly knocked him over. Maybe one of the bodies opened up and there's a leak or something, he thought. Or there's a couple of newbes in here stinking up the place. But he was especially sensitive to smells, like his dad. And his kind could pick up the scent of a rose three blocks away. Something this intense to begin with, locked in this frigid, enclosed space... it was impossible.

Impossible or not, he mounted the steps immediately to his left next to the exit circle. The stairwell was narrow, cold concrete, and oppressive; he felt trapped. If someone, or something was hiding in here... How about sticking with reality! he ordered himself.

He emerged on to the upper level, almost relieved. At least up here the two corridors connected, so he'd just have to walk straight through to the doors at the entrance, except for checking those damn branches!

He called her name as he went, desperate to break up the eerie feeling the Columbarium had on him, hoping for a reply that did not come. Periodically, when he went down a branch with a window, he would peer out of it, searching for, hoping for some sign of her. But the cemetery outside was still, still as death, he thought, lit only by the light of a half-hidden moon. And then he forced himself to return to the corridor and continue inside this oppressive, spooky environment. In here, where there was no air not laced with embalming fluid, where the cold weighed him down to the floor, where the lighting caused everything to seem artificial and created unusual shadow patterns, it felt as if the dead were about to come alive, like in so many horror movies he'd seen. You'd turn around and there would be one, mindless, less than human, sitting in the open drawer, staring at you with one thought in mind, one all-consuming passion. And behind that corpse, there would be another, and another...

Wow! he thought. This is how mortals see us. Maybe it was his mortal side that brought out such strange thoughts. This would be a great place for a Halloween party, it occurred to him, and that bit of lightness lifted his spirits.

But then, almost instantly, he broke into a cold, clammy sweat that clung to the shirt on his back and his pants at the back of his knees. "Now you're scaring yourself!" he muttered, faking it, as if his own voice would sound like the reassuring voice of another. As if he could convince himself that he was not as alone as he knew himself to be. Not as afraid.

Although he took one step, then another, the corridor seemed endless. And disappointing. He knew his aunt was not here, but he had to walk to the connecting circle at the end of the claustrophobia-inducing space anyway. Passing the many dozens of drawers that lined the walls containing mouldering bodies. Inhaling that god-awful odour. He glanced back over his shoulder despite telling himself how ridiculous that was.

And the branches! He half expected to come face to face with some Romero zombie, flesh rotting away, vacant gaze... And as he came to each branch he steeled himself then called up more steel in his backbone. He had to go down each branch because, at the far end, by the wall, there were those stupid indentations, body-sized pockets, where anyone could hide...

He moved back to the middle of the main corridor and continued down it, trying not to feel intimidated by the drawers of dead piled to the high ceilings. But the walls towered over him and made the space narrower than he knew it to be. Who had this weird idea, he wondered, of cramming the resting dead in drawers? Like the coroners' storage drawers he'd seen in so many movies and on TV shows, except these were not stainless steel but marble, and somehow that made them less antiseptic and more disturbing.

The carpet cushioned his boots so his movements became soundless. This corridor stretched endlessly in front of him. He knew there was nothing in the other corridor that led to the entrance except the odd tiny bench with angels and cherubs in the pattern of the fabric of the seat. It all made him feel suffocated. And this is so dumb! he reminded himself. Chloe is not here. You can't sense her. Which meant she had already gone and must be waiting outside for him. He knew it was the human part of him that made him call her name repeatedly. And loudly. Sensing would be enough. If there's something to sense, he reminded himself. All he could sense in here was that the walls were closing in on him, and the smell of embalming fluid made him almost dizzy. But he needed some reassurance, despite not wanting to need that, and the sound of her name on his lips helped.

The Columbarium wasn't that big, and it was taking him a long time to get through, but everything felt so unreal to him in this vault with hundreds of dead buried in one stifling space.

Finally, he reached the circle that led to the second corridor. He stopped to look at the small glass doors here, behind which were urns and boxes holding ashes. More pictures and names of the deceased. They reminded him of a movie he'd seen, set in the 1930s. The restaurant was an 'automat'. You put your money in the slot, opened the glass doors, and took out your food. What a hideous way to go out, he thought. Incinerated, and then stored in an automat for ninety-nine years or *in perpetuum*, depending on how much money your relatives wanted to spend.

A sound caught him off guard and he gasped. Above the bat, frightened, squeaking, flying towards the glass skylight, back and forth, back and forth. Michel judged that even if he could balance himself on the circular railing, he probably couldn't reach the poor creature. Still, its desperate struggle touched him and he figured he had to try.

Getting up onto the railing was not difficult and, even if he fell, it was only one floor and there was carpet below. Of course, there was also that hideous metallic sculpture of people floating up into space that went from the lower level almost to the skylight. He guessed it must have to do with souls floating up to heaven or something. If he got a few cuts and bruises, he would heal.

Once he had climbed up onto the railing, it was easy enough to balance himself on the flat metal surface. As long as he didn't move. The bat, of course, flitted back and forth, near the top of the skylight, which he could not nearly reach. Occasionally, it flew down a bit, almost within his grasp, and he knew if he waited long enough and stayed still, it would fly within snatching distance. It seemed to fly east and west, and he wondered if there was some kind of magnetic field, or ley lines or something — he'd have to ask Chloe. She knew things like that.

If he moved around the railing a bit, and took off his shirt, he would be in the best position to trap the bat. He could probably even use the shirt to knock it lower, then catch it in the fabric, and get it out of here. And himself too. There was no place on earth he'd prefer *not* to be than in the Columbarium. But he couldn't leave this poor creature, any more than he could leave himself in such a horrible atmosphere. David would have said it was symbolic. Whatever.

He pulled his T-shirt over his head, then began inching slowly around the railing. The bat squeaked loudly, unnerved by his presence, and became more frantic. "*Calme-toi, mon petit oiseau de nuit,*" he told the creature of the night. He waited, watching it flutter, and swiped at it once or twice, but the bat was more to his left. "All right," he said, "I can move over." He slid his feet slowly along the railing, thinking ahead to how he would catch the bat, take both of them to the entrance, release the night flyer into the dark sky, then go home. Something about that completion felt ominous. He would not find her. He would leave feeling far from relieved. He teetered and struggled for balance.

Once he'd regained it, he looked up and swung the shirt at the bat again. The bat eluded it. Suddenly, it perched on the railing directly across from him. The small bat, so rodent-like, sat perfectly still. Then it turned its head and stared at him with one beady eye.

Dread crept over Michel. Dread he tried to shake off. Why did it seem as if reaching the entrance would be somehow not a completion but the start of something? He couldn't ignore that feeling as he stepped a bit more to his left, so that he was now front-first with the entrance corridor.

At that moment, the bat flew up into the air again, just overhead, flapping at the glass above him, soaring back and forth, making him dizzy. Michel figured he could swing the shirt up and knock the bat down and catch it and, as he thought this, something caught his eye.

29

In the split second before he fell, Michel screamed.

Then instinct took over, and he clutched at the sculpture as he catapulted, and it was only quick reaction that helped him break the fall and land on his feet, with just a sliced inner forearm and no more damage.

But he was not worried about the damage to his body. Quickly, he found the stairs, raced back up, and around the circle and down the corridor to the entrance... and stopped dead.

What lay ahead he could not comprehend. His mind shut down completely. His body locked. Time freeze-dried. And then in a split second reality blew against him like a wave of freezing wind. Glacial sweat broke over his body.

Not far from the entrance lay... what? All he could fully acknowledge was the blood. Lots of it. Staining the walls and the carpet crimson. The smell of embalming fluid washed over him making him retch and nearly knocking him off his feet. He had an urge to turn and run, but that would mean returning through two corridors of hovering dead, just waiting to abandon their concrete tombs and attack him, the living. That's crazy, he told himself. *I'm the walking dead*, the one everybody on the planet fears... But these thoughts, he knew, were only distractions to keep him from recording the nature of the horror that lay before him.

Out of the mass of confusion and terror he felt, his mind finally did record some things — an amulet; a swatch of snowy hair; an eye, so blue, so familiar...

And finally his body burst into movement, racing for the entrance, leaping over... over... he could not think about it, even as he cried out, "No! No!" raising his hands to ward off whatever evil would touch him. What he saw could not be, and yet he recognised the hand, the clothing, ...everything.

As the door of the entrance crashed open, he glanced behind him, around him. What kind of mad creature had done this? Had the dead come to life? He must be in danger.

He could not think rationally, could only feel, and his instincts for safety overcame all but his terror, which it aligned with. Outside, senses fine-tuned, ready to pick up anything and everything that might warn him of danger, he bolted.

Dawn. The sun blazed above the horizon. Birds chirped. Small animals foraged for food. He could sense nothing in the cool dawn, nothing human or superhuman. Nothing to account for his terror. Nothing but what he had seen back there... who he had seen...

He fled, moving as fast as he could move, flying, like a homing pigeon, his destination clear. He tore a direct path through the cemetery, hopped the high fence as if he did it every hour, ran down the streets of the hillside to the plateau where his home lay. Michel felt himself move faster and faster, almost racing ahead of himself, trying to outpace thoughts and images. The motion was helping him keep at bay what his mind had finally and permanently recorded: his aunt's body torn to bits, parts scattered near the entrance, awash in blood that had splattered onto everything in the vicinity.

With speed-of-light thoughts, he made a story out of it: she had unlocked the door, not had time to relock it, had gotten no further than just inside... What was waiting for her? He saw her eye, hard like a marble, dead... is this death? Shouldn't she have turned to ash like the legends said?

A chill seared him with icy heat, and he began to shiver uncontrollably. Home. He took the stone steps two at a time. His hands shook and he could hardly find the right key to let himself into his house. The others: his father and mother, Gerlinde and Karl, would all be sleeping. What could he do? He did not know what to do. Who to tell. Who would help him? Despite what he knew, he hurried to the basement, to his parents' room.

They lay entwined on the large art deco bed. The familiarity of that, of seeing them together, their bodies as if blending, his father's hair dark as his own, his mother's lush chestnut hair splayed across the silver satin pillow case... so normal. Had he been dreaming about the Columbarium? What he saw there could not have been real. How he wished that were so.

31

His mother was new to this life by just a few years and could not wake in daylight. But his father, maybe. He called, "André. Papa! *Réveille-toi!* I need you!" He shook the arm of the sleeping form. His dad stirred in a minimal way — his head moved an inch or so, his arm twitched, but his eyes did not open. Michel knew it was impossible for him to grab onto consciousness. Chloe was the only one in this house who could remain awake after sunrise and she could not move.

Despite knowing that, because he had to be thorough, Michel went to Karl and Gerlinde's room. Only Karl lay sleeping on the large metallic bed of crisp, modern design. Gerlinde must have left for Austria already, as she'd been talking about.

Michel attempted to wake Karl, but with less result than with his father.

And then, just to make sure, hoping against hope that this was all some kind of hallucination, he checked Chloe's room. It was empty.

His heart beat too fast, too hard. He did not know what to do, but he knew he had to do something. He went down to the kitchen and sat at the table, burying his face in his shaking hands, trying to think in an orderly way, to make sense of this. He could not sort it all out now, but at least this much was clear: whatever had happened at the Columbarium, he could not let Chloe's remains be found by mortals. And despite a complete aversion to the idea, he knew he had to return to the cemetery and collect her body. And he had to do that soon, before the world of daylight took charge, before the cemetery workers arrived, and the mourners, new and old, came, and the world discovered Chloe and her secret. His secret. The secret of everyone who was important to him.

He stood, trembling. The morning summer sun blazed brilliant through the window pane. Normally he would see this as cheerful. Not today. He was mortal enough still that he could have felt exhausted, but he did not feel fatigued — a good thing. But the stress of the situation would cause his natural immunities to weaken and sunlight that might make his flesh only tingle, today could actually injure him.

At the front door, he donned his father's long Australian oilcloth coat, and a large-brimmed hat, and sunglasses. He looked in the mirror at the pale, slim young man dressed in oversized outerwear, shocking black, black as a mortician, he thought, feeling that that was his role today.

He returned to the kitchen and started to take a few green garbage bags from the cabinet but then just took the entire box.

There was no sense driving. The gates would be locked to vehicles for another hour, but they opened at sunrise to pedestrians. And the streets were so screwy it would take forever. He decided on his bike. It was the most direct way to get to the entrance on Côte des Neiges, and cycling was faster than walking through the neighbourhood streets or going through the woods, and far faster than a car since he could take short cuts through side streets. Besides, he didn't have a licence yet. He knew how to drive, but this was no time to risk getting caught.

The ten speed sped along the quiet streets of the city still largely sleeping. He decided to leave it at the bike rack outside a café across the street from the entrance gates. That was all right — the Columbarium was not far from the main gates, and he could pick up the bike any time.

As the building came into view, his nerves vibrated like the strings of a musical instrument. He could not stop shaking. He caught movement out of the corner of his eye. To his horror, he saw one of the grounds keepers beginning to head towards the Columbarium. The man was old and slow. He moved around the wide curved path near the building rather than crossing the grassy lawn, a more direct route. Maybe he doesn't like the place either, Michel thought.

The entrance door, inside of which lay Chloe's body, was a tenth of a kilometre from where the man stopped to light a cigarette and watch the squirrels. To Michel's dismay, the man turned and started over the grass and headed to the exit door.

Likely he planned to go into the building there, go to the upper level, along the corridor to the circle then along the corridor to the entrance and unlock that door from inside.

Michel sped across the grounds, moving faster than he had ever moved before, like black light, but skirting from shadow to shadow, using the trees to block him from view, ducking behind the taller tombstones, desperate to avoid detection. Once he reached the entrance doors, he yanked them open and slipped through. A dozen steps. Chloe's remains greeted him.

He had no time for terror now. No time to feel the rigid, chilling air. No time to gag on the stink of embalming fluid. No time to think about the dead lined up in drawers, eager to eat the living. No time to wonder who had done this and where they were now. He did not even have time to feel completely repelled by the carnage. He only had enough time to scoop up all of the solid parts of his aunt's body into bags, filling three of them, frantically scanning the area for anything he'd missed, acutely aware that when the grounds keeper found the exit door unlocked, it would make him suspicious.

Michel sensed him inside. He would be at the circle any minute. Michel knew he was leaving the blood, but what could he do? Blood. Great pools of it that painted the walls, stained the carpet, splattered onto the little cherubs on the fabric of the loveseat near the door, blood that spotted the marble of the drawers and even coloured the ceiling...

Suddenly, he sensed the grounds keeper at the connecting circle. Within seconds he would be around it enough to see down this corridor. And then Michel heard his footsteps. His gasp.

Michel's head snapped up. He felt like an animal caught in headlights. The grounds keeper, still half asleep, looked stunned, unsure of what he was seeing, which is how Michel had felt. And he didn't even see the body parts, Michel thought, grabbing the bags, hurtling himself back through the entrance doors and bursting through them with a crash, the voice of the old man screaming, "*Oy! Qu'est-ce que tu fais là, toi?*" loud in his ears.

Operating by pure instinct, Michel tore through the cemetery, hopping over graves and tombstones, scanning the grounds as he went, glancing behind him, seeing the old man, hearing him shout, moving like a blur, an apparition — had he gathered everything? He thought so. Maybe he missed something. He did a mental inventory and brought up an image of the scene in his mind. He saw clearly Chloe's amulet where the floor met the wall. Had he picked it up?

Soon he was at the fence, out of earshot of the old man, struggling to toss the three heavy bags over — he did not yet have the increased strength of the others — bulkiness was a problem. He vaulted the metal fence like an athlete.

He trotted quickly through the streets of Westmount, streets that now showed signs of human life.

He drew attention — a young male in a too-large black coat and hat, sunglasses, carrying three garbage bags. If he had allowed any of these mortals to get close enough, which he did not, they would have seen the bags smeared with blood. As was the hem of his father's coat. And his hands.

Not soon enough he reached his home. Inside, and safe, he reset the door alarms, deposited the bags in the kitchen — he could not bear to place them on the table but he also couldn't bear to put them on the floor so they ended up on the counter by the sink — and took off all of his clothing and had a shower. All the while, his mind had gone suddenly blank. He thought nothing, he felt nothing.

Finally, he returned to the kitchen, sat down at the table, and held his head up with his hands. Through his fingers, he stared at the bags with his aunt's remains, feeling an emotion surface. An emotion that was entirely new to him. One he found unpleasant as it grew, but a feeling he could readily identify from having seen humans displaying it in movies, on television, in real time. He guessed they called this grief. Now he knew what it was to mourn the loss of someone you loved.

# CHAPTER THREE

K ARL STRETCHED LUXURIOUSLY FOR ONCE. Normally, he stayed true to what Gerlinde called his "Minimalist Teutonic Nature" and sprang out of bed, quickly did the things necessary to prepare for his waking time, and then got to whatever he had planned to do that night without any delay. And normally, he was the first one up in the house. Today, though, for some unknown reason, he took his time. He felt a bit disoriented, not an unbearable feeling, but not an entirely comfortable one either. Maybe because Gerlinde was gone and he had the bed to himself, although that wasn't necessarily something desirable.

He wondered if she had stayed the day in Manchester, sleeping as she had talked about doing at David's ancestral estate, where David and Kathleen had gone for a few weeks. It was nearly impossible to get a flight from Montréal to Vienna that would avoid daylight. If she didn't phone tonight, he'd assume she stopped in Manchester, or found a connecting flight that left after dark so she hadn't been able to call. He thought about phoning Julien's place, but the time difference of six hours between Montréal and Vienna meant he'd have to do that by midnight to reach them before sunrise. It was only eight in the evening. He had a few hours to hear from Gerlinde. She might even have left a message on the machine.

He stretched again, yawned, and pressed the remote which opened the vertical blinds. He didn't need to see that the sun had set. Every cell that composed his altered body felt that keenly. He'd still be asleep if it hadn't set.

He'd often wondered about the strange effect of the sun on their bodies. The pull was as intense as the moon on the tides. Gerlinde believed it was just something to accept about their condition, like many of the other strengths and limitations. Most of the others of his kind — the ones he knew — felt the same way. But Karl tended to question everything. He saw his questioning clearly. It did not grow from the emotional roots that David's concerns stemmed from. David was a poet and tended to see things in imagery and laden with emotion. André rarely asked a question. His orientation was so inextricably bound up with his body, and everything he did sprang from a kind of instant reaction — very much an act first/think later reply. Karl found both of his friends' responses enviable at times. His mind functioned in a logical, ordered way, what they now identified neurologically as a left-brained approach. He liked order, rules and consistency because they gave him a framework from which he could analyse and try to make sense of problems. Sometimes, he knew, there were no answers. It wasn't in his make-up to accept that readily, and he tended to go overboard, 'off the deep end' as Gerlinde put it, and had a hard time letting go of the search. But if there were answers to be found, his means of deriving them came out of that structure. And besides, it was in his make-up; that's the way he was wired.

He pressed another remote and the television flickered to life. One of the strangest things about humanity was that it seemed so firmly planted in evolution, not revolution. He'd seen it over and over during the century plus of his existence. Television exemplified that. He'd first watched TV in its infancy in Germany, in the last months of the 1930s, during the war. The 30s, 40s and 50s had set the pattern of programming for all that followed. At least back then, when TV was in the developmental stages, the shows were live and spontaneous. They might have been crude by today's standards, but Karl valued spontaneity even if it was not his strength. Now, of course, live programming was unheard of. Despite having a dish that picked up one hundred and fifty plus stations worldwide, from station to station and hour to hour the shows of every country fitted neatly into slots that were consistent at best and predictable at worst: sit com; drama; game show; nature show; news/informational. And the movies, of course.

He flipped through fifty channels before pressing the 'off' button. Valuing order didn't mean he had to put up with being bored.

He climbed out of bed, stripped off the silk pyjamas Gerlinde had given him "for your sensuous soul", folded them neatly and placed them in the drawer of the night-table. It had taken her a decade to break him of the habit of putting them into the dresser drawer. "You're just going to put them back on in a few hours," she argued. They had compromised and he kept them in the night-table. Old habits die hard.

His mother had taught him pathological neatness. "At least you'll know where everything is, *liebkin*," she'd always said. He smiled at the memory of his mother. Her image flashed clear in his mind as if he had seen her yesterday, and not over a century and a half ago. The picture was of his mother as he remembered her from his childhood, and not the depressed, middle-aged woman who had died shortly after he altered, when he had been twenty-five. Died broken-hearted because she thought her favourite son was dead.

She had been a strong-faced woman of solid build, with sharp eyes and non-too-fragile skin; an extremely practical person, like himself. Vastly different from his father who was an idealist, a philosopher and a humanitarian, for which Karl had always been grateful. His father bequeathed to him a broad-based approach that lifted him out of the mundane by focusing on the larger picture. His father had been what had come to be called decades later an 'existentialist'. His mother gave him order, his father gave him permission to imagine within that ordered framework. Both qualities that allowed for hypothesising which Karl knew was his strength.

A quick shower, and he slipped into casual cotton pants and a long-sleeved shirt. Summer or no, he preferred long sleeves to short. This one was lime green which worked with the beige pants, the fabric a very light cotton. It wasn't a stylish outfit, but then he'd never been concerned with contemporary fashion as

André was, nor had he totally ignored the contemporary for the styles of another era, like David. He simply knew he had to wear clothing, that co-ordinated colours suited his disposition, and natural fabrics in classical designs gave him the liberty to dress and then forget about what he was wearing, as well as blend in with the normals.

As he buttoned the shirt from the waist up, he stared at his image. He did not look a day over twenty-five yet he had walked around on *terra firma* more than six times those years. Sandy hair, pale eyes, strong cheekbones and jaw, not thin but not excessively full lips. He continually marvelled at how his face always adapted to the images of the day. His hair might be long or short, and he might or might not have a beard, moustache, sideburns, wear glasses. Homo sapiens was a race of chameleons without knowing it. Now at the millennium, he was adopting casual all the way. He slipped on a pair of dark brown Birkenstock sandals — he'd been wearing them since the 50s before they were fashionable, through the 80s and 90s while they were fashionable, and now that they were becoming passé. He imagined they would be in vogue again some day, not that he really cared. They worked for his feet.

Karl left his room, closed the door and headed downstairs. He sensed something in the air which added to his disorientation and made him cautious. It wasn't a mortal — he would have been able to smell a warm-blooded being. And not one of his kind he did not know — that scent, too, would have been pungent. It wasn't danger exactly, but whatever it was, it unnerved him inexplicably and he walked faster, determined to find out the source of this odd energy, which would hopefully alleviate his reaction.

He moved to the kitchen because that was where the tension originated. Michel sat at the table, his head resting on his arms, asleep.

Right away, Karl noticed three large green garbage bags on the kitchen counter, and it would not have taken a blood drinker to smell the dried blood. Some blood clung to the outside of the slick plastic bags. It was not fresh, no, not fresh at all. In fact, if he had to name it, he would have called it 'recycled'. There was another smell, one he could not instantly identify, but it was familiar. His guard went up. He wondered what could be inside the bags and, careful not to disturb Michel, went to the counter to open one.

His steps must have woken the boy, who said in a heavy, level voice, "Don't open that! Please."

"All right," Karl turned and pulled out a chair to sit at the table with Michel, who looked terrible, now that he could see his face. Clearly the boy had not slept. His skin and lips were pale, his eyes flat-looking, as if they had been a picture of eyes stamped onto a mannikin. Michel's shoulders slumped slightly, in exhaustion, or in defeat, Karl thought, although why that came to him he did not know.

He'd known the boy since his birth, and even when he was gestating in Carol's womb. Michel was a lot like his father: physical, spontaneous. But he was also like his mother. Carol had given him a tremendous amount of love, more so because she had risked her life over and over to be with him and other than the first few weeks after his birth, had had to work hard to make up for lost time. Karl knew that her devotion had penetrated with Michel. His mother's love gave the boy a strength of character which allowed him to face things most would consider too difficult — and succeed!

But Michel had benefited from the love and understanding and support of the entire household. Both Gerlinde and Kathleen had been like second mothers to him, the light, airy, fun-to-be-with mothers, and Karl felt more an uncle who indulged his nephew and cultivated his mind. David offered the boy a soul connection through art that none of the others could provide, even Gerlinde, who loved to paint. But Chloe was the wise and warm grandmother who taught Michel so much of the natural order of the universe through a bond with the environment; she spanned the gap between the boy and a more senior generation, both because of the age at which she had turned and because she was older than any of the rest of them in this household. As a result of all this extended family attention, Michel was maturing into a solid, sweet, friendly, healthy, happy, and intelligent being. So far, he had had a rich life. And that was one of the reasons that now, across the table from him, Karl saw Michel under such stress that he was silenced.

Michel finally looked up at him. The boy's eyes were red-rimmed. He appeared exhausted, his face gaunt, haggard. The flickering of emotion in his eyes evoked pity from Karl, who held his gaze, and then finally said, "What's going on, Michel? What's in the bags?"

"Please. I want to wait till Mom and Dad get up. I don't think I can tell it twice."

"All right," Karl said. "I'll go wake them. And Chloe."

"Just Mom and Dad. Please?"

The desperation in Michel's face made Karl nod. It also sent a tremor of fear through him, but he did not know why. He got up and went to the doorway in the kitchen that led down the steps to the basement.

The large door at the far end of the basement had a bogus lock and chain system on the outside. The door could be opened from the outside without a key, although anyone who didn't know how to dismantle the fake lock would not be able to do it. It was there for security purposes. Carol and André could open the door from inside, and the others of their kind who knew the procedure could open it from the outside — in case of emergency. And there had been a couple of security breeches in the house — fortunately only mortals, which were easier to handle. Everyone who lived here took the precautions they deemed necessary for their own safety.

Karl knocked on the door three times with his knuckles, his signal. In a few seconds, the door opened. André stood naked on the other side. Karl could see Carol still in bed, the satin sheets over most of her inert form. She had only changed six years ago. He remembered his early days and how difficult it was waking, although sleep came in an instant. It shortened the awake time considerably, and Carol might lose an hour or even two compared to the rest of them, depending on a lot of variables.

"I think you should come upstairs right away."

"Okay," André said, picking up on the urgency in Karl's voice. In this instance, that he rarely asked questions was good; he didn't ask any now.

André reached for his robe, but Karl said, "Maybe you should dress."

André paused for a moment, said nothing, then slipped into a pair of tight Levis, a black sweatshirt and Nike running shoes. Karl noticed a look of tension on his friend's face. Whatever was bothering him this evening, also bothered André.

"Is Carol awake?" he asked.

"Carol?" André called. Her lack of response was the answer.

They walked up to the kitchen, André following Karl. Once there, André went to Michel immediately and placed his hand on the boy's shoulder, a look of concern on his face. Michel's head leaned towards that hand. "Where's mom?"

"Asleep."

"Probably best," Michel said.

"What's up?" Karl said, as he and André sat.

"Something's happened. Something... awful. It affects all of us." Michel's voice was low and small, and Karl saw the concern in André's face expand. André, of course, had noticed the bags immediately, and the blood, and the smell.

"Tell us, Michel," André coaxed, his tone a little harsh. André didn't handle tension well. His impulse was to act immediately. Waiting accelerated his impatience.

"I went for a walk last night, with Chloe."

We know this, Karl thought, aware of his own tension. Let him tell it at his pace, he thought.

"Chloe wanted to go to the cemeteries on the mountain. She wanted to go into the Columbarium, and I waited outside. We were supposed to meet up at the exit. She didn't show up so I went looking for her, and —"

Before he could finish, André was on his feet, tearing open one of the bags.

"Dad!... *Papa!...*" Michel sounded frantic and forlorn, his voice cracking.

Karl joined André just as the first bag split apart from top to bottom. A hand fell onto the floor. One they both recognised.

Suddenly, André was tearing open a second bag, and Karl the third. Karl could not believe what he was seeing. He could not believe this was Chloe's body, mutilated. He could not believe that Chloe was dead.

"All right, Michel, go over it all again, right from the start. We need to make sure you left nothing out," André said, just as Karl got off the phone from Vienna. He'd reported what had occurred to Julien, who wanted another call as soon as possible when new information came to light. Gerlinde had not yet arrived at his place and Karl had checked but there was no message from her on the machine. He tried the estate in Manchester, but no-one answered — likely Gerlinde, David and Kathleen were out together. Karl left a message with the answering service for them to phone immediately. In case Gerlinde was en route to Vienna, Julien said he would wait for her until tomorrow night, then he and Jeanette would fly over to Montréal. The children were in Paris — Claude — and Dublin — Susan — and he would attempt to contact them and have them at the house in Westmount asap. As well, he would contact all of the others of their kind, at least the ones contactable, and who wanted such connection. They would all meet in Montréal within the next two days.

Carol was up now, sitting in the living room with the rest of them, next to Michel, who was as pale as Karl had seen any of their kind. Carol insisted the boy take nourishment. They all had a glass of blood from the emergency stocks. And this was an emergency, one that required they all think clearly despite rampaging emotions.

Michel repeated the facts he had already gone over twice, and Karl in particular questioned him about details. André seemed more incapable than ever of formulating questions. Chloe was André's aunt, his father's sister, Michel's great aunt, family in the human sense of the word. André's last surviving ancestor. Karl could see that André was taking this very badly, much worse than the rest of them, and they were all devastated. With André, though, the feelings would surface in volatile bursts of dark emotion, like a poisonous gas emitted when you least expect it. At the moment, he was keeping it all under control, but that would not last.

"Did you sense anyone in the cemetery besides you and Chloe as you walked to the Columbarium?"

"Just the couple making love on the tombstone."

"Are you sure they were mortal?"

"Yes... at least I think so... I... I don't know —"

"Stick to what you remember," André snapped. At the same time, he put an arm protectively around his son. Karl could see him torn apart, maybe more so than the others. He'd known André so long... His heart went out to his friend.

"They must have been mortal," Carol said. "Chloe would have known."

"Yes," Karl agreed — he'd already thought of that. "Michel, what about when Chloe opened the door to go into the Columbarium? Did you sense anything then?"

"No."

"Did Chloe indicate she might have sensed any danger, or anything odd?"

"I... I don't think so. She didn't say that. I didn't see her do anything unusual."

"Did you watch her open the door?" Carol asked.

"Yes."

"And see her go in?"

"Yes. She went in and I remember seeing the outer door close before I wandered away."

"So, we can surmise that the killer was not in the Columbarium when she entered or she would have sensed him," Carol said.

"But if he were outside, Michel would have sensed him," André told her.

Karl had thought of that too and could only come up with one possibility. "Unless the killer or killers were cloaking themselves in a way that would deceive Michel."

"What do you mean 'cloaking themselves'?" Michel asked.

It was André who answered. "Some of the old ones devised a means of hiding themselves from one another. It's not easily done. There needs to be a container to hide in —"

"Lead," Karl said. "Like the containment tanks for heavy water at nuclear stations."

"Like Superman?" Michel said. "He's got X-ray vision but can't see through lead."

Exactly like Superman, Karl thought. We are supermen but with weaknesses.

"Well, wouldn't a lead container be quite large, not to mention heavy?" Carol asked.

"Not necessarily. It could be the size of a coffin," André said.

"But you're assuming this is one of our kind. Couldn't it have been a band of mortals?" Carol was so new to this life, and had not faced death as often as the rest of them — Karl could see the terror in her posture, hear it in the tone of her voice, feel it emanating from her being.

André felt it too. He put his other arm around her shoulder protectively and said, "Not possible. Both Michel and Chloe would have sensed them, and there would have had to be fifty to take out Chloe. Maybe more."

"The drawers,..." Michel began.

"What drawers?" his mother asked.

"At the Columbarium. The place is full of drawers. And I... I sensed something in them. That's all I can tell you, because I was too weirded out by it all."

"It could have been mortals," André turned to Karl for confirmation.

"A pack of them," Karl agreed. "Hiding in the drawers. The drawers would still have had to be lead-lined in order for their scent to be blocked. But how would they know to do that?"

"Maybe the drawers are already lead lined."

"Could be," Karl told him, "but unlikely. That's an unnecessary expense to inter mortal dead. More likely it was our kind hiding in there. They would know how to cloak. And they would know enough to wait until Chloe was inside."

"But she was just inside the double doors," Carol reminded them. "The closest drawer is what? I can't remember exactly, since it was so long ago I was there, but I don't think it's near the door."

"It's not," Michel said. "The closest is at least twenty feet from the entrance and the same from the exit."

"Chloe would have known when the first drawer opened, and she would have gotten out of there," Carol said.

This left them all stumped. It made sense. Whether it was their kind or mortals, Chloe would have known in an instant and raced from the building, if not to protect herself, to protect Michel. Karl couldn't make sense of it, at least not yet.

"Unless she killed herself," André said.

No-one could say a word. They all knew the suicidal tendency André was referring to. Karl could not envision such an option. Even in his bleakest moments, he had not sunk to such a level. But André knew, first hand. He had seen it before.

Karl shook off the shock of that statement first. He could not imagine Chloe arranging such a thing, and obviously she didn't rip off her own limbs.

"Tell us again what you did while Chloe was inside," Karl said, if only to wrench them all back to the reality at hand.

Michel went over it for maybe the fifth time. This time, while he didn't say he was lost in fantasy, it was clear to Karl that his daydreams preoccupied him. Still, Michel should have sensed anything odd. But he's a boy, Karl reminded himself. Half mortal still. His powers could not be accurately gauged or compared to the rest of them.

When Michel finished that portion of his story, Karl asked him to tell the rest: of when he had walked to the exit, the only other door, of what he did while he waited, when he entered and then when he exited the Columbarium. And Michel went over it all again, adding hardly any detail to what he had already said.

When he finished, they all sat back, stymied. Carol had her arm around Michel's shoulder now and André was leaning forward, elbows on knees. The boy sat between his parents. His head leaned towards Carol, but he kept physical contact with his father. Michel shut his eyes, and Karl was aware of the tremendous impact all this had had on him. He looked gutted, as if his insides had been sucked from his frame, leaving him an empty shell.

Carol looked horrified. She had been crying much of the night. Karl knew she was caught between a deep sadness and horror over Chloe's death, because they had been so close, and a fear for her own life and the lives of those she loved — for truly, if it could happen to Chloe, it could happen to any of them. They all knew this without it having to be said.

André had moved into fury. His immediate response was usually anger, followed by acute pain, which Karl expected to surface tomorrow night. For now, though, André's anger was valuable. That sharp edge kept them all from wallowing in despair which would have been easy to do.

Karl's thoughts roamed over the events. He could not see that mortals had done this. It just did not feel possible. He and André had looked at one another over the night. They both knew. It was Antoine. There could be no other answer. Neither of them voiced that, not wanting to upset Carol and Michel further. They would need to know, of course, but not just yet. And in truth they probably already did know, but voicing that would be too traumatising. Better to wait until Julien and Jeanette arrived, and their children, and David and Kathleen returned, and until Gerlinde came home — and the thought of her being so far away made him edgy. Once they were all together, including any of the others in their extended family, for this was a time to band together, they would be able to decide on a course of action. There was an enemy to track and fight, and they would need combined strength for the task ahead.

Antoine was the oldest of their kind, the strongest, the most cunning in many ways. And certainly the most insane. He had vowed revenge. He had sworn they would all suffer. Five years had passed, and that threat had gone from a roar to a barely-heard whisper. They had been lulled by its near-silence into complacency. Time, of course, meant little, and five years to their kind was as five days to a mortal. Antoine had existed so long that he could easily wait, biding his time, and strike when the moment was right. But why now? Why here? Why this moment? That was a question they would need to ask later, once they found him. Once they were in a position to destroy Antoine.

# CHAPTER FOUR

KARL AND ANDRÉ SPENT HOURS EXAMINING Chloe's remains thoroughly for clues, and for traces of the presence of another, mortal or otherwise. Their makeshift autopsy included dissecting organs: the heart, brain, lungs, stomach, liver and kidneys. They sliced into muscle. Even opened bones to investigate marrow. Michel participated to some extent. He helped reconstruct her body so they could determine just how the attack proceeded, and whether an object had been used to sever any of the parts — apparently none had been.

Carol could not bring herself to get too close to the body parts. Six years of this peculiar existence had not yet hardened her to the worst that could be encountered. Not that any of them had encountered anything like this before. Chloe and Carol had been like mother and daughter. Carol sat perched on the kitchen counter, away from the table they used for the examination and reconstruction. From time to time she left the room, and once Karl heard her sobbing.

He was glad Gerlinde was not here to see this. She had known Chloe for forty years. They were as different as day and night, but Gerlinde had said more than once that Chloe was so much like her grandmother. The bond was intense, from both sides, and Karl knew Gerlinde would be devastated when she found this out.

There were no remnants of an alien presence on any of Chloe's wounds, or at least nothing Karl and André could detect visually or through their olfactory nerves. The lack of both mortal odour and the scent of their own kind was a mystery that Karl could not fathom. Surely there should be something, even if the attacker wore rubber gloves, but there was not. Other than the revolting scent of embalming fluid, which permeated the Columbarium and which, naturally, clung to the remains, to the clothing, hair, everything.

From what Michel had told them, the quantity of blood at the Columbarium indicated that Chloe had not been drained, which pointed away from their kind.

"So it might be mortals," Michel said.

"That could be a red herring to throw us off track," André told him.

Karl looked closely at part of the back. It was as though the two halves of Chloe's back had been snapped apart, the way a chicken's back is broken. That took a strength a single mortal just did not possess.

"Yes, it's a clean break," André admitted when Karl showed him the two halves, both sides reflecting the clear-cut severing of skin, muscle and bone. "But her backbone is broken as well," André pointed out, showing him the vertical break between the fourteenth and fifteenth vertebrae, the small of the back, as if she'd been bent backwards.

For a kiss, Karl thought, and wondered why that thought came to him. "It's hard to say if that occurred before she died. If it did, such an injury would have killed her."

"A killing frenzy?"

"Likely."

"But then the blood would have been too much to resist, and one of ours would have taken it," Carol said.

Karl and André glanced at one another, and years of friendship let them communicate a thought they shared: Carol was trying hard to prove that it had been mortals. With mortals, there was a good chance they could be found and destroyed. If their own kind was responsible, the threat might be insurmountable.

"More likely," Karl said, "the blood was not the primary interest, and perhaps not even of secondary interest. And one of our kind would have fed well first to increase strength. I'm not saying some blood wasn't drunk — likely the perpetrator wouldn't have been able to resist entirely, and there appears to be teeth marks at the throat and at other places. This doesn't look random at all, but calculated, like a vendetta, a punishment." Karl was careful to avoid using Antoine's name. Carol was upset enough. "Whoever did this would have wanted Chloe to know she was being ripped apart."

"You mean she was alive through most of this?" Carol buried her shocked face in her hands and sobbed. André went to her, held her, and then led her from the kitchen.

"How come Antoine waited five years?" Michel asked once Carol was out of earshot.

Of course the boy would know it was Antoine, just as Carol knew. Michel could face it, though, and at this point Carol could not. Karl realised that Michel had been careful to say nothing while his mother was in the room and, once again, he was in awe of how sensitive and responsive the boy had turned out.

"That's the mystery, Michel. I don't know why he waited. Why he picked this method, other than that he knew it would reflect his physical power, and also show his overall superiority. He attacked us on our home turf, and killed one very special to all of us. But there's a certainty in all this," Karl said as André returned. "Chloe didn't struggle."

André stood stock still. His thought processes could not move along fast enough to formulate the questions he needed to ask, questions that would demand an explanation for such an outrageous statement.

Karl spared him the journey. "The reason I've come to that conclusion is because there's nothing under Chloe's fingernails to indicate she struggled, no skin, hair, blood, nothing. And nothing in her mouth either, which tells us she didn't try to bite her attacker or attackers. From the nature of the muscle tears, there's nothing to indicate that she pulled one way and the attacker pulled the other. Basically, it looks as though she just stood there and let herself be torn open."

Karl saw André twitch slightly. "Let's go to the Columbarium," André said in a tight voice, and turned and left the room without waiting for an answer. Action was his strength, and also his salvation when the stress got to be too much.

They stored Chloe's remains in the refrigerator, then headed out the door as a unit. The consensus was that all four of them should go. In fact, they would stick together from now on. With such a dangerous and cunning enemy, it was senseless to take chances.

They drove along Côte des Neiges, to the street leading to the cemetery's main entrance, and parked a block away. At two am. in this neighbourhood, it was easy enough to scale the iron fence that ran between the sidewalk and the cemetery grounds. Of course, after last night's carnage, the graveyard was far from empty. They sensed mortals right away — police officers, maybe a dozen of them — positioned at strategic locations, watching the gate, watching the Columbarium.

Both the entrance and the exit to the underground building had yellow police tape across the doors. As if the killer or killers would come back and do it all over again, Karl thought, wondering at the way mortals think.

André, whose senses were perhaps sharpest of them all, led them to the exit door of the Columbarium, which was only being watched by one guard, as opposed to the entrance where half a dozen stood talking and smoking. André took this policeman from behind, and Karl stared into his eyes long enough that he closed them in sleep. The door was unlocked and they entered easily.

The instant they stepped inside it was clear they were alone. Karl sensed no-one else, living or undead, in the building and knew the others sensed the same thing.

Nothing alive here, including the bat Michel had told them about.

The building reeked of embalming fluid mixed with the odour of decay. Their finely-tuned olfactory nerves could pick up even minute traces of scents, and the lamp oil and smell of dying flowers withering on the stem was enough to intoxicate them to the point of nausea. It was, Karl imagined, very much like a mortal being stuck in an elevator with a woman wearing an overdose of cheap perfume. Michel looked pale, and clearly did not want to be here. None of them did.

Karl placed a hand on his shoulder to steady the boy. "If they're going to watch the place, they should watch both entrances equally," Michel said in an effort to move to one side of his terror, pointing out the obvious, as youth tends to do, even when the obvious would not be in his favour.

The small group wound its way back towards the entrance by way of the upper floor which, because of the slope in the ground, became at the circle the only floor, the ground floor, of the other corridor. The intense air conditioning of this place added to the sense of alienation Karl felt, which so unnerved Michel. It was like being in a walk-in refrigerator that stank of too many noxious odours. And although the corridor was wide, the walls seemed to press in on you, like an icy birth canal. Why they kept it this temperature, Karl did not know. Likely it was for preservation purposes. He could not imagine how strong the embalming scent would be if the temperature was lower. He guessed mortals could not detect this odour, or at least most of them.

Michel looked nervous, but not as unglued as Carol. André, emotions contained by action, assumed the rear while Karl took the lead of this procession, sandwiching the two most vulnerable members between them.

At the far side of the circle where the corridor to the entrance took a right angle, they found a wall of more yellow tape blocking admittance. Ahead lay their goal — they could see the crimson from here.

Karl stretched the tape and they all passed between it. Soon, they were just feet from the entrance, standing surrounded by dried blood. At this temperature the blood was solid. It almost looked like red salt crystals.

The minute they had entered the Columbarium, Karl smelled the blood. The fragrance of so much dried *vitae* hit him like the powerful yet invisible scented oils the women in the

Middle Ages used to mask body odour. From what Michel said, the boy had not smelled blood when he searched for Chloe. Karl made a note to question him further on this.

He guessed the blood had not yet been removed because the police were waiting for all tests to be completed, and for everybody who was going to investigate this crime scene to do so before the big cleanup. Presumably DNA samples had been taken already, which was upsetting. Chloe's DNA would not be like anything mortal scientists had seen before. Even a cursory examination of her blood beneath a microscope would reveal not just the usual cells, but animal cells as well. That would be mystery enough, he thought, but let them try to grasp the two plant cells they would find in a sample! If there was a department for X files, this murder would end up there.

Of course, the police would not classify it as murder, since there was no body, simply blood, and buckets of it from the looks of the walls and floors, and even the ceiling where it had spurted from Chloe's arteries, flecking the beige paint with ruby dots. Researchers might assume kids had mixed human, animal and plant blood cells together, somehow, and had splattered it around simply to desecrate this place. With luck, Karl thought.

Karl and André examined the blood and André who had drunk from Chloe and who was the only one who could analyse what was hers and what was not from taste alone, collected some samples. He might be able to tell something about another presence by ingesting the reliquified blood later.

Carol stood to one side, facing the double doors of the entrance. Ostensibly she was keeping watch, although they were all capable of hearing, smelling, sensing in other ways if anyone came close to the door. She looked horrified.

Michel crouched beside Karl and whispered, although of course Carol could hear him, "I still can't figure why they left the blood."

"My guess," Karl said, "is that the killer knew we'd check this out, and wanted to show disdain. He's telling us he doesn't need the blood. He has control over his passions. He's saying we don't, which makes us vulnerable."

From the forward spray of the patterns on the walls and floor and ceiling, it looked to Karl as though Chloe had walked in through the door, taken several steps into the corridor and stopped.

He questioned Michel about where he had found which parts of her body.

"I'm not really sure, I mean, I was so scared I just collected... everything. I remember her hand with the ring was here, though." He pointed to the right wall.

"The other hand?"

"I'm not sure. I... I found her head there." He indicated a spot close to the inner entrance door. "The amulet was there. Did you find it? ...in the bags?"

"I didn't," Karl said. André shook his head.

"We've likely overlooked it," Karl said. "Where was most of the body, in relation to all this blood? What I mean is, would you say most of the blood was in front of the majority of body parts, or behind?"

"Um, I think most of her body was here, in front of the blood." Michel stood facing the length of the corridor, his back to the entrance, as Chloe must have stood. Most of the blood was behind him on the walls and floor.

Karl tried to construct in his mind what had occurred. He presumed there was no-one behind her, between Chloe and the entrance — nobody had followed her in. She would have been aware of that. And it seemed unlikely her attacker did that for another reason: Michel was near the entrance when Chloe stepped into the Columbarium. He would have sensed someone inside the entrance, that close, and certainly anyone who followed her in.

Antoine had been face to face with her, him facing the entrance, Chloe facing the length of the corridor. Which meant that Antoine probably came from the other corridor. She must have sensed him. And still, all indications were that she stood her ground, did not fight him, simply allowed him to pull her apart by bending her backwards.

Why had she stayed put when she sensed him, and then when she saw Antoine? Karl could not overcome his own abhorrence to this apparently passive suicidal action, yet everything seemed to point that way. He was too much the logician to ignore what he felt to be the truth.

When André was through collecting blood samples into the vials he'd brought along, they checked what Michel called 'the drawers'. In actuality, these were square marble slabs, bigger than the end of a coffin, one up against the next like tiles, the corners held in place with metal edges similar to the paper edges used in photo albums. Some of the drawers near the entrance had been dusted for fingerprints by the police. From what Karl could see, there were at least one or two sets of prints that appeared on several of the drawers. These, he felt, likely belonged to the workers who interred the deceased, although it was possible they could belong to Antoine and one or more accomplices. Still, they did not have Antoine's fingerprints, and in this world of the not-quite-dead, physical evidence proving guilt was not as crucial as it would be in the mortal realm.

All four of them pried open one of the squares, then the next one, and the one after that. When they had a dozen open, they examined the coffins within. Standard, modern coffins, metal and fibreglass. No lead surrounding any of them.

André and Karl pulled up the coffin lids — no lead linings in these caskets, just corpses in varying stages of decay, the stench of rot and the components of embalming fluid mixing into a revolting odour that assaulted their nostrils. They removed marble squares on the other side of the corridor as well, and broke open the coffin lids, to find... nothing remarkable. There were more bodies, and more embalming fluid and decay filled the air.

Michel said, "You'd think they'd make an effort to mask the odour."

"They do," Karl told him. "Formalin is made up mostly of formaldehyde which has a distinctive foul odour. The rest is water, dyes, stabilisers and floral scents."

"Well, they didn't do a very good job with these guys. They should add more perfume."

Karl had to agree. The formaldehyde odour was extreme here, and it should have dissipated in most of these corpses. Of course, they were picking up minute traces that expanded and became excessive because of their acute sense of smell. And formulas changed from brand to brand; some brands of embalming fluid would not be this intense.

There was no trace of any presence, mortal or immortal, just the dead and buried, which was a good case for Michel's theory that these dead had come to life and murdered Chloe. Karl could not accept that, of course. But given that the murder was so odd, he forced himself to keep an open mind to that option while not dwelling on it.

They worked their way back to the circle, and investigated the glass windows which held urns and boxes of ashes. None of these windows were nearly large enough for a body, unless the killer was an infant.

As they moved along the other corridor, towards the exit, André began yanking marble tiles from the wall.

"I don't think we need to bother," Karl said. "It's clear that this second corridor would have been too far for him or them to travel without Chloe sensing them and getting out."

André looked annoyed. It seemed like he intended to check every burial space in the Columbarium until he found one which could house a group of vampires. But he was not stupid and saw Karl's reasoning, even though it left him with nothing to do, which left him agitated.

They climbed down the stairs near the exit. The policeman outside still slept, as Karl had directed him to, but there were four more in the area. Karl focused on the entrance and determined there were just two policemen near it, which meant that was their best route out.

The group retraced their steps back up the stairs, along the corridor, past the circle, and walked past the blood to the entrance. There they paused long enough to assess that the two policemen were drinking coffee and talking, and walking towards the exit to join the others.

"Good thing they take coffee breaks," Michel whispered.

It would have been easy enough to overcome any guards, but it would also have been risky with so many police in the vicinity. They were not in physical danger, but Karl did not want to chance any of them being spotted and later recognised. Nor did he want any gunplay. A wound that produced more blood that analysed as abnormal would mean they might have to leave the city. He always preferred the easy, non-confrontational path.

The four took their golden opportunity and made their way quietly and quickly out the Columbarium's entrance door.

Just after four am. the frazzled group staggered through their front door. This night had been an ordeal for each of them, and it wasn't over yet. André went about the business of liquifying some of the blood from Chloe's wounds, and some from the Columbarium to ingest, hoping to catch the trace of a foreigner, the blood of someone other than Chloe.

Karl took some of the blood samples from the body and from the walls, and liquified it with a saline solution. He waited until the cells sank to the bottom of the vial and the plasma had separated. Then he checked the blood cells beneath a microscope.

The cells were not stained, but his practised eye could distinguish the different types of cells anyway. About 45 per cent of blood was cells, mostly the doughnut-shaped red, which outnumbered the white cells about ten to one. There were other cells — Neutrophils, Lymphocytes, Monocytes, Eosinophiles, Basophiles, a few that resembled animal cells, and two harder-edged green pigmented cells, because of chlorophyll. Their bodies were such a hybrid, composed of human, animal and plant cells, and after all the years of research he'd done, he still had only the sketchiest idea of why this particular mixture produced beings like him. Still, none of what was in Chloe's blood seemed unusual. Well, that was not strictly true. One of the red blood cells had a nucleus.

He studied that cell in particular. Normally, the nucleus shrank as the red blood cells developed and eventually was expelled when the cell was fully formed. He had examined his own blood innumerable times, as well as the blood of many of the others in his community, including Chloe's. They were always on the search for the roots of their mutation, as well as researching methods to go without blood, to repel the dangerous effects of sunlight, to unearth the element that kept them from dying. He had never seen a mature red blood cell with a nucleus in his kind. In mortals, it was a clear indication that a cell had gone haywire. A sign of a cell that was necrophilic.

Despite that anomaly, he felt the answer to this puzzle might not be in the cells but in the plasma, the other fifty five per cent of blood. How to analyse that was the problem. He did not own a HPLC — high phase liquid chromatography machine. He would need to go to a research facility, possibly a hospital to use their forensics lab.

Karl couldn't do more tonight. The hour was late and any tests he would run, once he managed to gain access to a lab, would take hours.

He thought about questioning Michel more as to why he didn't smell all the blood when he entered the Columbarium, but the boy needed a break. And also, Karl was beginning to feel anxious: Gerlinde had not phoned, nor had David and Kathy. Still, the time difference alone could account for that. It was after sunrise now in Manchester, no use phoning there again. And seven pm. Manchester time was one in the afternoon Montréal time, which meant if they phoned today, Karl would not get a message until sunset. But still, even if they got in just at sunrise, they would have gotten the message he'd left, and they could have called and left a quick reply on the machine here.

He decided to phone Julien to leave word on his machine about the latest developments, and was surprised when Julien answered. This one who had altered in the Middle Ages possessed the most ability to stay awake during daylight hours, although he could not move well, and needed complete darkness. His voice betrayed his lethargic state.

"Karl, I agree with your hypothesis. Undoubtedly Antoine is responsible, and I too believe he acted alone. I also believe you are correct — Chloe did not attempt to defend herself."

"Why?" Karl asked. More than anything else, that was the question for which he could find no reasonable explanation.

"I think it would be good to discuss all aspects of this tragedy in person. I am not at the moment at the height of my powers. Our flight departs Vienna for London shortly after sunset. It is already arranged that Claude and Susan will join us at Heathrow. We will leave a note here and a message on my machine for Gerlinde to return to Montréal as soon as possible."

"Has she phoned?"

"No."

"Instruct her to phone me right away," Karl said.

The worry in his voice caused Julien to pause. "Yes, of course," he finally said, but a slight hesitation left Karl feeling even more uneasy. He tried to write it off to Julien not being as sharp as usual.

# CHAPTER FIVE

KARL AWOKE THE SECOND THE SUN HAD SET. He checked the machine and found no message, then immediately made another call to the stately home in Manchester, and got the answering service again. The service operator told him that his message of the previous night had not as yet been picked up. His unease turned to full-blown worry bordering on panic.

He knew he should head out to a lab right away — the tests took hours — but he could not ignore the worm gnawing at him. He decided to forego sustenance and instead went upstairs and sat alone in Gerlinde's studio on the third floor, under the skylight roof, the blackening sky above his head, and began to track her.

Her essence permeated this space where she painted under the stars. She had designed the room, selected the colours, the furnishings — what little there were — and her artwork and the pieces she loved by others adorned the walls.

Karl was filled with Gerlinde as he knew her, as he loved her most — vibrant, free, a joyous spirit. He closed his eyes and focused on that essence in the space between his eyes, where the pituitary gland lies, where the mystics have always claimed the third eye waits to blossom like a lotus flower when the time is right. Simultaneously, he slowed his breathing to a steady, comfortable rate, inhaling her essence with each breath, exhaling all other energies he carried that would distract him, until he had only Gerlinde residing within his skin so close beside him. Then he permitted her energy to descend to his heart, which knew her so well.

Heat swelled within him, and the beating of his most vital organ intensified. Each pulsing spread awareness of her through his body until he felt her life force throb within him, expanding from his torso to his limbs, through muscle and bone and organs, running through his veins and arteries and through the tiniest blood vessels like a racing river, until finally, finally, his heart flooded and overflowed and the liquid presence flowed eternally through him, an artesian well that will always nourish and always be replenished.

It was only because he had ingested her blood when he turned her that he could track her like a magnet picking up iron, or that's how he thought about it. Whatever traces of her blood he had consumed which still resided in the cells of his body recognised Gerlinde and aligned with her. He and she were each a disparate sound, an orchestra tuning instruments, creating discord, a cacophony that dissolved instantly when they began to play together as a symphony, when they became as one sound, two parts blending to form a consistent whole. His soul and Gerlinde's became melded and overlapped, and eventually he recognised not so much by a mental process as by an innate process where she was; he could 'see' through her eyes and feel the flavour of her environment through her senses.

With a start, his eyes snapped open. Gerlinde was in Germany! Somewhere in the western part, along the Rhine!

Rather than reassuring him, this knowledge caused him even more consternation. There was no reason she should be in Germany, none at all. She was headed for Vienna, possibly stopping in Manchester, and Germany was not en route. Of course, it was possible she might have found a flight that took her farther than Manchester, but not as far as Vienna — after all, Karl did not know every single airline's routes from Montréal to Europe. But Gerlinde did not like Germany. And why the Rhine? It made sense that if she did make a stopover in Germany it would have been Munich, or even Frankfurt. Or Berlin, the place of her birth.

Gerlinde was impulsive, yet predictable in her spontaneity, or at least enough that Karl could count on her. And after forty years, he knew her very well. She could have gone to Germany. She might have had a reason to travel to western Germany, even if she didn't mention that reason to him, which normally she would have. But surely she should have phoned home by now — it was unlike her not to. And if she didn't phone here, she would have phoned Julien's place to say she'd be arriving a bit later. Although maybe not. If the stop-over was brief — she could have stayed at an airport hotel and flown out at sunset and have arrived in Vienna in an hour. But then she or Julien would have called. It was now only about three am. in Vienna, long before sunrise. And where were David and Kathy? Why hadn't they picked up the message? They knew Gerlinde was coming, so they should have been there, unless they met her somewhere along the way and were going to Vienna with her. Maybe they wanted to stop off in Germany...

Such speculation, he knew, was more than useless. There could be an infinite number of reasons why she went to Germany, and he would not know why until she told him.

The only thing he could think to do was to track her again before the sun rose in Germany, which would be six hours difference. Which meant he could track her until around midnight, one am. at the latest, Montréal time. After that, it was pointless to track her since where she was it would be daytime and she'd be in the same place.

Tracking exhausted him, as it did most of his kind. Normally, a tracking session took place once in an evening, after which the tracker was famished. Tracking was best accomplished on an empty stomach. If he ingested blood tonight, it would act as a barrier to be overcome, almost a third presence crowding out Gerlinde and himself, and that would make the job even harder and the results possibly tainted. He'd need to fast, there was no way around it; he could feed once he had tracked her again. Unfortunately, lack of blood added to his agitation. And left him weak for the job ahead, which was breaking into the police forensics lab.

It was already eight pm. Late, but at least he would find most of the personnel gone for the day. He hurried through the downtown going east by taxi to the nondescript building on rue Parthenais, near the Pont Jacques Cartier. High fencing surrounded the greyish structure. Formerly, it had been a detainment centre for hardened criminals. Now it was headquarters for the Sureté du Québec — police headquarters. The coroner's office was in the basement and forensics sciences took up the entire fifth floor.

Forensics was the place where autopsies were conducted and tests run on the dead to determine why they were in that state. Karl had used the facilities a couple of times before, unbeknownst to anyone. Entrance to this heavily guarded building would have been nearly impossible for a mortal. For Karl, gaining access was not difficult. Through a mental process akin to hypnotism he persuaded the guard at the front desk that he had a pass. And eye contact along the way made all the difference.

Karl was lucky that no-one was working overtime on five. Apparently there had been no murders or suspicious deaths in Montréal for a couple of days and so no test results were urgently needed. He was also lucky that the icromatography equipment was not running. Once he had been here when the personnel had left it on to complete an analysis overnight. Tonight, though, the machine that resembled Dr. Frankenstein's equipment was free.

He shook his head and smiled a little — the turn of a millennium, and look at this: a rectangle of plastic, on top of which sat two brown jugs of solvent. A haphazard silver wire extended from a beaker into the machine and up and out of it, passing through a kind of bar that held a filter, then onward to be draped casually over a wire like a clothes line. The plasma from Chloe's blood contained elements that would be passed through the cilia-like filters in the bar, the smallest particles first. It was a fairly straightforward process. Regrettably, he could only run one sample at a time, making it a painstaking process, but at least that would be something.

Karl had always loved chemistry. Nothing fascinated him more than deconstructing substances, and elemental forms of matter. Unless it was combining them. If there's a god, he'd often thought, he would be a chemist, or at least an alchemist.

He set up the equipment and started the process that would take up to six hours to complete. In the meantime, he walked around the lab to see what was new. A quick tour of the space revealed equipment he'd seen and used before. Except for the GPC. He'd only read about them, and now he was looking at one.

The Gas Phase Chromatographer was such a specialised piece of equipment. It was able to determine what gases were present in a small quantity of organic material simply by burning the material. Why not, he thought? He'd never used one, but it wouldn't take a genius to figure it out.

He turned on the GPC and the computer next to it which would calculate the results and display a graph on the screen as the gases were sorted out one from the other. There would be a book of patterns in this room somewhere but he decided to try the computer first, to see how much information it held. He was in luck. There were files of patterns from all the previous machine runs identifying the characteristics of all the gasses sampled. That meant he could burn some of Chloe's blood and let the machine match up the patterns that indicated what was in the plasma. And then once that was known, he could determine what, if anything, couldn't be accounted for. After all, science was mostly a process of elimination. And it would give him something to do while he waited for the HPLC to do its job. And while he waited for midnight, when he could again track Gerlinde.

He took a chip of Chloe's dried blood, placed it inside the equipment's containment chamber, and ignited it. The gas emitted was mildly visible, which meant little. He wondered how long it would take to process all the different gases in blood.

While he waited, he sat in one of the overstuffed chairs and his thoughts turned to Gerlinde.

Even after all this time together, he still found her more attractive than any other female, mortal or immortal. And that was saying something. Each of the women of his species had their appeal, and it was intense: Carol possessed a slow, sensual, quiet eroticism. Jeanette was more sophisticated, almost metaphysical in her seduction. Kathy had a physicalness the others lacked — her sexuality was direct and down-to-earth. Morianna was like a mother goddess, a bit aloof but wise and all encompassing in her allure.

But Gerlinde had something the others didn't. She possessed a playfulness of spirit that he still found refreshing and appealing. She was passionate in a carnal way, yet also immensely vulnerable — this gave him the scope to be himself, always. She surrounded him with a relaxed, amorous acceptance that offered freedom. And that always made him want her.

They had made love just before she left. She liked being on top, and he liked it too. The position gave her more liberty and led to a strong arousal, and it allowed him to control his passions while still enjoying an incredible amount of stimulation.

"Kiss me," she whispered melodramatically, imitating Marlene Dietrich. "Kiss me hard. Kiss me as though you'll never kiss me again!"

And he had. He brought her mouth to his, and her lips parted. Their tongues played and she gasped and panted and moaned and breathed hot words into his ear as her hips moved rhythmically over his.

The feel of her slim, girlish waist, the swell of her breasts, of her buttock, the moist hotness of her vagina... These were eternal moments like what he envisioned heaven to be, or nirvana, or any place in the universe where bliss could be attained. Where the mind shut down and the loneliness dissipated. Where he knew for certain he was not the only extant being because conceptualisation gave way to the concrete...

He became aware of a computer beeping. The HPLC was already spewing forth results. He jumped to his feet and went to look at the screen. The plasma contained just what he expected it to contain: albumins, globulins, fibrinogen, electrolytes, nutriments, general gas, some vitamins, and waste products. The unknown factor would be in the waste products, of that he was convinced. It was about midnight, and he tracked Gerlinde again. She had moved a bit further north, not enough to warrant the effort he expended.

The double tracking had exhausted him. He felt skeletal, flesh stretched around bones. He knew it was probably pointless, but he searched the lab for blood like a rodent sniffing for food. There was hardly anything that would replenish him. This was not the type of facility which stored blood or plasma in quantity. Here, they saved small samples for analysis. Even in the autopsy room he would find nothing — there, they simply washed it down the drain. At the moment, that thought revolted him.

He did manage to find one small bag of blood. He tore open the plastic and downed it in one gulp. Rh negative from the taste of it. It was hardly enough to sustain him but it was better than nothing.

He returned to the lab and checked the Gas Phase Chromatographer. Results were pouring onto the computer screen. He managed to identify most of the gases, the common ones in blood which he had expected to find: $H_2O$, $O_2$, etc. And then he found something that could not be identified. Now was the time for detective work.

The computer held thousands of files of graphs. Whatever this substance was, it was not normally found in blood, so it required a further search. The Pentium went about searching and meanwhile Karl checked the HPLC. Ninety per cent of the readings had come through. There were no surprises. Nothing at all. This machine would not identify any substance that it was not asked to identify. Karl had asked it to identify the levels of the known ingredients in plasma, and it did. Everything else was lumped together as 'other'. He would need to know what was in the 'other' to get from this machine a confirmation or negation of its existence.

When he returned to the GPC, he got the shock of his life: the plasma contained formaldehyde. In abundance!

When Karl returned home, the first thing he told André, Carol and Michel about was tracking Gerlinde.

"It's a bit early to worry," Carol said, although her voice did not convey calm. Still, the overall situation was such that it was understandable she would be far from peaceful.

"David and Kathy might be travelling," André said.

"Gerlinde phoned and told them she was coming this week. If they were planning on being away, she didn't tell me that." Karl looked hopefully to André and Carol, but they did not offer any new information.

As if to move the subject onto more solid ground, André said, "Last night before we slept and then again when I awoke tonight, I tasted some of the blood, both what was at the Columbarium and traces of what clung to her body."

"And?" Karl said.

"Her fear is evident."

That left them all silenced until Karl said, "Did you determine anything else?"

"Only this: Michel said that Chloe did not drink the night she was killed."

"She often waited until near sunrise," Carol reminded them, and André, who knew Chloe's habits better than anyone, nodded.

"I found Chloe, of course — I know her essence. But there was no new blood which confirms that she did not drink that night. And no trace of the blood of another — as you suggested, Karl, I took my samples from the wounds in the throat, elbows and behind the knees where the bite marks are."

Karl nodded. If one of their kind was going to drink from her, they would want the easiest route, the least messy, the largest veins or arteries that are most accessible.

"There wasn't much else," André said, "but there was one element I can't quite place."

"What do you mean?"

"Well, it's not mortal blood. And not blood filtered through our kind. It's not even blood."

"Do you have a sense of what it is?"

"I wish I knew. All I can tell you is that it has a kind of... personality."

"Personality?" Don't start becoming David on me, Karl thought, trying to keep his impatience in check. "What's that supposed to mean, André?" His tone was harsher than he had wanted it to be, probably because he was hungry and all this talk about blood only fuelled his appetite.

André stiffened. "If I could be more specific, Karl, I would be. I only know that there's something there that shouldn't be there. I've liquified a bit more of the samples. Maybe you can be more exact than me."

Karl said. "All right. I'll try." Then added, "I've been fasting. To track. I'm hungry."

André nodded, and relaxed. He got up, went to the kitchen, and returned with two vials, one of which he handed to Karl.

Karl sniffed from the vial — the scent of blood. He lifted the vial to his mouth and just let the blood wet his lips. He licked it off. Stale blood, as they called what came from anything but a living, breathing human. Blood that had dried and been reliquified had gone through a natural process towards decay and a great deal of its vitality was lost. Add to that the fact that this was blood Chloe had ingested twenty four hours or more before her demise, making it not just a secondary source, but a third level source, and over forty-eight hours old...

Despite all these drawbacks, this was preciously aged wine to a connoisseur, a rare mushroom to a gourmet. The richness of even this small taste of *vitae* filled Karl's mouth, his throat, slid down into his stomach and created a passionate fire that burned through his body. A fire he craved, and that left him weak even as it built his strength. This was the closest experience to a sexual orgasm Karl knew, but, unlike orgasm, blood always always always tasted superb.

69

Only the aftertaste betrayed the staleness, leaving his mouth filled with something bordering on the unpleasant. Still, this was nourishment and that outweighed all else, or normally would have. Because André was right. There was something else in this blood. Something not blood, nor any of its derivatives. And it had no scent. Or taste. More, it had a texture or a weight.

Karl, like all of the others, had run across alcohol in those he drank from, and various drugs, street and prescription. This had more of the feel of a drug, yet it was nothing familiar. And although it had no real taste, it struck him as foul.

He looked up at André, who said, "That's from the Columbarium." He handed Karl the other vial, the one with blood from Chloe's body.

Karl smelled the contents — no odour but blood. Yet there was something... some trace of something... He lifted the vial and again just wet his lips. That taste of richness, of wondrous fullness, and then the release — a parched man drinking water. The blood tasted similar to the first vial to him, down to the aftertaste. And that alien element.

"It's a peculiar additive," André said. "Like a pharmaceutical, but not. Or so it seems to me," André said, looking both relieved and also unsure — science was not his *forté*.

Karl could see that André had been doubting himself. Chloe's essence would have overridden all else for him and he might well have been confused as to what lay hidden between the corpuscles.

"I've done some tests with the microscope on the cells and at the forensic lab on the plasma, isolating the elements," Karl said.

André nodded.

"I'm thinking the perpetrator must have drunk a bit from her, from the places where we discovered teeth marks, from where you've taken the samples, and he's infected those spots. It would affect what shot out of her arteries and hit the walls and would also have entered her blood stream and circulated through her entire body along with her blood in about four minutes. That's the normal time. Blood circulates faster, during orgasm, when someone is panicked —"

"I took samples from several of her wounds and from several spots at the Columbarium, and tasted them all. They are all the same," André said.

Karl was quiet for a moment, wondering what this odd business was about. He thought he should know how this fitted together, but he didn't. The awareness was just beyond his consciousness. "What I've discovered in the lab is that Chloe's blood contains formaldehyde," he told them. "Which I imagine is what you and I are tasting in the blood. Formaldehyde loses its potency after a while so we can't smell it in her blood samples. And likely it would not have been more than a trace anyway."

"Where's it from?" Michel said.

"I can't see the formaldehyde being from a living body — some of the blood is from the bite marks. It might be from a dead body, odd as that sounds."

"Man, I was right about the dead coming to life!"

Karl ignored that. "I don't envision it as coming from one of our kind. Still, we can't rule out any possibilities. We've got to keep all options open."

Carol, who had been silent for some time, said in a small voice, "If this wasn't one of our kind, and it wasn't mortals, then we might be facing something we can't contend with. Something we can't defeat."

André just looked at her, as did Karl. There was nothing to say. Yet. They all knew very well that whatever had happened to Chloe could happen again to any of them, at any time. And if the threat was severe enough, they were not safe even in a group.

# CHAPTER SIX

THE OTHERS BEGAN ARRIVING EARLY THE NEXT evening: Julien and Jeanette with their children Claude and Susan appeared just as the household was rising. Morianna came about midnight and Wing rang the bell a half hour after her. A few that Karl only knew peripherally, from when they had all travelled to Fire Island, showed up as well. Soon the living room was crowded to seating capacity.

There were no messages on the answering machine other than from Julien, telling them the time he and his family would fly in to Montréal.

Karl left it to André, Carol and Michel to fill in Julien, and took the early part of the evening to once more track Gerlinde. He intended to fast all night again in order to keep tabs on her movements. He discovered, to his dismay, that she was still in Germany, still along the Rhine but a bit farther north than where she had been the night before. Tonight she was in the region of Köln. This told him she was moving away from Vienna and that left him really rattled.

His major concern was contacting Gerlinde and getting her home safely. But there was nothing more he could do there, for the moment. His secondary concern, a very close second, was revealing the results of the analysis of Chloe's blood to the others in the community, some of whom were also scientifically inclined, and getting some feedback. There were many avenues of thought they could pursue, many options to investigate.

About two in the morning enough of the others had arrived that Karl felt he could safely reveal what he had learned without having to repeat himself too many times. But the new arrivals were being filled in, and it made sense that they all start at the same place with the same knowledge, so he waited. It was important that they be together. The collective energy that came from bouncing information around and the ideas generated by a group would surely outweigh a one-on-one conveyance, although he realised that most of the others preferred the more personal touch. Theirs was a alienated species. Trust took time to build and was never truly secure.

He felt famished. Carol and André passed around glasses of blood from the household's stores. Karl watched the crimson liquid glitter like rubies in the glasses. The blood seemed to call to him; the perfect liquid. The most appealing beverage in this or any other universe.

His stomach contracted sharply with hunger. At the same time, his thoughts rang clear as a crystal bell. Mentally he was blade-sharp, physically at the cutting edge of his powers and closely aligned with his senses. He also felt excited, on the verge of discovering something important, and expected that when he revealed the results of the tests, he could count on a few answers to the myriad of questions forming as more and more of their kind gathered. If only Gerlinde would call, his excitement would be untainted.

While the recap took place, Karl phoned Manchester again. David and Kathy still had not picked up the message. They might be with Gerlinde.

Gerlinde. He left the living room and stepped out onto the deck at the back of the house. The fall evening was cool but the temperature a bit higher than normal for this time of year. The slope of the woods behind rose up the side of the mountain. The leaves of the deciduous trees had changed colour and were in the process of dropping from their branches. If he walked up through the dense woods, up Mont Royal so packed with coniferous trees — Pine, Cedar, Birch — all the way to the top, and then began to descend on the other side, he would come to the cemetery. And the Columbarium. That place where a split in the fabric of their world occurred. Where Chloe was murdered.

He was really beginning to worry about Gerlinde. And David and Kathy. What happened to Chloe might be an isolated incident, but he didn't think so. None of the others thought that way either, that was obvious. No matter how much energy he expended, he could not come up with one good reason why Gerlinde would be in Germany.

What was she doing in Köln? They had visited there together. The first time was in 1960, two years after they met and went on a 'vacation' — a little trip to see if they could actually be together in new places and get along. That would be a necessary ingredient to a companionship. He was thinking of turning her. But they were still 'dating' as she had called it. In love. Then. Now.

It had been a peculiar time in Berlin. What the Americans coined as the 'Beatnik Era' had ended, and the 'Psychedelic Era' was some years away. For a time, the clubs were evolving. The black walls and café tables remained, but there were no more bongo drums accompanying Ginsberg-like poetry to be heard. New outrageous electric sounds rang through the air. The dark spaces were lit by spots and iridescent posters flowers on the walls.

He had returned to Germany in 1958 from New York. Things had fallen apart there for him, for André and David as well. Ariel wasn't the real problem, at least as far as he was concerned — she just reflected the loneliness, the alienation he was already feeling. Going home seemed to be the right move, although Berlin was as close as he wanted to get to the town where he was born.

The club scene in Berlin was small. One of his favourites was Klub Hole, a pit-like space in the basement of a building burned out during the war and still awaiting demolition. He went there frequently, and it wasn't long before he became a fixture in this evolving scene. It also wasn't long before he met Gerlinde.

She was small, slim, with flaming hair and enormous brown eyes that seemed about to go liquid to him. She wasn't much past twenty — fortunately he looked the age at which he'd changed. What began as a casual encounter grew organically until they were spending all their time together, at least the night hours.

Gerlinde worked as a sales clerk in an art supply store. Since she painted, this helped her financially, and kept her focus on the world she loved, the art world.

He found her personal style fascinating, and reflective of her artistic style. She often wore oddly cut clothing, very daring, the styles *avant garde*, although she leaned toward the 'beat' look, which was mainly black. She accentuated what she wore with vivid and unique jewellery. But it was her personality that affected him most.

He had never been with a woman so naturally buoyant. He loved how her spirit seemed to move at the speed of light, like a butterfly, touching this flower, then the next, lighter than air. Words poured from her, clever comments, pithy phrases, in a way he had no hope of emulating. She was fresh and alive to him, open to new experiences, living her life at the cutting edge in every way.

Over the nearly two years they were seeing one another, he had taken her blood from time to time, as part of the foreplay of their lovemaking. Gerlinde called him 'kinky', and perhaps because of her artistic nature, she could readily accept what normal people could not. She was so experimental — he'd never met a mortal female like her. The era encouraged exploration, but still, most of the females were conventional. And the ones who were not frequently had such severe emotional problems that he steered clear for mental health reasons.

One evening, they made love at her four-room, quirkily-furnished apartment where it seemed the decor changed every time he visited.

He arrived just after sunset. She met him at the door wearing a skimpy outfit that was like something a cave woman would have worn: a piece of fabric wrapped around the waist like a short skirt, a scarf tied around her breasts, a band at her wrist, and all of it leopard skin. She rubbed against him, and the feel of the fur alone stimulated him. She used the animal claw hanging around her throat to lightly scratch his chest where she'd opened his shirt.

Once they reached the bedroom, she snapped a chain to the wrist band, handed him the other end, then got down on all fours on a bearskin rug and growled. He could only laugh in delight, and make passionate love to her.

Later that night, they went to Klub Hole and listened to a band from England called The Rolling Stones. Karl had seen the band before — they liked to play small clubs, to keep in touch with the people. He had a feeling they were about to make it big.

When the show was over, Gerlinde leaned over and said, "I wish this could last forever!"

He was so caught up in the moment that he said, "Maybe it can."

"How?"

"The blood."

"Okay, *Nosferatu*. Take me, I'm yours!"

She'd called him *Nosferatu* ever since he began taking her blood. Of course, she hadn't believed he was a vampire. Why would she? It was outlandish, and he relied on that to protect him.

But now he didn't want to be protected. To the contrary, he wanted to expose his soul to this woman. He had grown so fond of her, no, not *fond*, he had grown to love her. The idea that he would lose her to time, to age... he couldn't bear the thought.

"I'll take you if you want that," he said, so seriously her usual animation ceased and she became as still as a lizard. She looked deeply into his eyes, as if searching for something.

"You're not kidding, are you?"

"No."

She just stared at him.

"I'm *der vampire*. Not like in the movies and books. I'm like a human being but I'm not. I need blood to survive, and I can only function in darkness."

"You've... you've drunk my blood. Will I be like you?"

"Not unless you drink mine. What I've taken from you has been very little. I haven't drunk from you to sustain myself, more to highlight and prolong the pleasure of our love making."

She sat back stunned. The band came on for another set, and they listened to the music, but he knew she was as preoccupied as he was.

When the band finished, Gerlinde seemed upset. She wanted to go home. Alone. And he let her go.

The next weeks were hell. They came together and broke up so many times. Knowing what he was and accepting it were two different things, and she had a hard time accepting that her lover was undead.

Two weeks later they were both at Klub Hole again. She had ended the relationship two nights before, and this time it seemed final to him. Karl was just on the edge of coming to grips with the fact that she would never be his, that he would need to leave Berlin soon. He couldn't bear the thought of seeing her, knowing she could be his but would not be. He had never been experimental in his lifestyle. He was monogamous by nature, and needed the stability of a relationship for balance. Now that he'd found a woman he wanted to be with, he knew it would be hell without her, and staying here would make that worse.

They saw one another through the crowd. She came to him. "Let's talk."

They sat in a little alcove, dark, as quiet as was possible. "Okay," she said.

"Okay what?"

"Do it. I want to be with you."

He sat back, wary. "There are things you need to know to make an informed decision."

"Like?"

"The drawbacks. No family, no friends. A world of darkness. Blood as your only food."

"Any benefits, or is it all hell on wheels?" He grinned a little — she had a way of lightening everything that he adored.

"Well, there's increased sensation, and strength. I like to think those things outweigh what I've lost."

"Is it reversible?"

"No."

"What about that stake through the heart business. Seems like a nasty way to exit."

"Well, I don't know for certain, but I suppose that could kill us. It could kill you as you are right now."

"Yeah, but nobody's after me with any stakes. How about you?"

"No-one is after me at all, that I know of."

"That's a relief. So, I guess sunlight's not so good. Would Coppertone help?"

He shook his head.

"What about garlic, and crosses —"

"Well, you've seen me enter a church with you, with your own eyes."

"Yeah, I forgot about that. Not that I go to church myself, but it's nice to have the option. Especially if somebody with a stake is chasing you."

"The garlic and the other things, they're all mythology. Basically, it's the night and the blood. And that means a lifestyle that isn't normal."

"Well, I'm not exactly normal now. It's not going to make me nuts, is it? I mean, will I want to move to the suburbs and have kids or something?"

"It's possible. I don't know how you'll react. I've never created anybody before."

"You're sure you can do it, right? I mean, I'm not going to end up like some kind of ghoul or something prowling around cemeteries and garbage dumps."

"I hope not."

"But I might end up dead."

"I don't think that's likely."

"No money back guarantees?"

He said nothing.

"Well, okay, let's go for it. Nothing ventured, nothing gained. Or lost, but who's thinking negatively? Where's that Norman Vincent Peal book when you need it?"

He had misgivings, of course. What if he couldn't accomplish this? André had tried it. And failed. But that wasn't it, not really. More, he worried that things would be different, that he and Gerlinde wouldn't be as close, or *couldn't* be as close. They might become competitors — that wasn't unheard of. And with her new powers of seduction, she might decide that life with only him would be too boring, although she denied she would feel this way.

He had tried to be straight with her about everything. Especially this: for every successful transformation that he knew about, there was at least one unsuccessful attempt.

"Look," she said with an exasperated sigh, "we can huddle together, biting our nails to the quick, pulling the hair out of each other's head, but what's the point? I think we should go on a holiday together, just to check out that we can actually stand being together in new places. Hey, I've always wanted to see that huge cathedral at Köln! Want to go there?"

They arrived in Köln late in the evening. She went to the cathedral in daylight the following day, alone. He joined her just after sunset.

The Köln Bishopric's history stretched back to the fourth century, although the exterior was not conceived until the year 1020 and construction had not actually begun until 1248. It took six centuries to complete the Gothic masterpiece. Karl had seen the cathedral before, but with her by his side, he viewed the immense structure with new vision. He saw it not only through his own eyes, but through hers — a more artistic concept to complement his practical and scientific view.

They stood before the enormous doors, staring straight up at the two tallest grey stone towers, their spires piercing the heavens. Silently, she took his cool hand in her warm one, and he turned to see her profile. So breathtaking. "I want it," she said, her eyes clear. She looked lucid. "I want to be like you, Karl, and I want to be yours."

That picture of her face and another snapshot he stored in his mental files of later in the evening when he brought her over, those would be imprinted into his memory for all eternity.

She was still human then, but the marks on her throat were evidence that she belonged to him. Seeing her so open and vulnerable, her youthful profile alive with the majesty of this edifice, so in awe of the power that it represented, that visage left him feeling like a predator, luring the lamb to the slaughter. He had never turned anyone before or since. He was nervous about the process. His doubts had caused him to retreat from her periodically, but his desire for her brought him back again. And that night desire won out.

They were staying in a small hotel not far from the cathedral, on the street with the bronze sculpture of odd-looking cherubs, their room overlooking the Rhine.

"Are you comfortable?" he asked.

"Of course! I'm always comfortable with you."

She smiled up at him from the bed, so trusting, her short red hair capping her sweet, vivacious features. That alone ignited his passions.

He made love to her as if it was their 'wedding night' as she called it. She had never been more responsive to him, physically, emotionally, with her whole being. It was while he penetrated her in the sex act that his teeth did the same at her throat, reopening the wounds he had made over the past two years, where he had drunk from her.

Her body rose to meet his, quivering. He grasped her tightly and clutched her to him, and that caused her to moan softly, "I love you so!"

There were different ways to take the blood and he could have done it quickly, but he decided to savour it by taking it slowly, as she asked him to do. She was an artist, always seeking experience. He did not want to deny her that.

His own transformation had been so abrupt — he could not say what value was in the process because he did not know. Karl had been aware of a darkness overwhelming him, of a sharp and consistent pain, of passing out and reviving, and feeling brutalised, all in less than two minutes.

The night he brought Gerlinde over, he fed her blood from his wrist. Back and forth, he fed her, he fed from her, slowly, an orgasmic pleasure/pain experience over all the dark hours. The process was so slow that her body had already begun producing lymphocytes in large numbers, to fight the alien presence. Never once did she complain or pull away. He had been astonished.

Through it all she was as steady as the cathedral, standing firm in her goal to be with him, to be like him, to love him forever, as they had talked then, in the first flush of love. And at one point, where he wavered, so subtly, internally, her sensitivity to him recognised that shift. She stared at him with a soft, loving look and said, "The cathedral we saw earlier, it took centuries to become what it is. It only gets better with time."

Forever, he knew from experience, stretches the concept of time. They both came to understand that. Yet all the decades that passed had not dimmed their affection for one another. Despite the odds, they were in love still and the attraction held. That, more than anything, astounded him.

Karl knew that his strong personality, the mathematical precision of his thinking patterns, would have put off most females. Yet here was Gerlinde, his polar opposite, and perhaps because of that opposition, so like a positive and negative charge, the bond held. She was an artist who perceived the world conceptually in terms of light and shadow, colour, contrast, shape and form... very unlike the way he saw things. He had never noticed what she saw. His view took in more the arrangement of things, the nature of the materials used, and how those materials came to be rearranged into that form. He was the first to be amazed that his seriousness, his penchant for pure reason was never diluted by her whimsy but expanded by it. In a sense, she enabled him to separate the wheat from the chaff and give a deeper meaning to existence.

That night in Köln, before he turned her, as they stared up at the giant structure that humbled both of them, Karl could well understand how the concept of opposites, like thinking and intuition, heaven and hell, how they must, of necessity, come together to create an entirely new element. A stable element that would move evolution ahead.

Gerlinde remarked softly, "It's as though we're only bees. But we're so busy making honey in our little hives, thinking that's everything, unaware of the big picture. We're so small in the universe. We could be squished any second."

"If there were a being who could squish us," Karl said, touched by her vulnerability. That was one of the few times he had seen her so thoughtful.

Suddenly, she turned and smiled at him with that impish smile of hers, the one that caused her eyes to twinkle like brown diamonds, and her naturally turned-up lips to curve further. The effect was of light pouring out of a translucent container, and through her he could understand the nature of 'soul'.

"Sometimes," she laughed, "the divine has a macabre sense of humour. This church could collapse on us right now. God's little practical joke."

Just before sunrise, when the process was almost finished, he took her remaining blood. Seeing her still, cold and lifeless upset him. More than he had anticipated. He remembered that joke about 'God's little practical joke', and terror snaked through him.

He should have waited for her to begin to revive on her own, but he could not wait. The following evening he brought her back like the nosferatu of old. Calling her into a new life. The relief that flooded him when her eyes opened brought pink-tinged tears to his eyes. And he knew then that 'forever' was the right word. They would be together forever.

They had visited Köln one other time, for only a day, en route to Bonn, further north. That had been when Michel was an infant and they had fled the house in Bordeaux to protect him. On that trip, Gerlinde found a postcard of the cathedral standing tall amidst the rubble left by the bombs dropped at the end of World War II. She loved that postcard. She taped it to the west wall of the studio where she had constructed a collage. The black and white card sat near the middle of the construction. The postcard showed the cathedral and the surrounding area; every building had been destroyed, all but the church.

Karl discovered later that the allies had instructions to leave the cathedral standing, if possible — the church was world renowned and a masterpiece of architecture. He wondered if there had been similar instructions concerning any of the oldest temples when Japan was bombed. Of course, those two wars were definitely another era. He thought about some of the wars since then, and the massive, anonymous destruction that human beings had come to accept as normal. 'Smart bombs dropped by dumb people,' Gerlinde had said once.

But apart from the cathedral, Gerlinde did not like Köln much. In fact, she did not like Germany for the most part, although she had been born there, as had Karl. The five years they'd hidden in Bonn left her not exactly depressed, but her joyous spirit had dimmed. Michel was the single light source for all of them then. The remarkable being that gave them hope and represented possibility. The boy had had so many loving parents, and no-one loved him more than Gerlinde, who treated him as if he were a son she'd given birth to.

Karl struggled for composure. There was absolutely no reason for Gerlinde to be in Germany.

He headed downstairs where events were being reviewed again and again, and Michel was asked the same questions over and over, including why he had not smelled blood in the Columbarium. It seemed that the overwhelming scent of embalming fluid was the cause.

Karl sat next to Morianna and said, "Gerlinde has not contacted us yet. She hasn't left a message on Julien's machine either — I asked him and he just phoned his machine to check."

"This does not present a picture that entirely comforts me," she said. "Still, there could be a reasonable explanation. And the fact that David and Kathy are apparently not in Manchester indicates the three are travelling together."

He knew she was making an effort to calm him and appreciated that.

"We have yet to hear from some of the others," Morianna said. This striking female emitted the wisdom of the ages. Profound knowledge was locked firmly in her almond-shaped, violet eyes, displayed in her regal bearing which commanded respect. She appeared Eurasian but her origins were a mystery; Karl did not expect ever to learn of her history. As with the other times he had seen her, Morianna wore many layers of elegant clothing draped over her subtle frame. Gerlinde had said about her, 'She's the most womanly woman I've ever met, and to think, she's a blood drinker!' Julien might be the eldest in their circle but Morianna was not far behind.

Nor was Wing who once told Karl he had existed for over three centuries. Wing came from a time when inscrutable described the Chinese. Today, of course, that was not so, especially since what McLuhan had identified as the 'global village' had become a reality through the media. First the media and communication explosions, and more recently China — through Hong Kong — a land locked in on itself for a millennium, opened to the influences of the rest of the world. These were not easy changes for Wing, reserved by nature, to accept. He looked and dressed the part of the Oriental ancient — short, stocky, nearly bald, his black eyes too intense to be readable; he held his insights close to his chest and one could not understand him easily.

In fact, all of the old ones were difficult to assess. They had a tendency to become inert at times, like lizards, especially when decisions were to be made. Their features seemed to flatten so that they appeared to be almost two dimensional stone carvings.

They resembled works of art, neither proactive nor reactive, and when finally they did move or speak, they demanded attention.

Morianna said that she, Julien and Wing had tried to contact several of the others with no luck. "There are four still unaccounted for, one of whom is Kaellie."

Another old one. Karl felt very uneasy with this news. "Gertig has not been able to contact her either. As you know, she is not easy to locate. None here have shared her blood, only Gertig. He has tracked her and is now travelling to a secret place they share. Before sunrise, we hope to hear from them."

"There's also David and Kathy. And Gerlinde," Karl reminded her. "That's seven missing, altogether."

Morianna's look silenced him. He knew that she understood his worries. "Tell us of your efforts again," she said, for the benefit of new arrivals.

Karl had just started to discuss his phone calls and the tracking of Gerlinde, hoping to lead into the results of the blood tests when the doorbell rang. Carol went to answer it and returned a moment later with David and Kathy.

Karl, relieved, rushed to them, embracing them. André, Carol and Michel felt the same relief, and soon they were all crowded together in the doorway of the living room, Karl firing questions at them.

David said, "We picked up your message this evening. We were en route here anyway, as you know."

"En route here?" Karl said. "How did you know to come?"

Both David and Kathy paused a moment, glanced at one another, then Kathy said, "Well, Gerlinde told us to come here. She said you were all waiting."

"When did you see Gerlinde?" Karl asked anxiously.

"We didn't see her," David said, "but she contacted us, what...? Three evenings ago?" He looked at Kathy for confirmation, and she nodded.

"That's the night she left," Karl said. "The night Chloe died."

"What?" David shouted, and Kathy gasped. "Chloe's dead?" David turned to André who had been holding up fairly well until this moment. Suddenly, as Karl had expected would happen, André went to pieces.

General chaos ensued in the room. David, Carol and Michel comforted André who could not stop crying. André rarely lost control. In the many decades since they had known one another, this might only be the third time Karl had seen a display of any of the more vulnerable emotions coming from him. His strength was in anger but that was also his weakness. Beneath the anger were emotions that left him perhaps the most vulnerable of their kind. Like many of the others, André, in his way, was an enigma.

The room descended further into a state of confusion, everyone buzzing around, André being the focus of it all. Kathy, though, came up to Karl privately. "We didn't know about Chloe," she said, her voice shaking. "It's awful. Chloe was so nice. I didn't know her real well, but she reminded me of this woman Mae in New York. I really liked Chloe. How did she die?"

"I'll tell you that in a minute," Karl said, more than frustrated. He needed answers and he needed them now. "Tell me first about your conversation with Gerlinde. It's imperative that I know what was said. Did you speak with her or did David?"

"Both of us."

"Were you in Manchester?"

"Yeah."

"Where did Gerlinde say she was calling from?"

"Uh, I don't know, but I guess I figured it was from here. She said she was leaving that night for Julien's place."

"What else did she say to you?"

"That's pretty much it. She said she might not be stopping in Manchester — she wanted to — but there probably wouldn't be time. She was in a hurry. She was sorry she'd miss us. Then she talked with David about us coming here."

André was seated in a chair, his head in his hands, sobbing. Michel and Carol sat beside him, and Morianna stood behind him, her hand on the top of his head. Karl saw that David was free for the moment and motioned him over. Although David was shattered by the news, he filled in the blanks.

"She told us we should come here tonight. She said it was important, she couldn't tell me why, and that we dare not contact you or it would spoil the surprise."

"Didn't you think that was odd?" Karl asked.

"Yes and no. Gerlinde is rather mischievous at times, and I suppose I expected this was some sort of surprise party. Your birthday. Or an anniversary, or something like that. But, no, I was not unduly concerned."

This sounded like Gerlinde, but not like her. But Karl did have a sudden recollection of an anniversary, *their* anniversary, of when he had brought Gerlinde into this life. "When you spoke, did she seem to be under any stress?"

"No, not really. She sounded the same as always. Why?"

"Nothing's happened to her, has it?" Kathy said, rattled. She and Gerlinde were about the same age, or at least when they had both been mortal, although Gerlinde had existed closer to half a century, while Kathy had been changed just a few years ago. Gerlinde's lighter-than-air spirit fitted nicely with Kathy's street-smart, spontaneous aggression, and the two had become close quickly. 'G-friends,' Gerlinde laughed.

"I don't know, Kathy," Karl had to admit. "All I can tell you is that I don't know why she told you to come here. And she never made it to Julien's place. I've tracked her to Germany."

"Germany?" David said.

"Yes, and that does not make any sense. But it also doesn't make sense that she would tell you to come here."

"I'm afraid it makes perfect sense," Wing said, and Karl turned to find both Wing and Morianna behind him, like two immense gargoyles, guarding the secrets of the ages. Secrets they had gleaned by hovering over both living and undead and studying their movements. Secrets they would not or could not reveal. And if the looks on their faces could be interpreted in any way at all, Karl would have had to call those looks ominous.

Morianna said in a voice commanding attention, "It is best we all join together and share what information we have."

They began sitting on the classical sofas and chairs, and the Oriental carpet on the floor, facing the large, round coffee table with the black sculpture of the mermaid and the dolphin in the centre, slowly binding together the way a community in grief will knit itself into one unit. Karl had been to funerals in his mortal youth. His memories of those mourning sessions had him identifying more with Michel, Claude and Susan than with the 'adults' in this room of ageless beings. It was only his close and long association with Chloe, a woman he had known over a span of close to half a century, from the time he, André and David had met, that brought the reality of all this home to him in a personal way.

Chloe had been a kind and generous spirit, nurturing, wise in the ways of nature, a woman who had been there for him, for his friends, so many times. She had been instrumental in establishing a bond that said they could be more than predators, jealous of one another's food, prepared at any moment to undermine and harm and betray each other by instinct. She had been in the vanguard of incorporating both their higher instincts and their baser instincts and making sense of it all in a manner that would allow community, something they all craved, as well as preserving their autonomy. A situation the change had seemed to deny them.

And yet even as Karl felt all of the remarkable achievements of this loving female of their kind, he was aware he barely knew her. Chloe was not much older than he to this life. And yet she seemed to have changed old, and it was more than her chronological age at the time she was brought over. Something in her nature aligned her with the old ones. She did not possess their powers yet she was not as 'young' as the others, including himself.

"We are here to share a sad moment," Morianna said. "And at the same time, we must look beyond our sadness for we are all in jeopardy." She did not need to spell it out. Each of them understood the ramifications of murder.

"Before we proceed, we must once again go over what has occurred up to the present. In that way, we have a collective strength that derives from knowledge."

"And it is only knowledge which will save us," Julien added.

Wing said, "If salvation is possible." This left them all contemplating what the old ones were thinking, which would be revealed in time, no doubt.

David and Kathy were filled in and they presented what information they had, which was what they had already told Karl.

And finally Karl had a chance to tell what he knew, about tracking Gerlinde, about her dislike of Germany, and then about his analysis of Chloe's blood. "I managed to isolate the alien element in Chloe's blood. It explains one thing and raises a great number of new questions. Embalming fluid."

"You found... embalming fluid? In both samples?" Jeanette asked.

"Yes. These are trace elements, you understand."

"Do you mean formaldehyde?" David asked.

"Yes, mostly."

"But formaldehyde is a gas, is it not? Could this have come into her blood as vapours?"

"Formaldehyde is a gas, but this was in a liquified form and it's more than formaldehyde: it's embalming fluid."

"Let me get this clear, Karl, if you don't mind," Jeanette said. "You're saying you found traces of embalming fluid in Chloe's blood?"

"Yes."

"What, exactly, does embalming fluid consist of?"

"Formalin is the official word for what is pumped into the veins of a corpse as the blood is being pumped out. It's thirty to forty percent pure formaldehyde, about twelve per cent methyl alcohol — another version of formaldehyde — and maybe another twelve percent methanol — yet more formaldehyde. The rest is water, dyes, stabilisers, and sometimes they add scents, because formaldehyde has such an overpowering odour."

There was a slight pause, then Julien asked, "Do you have a hypothesis as to how this fluid became mixed with her blood?"

Karl had thought quite a bit about it. "One possibility is that Chloe was... interacting with one or more of the bodies in the Columbarium."

"Interacting?" André repeated.

"Michel did mention the intensity of the odour when he entered the Columbarium."

"Yes, but when we reached the entrance of the Columbarium the following evening, we were overwhelmed by the scent of blood first, then formaldehyde," André reminded him.

"Formaldehyde has a powerful smell, but it dissipates quickly when exposed to air. Twenty-four hours would be sufficient time for a good deal of the odour to evaporate."

Karl could feel the unease in the room. He was afraid to say what was truly on his mind, but Julien said it for him.

"Your feeling is that Chloe, for some reason, opened one or more vaults — perhaps a fresh corpse, newly interred — and... consumed this fluid?"

"Not consumed, no. It went directly into her veins as her blood was being drained. As you know, normally we take in blood the way mortals take food, into the stomach. But with us, there is no complicated digestion process and it moves into our veins very quickly, within ten minutes. There was no blood in her stomach — I checked. It's more like..."

"Go on."

"I know this sounds impossible, and I'm not suggesting it, simply saying what it's like."

No-one said a word for a moment. Karl felt a little uncomfortable and decided to take the long way around. "Let me present this slowly. I think we can surmise that a vein or artery ruptured — I'm thinking artery because of the blood on the ceiling. As you all know, it would have had to spurt to reach that height and only an artery could do that —"

"Yes, we know, but she hadn't drunk," André reminded him, his voice tense, intuiting what was coming.

"But she would have had sufficient blood in her body from the night before to bleed like that, if she were upset. What blood was inside her would have pumped much faster and, when the artery was pierced, it would have come out like a fountain."

Julien said, "I think we can all agree that this is likely what occurred."

"You were about to tell us about the traces of embalming fluid," Jeanette said.

"Yes. Well, I don't have an answer, but I think if we're going to be searching for an answer, this pattern might help point us in the right direction. It's as though one of the newly buried, and I do mean newly, was not dead but rose up and bit her."

"Like a vampire?" Kathy gasped. "I mean, one of the ones you see in movies —"

"I believe we all caught your drift," David said.

"Like a zombie," Carol clarified for all of them. "Something not alive, since it was embalmed and had no blood, but something still animated. Something that might stun Chloe so much she wouldn't be able to defend herself."

"Wait a minute!" André said. "Do you know how ridiculous this sounds? This is crazy."

"Dad, it makes sense. That's what I was feeling in there, that the dead were alive —"

"Michel, stop it! Karl, in all the time I've known you, I've always respected your intellect. This, though, is nonsense. And personally, I'm offended. Chloe was my relative —"

"Hold on, André," Karl said. "We all cared about Chloe."

"I think," David said, "Karl might be speaking in a metaphoric sense and not a literal sense, André. I don't want to put words in your mouth, Karl, but I can't believe you believe in zombies."

Karl felt a little offended himself. He knew his emotions were stronger than usual because of the lack of blood, because of worry about Gerlinde, and because of this whole damned situation. "Thank you, David," he said, his voice in his own ears strained. "No, I do not believe in zombies, although I suspect most mortals don't believe in us, and we could draw a parallel."

"There are days," André said, "when I don't believe in mortals."

Karl smiled a little, knowing André was trying hard to ease down. "What I'm saying is this is a template. It's one way formalin could have gotten into her blood in trace elements. If we think along the lines of the improbable, then we keep open to not only the possible but the probable. There are obviously other possibilities, if any of you would like to hear them."

"Please," Carol said. "I want to hear."

Several of the others encouraged him, and Karl went on. "She might have fallen into embalming fluid or touched it, then touched a wound at her throat during or after she was attacked."

Michel said, "But where did the embalming fluid come from?"

"From inside the Columbarium, obviously," David said. "One would expect to find it there."

Suddenly, Karl had an odd feeling, one he could not pinpoint. A feeling of a long-lost connection, but out of reach. He stored the feeling in his memory to revive and investigate later. Just then, the phone rang. His heart leapt with hope.

Carol answered and handed it over to Julien, who spoke for perhaps ten minutes. Immediately, it became clear to Karl that Gertig was on the other end of the line, and that the news was not good.

When Julien hung up he reported that Kaellie was found. Her body had been torn to pieces like Chloe's, bite marks at the important veins and arteries, but blood everywhere so she had not been drained. "It appears she did not struggle," Julien said, his voice even, but his aura dark.

The stunned silence reflected how unnerved each of them felt. That one so old had been mutilated...

"A malevolent energy stalks us," Morianna said soberly. "We are in grave danger. Grave danger, indeed."

# CHAPTER SEVEN

T HE EXPLOSION OF VERBIAGE RANG OF CHAOS TO Karl's ears. There were more opinions than bodies in the room. He listened carefully to all of it, trying to get a feel for the turn of the tide. Eventually everyone calmed down enough that they were beginning to listen to one speaker at a time.

"We cannot allow these acts of violence to go unavenged," André said for maybe the fifth time.

Jeanette said, "But we don't know who's responsible —"

"Of course we do! It's Antoine."

David said, "I tend to agree with you, André, but until we have evidence linking him directly we need to proceed as though it could be anyone."

"What more evidence do we need? A business card left behind?"

Carol put her hand on André's shoulder. He had returned to the fury that usually charged him and the circumstances were so personal for him that Karl knew he would be out of control much of the time.

David said, "André, we all loved Chloe."

Carol's simple act and David's plain expression combined to dent the armour that protected André and, for a moment, he looked subdued.

"Look," Kathy said, "if Antoine did it, wouldn't he want us to know? I mean, he promised revenge, right?"

"He doesn't need to hit us over the head," Jeanette said. "His power is in mystifying us. Don't forget, he's old." She looked at Julien, who nodded imperceptibly. "He travels along routes that most of us in this room are not familiar with. I think Julien, Morianna and Wing are the best ones to assess Antoine's moves and motives."

"If it is Antoine," David added. His experiences on Fire Island had taught him clarity of thinking, if nothing else, Karl thought. David had been through so much that he had come to reject face value and to be more analytical. Despite the grim circumstances of the present, Karl smiled a little smile to himself and thought: how the three of us have changed! David, once so poetic and dreamy, now focused more logically. André, victim of his own defensiveness, had become far more expressive of a range of emotions. And Karl knew he, too, must have altered — he just couldn't get a grip on how. He did know, though, that the changes had come about in each of them because of the mortal women they had altered. The love of Kathy forced David to fight for something of value. Carol had brought out André's deeply buried emotions through her perseverance and their connection through their son Michel. And Karl knew Gerlinde had changed him.

Before meeting her in the 1950s his life had been so empty. He had drifted in an aquarium of concepts. Life was a giant philosophical game to him. Divorced from real needs, a good debate was the best he could hope for. He had been mostly content to fill his waking hours with mental gymnastics. But he could not escape altogether the feeling of desolation that crept over him as he fell asleep at dawn and woke at sunset.

Gerlinde had been like a splash of colour to a black and white life. Of course, he had had women before. He expected nothing more than that they be temporary distractions, and they were. Each may have cared about him in her own way, but none could accept him as he was, for *what* he was. And none could pierce his intellectual armour. Gerlinde did. She loved him — enough to want to be with him for eternity, which meant the change. And her love was not the slavish kind which he would not have been able to tolerate for very long. She was true to her own self, possessing her own deep-seated interests. She was always ready for action and held strong values which she was not afraid to express, even if she stood alone. He always marvelled at the myriad of ways they were so different yet so compatible. It must be true in all areas of life, he thought — opposites attract.

Gerlinde. Why was he thinking of her in the past tense? He wondered where she was and worried about her safety. She must be all right. He could track her which meant she was alive. But why was she in Germany? And not making contact...

The volume rose and opinions ran rampant again, and Karl felt he had to contribute some stability to the discussion which was threatening to get out of hand by going nowhere. As always, when he spoke, everyone listened. "My thinking is aligned with David's, and some of the rest of you: it appears to be Antoine, but we cannot be naive and rule out the possibility that it might be some other being or beings. To do that would be suicidal. Think about what it would mean if we direct our energy towards Antoine when the source might be elsewhere. That would leave us even more vulnerable than we apparently are."

"*Merde!*" André suddenly shouted. "Who else could have done this? He's destroyed Chloe, Kaellie, three others —"

"We don't know about the other three, and we have yet to get the details about Kaellie's death —"

"Well, we can surmise!" André snarled, as if the obvious eluded Karl. "And from what Gertig has said, Kaellie's murder fits the pattern. She was torn limb from limb, and appears to have been caught unawares —"

"Or at the least it appears as though she didn't fight back either," Karl reminded him.

This was not what André wanted to hear. If Kaellie, and more to the point for him, if Chloe had submitted to this violence, he didn't want to know about it. And Karl could understand. In André's family there was a precedent, one which he was trying hard to reverse.

"I think," Jeanette spoke quietly, "Chloe, and Kaellie would have fought if they could. I don't know why it appears that they did not, but I knew both of them in a way that convinces me they did not just submit to Antoine, or whoever was responsible. They didn't fight because for some reason they couldn't fight."

"I believe that we three might provide some of the missing pieces to what is puzzling you all," Morianna said. The elegant old one folded her hands gracefully in her lap, which looked more like an elaborate Thai dance movement than anything else.

Wing took the lead. "We three have lived a long time, collectively our existence totals more than fifteen hundred years," he said, meaning he, Morianna and Julien. "Our knowledge comes from much time alone, meditating on the movements of the universe. In my culture, the *I CHING* best expresses those movements."

Karl had, of course, seen the *I CHING. The Book of Changes*, as the translation went, allowed one to ask a question, to sort out a confusion. Wing assumed that everyone knew about the *I CHING*, and Karl was certain most did, until Kathy said, "What's the... *I CHING?*"

Wing explained simply for her and for any others who were unfamiliar with the ancient procedure. "By tossing yarrow stalks six times, a questioner creates a pattern — six lines composed of broken and solid lines. The six lines together form a hexagram and there are sixty-four possible hexagrams, or combinations of broken and solid lines. By reading the lines from low to high and focusing on particularly obvious energies, the questioner can locate his or her position in the flow of time."

While Wing continued, Kathy looked perplexed. Of course she would be confused. She was a neophyte and a concrete thinker besides, who needed to see things in order to understand them. "It's a bit like Tarot cards," Jeanette explained to her. "A divination tool."

Kathy nodded. She, like most westerners, was familiar with Tarot cards, and predicting the future. But from Karl's reading of the *I CHING* — and he was mostly familiar with the Bollingen translation by Richard Wilhelm, the one with an introduction by Carl Jung — he understood that this perspective on universal patterns was meant to be seen as a brief pause in an ever-changing state. *The Book of Changes* required reflection from the questioner who was cautioned to not ask too many questions, but to wait

97

until, like a flower ready to burst into bloom, the time was right to ask — because only then could the knowledge embedded in the answer be incorporated.

"This is fascinating," André said dryly, "but let's stick to the point."

"Patience," Morianna reminded him, and the old ones were the only ones who could say such a thing to André and get away with it.

"The flow of the universe," Wing continued, "presumes change. We especially are not immune to it."

"One might say we are more subject to change," Julien added cryptically.

"Why?" Karl wanted to know.

"Because we are beings who have experienced more change than any other lifeform on this planet. To be born, to die, to be reborn..."

"Of course," Morianna clarified, "there are those mortals whose beliefs allow for this concept yet, for us, it is a reality. Mortals think of little deaths only. We cannot dismiss mortals. And yet, we have a conscious knowledge of the progression that expands our views. Because of expanded time. And also the nature of our existence."

"Process for us becomes praxis," Karl said, and Morianna nodded.

"Antoine has an expanded view, doesn't he?" André snapped, but the others let it pass.

"What does this have to do with the murders?" Karl asked, sensing that André was about to explode again in frustration and wanting to temper his passions.

"We three come from eras far different from those of you who were altered in this century, or even the last," Morianna said. "Antoine is like us. We understand a... phase which none of you can yet conceive of, although you may have tasted it. The eldest of you is but two hundred years walking the earth. This is like a drop of dew on one leaf, in one garden, in one country of a very large planet filled with dew on leaves in gardens and fields every morning."

Karl though it odd that her metaphor would focus on dew, since undoubtedly she had not seen any for hundreds of years. Perhaps that image became numinous for her precisely because it was out of reach.

"Do any of you three think it was Antoine?" Carol asked.

None of the three would speak at first until Julien finally said, "What we know is that those who have died have been old ones —"

"Chloe was not an old one," André said.

"Not in time, but in spirit," Morianna told him. "Chloe was exceptional in that her wisdom exceeded her span of existence. She felt the rhythms of the universe acutely, as do we."

"And also," Julien continued, "if the three we have yet to hear from are dead, then those who have died have all been not only old, but the children of Antoine."

"Three we haven't heard from, plus Gerlinde," Karl reminded them. "But Antoine did not create Kaellie. Or did he?"

"Kaellie's origins are a mystery, even to us," Morianna said.

"But she said she was created six hundred years ago, a century after Antoine, or what we guestimate to be Antoine's change," André said.

Julien said, "From what we know of Kaellie, we believe she may have created Antoine."

This stunned every one of them to silence. It had not occurred to Karl although, of course, someone must have created Antoine. But this made no sense. "I thought Kaellie was not as old as you, Julien. Am I wrong? We were told you are the oldest, other than Antoine."

"Karl, you are far from wrong, but you are not right," Julien said. "I am the eldest of our community, yet all is not as it seems."

"Well, how is it then?" André snapped.

"May I?" Morianna said, and Julien deferred to her. "Kaellie is unique. She has lived many existences, in many forms."

"I have no idea what you're talking about," André said, losing what little patience he held on to.

"Please explain," Jeannette said. "We're all so very confused."

"Kaellie," Morianna said, "holds the secret of not just birth, death and rebirth, but beyond that, to death, birth and rebirth again, and again."

The clock ticked loudly for several moments while they all digested the ramifications of these remarks. It was Kathy who put it together succinctly, "She's figured out how to die as a vampire and come back again."

Morianna nodded.

"How is that done?" Karl asked.

"We are not certain," Julien said. "There are ways we can die, as each of you know, but full regeneration is not within our knowledge."

"Didn't you ask her?" Karl said, stunned.

"Of course."

Wing said, "Her ways are her own, and she would only reveal them in her time, which is how it must be."

"Meaning," David said, "she died for good before she had a chance to reveal this vital information. Or will she regenerate?"

"We have no way of knowing."

"Maybe Gertig —"

"Gertig does not know," Morianna said, "nor can he confirm that Kaellie created Antoine."

"Then this is as much speculation as is whether or not Antoine committed the murders," Karl said, feeling frustrated. He respected the mystical ways of the old ones but they were not as scientific as he liked, and he did not always grasp enough of their meaning to put things together in a manner that allowed him to feel grounded with understanding.

Julien, Morianna and Wing glanced at one another. Their eyes seemed to convey information that Karl could not fathom.

Wing stood and moved across the room. He always carried a satchel with him, usually slung across his body, the leather so worn the colour was unidentifiable. Into the hide he had carved Chinese characters, the etchings painted in black India ink that Wing refreshed from time to time. Mandarin Karl knew, because he recognised one as the figure of a man striding in a carefree manner.

Wing returned with two books, one in Chinese and the other the *I CHING*, the version Karl knew. He paused for a moment, then handed the English version to Julien, who accepted the book, and Karl understood that Julien would read to them the English translation. To Morianna, Wing handed a square of pale rice paper with a gold impression in the centre, a smooth board onto which the rice paper fitted perfectly, a small bottle of black ink, and a fine sable-tipped brush with a bamboo handle. Besides the book in Chinese, Wing also held in his hands a piece of bright yellow silk and a considerable number of stalks, which Karl suspected were yarrow, and that meant there must be forty-nine of them, although he'd never seen them used. Normally, Westerners threw three coins, heads representing a solid line, tails a broken line, and in each toss whatever dominated determined the type of line.

Wing said, "The yarrow creates a picture of the moment. It encompasses every element of the moment, down to seemingly nonessential details."

"Because you never know what will be relevant?" Jeanette asked.

Wing nodded. He composed himself in a meditative posture on his knees, opened the piece of silk and placed it before him on the Oriental carpet, then lay the book on top of the silk. He held the yarrow stalks upright in both hands and closed his eyes. The room fell silent. After a time, he dropped the stalks onto the book. Some stayed on the book, and many scattered over the silk.

From the satchel, he removed a small but beautiful abacus of oiled rosewood and ebony beads. Silently, Wing counted the stalks — although Karl could not figure out how he was counting on the abacus. Eventually, he came up with a total. He turned to

Morianna and said something in Mandarin, which presumably Morianna understood. She dipped the tip of the paintbrush into the ink and painted on the square of rice paper a broken line. To the right of it, she painted a small circle.

Wing gathered the stalks together and, when the moment seemed right, dropped them again, and counted again. From what he said to her, Morianna painted another broken line, with a small circle next to it.

Once six lines were painted onto the rice paper, Wing gathered up the yarrow stalks, tied them together with the black and red tie with gold dragons painted on it, and opened the book he held. While he did this, Julien opened the English version.

"I have gathered the energy of this assembly, which is composed of large questions we all share, and the individual questions each of you is asking," Wing told them. "The *I CHING* will respond to you individually and collectively. It will also convey to those of you who are ready to understand it what we three fathom so well, and which we cannot adequately express in words."

Wing began to read from the Chinese book and, at the same time, Julien read the English version. The two voices did not drown one another out, but somehow overlapped and, oddly, Karl felt he almost understood the Mandarin.

"The hexagram created is number twenty-three, PO, which means Splitting Apart," Julien said.

Karl could almost feel the quiver of terror vibrate throughout the room. From the drawing Morianna had made, he saw five broken lines and the sixth one, on the top, solid. Even he could see that this was an extremely unstable image, because the broken lines could not support the heavy, solid line.

Julien read from the book about how the darkness is about to move up and overthrow the last line by exerting a disintegrating influence. He read how dark forces overcome what is strong by a gradual undermining until everything collapses.

"The Judgement," Julien read, "is Splitting Apart. It does not further one to go anywhere."

He continued reading, and the essence of what Karl gleaned seemed to be that they should remain still and do nothing. It was a dangerous time with collapse inevitable. It was a question of how one dealt with the inevitable.

Finally Wing and Julien reached the individual lines. All six were read out. Then Wing explained that certain lines that are overwhelmingly broken or solid have special significance. "These will direct us, show us fate," Wing said. It was as if a collective breath were drawn in the room.

Karl could see that Morianna had made a symbol next to four of the six lines, and he presumed these were the significant lines.

The broken line at the beginning talked about the leg of a bed as split. "Should you persevere, you will be destroyed. Misfortune would be the outcome."

The broken line in the second place was also prominent. Here, the edge of the bed is split. Again, destruction for those foolish enough to persevere.

The fourth line showed the bed split to the skin — Karl thought this must refer to the beds of the ancients, made of animal hide. The result — misfortune.

Finally, the last primary line was the solid line at the top. The writing painted pictures of a large fruit uneaten. For the ancients, this would have signified a great waste of something valuable and important to existence, although clearly this fruit falls to the ground, which means a re-seeding, a positive note amidst the gloom. A further image reveals that the superior man receives a carriage, a great and wondrous gift, one which permits movement. At this point, the inferior man's house is split apart.

Wing closed the book, and Julien did the same. "As the *I CHING* tells us," Wing said, "these are the laws of nature. Evil does not destroy only good, but must, of necessity, destroy itself. Evil negates, and possesses no innate strength on its own."

After a pause, André said, "Is this positive or negative?"

Kathy said, "The ending's not bad, but it sure sounds like hell to get there and we're in for it."

"That is very close to the truth," Morianna said.

Julien added, "A cruel destiny awaits us and one cannot alter destiny."

"A superior man or woman will assume the proper position until destiny plays itself out," Wing said. "That way leads to the best position for survival."

The group paused for refreshment. Carol passed around juice glasses of blood from the freezer, defrosted in the microwave. Karl declined, because he wanted to track Gerlinde again before the rise of the sun in two hours. He felt inordinately weak. He had not drunk yet tonight, and last night he had only drunk before sunrise, which meant he had not derived the benefits of nourishment when he needed them, when he was awake. Still, it was important to keep tabs on Gerlinde and he was the only one who could.

"What about tracking Antoine?" André asked. "He created David and Karl. And indirectly he created me. And Julien, wasn't the girl who bit you turned by Antoine?"

"I was bitten by another," Julien said.

Karl suddenly realised he did not know Julien's vampiric origins. Julien had never revealed them. The old ones were like that.

"Well, there are still three of us," André said.

"You cannot track him," Julien told him. "Chloe's blood contained trace elements of Antoine but that would not dominate in your change. They were too faint for her to track and far too faint for you to identify."

"Are you certain, Julien? After all, Ariel could track David and, more to the point, Michel tracked Ariel, tasting only a drop of her blood. And Michel was a child, still more human than not."

"Michel is exceptional. And blood shared by equals is not the same as the draining that takes place between the mentor and the apprentice."

"Mentor!" André snarled. "I can't see Antoine in that role."

Julien waited patiently. He knew André very well. There was more.

André, frustrated, said, "All right, then David and Karl can do it since Antoine took both of them."

"One cannot easily track one's creator," Morianna said. "The creators are like mothers, they created their children. A mother always possesses a sixth sense regarding her child. She knows the whereabouts and wellbeing of the child intuitively. But the child cannot sense the mother. It is not evolved yet. This is the way nature protects children."

"David and Karl aren't children. David's existed over one hundred years and Karl close to two hundred —"

"This brief time on our plane is like an infant to a mother," Morianna assured him.

"We don't know that," André argued. "They could try."

David said, "I've tried to track Antoine."

"And?"

David shook his head.

"I've had no success either," Karl added before André could pursue this line.

Karl thought back to when he had been altered, so abruptly, so violently, with but a glimpse of the being who stalked him down at the wharf by the Rhine, then through the streets of Düsseldorf to the house where he was staying, who beat him viciously, leaving him barely conscious, then siphoned the blood from his jugular so quickly he went into shock, all with a diabolical laugh. And then left him to die. But Karl did not die, and there were many times later when he wished he'd had. Because, despite the hatred and fear he felt, Karl was soon lonely for that being who had done him such harm by not only taking his blood but forcing Karl to drink his. He supposed it was the same for all 'children' as Morianna put it. Whether the parent is nurturing or rejecting, tender or violent, it makes no difference. The child needs the parent.

He had searched for Antoine — and of course it was only later, when he met David, and Chloe, and still later when he met some of the others whom Antoine had begat that he came to realise just how much of the community the old one had created. But long before he had met others of his kind, when he was alone, struggling with his 'condition' as he had at first conceptualised it, Karl had searched.

Those early days he had been off-balance all the time. Existing only during the night hours caused him consternation and would not gibe with his logic, but lethargy proved to be a friend in disguise, forcing him to wake and sleep on the safe side of both dusk and dawn, despite thinking this made no sense.

What got to him most was the blood drinking. A normally sedate human being, he became ravaged by the blood thirst. He had always been able to control his impulses and his physical drives, but the lust for *vitae* was something else.

His scientific brain led him to experiment. He tried raw meat and found it indigestible. He substituted animal blood for human blood — he could drink it but it did nothing to cut the craving. He drank plasma which he found sustained him, but acquiring a sufficient supply was nearly impossible. The synthetic blood he was hoping would be developed hadn't been, or he would have tried that too.

He also explored abstinence and its variations. He tried to regulate his intake, drinking less and less, or measured amounts consistently. He even starved himself in an effort to gain supremacy over what dominated his every waking moment. Those efforts, naturally, caused a severe reaction and swung him sharply to the other side of the pendulum. Nightly, like an alcoholic battling an addiction, he grabbed and drank. Young, old, male, female, sick, healthy, he preyed on them all, anyone with human blood still pulsing through their veins. It took over a decade to gain an upper hand in the regulatory process, and another two decades to feel some confidence regarding that delicate dependency.

And during all that time, he searched for Antoine. Then, he had not known about tracking. But instinctively, he guessed that the connection between them must be strong. He knew the *Nosferatu* had sussed him out — he was prey. Surely he might be sensitised to his predator. There was so much Karl needed to know and wanted to share, and he felt desperate for contact with one like himself. And now that he thought of it, again, Morianna's metaphor of mother and child rang true. He needed Antoine, but Antoine did not need him.

Try as he might, Karl could not locate this one who had forced him through a demise, leaving him desolate and alone in this nether-world state that resembled being half-alive and half-dead.

At points, he came within range of others of his kind and quickly became aware of their threat to one another. But eventually, miraculously, he met André and David, and found kindred spirits — perhaps because they were all 'new'. They had not existed for centuries, had not become callous, did not feel the urge to compete with one another. André's aunt, Chloe, seemed to be the source of his co-operative spirit, although André possessed a defensiveness borne of traumatising experiences that forever tormented him. David's gentle but agonising nature allowed him an emotional openness the old ones no longer possessed. And Karl had always been noncompetitive. The change did not alter the basic chemistry of his personality.

Karl, David and André shared what they knew. Each of them had experimented with tracking in their own way, and the combined knowledge helped them refine the technique. Still, Karl had never been able to sense Antoine. And even on Fire Island, when he and Antoine were only a few feet apart, when the power of that being radiated through the night like the energy of a black hole, pulling Karl's allegiance away from David, away from André, from his friends, and towards that sucking, swallowing source that had so altered his destiny, even then, as Karl fought hard to maintain his loyalties, his integrity, his autonomy, he had not been able to sense Antoine other than as another being like himself. But he knew Antoine could track him. And on Fire Island he had strongly felt Antoine's efforts to control him.

Suddenly, he heard Morianna say, "I have not been able to track my creator."

Of all of their kind that Karl knew, Morianna and Kaellie were the two whose origins were most shrouded in mystery. Neither had ever even alluded to their change. Karl asked, afraid he might offend her with such a direct question, "Who created you?"

He was surprised she answered him, but even more surprised to hear her say, "Antoine."

We are an incestuous breed, he thought. So tied to one another through the exchange of blood. One begat the next, who begat the next, and so on. And there was one of their number at least who had begat many. Antoine had created a plethora, a world of dark beings. He could destroy his offspring as well. Apparently at will. Infanticide? Karl wondered.

He thought of the chain: Chloe had created André, he created Carol. Michel was birthed like a human. David changed Kathy. Julien changed Jeanette and together they brought over Susan and Claude. Wing never identified his creator, but it was not Antoine — he had made it clear it was an ancestor. Kaellie had made Gertig. And Karl had altered Gerlinde.

Of the others, three had been created by Antoine — the three who might be dead — and the others had all been changed by someone in the community.

If the three were dead, that meant that David, Karl and Morianna were Antoine's only direct descendants still in existence.

As if his thought were a universal one, Karl, David and Morianna glanced at one another. It's clear, Karl thought. Our days are numbered.

The three got up as a unit and moved to a small room down the hall. The others understood — intuition tended to reverberate through their community, and they let them go.

# CHAPTER EIGHT

O NCE THEY WERE SEATED TOGETHER IN A ROOM only large enough for a loveseat, two small armchairs, a two-foot long footstool and a little table, plus a wallshelf that contained a CD player and a few dozen CDs, Karl said, "Antoine vowed to kill us all. He's starting with his brood."

"But how does he attack?" David said. "So that they don't fight back? Is it simply because they were turned by him? Could they be that much in awe of his powers?"

"I know you were preoccupied David, but trust me, I felt his power on Fire Island."

"As did I," Morianna admitted. "I doubt one ever becomes entirely immune to the mother — the cellular tie alone is enormous."

This was not good news. If Morianna felt it too, and she had existed for half a millennium, what hope did Karl and David have of resisting Antoine?

David turned to Karl. "Are you telling me that the pull would have caused you to simply let him rip you to shreds?"

"I don't know," Karl admitted. "It was intense and I fought it, but I have the feeling I succeeded only because so much was happening, and he was distracted by other events."

Morianna said, "The difficulty with the creator which I see is that as one is 'birthed', if I may use that word, so the relationship is solidified for both. In other words, Antoine took each of us forcefully. We will always be susceptible to his use of force, and it would take much to overcome our natural inclination to submit."

"Because the pattern has been established?" Karl said. "And we, like humans, are creatures of habit?"

"Yes."

"I'm proof, am I not, that patterns can be overcome," David pointed out.

"Indeed," Morianna told him. "But Ariel was not your creator."

Karl could only conjure up a picture using mortals as the template: abused children of an alcoholic, who always fall prey to their fears of that powerful, dominant force. It was not a picture he wanted to look at for very long and, like David, a part of him would not acknowledge such helplessness.

Michel had been standing in the doorway and Morianna motioned him in, saying, "Young and precious one, instinctively I believe you must hear what we say. Join us."

Michel, looking pensive, took a seat on the footstool in front of the chair on which she sat.

"All right, aside from the issue of dominance, and even admitting we cannot sense our creator, wouldn't those who died have sensed him just because he's another of our kind?" David asked.

"You would think so," Karl said. "That's what is so baffling."

"I've been thinking," Michel said. "About how come I smelled embalming fluid so strongly and didn't smell the blood. I didn't see any drawers open or any bodies lying around... except Chloe."

"Yes, I've been thinking about that too," Karl said. "Did you notice the smell as being stronger near Chloe's body?"

"Yeah."

"Near either of the walls?"

"Uh, not really. I mean, I was so weirded out by then, I didn't notice much of anything else. But I did look around me, because I was afraid that whoever did it was still there."

Karl nodded. "We did not find any containers of formalin, or find it in any of the vaults, nor did we find any of the coffins open or any of the bodies leaking fluid. I think we have to assume that the formalin was not from one of the dead bodies but was something brought into the Columbarium. It infected her blood because something or someone touched Chloe and bit her with formalin on the skin and teeth, or she touched someone or something with formalin on their body. This formalin infected the blood going through her veins. And that all this took place just inside the entrance to the Columbarium."

David said, "That doesn't move us much ahead in this game of wits with the murderer."

"No, it doesn't," Karl agreed. "We're missing some large pieces of this puzzle. One of the biggest is why Chloe, and Kaellie apparently, did not resist. Do we know where Kaellie died?"

"I cannot tell you the exact location," Morianna said, "but Julien learned from Gertig that she, too, died in a place of death — a funeral home."

"What?" Karl said, astonished.

"This boggles the mind." David shook his head. "What was she doing in such a place?"

"Apparently," Morianna said, "she and Gertig own a chain of such establishments."

"I knew they had one..." Karl said. "I remember Julien talking about it. In London."

"They own a dozen or more."

"Man, this is too sick!" Michel said. "I mean, are all you guys into hanging around the dead all the time?"

Karl saw a look of fear on Michel's face. This was something the boy had not considered before. But neither had Karl. It just struck him now how important death seemed to be to some of their kind. How had he missed the obvious?

"I may be able to shed light on this," Morianna said to all of them. "Please bear with me. What I have to relate is not an easy concept to convey, and I have not expressed it before. The old ones know this instinctively — we all have heart knowledge. Therefore, we have never spoken about it because there has been no need. Wing tried to impart this with the *I CHING* and perhaps, in time, that wisdom will surface on the pond of understanding and become clear to others. Unfortunately, though, I believe that words alone cannot truly convey some things. Only experience.

111

"My years are long and, of course, I have been through much during the centuries of inhabiting this planet. The external changes of cultures, nations, even of the biological life of the planet herself, that living entity which supports us all, they have paralleled my interior life. Consequently, I have been forced to undergo a kind of... renaissance in my being from time to time.

"You see, you are male and have always been so. You cannot easily comprehend this. For mortal females, hormonal shifts by the moon preordain that a woman will experience cycles."

"Uh, isn't this kind of sexist," Michel blurted. "I mean, even human beings don't think like that anymore."

"Young one, I speak beyond cultural developments and tap back to what is larger, to what cannot be denied. To biology."

Michel had that youthful brashness that let him plunge in with what knowledge he possessed, as if it were all the knowledge in the universe. As if those who were older could not possibly comprehend where he was coming from. Karl was glad they had raised Michel to participate. The boy felt free to question and that was always a good thing. And he managed it without being obnoxious.

"Think of the glaciers," Morianna was saying. "Does it make sense to call them useless because they are from another age? Or the appendix in a human body. No-one knows why it is there, and yet to say it should not be there presumes a godlike view. That type of thinking is a cultural interpretation of what precedes human history. Biological fact is unalterable. All the jargon in the world cannot dismiss what nature deems truth by the actuality of its existence and, in this regard, what I am alluding to is this: monthly, a woman is brought to her knees, close to the ground, where she may, if she listens, hear the heartbeat of what certain peoples call the Great Mother. She must undergo an ordeal from within that leads her to this, whether she wants to undergo it or not. Each month she faces death and 'dies'.

"For you males, it is not the same. Your challenges are external, always, and without them you will never feel rooted in the universe because death eludes you."

112

"I understand what you're saying," Karl said. He knew her analysis was correct, if quaintly put. He had long felt it was one of the reasons for the attraction between the genders. From his side, he knew Gerlinde understood this passing through phases, this rite of passage to the core of her being. What would be to him and other males an initiation which hopefully they would be subjected to in order to mature, females are subjected to automatically. Gerlinde encouraged him and assured him that he could survive anything. And he trusted that because she had.

"I do not disagree with you," David said, "but we have all died."

"*You* have," Michel said.

Morianna touched his arm in much the same way she had touched his father earlier that evening.

"We have died or have imitated death, for we still walk. We still take nourishment, and so forth," Morianna went on. "I tell you of mortal biology for this reason: because I lived my entire mortal life as a female, from menstruation, through the years of conception, to menopause, because I experienced the birth, death, and rebirth monthly for forty years, I recognise the nature of patterns from my mortal experience. There are patterns to our preternatural existence as well. The shadow of these patterns predates my change from mortal to this state, so the only correlation I can present to you is from my mortal state. I call these female patterns, or feminine, if you will, which might make more sense. Especially since you males undergo similar patterns but, as I say, they are external. And, of course, you possess a feminine energy, as females possess a masculine energy. It is only biology that determines on which side we fall, but that is a digression at this point in what I am saying."

"These patterns, are they like archetypes?" Michel asked.

The boy had a strong interest in Jungian psychology. Karl knew it had been Chloe who had directed him that way. Michel would miss her deeply.

"In a sense, yes, Michel. But in another sense these patterns are more like phases and cannot be easily personified or imaged as archetypes often are. In much the way Carl Jung mapped out the archetypical energies present in the collective unconscious, I have identified major patterns or phases which affect all life, and affect our kind in a particular manner.

"Let me tell you a story, a brief glimpse from my life, out of which, perhaps, you may know some of what I know, and this may explain in a simple manner what appears to be incomprehensible behaviour in Chloe, Kaellie, and possibly the others as well.

"Three centuries ago, that would have been the early 1700s, I found myself in Belgium in what was then still a town, Gent. I spent much time there and in Brugge. The canals, the lovely architecture along the water, the castles and churches, all so picturesque, the flavour distinctly Dutch — these places fed my soul.

"There is in Gent a cathedral, Saint Bavo's. Even on my first visit there, that cathedral was much as it is today. The earliest part had been constructed in the Twelfth Century and had already vanished by the 1700s. As with every cathedral in Europe, Saint Bavo's was built over centuries, in this case between 1300 and 1559, and the bulk of what was built over those two and a half centuries was available to me. And of course, Saint Bavo's is famous for one particular work, *The Lamb of God*, painted in 1432 by Jan Van Eyck.

"What can I tell you about the painting? Karl, you have seen it. And you, David?"

David nodded.

"Yes," Karl said. "It's a marvellous work of art." He had visited the cathedral with Gerlinde who was utterly overcome with this very early painting, so well preserved. The colours — still vivid after centuries — the expressive faces, the very Flemish quality of the postures and style of dress had entranced her. *The Lamb of God* was an enormous painting, composed of smaller

114

panels which folded in, screen-like, on a large main panel. The focus of it all was depicted in that central panel — the appearance of Christ, the Lamb. The panels around the Lamb specialised: angels, church officials, saints, ordinary people, all concentrated on the centre. Karl had been particularly taken with the painting of the Virgin.

"What attracted me initially," Morianna said, "is the rendering of Christ as an actual lamb. The artist took the metaphor and made it obvious. Everyone in the painting congregates worshipfully around the white lamb with the halo. *The Lamb of God* as a lamb! Such simplicity is touching, is it not? I found it endearing.

"As I stood meditating on the painting, I began to understand the nature of the lamb, of the Christ, a metaphor for sacrifice. A lamb led to the slaughter. One sacrifices oneself and blood is spilled for the good of the many.

"To say that the metaphor appealed to me is to understate what I experienced. I am from a culture rooted in Buddhism. In that religion, the concept of sacrifice towards enlightenment comes close to the Christian concepts. Every religion has a version of this: the Hindus, the Moslems... Did not Moses lead his people to freedom yet he was required to sacrifice his passion to see the Promised Land? Something about the Christian metaphor struck a cord in me. I believe I was in the right place at the right time, as mortals say. Or, as Carl Jung would have put it,..." She looked at Michel, who looked at her, "...synchronicity occurred. My inner and outer realities aligned and were mirror reflections of one another.

"Over the following decade I became obsessed with the metaphor of the sacrificial lamb as one that would give my existence meaning. You must realise that I, as with all of our kind — all but Michel — had spent most of my waking hours alone. Then, I was apart from my own kind, apart from humanity, an alienated being adrift in the universe, like an embryo floating in amniotic fluid. For those of us who are older, the path was more painful. We did not possess the ability — due to our fears of course — to amalgamate. Isolation was what we expected, our existence from conception had been founded on it. We did not see another way. Had we had the benefits of community, we might be different today. Or, perhaps not.

"In any event, as my obsession grew, I began to believe that my sacrifice would bring together those others who existed. I did not know them, but knew *of* them, catching fleeting glimpses here and there, but we avoided one another for safety's sake. This led to despair, naturally. I constructed a scenario in my mind, very elaborate and detailed, wherein if I could find a way to extinguish myself, it would in some way affect the others, for we have always felt the loss of any of our own. I will spare you the details of my thought processes. Suffice it to say that I believed that if they could understand that I had not died at the hands of one of us, nor at the hands of mortals, but had willingly brought myself like a lamb to the slaughter, my death, like the death of Christ, might signify a giving that transcends the norm. A sacrifice that can lead to a higher value. And through it, the others could be saved from the excruciating isolation. I hoped that those others, the ones who had come before me, and the ones still to be brought over, might find a way to overcome their fears and bond together, although I did not have a specific method as to how this could be accomplished. But my death would tell them that someone cared for our species, enough to sacrifice herself. And more importantly, this would give meaning to my birth into the world of darkness. Like the lamb, you see. Born to be sacrificed, it has a purpose."

Morianna paused. She looked drained, the first time Karl had seen her vulnerable. "I suspect we could all use refreshment," he said, and nodded to Michel, who got up immediately and went to the stocks.

Morianna glanced at Karl, and he saw gratitude and hostility in her eyes. This was natural enough. Whatever co-operation their kind had been able to achieve, their inherent nature did not vanish. They were most vulnerable to their own kind. They could sense one another's presence and read one another so well, strengths and weaknesses, and prey on those weaknesses, if they so desired.

Michel returned shortly and passed around demitasse cups of blood. Karl let his sit on the table untouched. Morianna sipped hers slowly, as did David, while Michel downed his quickly, like any teenager with a Coke.

"Thank you," Morianna said. "I am refreshed and can proceed."

She shifted slightly in her seat before beginning again. David sat back in the armchair, a look of amazement on his face. When Michel sat down, he joined Karl on the loveseat. Karl sensed the boy was both intrigued and confused. Karl had an uncanny feeling about where Morianna's story was leading, and that made him uncomfortable. That plus the scent of blood — he was very very hungry. Still, he needed to track Gerlinde and wanted to be most receptive to her energy.

Morianna said, "This time of which I speak is a period when I was attracted to death. It is a part of the pattern of our existence. We are beings caught between planes. We are not alive, we are not dead. David, I believe it was you who put it so well once, when you described our souls as having begun to depart the body and gotten part-way out. That resonates with me. And because we are neither here nor there, we are at the mercy of those opposites."

David said, "I think I know what you're getting at. I've felt this pull within myself, a kind of swing between the dark and the light. I felt caught in the death throes myself, in Manchester, before meeting Kathy."

"Yes, that is precisely what I'm getting at," Morianna said, "although as painful as it must have been for you, I believe that was but a taste. Because we dwell in a middle realm, we are pulled to one side and then the other constantly. Young ones feel it more intensely and more frequently; they have not as yet had time, in perpetuity, to dwell on the meaning of it all. Consequently, they move into and out of this phase so quickly it does not clamp onto them or hold them in the same manner. We who are older see it for what it is. With us, these periods last longer. Much longer. The experience cannot be assimilated quickly, and the energy lingers in the pit, which makes it all the more debilitating."

Karl felt his own understanding was more theoretical than practical. Yes, he had been depressed, if that was the word for what she was describing. Before meeting Gerlinde. But the extremes that André and David had gone through, and what Morianna was talking about, these were foreign to him.

Finally, Michel said with the directness of youth, "So, you wanted to die. Is that what happened to Chloe?"

"Yes."

"But she loved life," Michel said. The boy was clearly upset. "I mean, she was always talking about nature and her eyes sparkled, and she laughed like she enjoyed a lot of things and —"

Morianna motioned for Michel to join her. The boy got up, went to the footstool, and sat, facing her. She put her arms around him, wrapping him in protection, it seemed to Karl. An expression that most teenage boys might have rebelled against but which Michel felt confident enough to receive. "You are very very young. You cannot be expected to understand. Our despair is not always visible. And in truth, even from those we trust, we are still removed. We suffer our own pain, our own grief, and mostly in silence.

"And in this way I call the energy feminine, though it affects both genders — the death phase comes without warning, and departs abruptly, like the menses, the menopause. One cannot prepare."

"Yes," David said, "that's what I felt. One moment I was fine, the next I had taken to lying in a coffin, barely eating. And it was not over for me until my experience on Fire Island."

Morianna nodded.

Michel looked devastated. It was as though he had not envisioned this drawback to their existence. As though he had expected all would be easy and fun, that the benefits far outweighed the liabilities. And while Karl did not experience that joy and hope that Michel's youth automatically bequeathed to him, he knew his own time of true despair had not yet arrived. Or, maybe, he thought, I'm different, and I'll never enter such a dark realm.

Morianna sat back. "I will not give the details of my ordeal which lasted two decades in total. I will only tell you that this attraction to death caused me to see everything through biased eyes. My own demise was the primary thought in my head, its value and how to accomplish it in the most meaningful way. And my emotions replicated this thought a thousand times a night. I found myself drawn to the accoutrements of death, to houses where a death had recently occurred or was about to, to cemeteries, to funerals. I drank from the bereaved. I dug up corpses with my bare hands and cradled their decomposing bodies. I slept with the skeletons of young children, clutching them to my breast as a mother would her child. And I attempted suicide many times in a variety of ways. Yet throughout all this I must have possessed a strong survival instinct as well, for my efforts failed, as you can see, and I sit before you now, over two centuries later."

Karl, David and Michel stared at Morianna. She *was* like a living gargoyle. A being that knew the heights of heaven and the depths of hell. One that had survived and now sat apart from it all, looking down at the simple concerns of those below her, seeing their naiveté, knowing what awaited them. She has the keys to the universe, Karl thought, and would be someone to seek out if he ever encountered a locked door.

"What I am saying to you all is that Chloe, Kaellie, and I suspect the others were in a death phase. Drawn to death. Weaving a story in their minds, *their* story, in which they were the protagonist whose disappearance would, in some way, give meaning to their existence."

119

Michel had half turned. His head against Morianna's shoulder, he said, "It sounds like she was psychotic. They all were. Paranoid."

"If labels like these help you to cope with what you see before you, then they are useful. But it is not for you or me or anyone to judge any of them. No-one can know the scope of the universe and how these constantly evolving phases effect what follows. We live in a causal reality with synchronistic overtones; meaning, we are part of a continuum that is effected by all that occurred before and which will determine what comes later. It is the paradox of existence that at the same time we are locked in an eternal, universal, yet very personal moment, each moment of existence is all there is to life. That one moment encapsulates our being and gives meaning to our time on this planet. I can only tell you that when the death phase is in process, it is not something we can easily struggle against, but must move through organically. It must be gone through and it must reach its inevitable, natural conclusion, whatever that is. We cannot determine who will succumb and who the death angel will pass by. But survivors are catapulted to the other end of the spectrum. In my own case, the outcome was continuation. For Chloe, Kaellie and the others it was termination. Ultimately, I have learned what my early Buddhist teaching tried to convey — both extremes of the pendulum are to be avoided, and yet they cannot be avoided."

"It sounds so harsh," Michel said. "And I can't believe we can't do anything about it."

"Oh, we must do what we must do, and we cannot predict what will effect the outcome, if the outcome can be effected. It may be preordained, no-one knows. Again, this is a paradox, and paradox is difficult to accept."

Karl said, "Are you saying that Antoine, as their creator, knew they were in this phase? And took advantage of it?"

"I believe so."

"But why now?" Michel said. "I mean, how come he didn't kill you?"

"Antoine had other concerns then. But since your birth, Michel, all has changed. You are a symbol to him. And he is vengeful. Or, he has convinced himself that revenge is his goal, his right. I suspect more that it is simply his own drive towards extinction."

"What do you mean?" Karl asked.

"In any death game, one will live and one will not. Antoine will, of course, try to live, even as he hopes to die."

"But why would he want to die?" Karl asked, still very confused by this extreme attraction to entropy. "And how does this fit into your concept of sacrifice?"

Morianna smiled a small smile, one filled with pain. One which told him that, in time, he would truly understand. "Despite your feelings about him, Antoine is like us, and must have a *raison d'être*. Karl, you have thought yourself, no doubt, that eternity can be a very long time. Imagine your thoughts, your feelings and the weight of your experiences after five more centuries."

# CHAPTER NINE

B Y THE FOLLOWING EVENING, KARL HAD COME to some conclusions. New information brought this about.

Two of the missing three had been accounted for. They were discovered mutilated, one in Greece on the island of Santorini, lying in a newly dug grave next to the corpse of a recently-buried relative, the other in a cryonics lab in California. Both bodies had been found in time, meaning mortals had not examined the remains. By all appearances, neither had fought their attacker.

At Julien's request, Gertig had sent by overnight courier a sample of blood from Kaellie's body and one of blood in the immediate vicinity. Another trip to the forensics lab and a session with the Gas Phase Chromatographer revealed to Karl what he expected to find: traces of formalin. Samples from the two bodies from Santorini and California had not yet arrived but Karl suspected they would not show formaldehyde in the blood. For one thing, formaldehyde was not used in cryonic suspension. And from what he knew of burial practises in the remote areas of Greece, embalming was an expensive proposition which most people could not afford; it would not be prevalent in a cemetery on a small island in the middle of nowhere with a population of less than seven thousand people.

Whether or not the two bodies were embalmed didn't matter. Karl had figured out what was happening and told the others his conclusions.

"My theory is that Antoine used the scent of death as a disguise."

"Meaning?" David asked.

"Meaning that wherever the mutilated body was found, the overwhelming scent associated with death would be what he would use to mask his own blood scent, his presence."

"So at the Columbarium," Michel said, "he used formaldehyde so Chloe wouldn't be aware of him. She'd be prepared for that smell."

"She would have found the smell stronger than usual," Carol said slowly, "but not out of the ordinary. It might put her offguard, but it might not. Either way, she wouldn't be expecting Antoine. Is that what you're getting at?"

"Yes, and from what Michel told us," Karl said, "Chloe was attracted to that place because it reminded her of her own death. According to what Morianna told David, Michel and me last night that makes sense. Chloe would be attracted for that reason if she were in a... a death phase." He looked to Morianna, who supported him with a nod.

"Death phase?" Kathy asked.

"I'll try to explain it to you later," David told her.

Carol looked to André, who shrugged, then to Michel who said, "I think I understand. At least I can tell you guys the stuff Morianna said."

"When the samples arrive from California, I suspect we will find traces of liquid nitrogen in the blood. That would make the air in the lab the same as what was in the cryonic storage bins."

"But can you smell liquid nitrogen?" David asked.

"No, but the substance would replace the blood in the body."

"How?"

"By being injected."

"*Mon Dieu!*" André said. "Are you telling us that if Antoine injects embalming fluid or liquid nitrogen or whatever into his veins, we can't sense even his presence?"

"If we are in a place of death where that scent is prevalent, and if we are... how can I put it... obsessed with that place, yes."

Carol said, "But supposing Antoine injected embalming fluid into his veins, and supposing that Chloe couldn't sense him, that still doesn't explain why she didn't resist. Even if he came up behind her, she should have fought."

"This is the part that's hard to accept," Karl said. "The death phase, as Morianna described it, means not just an attraction to death, but an attraction to suicide."

"So Chloe wanted to die. And Kaellie. And the others."

Morianna said, "It might be more relevant to say that Death called to them and they answered."

A chill ran through the room. Karl could feel it. They all intuited that this state awaited each one of them. Now. Later. It didn't matter. And when it did, they would be vulnerable. To the state itself. To a killer. They would live a long time — possibly forever — but so would Antoine — he could wait.

Julien said, "That Antoine has extinguished five of our number so quickly, within a week, devastates our community — as he intended."

"We've got to fight back," André said.

"Yes," David agreed. "We cannot let this monster destroy what has taken so long to build."

"If we stick together," Kathy said, "he can't get us."

Carol said, "That's probably the best plan."

Jeanette shook her head. "We can't stay together twenty-four hours a day. It's not possible. And we're vulnerable when we sleep. It's a wonder Antoine hasn't found a way to attack us in the day."

Wing said, "It is unlikely he would resort to this."

Morianna agreed. "Antoine plays a game of integrity."

"What?" André yelled. "Not at all!"

"*Au contraire, mon ami*," Julien said. "Antoine has his own rules — his own agenda — and within those parameters he abides by a code. We must respect the enemy's rules or he has already won."

Morianna added, "In his way of thinking, to destroy us in daylight would require the help of mortals. And while we have seen in the past that he is not averse to using them on occasion in minor roles of his passion play, he far prefers a challenge."

"How do you know that?" André said.

"Look at those he has brought over. There is not one who is weak, not one unworthy of being his child, the offspring of a powerful force. Antoine did not bring over any impotent mortals because that would have offended his sense of ethics."

André snorted. "We don't know about the ones he tried to bring over who died in the process."

"No, we do not, but we can surmise. He is no fool. And his instincts are strong," Karl said.

Julien directed them back to the issue at hand. "Thinking along the same lines, he cannot bring himself to resort to stupid ploys and unsophisticated trickery. He will not enter by the back door. He is compelled to face his creation and destroy it. He wants those he has made to know him as the creator/destroyer god. For such knowledge to be evident, the created must be awake to his or her own destruction."

Morianna added, "Antoine, as with each of us, creates his own story in which he plays the starring role. Without conflict, there is no story. I believe he views himself as an archetype."

"Antoine," Wing explained, "has made the stakes high for himself. Only in that way can victory or defeat have an impact. You must understand, after so long an existence, there is not much that will engage his energies. One either turns outward or inward, and his make-up does not allow for the type of introspection which of necessity we gravitate towards as we mature."

"So," André said, "we just sit around and wait for the death phase to strike us, then we hope Antoine comes and rips us apart quickly. That's ridiculous!"

Julien said, "I do not believe anyone here sees that as an option. But we cannot protect ourselves from the death phase."

"Maybe," Jeanette said, "we can protect one another."

The discussion now focused around ways in which they might evaluate one another. It made sense that if one of them entered the death phase, others could stand watch, even for decades. It had never been tried in the community, Morianna

125

said, and there was no way to know whether or not it would be an effective approach. Still, most of those present believed it was something that could be done, in the face of what felt like a formidable opponent.

"Antoine is the big problem," Michel said, "but this death-phase stuff makes us kind of our own worst enemy."

Keeping watch meant being together more and keeping tabs on one another when they were apart. And most agreed it seemed to be a good idea to stay in groups. David and Kathy would be together, as would André, Carol and Michel. Julien and his family were a unit. As were most of the others. Those groups could come together and make larger groups, then reform into other groups. Wing and Morianna, though, would not hear of this.

"We were unsuited to your era, and we have not built a condition similar to what Julien has found for himself," Wing said, meaning a family-type situation.

"I could no more travel with someone endlessly than I could walk in daylight," Morianna added. "It is against my nature. I know Wing feels the same."

Jeanette said, "Well, we can at least keep in touch with you both on a regular basis. That's possible, isn't it?"

Both Wing and Morianna paused. "Arrangements can be made," Wing finally said a bit reluctantly, and Karl had the sense that he and Morianna would keep in touch not so much for themselves, but because the others needed the reassurance that they were okay.

How to evaluate the death phase was a problem since they were all so secretive to begin with. Even the most extroverted of them was introverted in many ways, especially when it came to the very personal experiences.

David said, "Of course, it will be obvious to a companion when the one they are with becomes obsessive."

Karl was aware that none said what they were all thinking: how could they determine if Morianna and/or Wing were losing it? And there were others alone like Gertig and the third one they had yet to hear from. And Gerlinde. They might all be in the death phase for all any of them knew.

"I have another piece of information that might be helpful," Karl said. "The samples of Chloe's and Kaellie's blood which I examined under the microscope contained one human red cell with a nucleus. This is unusual. Mature red cells do not have a nucleus."

"Well, our cells are different —" Jeanette began.

"Yes, but I've examined enough blood from our kind to know the pattern, and we all fit the pattern."

"What's the significance of a nucleus in a red blood cell?" David asked.

"With mortals, it means an aberrant cell. A deviant. A distortion. Usually, it signifies illness. I'm betting that when the death phase comes over us, it will show up in the cells. We will have one or more cells in a sample with a nucleus. Cells with a nucleus are necrophilic."

"In other words," Jeanette filled in for him, "the distorted cell makes us sick."

"Or the state of entering the death phase brings about a change in some of our cells. We won't know until we do more research, and determine first of all if this is related to the death phase, or not. Maybe it's just an anomaly that appears in the blood samples I analysed. And it's possible the killer somehow distorted cells, but that's unlikely. I can't see that happening at the time of death."

While this new information created a buzz around the room, Karl sat back thinking about Gerlinde.

She was always on his mind now. He tracked her first thing after sunset and located her in Düsseldorf, the place where Antoine had attacked him and brought him over. Gerlinde being there in the midst of all this murder was like a neon sign with the name 'Karl' flashing. He knew in his heart that she was with Antoine and that he was being lured to the place of his mortal death.

Despite knowing this, despite the new information which made Antoine's *modus operandi* clear, Karl was determined to rescue Gerlinde. He told the others his intentions.

"Absolutely not!" André said. "It's suicidal."

David was adamant too. "Antoine might be trying to draw you there or Gerlinde may just be travelling by herself but, either way, this is not the time to go off on your own."

"Remember what the *I CHING* said," Kathy reminded him. "You're not supposed to go anywhere right now."

"I've got to help Gerlinde," Karl said. "She would do the same for me and for any of you. Remember, David, it was Gerlinde who helped Kathy persuade the others to fight. I thought you all were her friends."

"We are," André said, annoyed. "She and I may not always have seen eye to eye, but you know I care deeply about her. We all do. That you would say that makes me wonder what's going on in your head."

"What's going on in my head is that Gerlinde is missing and hasn't made contact. That she left a strange message with David. That I've tracked her to Düsseldorf, the city where Antoine brought me over. That Antoine is killing off our friends one by one, and Gerlinde might be in a death phase. And clearly, she's been kidnapped."

"But Antoine didn't create her," Carol said.

"No, he didn't. But maybe he's expanding his repertoire. He did promise to kill everyone on Fire Island that night, not just the ones he made."

"Well, if you're going, I'm going with you," David said.

"Not possible," Karl told him.

"Why not?"

"He would be able to track you since he brought you over."

"He can track you for the same reason."

"Yes, but if he finds two of us coming, he might kill her. Obviously he's trying to draw me there."

"To kill you," André said. "I'll come, then, since he can't track me."

"He can't track you, but when we get within his sensing range, which I imagine is more extensive than our own, he'll know there are two of us and again, he might kill her."

"You going there alone doesn't make sense," André said, clearly frustrated.

"I agree. We can't let you go alone," David said.

"I don't think we should let you go at all," Carol told him.

Karl suddenly felt defensive. "You can't stop me. None of you can. I'm going, and going by myself."

"Maybe," Michel said, "you're in a death phase."

"If I am, Michel, then I'll have to go through it, just like everyone else."

"But if Antoine kills you first —"

"I hope that won't happen. I know how he's working, which will give me an edge."

"All right, you know his methods, but he'll destroy you the moment he can," David said. "What are you planning on doing if you meet up with him? How are you going to defend yourself?"

"I don't know yet. The first thing is to get to Gerlinde, and see what's what. Maybe she *is* just travelling. I don't believe that, but you never know. If she's alone, then there's no problem and we'll return here right away. If Antoine is holding her hostage, well, I guess I'll start by trying to talk with him."

"*Merde!*" André snapped. "Have you lost your mind?"

"That is ludicrous!" David said.

"It may not work," Karl admitted, "but I doubt anyone has tried this approach. And frankly, I don't hear anybody coming up with a better idea."

Clearly this was something that none of them had anticipated as a plan of action. None believed Antoine capable of reason. Especially after the murders. And Fire Island. Not to mention the violent way Antoine had brought over so many of them. Karl didn't kid himself that this was some foolproof plan. It probably wouldn't work, but he didn't want to rule out the obvious just because it *was* obvious.

No-one said anything for a few seconds until Julien spoke. "I believe it was Winston Churchill who made this memorable remark: an appeaser is one who feeds a crocodile hoping it will eat him last."

Karl was able to catch a flight to London. He arrived at Heathrow close to sun-up. He booked a room at an airport hotel and a flight to Köln first thing the following evening. From Köln, he would travel to Düsseldorf, less than an hour's train ride.

He had had a lot of time on the flight to London to plan his course of action. Unfortunately, there seemed to be few options. And overlaying all of it were two major fears. The first was that Gerlinde had been harmed. He knew she was still alive, because he'd just tracked her — she was still in Düsseldorf. But his strongest fear by far was the terror he felt at the thought of having to face Antoine again and experience the power of the dominant will that he sensed could so easily crush him and, given a chance, would.

Still, he had to help Gerlinde. He loved her. And he could not exist without her. That, above everything else, had become crystal clear to him over the last few days. He would do whatever it took to free her, even if it meant relinquishing his own existence.

# Part II

"Of all escape mechanisms, death is the most efficient."
H. L. Mencken

# CHAPTER TEN

KARL ARRIVED IN DÜSSELDORF WITH A premonition. He did not normally experience premonitions. It occurred to him that this could easily be the product of fears clashing with a situation that seemed if not impossible, then one for which answers were not as yet apparent. Whatever the source, the premonition was not good. It felt as if this were a film *noir* and the ending was going to be dismal. Gerlinde had always told him to listen to his feelings, but tonight he was bent on ignoring them.

The city had suffered since his last visit here. That had been in the early part of 1930 as Adolf Hitler was gaining power in Germany. The events in Düsseldorf then were a precursor to the blood that would be shed later.

Karl walked from the train station towards the old city not far away, automatically, out of habit, he guessed. He had lived in the area. Twice. And indeed, the street held a peculiar history on both occasions, one a footnote to which Karl had been privy.

But since the second world war when much of Germany had been destroyed by allied bombs, this area looked nothing like it had. Today, Mettmannerstrasse was lined on both sides with Moroccan shops that gave way to a string of dirty and dismal apartment blocks, built when architecture had not been a concern and the goal was to put up as much housing as possible in the shortest time for the least amount of money. But back before the war, the houses had been lovely, traditionally German. Three, four, five story buildings with pointed roofs and latticed fronts, some of which dated back several hundred years. There was the square — every German town had one — composed of a church with bell tower, a town hall and shops strung along the streets running off the square. This city had once been so beautiful. Karl thought about what Goethe said and recognised the truth in it: "The Germans make everything difficult, both for themselves, and for everyone else."

As Karl walked, he knew the house where Peter Kurten had lived with his wife would be gone. It had been an ordinary house, as he remembered it. Not a place where you'd expect a vampire to live.

He strolled along Mettmannerstrasse, thinking back to the events in Düsseldorf the last time he'd lived in the city. That had been a peculiar era. Germany had been forced to pay reparations for World War I and poverty abounded. He recalled watching a woman one night who had walked into the city from the surrounding countryside, her brood in tow. She pushed a wheelbarrow overflowing with marks, hoping to exchange the cash for a loaf of bread to feed her children. Someone took pity on her and gave her half a loaf, telling her they didn't want the worthless currency.

The time had been right for a dictator to take power and Hitler was in the wings. The German people were being bled dry. Peter Kurten and Adolf Hitler were there to lap up the blood. And others before them, but Karl did not want to dwell on events too far back in the past.

From what Karl pieced together later through newspaper accounts and local gossip, Kurten had been disturbed from childhood. He was born in 1883 in Mulheim, not a pleasant place in the south near the French border.

The year Kurten was born, Karl had already been alive for sixty three years, thirty eight of them as a blood drinker. He recognised another blood drinker when he saw one. And he saw such in Peter Kurten — a drab, low-key, mild-mannered man, always impeccably dressed in a suit and tie with a handkerchief in his breast pocket. His flat pale eyes and a very tense mouth gave him away, at least to Karl. Kurten was the type who worried a lot but presented a stable, pillar-of-the-community image that most people accepted. Yet beneath all that normality lay a savage spirit and, seeing him walking the streets, Karl knew that something of the veneer of socialisation had either been ripped away or had never been constructed.

All this made Karl fascinated after the fact, after they found out what the *vampire* had been doing throughout most of his life. He read everything he could find on Kurten's life, as if studying the reports on abnormality in a mortal might in some way shed light on his own condition.

Why Kurten and his wife came to Düsseldorf in 1925 is anybody's guess. Newspaper reports that appeared after Kurten had been arrested, said he was one of ten children, but that was not uncommon then. His father, an alcoholic, beat him. That, too, was not uncommon.

As a boy, Kurten enjoyed slaughtering animals. One report said he lived with the town dogcatcher for a while and learned to kill stray dogs.

When he was nine years old, he 'accidentally' drowned a playmate, then tried to drown another friend who attempted to rescue the victim. At seventeen, Kurten attempted to rape and murder a young girl. Because of this and other acts, he spent twenty-four years of his life in and out of jails where, it appears, he killed two inmates, or so he boasted. When not inside, he married and by the time he and his wife were living in Düsseldorf, he was well into a killing spree that lasted seventeen years, the likes of which put most contemporary serial killers to shame.

Even before a finger had been pointed at Kurten, Karl found himself observing the man often as he roamed the streets after dark. So even-tempered, such an incredibly passive-looking *Herr*, but possessing a primal energy-urge that reminded Karl of an animal on a leash yet still on the prowl. Kurten emitted a peculiar energy for a human being — the same energy Karl would, a few years later, feel coming off Hitler when he gained supremacy. The same energy he had felt almost a century before on the night Antoine attacked him. It was the same force Karl recognised when the blood lust threatened to overtake him. But he, unlike the others — the mortal and immortal bloodlusters — had always been able to control his obsessions.

Kurten managed to kill quite a number of people over the years, mainly children, before getting caught. Amazingly, despite his history of violence, the police did not suspect him of the increasing numbers of disappearances — they preferred to believe Kurten was an upstanding citizen. In fact, the authorities even executed an insane man in the town for murdering one of the missing children. But of course the murders continued.

Mostly, Kurten preferred the knife, he told a reporter later, slicing the throats of his victims or stabbing them in the chest; although he also enjoyed strangulation beforehand to subdue his victims. He adored the sight of blood. The smell of it. The taste of it. He took to writing Jack-the-Ripper style notes to the newspapers anonymously, mocking the police, describing himself as a blood-drinker. Karl found the style of the letters high melodrama, the stuff of tabloids, and that added a piece to the puzzle of what made this serial killer tick.

Blood, Kurten said, put him under a spell. Karl could relate to that. And because of that bewitchment, Kurten was driven to kill more and more and must have murdered dozens in the course of an escalating horror. All so that he could touch and taste their blood.

Finally, he kidnapped Maria Budlik and took her to his home. He tried to strangle the girl but she talked him into releasing her which, surprisingly, he did. She went to the police, of course, and gave them the name and address of her would-be killer. The authorities visited Kurten's home and told his wife of these allegations, but they still thought him so upstanding that even with a jail record, they could not bring themselves to believe he was a mass-murderer.

Later that night Mrs. Kurten confronted her husband and, astonishingly, he confessed to her. Together they planned to leave the city, but then his wife lost her nerve. She collaborated with the police and set up a meeting with her husband at the church in the square where he was arrested. Even then, it wasn't until Kurten provided details of the many murders to the police that the authorities truly believed him guilty.

Unlike the Hanover vampire who arrived in the course of human history later and had a trade that supported his habit of murder, Kurten's appetites were clearly sexual. Karl had watched him on one occasion. Fear mixed with lust. The lines gouged even more deeply into the always-worried face. He acted as if somehow he found himself in a bizarre situation which left him holding the bag, so to speak. As if it was someone else who had raped, strangled and killed so many. Karl could relate to that. He had often felt that dissociation himself in the early days. The Karl he was before he drank and the one who pulled his lips from the ragged wound that had fed him, were two different beings. It allowed him to feel not pity but at least some empathy for Kurten that, even if he had been able to verbalise it, no mortal could possibly understand.

Kurten was sentenced to death on nine counts of murder and, in 1930, decapitated in the Klingelputz jail. In the same year Hitler's party made a great leap in the polls and became the second largest. Soon it would be the party that created the Third Reich — the Nazi party.

All of this had interested Karl — history in the making. Here were human beings who found blood as powerful as he did. Who would go to any lengths to get it. But Karl had never intervened in Kurten's activities — nor in Hitler's — as a disinterested observer of an entirely different species, he did not feel it was his business to. When he told her the story of Kurten, Gerlinde had said, "What a very German approach! MYOB. That's the trait that allowed Hitler to trap a whole country."

She was right, of course, but he felt he couldn't change his nature. He had been born German and what could he do about that? Not much, it seemed. He was a German and a predator. Karl could not change those two things in himself anymore than Kurten could, or Hitler. Even many of the greatest German philosophers have believed we cannot change who we are; the best we can do is to live from moment to moment, trying to make each of our decisions the right one.

Karl stopped where he believed the Kurten house to have been, if he remembered correctly. He should have known it well. A long time before Peter Kurten shed blood, Karl had lived in the same house. And it was only when he stood before the cement apartment block that had obliterated all traces of the house, only then did Karl become aware that he had not walked here by chance. He had been drawn this way. Not only had Kurten killed here, but another death had occurred on this spot. This was the site of the house in which Karl had taken up residence in the middle of the nineteenth century, thirty-eight years before the birth of the Vampire of Düsseldorf as Kurten came to be dubbed.

Karl had been attacked almost at the front door of this house.

It was late autumn. Dying leaves shrouded the road and the wind howled mercilessly. He had been chilly that night, he remembered. He wanted to escape the harsh elements and retreat to the room he had rented in the house. It was a modest home, the residence of a widow and one of her daughters and her daughter's husband. The daughter had miscarried because she had contracted Rubella, a disease that the living could cope with, but one that damaged the foetus. Karl came to Düsseldorf to work on a cure for what would come to be called German Measles, and the woman who owned the house had been eager to have the young scientist lodge at her home.

Suddenly, the energy emitted from this spot felt like a living, breathing entity about to invade him. A swirling eddy of blood and transformation which straddled time. Now that he was paying attention, he recognised the energy at once. Antoine. Inside the modern building somewhere. Lurking in one of the apartments. And with him, Gerlinde!

Memories flooded Karl. Unconsciously, he backed away from the apartment complex and only noticed he did so when he found himself on the other side of the street, holding onto a lamppost for support. Air caught in his chest, pressing against his heart, making his head swim.

That night, more than one hundred and fifty years earlier, Antoine had emerged from the alleyway beside the house, a *schwartz geist*. Even before contact had been made, evil and corruption clogged Karl's pores. It was as if the fabric of the universe tore and a powerful negative energy sucked him into its maw, swallowing him, rending his flesh en route, ripping him out of his body, siphoning the blood from his veins by a monstrous extraction that had him depleted in minutes before he could react. Held in a vicelike grip and against his will, cold, slimy liquid penetrated between his lips and slid down his throat, chilling him with the realisation that this recycled blood was his own. He gagged but the black blood stayed down, as if it recognised its rightful home and wanted to return. Even as he swallowed and choked, Karl thought, 'This is not the way to replenish me', but that rational thought did not alter the horror of the reality he lived, and what would follow.

Left for dead, he managed to revive before sunrise, the only memory at first an ugly one: the sound of coarse, demonic laughter. He did not know where he was, who he was, and only strength of character led him out of the chasm of a distorted reality more like a nightmare and back to planet Earth.

By instinct, he crawled to the door, used his key, and entered his room. Again, by instinct, he locked the door to his room, closed and bolted the shutters, and wrapped himself in three blankets, for he felt frozen to the bone. His body trembled uncontrollably. Sound was distorted, and every tick of the grandfather clock, every creak of a floorboard, every dog howling outside the window was magnified tenfold. And as the light began to emerge in the sky, exhaustion that bordered on annihilation overwhelmed him, and he could do nothing but capitulate to what he anticipated, even hoped would be death. He could not have been more surprised when he woke the next sunset.

The dark being that had forced him into an altered state was the catalyst for a change that would transform every last part of him both genetically and emotionally. And now, the cold and hellish creature that he had come to know as Antoine, waited with no sympathy, no empathy and no remorse, like an enormous poisonous spider lurking in a web which Karl was drawn towards as if the silken threads were his home. He felt in every cell of his being that Morianna had been right — Antoine was his parent. He was the helpless offspring of a despot.

Terror gripped him as if he were caught in the jaws of a metal monster. Despite that, Karl found himself pushing forward, one step at a time, moving towards the apartment complex door. Moving, he suspected, towards his demise.

He gained access through the street door, then the inner door, and proceeded up the steps. From the number of mailboxes he passed, there might be a dozen apartments. He did not need a name. It was clear which one Antoine and Gerlinde were in. He would have had to be truly dead to miss the energy they emitted.

On the second floor, at the end of the faded marble hallway, the door stood ajar, as if he were expected. Of course, he *was* expected. They knew he was in the vicinity just as he knew they were.

Karl reached the door, pushed it open, and entered the apartment. Gerlinde sat on a small marble ledge for plants in front of the window. She looks tense, he thought. Her brown eyes bright, feverish and focused on him. Her hands gripped the edge of the ledge. She wore the outfit he'd last seen her in: black tights and a long-sleeved asymmetrical dress, the neck cut at a peculiar angle. She turned her head slightly and her short red hair flipped away from her face, back from her neck, as if she wanted him to see the marks at her throat.

Antoine was behind him. Karl didn't see him, but felt paralysed by the energy, as if a wall were pressed up against his back, an intangible wall that was just as effective as if it were three feet of steel. It blocked him, held him in place. He told himself he had no need to turn, but he knew he could not. It was not in him to face the beast. Not yet.

139

And then a rumble began, as if the earth quaked beneath his feet. It was a deep sound, hideously evil. Had a pit in hell opened and released all of the dark forces into a realm where they did not belong? He recognised the sound because he had heard it before. Antoine, laughing. At him. It left Karl shaking in terror, submissive to a power that was beyond his abilities to confront.

Abruptly, the sound died as if a head had just been chopped off with a sharp axe. Karl felt Antoine leave the apartment, leave the hallway, leave the building. The evil energy faded as he went, leaving Karl weak and fragile. But he had found Gerlinde and that gave him strength.

He took a step towards her.

"Don't!" she said sharply, holding her hand out. "Don't come near me."

"He's hurt you," Karl said lamely, startled by the rejection, justifying it in his mind. Of course Antoine had abused her. He moved forward.

Gerlinde jumped to her feet and snarled like an animal. "I said, don't come near me!" Her voice rose an octave and her face turned feral before his eyes. She looked about ready to attack him.

"All right. Stay calm. It's all right," he said, as much for himself as for her. He had seen her geared for attack a few times, but never directed his way, and it unnerved him to be on the receiving end.

She did not sit but she did not attack. "He's gone," Karl said, hearing how hollow the obvious sounded when spoken, but maybe she needed that reassurance. "Come. We'll go to the airport right away and get a flight to Montréal where the others are waiting and —"

"I'm not going back with you."

"What? You're... you're not yourself. He's used you. I know how he works. I understand how you're feeling, but —"

"You understand nothing about me! You never have."

That, more than anything, cut deep into him as if she had used a knife. And it found the target, his heart. Still, Antoine had affected her, that was clear. She must be under his spell to be saying such things.

"I know what you're thinking," Gerlinde said. "He isn't controlling me. I came to him. Of my own volition. I sought him out."

"No. He called you, you just didn't know it. He used his tie to me, to track you through me. He's powerful —"

"Yes he is. That's why I want him. Karl. I'm tired of how it's been with you, with the others. We're not a breed meant for such compatibility. We're demons, ruthless, and the more power we gain, the more in control of our fate we become."

"Gerlinde, this is not you. You've never talked this way —"

"I've felt this way, but you've never wanted to know about it. You've always been so busy trying to get along —"

"You made quite a few conciliatory efforts yourself —"

"Because it's all I knew. Because you and David and André wanted it that way. It's not how I wanted it. You acquiesce to their every wish. Well, where were your own wishes? What did you ever want?"

"I wanted you."

"Did you? I doubt it."

Now he felt angry. Whatever Antoine had done could be undone, or at least he hoped so. But he had no intention of letting this go on. "You know I care deeply for you —"

"Care deeply? After forty years together? What about the word *love*?"

"I love you, you know that —"

"Don't be ridiculous. We're incapable of love. You can't love me, I can't love you. And the others, with their notions of attachment are deluding themselves. You can't even be as open with me or give me as much as a mortal man can."

"I have been open with you. I've told you all there is to know about me."

141

"Have you?"

"Look, this is ridiculous. You must come with me."

"I don't have to go with you and I won't. You just don't get it, do you? We are an isolated species, always have been, always will be. We band together for selfish purposes. I was with you out of fear of being alone. You created me, what choice did I have?"

"You had all the choice in the world. You wanted this. Begged me for it —"

"But I didn't know what to expect. What I'd have to give up. You never made that clear."

"I tried —"

"And failed, Karl. You failed. I was with you because you were my creator, more powerful than me, because of the blood. But now I want something more. And you can't give it to me."

"You think Antoine can? You think he can love you?"

"No. He admits he can't love. At least he's honest."

That stung him to silence. Whatever Antoine had done to her, her words, words he'd never heard from her lips before, rang true somehow. This makes no sense, he told himself. She's mesmerised... But he knew that wasn't it. She did not look mesmerised. She looked clearer than he had ever seen her before.

"What are you telling me?" he finally said.

"I'm telling you to leave. I don't want to go with you. You can force me, of course —"

"Why would I do that? What would I get out of it?"

For a moment he saw a peculiar look on her face, one he could not identify. He didn't know if he was reading her correctly, but he thought she looked hurt. Then, in an instant, her features shifted, hardened, and she said, "Then go. I've made my decision. I want to be with Antoine."

Karl felt that dark pit of hell beneath his feet and his legs trembled. "I... I came to rescue you —"

"Do I look as though I need rescuing?"

"But... what can he offer you? If not love, what?"

"He offers me what you never could, what you never can. Potency. Now, go!"

But Karl could not move. He felt rooted to this spot with the black chasm widening beneath his feet. And while he stood there, stunned, Gerlinde pushed herself away from the window, saying, "If you can't leave me, I'll leave you." She brushed past him and headed down the hallway. He heard her boots clack against the marble steps, heard the door open, felt her moving away, down the street, in the direction in which Antoine had gone. He felt her energy fade.

An enormous cavity opened beneath him that expanded to surround him until a corrosive nothingness encased him. He felt hollow. His senses picked up nothing. He had no thoughts, no emotions. Suspended in time, the realisation dawned on him: *So this is how it feels to be dead!*

# CHAPTER ELEVEN

K ARL'S FIRST INSTINCT WAS TO PHONE HOME. Like any alien being, he needed some kind of connection to what was familiar, if only to preserve his sanity.

From those first hours of numbness, an ache had set in, growing slowly like a fungus, becoming emotionally acidic, eating away at him until he recognised what it had transformed into: pain. The intensity he sensed developing on the horizon of his psyche frightened him. He did not know what to do, where to turn. Ultimately he turned to his friends.

"Come home, *mon ami*," André said.

"Yes, do. Take the next flight," David added from the extension phone. "We'll meet you at the airport."

"What can you do in Germany? Nothing. You've got to be here where it's safe. Then we can think of a plan."

"It's too dangerous out there with Antoine at your heels."

"If he had wanted to harm me," Karl told them dully, "it would have been easy enough."

"It seems he *has* harmed you," David said.

While they talked, Karl felt more and more determined not to return to Montréal. He knew André and David cared about him. They had all been through so much together and yet somehow remained loyal friends. But this was a situation he felt he could not truly share with them, or with anyone. It was his own very personal grief.

"We know what you're going through," David said. "We've both been there."

But they hadn't. Not really. What had occurred between André and Carol, and between David and Kathy had been nothing like this. Nothing at all. He and Gerlinde had been together almost half a century. She had been by his side always it seemed, although that was not true. But how he had lived without her before he met her, he did not know. And how he could continue now that she was gone...

"We've both been rejected," André said.

But neither had suffered anything so outright, so final.

"It's Antoine, really." David knew Antoine as well as Karl did, if not better. Antoine, the furtive monster that appeared out of nowhere, destroyed, then faded quickly into the night as a black mist. A force so evil, so devoid of any bonds that he seemed all powerful, if only by virtue of his complete autonomy and total unpredictability.

"He's manipulating her," David went on. "Look how he controlled Ariel. And Kathy. And me, for that matter. Surely you recall the night he took you —"

"Of course I remember that night," Karl snapped. Instantly he regretted his tone. His friends were only trying to help. "I'm sorry. My nerves are on edge."

"It's no wonder," André said. "You've got to come home."

"I have no home," Karl told him, and the two on the other end were silent as if they had been verbally slapped.

David tried again, but spoke softly so that Karl could not easily interrupt him. "If you think about the night you were brought over, you will remember, as do I, the overwhelming sense of helplessness. Antoine invokes that feeling in his victims, then feeds on it. You know it as well as I do. He's turned Gerlinde's head in some manner, and he's done that to harm you. He wants you helpless and it's the only way to do it, now that you've got distance from him. Don't let him succeed."

"David's right," André said. "Antoine is using Gerlinde to get to you. That's obvious."

"I'm not stupid!" Karl said. He was losing it with his friends. He should get off the phone and stop torturing them. He sighed then said, "I know you're telling me the truth. But whatever Antoine's underlying motives, the result for me is the same: without her, I see no point to survival."

Hearing the words come out of his mouth crystallised the pain that had been washing over him in waves. Antoine might be manipulating Gerlinde, and him. After all, he had stated he was bent on destroying more of their kind. But if so, then he had already won. Karl could not fight him, that was clear. And Gerlinde was gone, which meant a part of him had vanished. He felt like an amputee, as if all of his limbs had been severed from his body and only a bloody, eternally-aching torso remained. And yet, despite it all, he felt curiously detached, as if this pain were happening to someone else. Ever the scientist, he was busy analysing it even as it was occurring, and that alienation from his own existence did more to swell his despair than anything else.

What have I become? he wondered. Over one hundred and fifty years on this planet has made me rocklike. The part of me that died at Antoine's hands has grown. Where am I headed, if not to oblivion?

David and André were busy protesting Karl's fatalistic statements with all the arguments that Karl would have made and had made to both of them over the years. But their words did not ease his suffering. He suspected nothing would ease his suffering.

At one point Morianna came on the line with Julien and Michel on the extensions. "Time will heal the wound," Morianna said lamely, her voice halfhearted to his ears. She sounded banal, like any mortal not knowing what to say to someone who had received a terminal diagnosis. And he had never perceived her as banal before.

Julien said nothing.

Michel's traumatised tone infiltrated his words. "You've got to come back. Please, Karl. Don't stay away. We'll find a way to get Gerlinde back, all of us together. But you're alone out there. Please."

The boy's love for him came through and these were the first words that scraped against his armour of agony. But in the end, Karl knew that to return to Montréal would be to fall into a coma. "I can't come back. Not right now."

"But Antoine will be tracking you —"

"He has always been able to track me. If he wanted to destroy me he could have done it many many times."

"His plan is more treacherous," Julien said. The tenor of what this old one said usually ran deep and forced Karl to listen. "As a mortal writer told us, the heart is indeed a lonely hunter. You would do well to remember that and to remember Morianna's words to you before you left."

"About the death phase? Well, if I'm destined for it, I am. And it appears I can only enter it and see where it leads."

"But we can help you," Michel said, stretching, reaching, clinging to hope as flimsy as a cloud, the way youth does, and it moved Karl. If anyone could have swayed him from his course, it would have been Michel.

"Maybe communal help is possible," Karl said, "but not now. Now I need to be alone."

Over two hours, he spoke with all of them. Their concern was palpable. And yet nothing moved him from his course because he could not be moved. Despair weighed him down. He could not be with them. He had nothing to offer and could not receive. If being alone meant that Antoine would kill him, or he would self-destruct in the death phase, then he would bow, hopefully gracefully, to his fate. That might be all that remained that he could control.

By the time Karl hung up, he knew where he was headed. It was not towards Gerlinde whom he sensed had left Düsseldorf. He tracked her north east to Hanover. He could not track Antoine, of course, but believed they were together. Hanover. Another German city that had produced a human 'vampire', Karl thought wryly, bitterly. Maybe Antoine has a sense of humour after all.

He could not follow them. What was the point? Gerlinde may or may not be under a spell, but Antoine outclassed Karl by miles. How could he fight his creator? Well, he could, but he would die instantly. And while fighting for and dying in front of the woman he loved appealed to the slumbering romantic in him, that was really just a daydream. In reality, it would be a horrid death. Antoine would rip him to shreds, and Karl would probably be forced to plead for mercy. That was not an end he would like to leave as his legacy. And in his mind he had a clear picture of Gerlinde sneering at such a demise.

No, if existence were impossible, the one element of control he just might retain was his own death. How and when he would die. Antoine might attack him, but he doubted it. As he'd said and thought, there had been too many occasions. And Antoine did like a challenge. Karl was not a fit opponent. Antoine knew his offspring and determined that Karl, if left to his own devices, would kill himself.

Playing into Antoine's hands did not appeal to Karl, but what was the alternative? He did not see any. This all-powerful father could make or break him. And had done both.

With a heavy heart, Karl caught a train south to Oberwesel. What better place to die than the place where he was born?

# CHAPTER TWELVE

T HE TRAIN CHUGGED ALONG THE RHINE VALLEY, stopping briefly in the small towns along the way for passengers who wanted to embark or disembark — Porz; Bad Honnef — and then Bonn, a low city with high churches and long industrial parks; busy, clean and efficient. As he glanced upward along the picturesque route at the dozens of mediaeval castles lodged high into the mountain tops, as the scent of fertile, familiar earth filled his nostrils and the faces of the people on the train, looking so much like their predecessors began to imprint themselves into his brain and overlap his memories, Karl felt that he had come home.

The river Rhine wound through the mountains. Slopes spread with squared-off vineyards over the land of the white grapes that produced the beloved Rhine wine Karl had grown up on. This land had formed him.

The train whistle sounded, needlessly it seemed to him — at this time of night there would be no other traffic on the tracks, neither the highspeed European train that did not stop at these small places, nor the boxcars of goods being transported between the north and south. This simple wooden train, so narcissistically disposed, consisted of two cars and an engine. It had been built in the 1930s, around the time of the war, and was the type they made miniatures of that raced around the tracks beneath Christmas trees.

The train rounded a wide bend. The river was low tonight and ahead Karl could make out the tip *die Loreley*, the rock formations beneath the water that, like the sirens of Greek mythology, had lured so many sailors to their death in shipwrecks when this waterway had been the only route between north and south. Heinrich Heine was a contemporary of Karl's, and the words of his famous poem came to mind:

There's sitting high up in the light
A maiden so beautiful, fair,
Her jewels are glistening bright
She combs her gold shimmering hair.

Her comb is of most precious gold.
She's combing and singing so sweet
Bewitching young fishers and old
Their hearts start to quiver and beat.

There's a man in his boat on the river,
He cannot but listen and stare,
A longing is making him shiver,
Look out, the rock's ledge, oh beware!

I fear there's a crash, the boat sinking,
The man will be swallowed and gone,
And that with melodious singing
The Lorelei will have done.

It was not the most beautifully written poem, but the words struck Karl in the heart. Yes, he was that man in the boat, listening, staring, longing... and headed towards his death.

Suddenly, the small town of Oberwesel burst into view. Home. It had changed and not changed since his childhood. Oberwesel was still only a village to him that had not altered since his birth in 1820, and, he suspected, not much in the last five hundred years. His eyes selectively scanned out what did not superimpose perfectly with his memory. What he saw was not the Oberwesel of today but the one from his past.

It had been smaller, of course. All of these towns and cities had been. This same trip along the Rhine would have taken perhaps a week, or longer. There were no roads then, and barely beaten-out dirt paths from town to town. The river was the source of life. No pleasure craft dotted the waters, just merchant ships relying on the wind to catch their sails. And if there was no wind, horses on land would pull them with ropes so they could dock. These boats arrived infrequently, mainly to load and unload supplies to the isolated fiefdoms. There had been little need back then to go anywhere else and people did not travel.

Ahead he saw memories transform into reality — he remembered *der Mauseturm* — the Mouse Tower — and the Cat Tower, and the other one — yes, the Ox Tower — all of them standing since the Middle Ages but now lit at night by electricity. In his day they were lit by candlelight to a similar effect — yellow beacons along the dark and twisting river. The towers were in the old part of the town, which, when he had been a boy, had been the entire town. Then, Oberwesel consisted of perhaps one hundred houses — the population did not total more than one thousand — the cathedral, Our Lady's Church, by the port, and St. Martin's further inland, the cloisters, and towering above it all at the top of the highest hill, *die Schönburg*.

By moonlight Karl saw the red brick of the reconstructed wing in glaring contrast to the original grey-brown stones of the massive fortress. An architectural quirk created a vogue for this type of restoration. Many castles along the Rhine had been reconditioned and there were a hundred along the Rhine. It was not aesthetically pleasing, but at least, Karl thought, it's clear to everyone what was original and what was not.

Castle *Schönburg* had always been here, or so it seemed. Construction begun a thousand years ago, built in increments by the many warring princes who had dwelled in this place. Ownership had frequently been in question over the centuries.

From the train station, Karl phoned one of the two taxis in the town and directed the driver to Castle *Schönburg*. If he had learned one thing in his century and a half of existence it was that the wealthy could afford to be eccentric. It was expected of them. Far easier to demand that his room be cleaned after eight pm. at night here, where he was paying for specialised service, than at an inn where his request would be ignored no matter how much he paid.

The taxi finally arrived at the station and the driver, a matron, with the customary *"Guten Abend!"* drove him along

151

the twisting highway that ascended the mountain. She tried to engage him in conversation but Karl resisted the overtures. Oberwesel had always been small. It was still small. He was a stranger arriving in the middle of the night. News of his arrival, a description of him, anything and everything would be grist for the gossip mill. By noon, the entire town would know he was here.

It had been the same when he was growing up. His every action had been known. He could go out in the evening and in the morning his grandfather would tell him where he had been, with whom, and what they had talked about, in detail. Someone would have seen this, another heard that, a third noticed such and such. Small town life. No wonder the undead preferred cities! Anonymity had its rewards.

Directly above, drawing closer and closer, was an enormous collar wall, one of the most immense ramparts Karl had seen in Germany. Within the wall were five battlements and the old chapel. Finally they arrived at a wooden-plank overlook and the taxi could go no further. From here he went by foot up the ascending cobblestones, over the drawbridge that spanned the moat and into the courtyard. Ahead lay a peaked arch doorway, and behind him the massive tower gate of stone and metal. Despite the chill wind that whipped around him this high up into the clouds, he stopped for a moment to view the castle from this courtyard.

Karl, like every other lad of his day, had learned the history of the castle in his youth. Oberwesel had once, a thousand years ago, been a Roman encampment called Voslvia or Ficelia — he could not quite recall. Excavations of the town over the years before his time and what he'd read about since in *National Geographic*, revealed the remnants of Roman mansions with columns, water ducts, wells, floors. The castle itself may have served as a watch tower. After all, the vantage point was the best along the Rhine and the positioning of this fortress would have made it easy to defend.

Serfs had built the castle between 966 and 1166. The family *Schönburg* originated in Oberwesel — Karl was distantly related, as, he suspected, were many from the town. Above the doorway he noticed a shield — the family arms, bestowed on a *Schönburg* knight by Charlemagne in 744 as thanks for bravery in battle and, especially, for saving the King's life.

Over the centuries there had been many intrigues and as many deaths. Count Palatine was said to have held his rival, the young Otto of Rheineck, Junior, captive in the dungeon and finally strangled him there. Espionage and political conspiracies abounded. One complicated ploy resulted in a confrontation between the then Emperor and the Pope and, when promises were broken, it was the ownership of the land that was wrestled from the hands of the *Schönburgs*, although the family still was permitted to reside there. Overnight, the Free Imperial City of Oberwesel reverted to a fiefdom which was ruled by a succession of different lords. Later the castle was divided into thirds and each third given to a different clan of the *Schönburg* family. As many as two hundred and fifty persons might have lived in this spacious structure at any one time.

He glanced around. These thick walls had stood for centuries. What secrets they knew! The two rounded towers in view on this side — one had collapsed in 1880 — were impressive. He knew there were more on the other side because, as a child, he had played in the forest covering the mountain slopes behind. This courtyard held cast-iron cannons flanking the wall facing east to the river. To one side was a mound of "bullets", huge stone balls which had been used in catapults, ready to be flung at enemy vessels — remnants of the major battles that had occurred here over the years, each one inflicting damage. Most recently, it had begun with Frederick II; followed by the Spanish in 1632, the Swedes in 1639 and the French in 1646 — there was no way to determine which scars were left by whom. Karl recalled Victor Hugo's description of Castle *Schönburg's* ruins, and laughed: "One of the most venerable hills of rubble of all Europe."

By 1820, the year Karl was born, there were no *Schönburgs* at the ruined castle. But their legacy remained. Karl recalled reading in his youth "*Dialogus miraculorum*" by Césarius von Heisterbach, a chronicler of the late twelfth and early part of the thirteenth centuries. That work made clear the constant arguments between the town's people and the *Schönburgs*. And always, Karl mused, the citizens were the losers in such situations. One *Otto Schönburg* had tried to blackmail some of Oberwesel's more prosperous men, mistreating the wives and children of all those who went into hiding to escape the threats. The *Schönburgs* had also used their position in the church and in government to fortify themselves, and had aided in the Eastern colonisation in the twelfth century, especially in the Saxon regions — at least they had a good reputation outside their own region. But within, betrayals abounded, and it was commonly felt that the sacking of the town by the French in the mid 1600s was not by chance. It left the town and the castle in ruins. Oberwesel did not recover quickly and memories are long. Karl suspected that the name *Schönburg* still did not sit well with the locals.

He knew more of the history than he knew of the restoration. Hopefully, he might discover some of that information once he checked in.

He entered through the stone doorway, up the stone steps, and immediately came to a small reception desk behind a glass. Handel's *Canon* played softly in the background from a CD. An older gentleman greeted him deferentially, as was the German way. "How long will you be staying?" he asked.

"I'm not certain yet."

The gold AmEx card was run through the machine for a deposit. Karl was asked if he would like this plan or that plan, some of which included breakfast, some dinner. He declined all of them, only making the request about the cleaning of his room. "I write in the evenings and sleep in the day," he explained.

"Oh, you are a writer!" the host said, perking up. "I read. Fiction?"

"Nonfiction. I'm doing a book on the castles of Germany." That, he knew, would provide him with special status and the manager would ensure that he was not disturbed during the day.

A Vietnamese girl appeared to show him to his room. How times have changed, he thought. Truly, the world is a global village.

The tiny elevator moved up the tower slowly while the friendly, smiling girl talked fluently in German about the facilities available, the times dinner and breakfast were served, the town below and what it had to offer. She said again and again that if he needed anything at all, he should be sure to phone the desk.

Once the elevator stopped, she led him down a narrow, sloped hallway crammed with artifacts from the past to a door — number twenty-three — coincidentally the number of the hexagram Wing had thrown.

While the girl chatted, she unlocked the door, ushered him in, then left. The space was lavishly appointed. A large antique bed of dark wood dominated the room with the rest of the decoration pleasingly eclectic: to one side, a walnut desk carried the incongruous mixture of an imitation quill standing proudly from a silver ink pot, an old valve radio and half a dozen history books on the region. Iron curtain rods that folded over one another and held heavy red velvet curtains like banners graced the lead-latticed windows — very Mediaeval, he thought. The management had thoughtfully provided an iced bottle of Rhine wine, a decanter of port, crystal glasses, a bowl of fruit, and a paring knife and plate on a small round table. Plush velvet armchairs and a settee. Coats of arms and paintings of wildlife against the tiny flower-print wallpaper. Ornately framed mirrors. A crystal chandelier. A vase of fresh flowers. Chocolates on the pillows. Gerlinde would have loved it. She would have hated it. She would have laughed at it in delight.

But he would never hear her laughter again, except in his memory. And he knew that he would no longer laugh either. Or cry. Hope had been crushed out of him, leaving a heart like one of the stones that composed the outer walls of this fortress. What was it G. K. Chesterton had said? The insane man isn't the one who has lost his reason, but the one who has lost everything *but* his reason.

He sat and stared out the open window for a while, at the water below, the moon hanging in a clear, star-filled sky, and eventually picked up one of the books. It told the story of someone named Herr Rhinelander, an American of German extraction — his ancestors had hailed from the other side of the Rhine. In the late 1800s, Rhinelander acquired the castle and sank millions of Gold Marks into restoring the infrastructure to its original glory, recreating the layout from ancient drawings and etchings. In 1950 his son sold the castle to the town. Now it was owned privately again and run as a first-class hotel.

Change. Life is change, everyone said. But how could Karl accept the change when it meant only pain for him? The castle had always been in his life, in his blood. It was as good a place as any to die.

He closed the book and decided on a walk. The night air felt crisp and he wore a heavy jacket to avoid suspicion, although the cold would not affect him. He felt hungry but was not hungry, like a mortal too depressed to care about food.

Instead of the paved road, he climbed one of the walls and took a route he had employed so often in his early years down through the forest. The path was not overgrown which suggested that children still used it. At least some things never change.

Gerlinde had never been to Oberwesel. Well, that was his fault. He had not really wanted to return. Like so many beings who manage to cut the ties to their roots, he had his reasons and some of them involved tainted memories. Maybe he should have been more open with her, as she said. He thought he had been open, with his past, with his feelings. Apparently that was not so. Or maybe that didn't matter.

*Oberwesel am Rhine* looked to him as the town had always looked at night — narrow, gently curving streets blanketed by darkness. Not a shop was open on the main street, of course — it was night. Even the *bierlokals* were closed tight, not that he would drink beer.

The town was thick with traditional German housing, peaked roofs and lattice work from the second floor up. He walked past the *Hauptstadt* and paused for a moment to look at the enormous wine press made of sturdy oak beams that had survived for three centuries. His father, as had most of the men in Oberwesel, pressed grapes here.

He wandered through the residential streets up to the cloisters now mostly in ruins. What remained standing had been turned into chic apartments. This startled him and he recognised a truth about himself: although he knew change occurred, he was never prepared to face it.

The oldest part of the city drew him. He climbed the *Katzenturm* to the highest point — he had done this so often as a boy. This tower gave a nice overview of Oberwesel and the river. It was not nearly as high as the castle but provided a more human perspective. Human, he thought. I'm seeing all this like a human being, a mortal. And of course, he again recognised that he wanted to see things through the lens of the past.

There was another tower further along the waterfront and he climbed that to discover a tiny church, which he entered. It had been some time since he had been in a church. This one was quite simple, yet on both side walls were ornate painting in frames, the artwork dating back at least to his era for he recognised the styles. Yet this church was new to him. It had not been here before.

The sound of a door opening disturbed him and he felt someone was coming. He did not wish companionship at that moment and left quickly. Perhaps it was a priest expecting to hear the confession of a troubled parishioner.

As he hurried down the stone and wooden steps, he wondered just what it was he would confess. That he had taken the blood of a mortal every night for one hundred and fifty years.

157

Over fifty thousand mortals had fed him but he had never killed even one — unless bringing Gerlinde over counted as a killing — and perhaps that would provide some dispensation. Or not. His other sins paled by comparison. But he had brought another into this existence — there were some sins for which there was no way to atone.

He walked uphill to St. Martin's, a church that had been old when he was a boy, the church where he and his family had worshipped. Where his parents and grandparents, and those who had come before were buried. Where he had expected to find his siblings and their children. Where a plot no doubt still awaited him in the midst of his family.

Once he had changed, he had chosen not to return home. He had longed to see his family but knew it would create an impossible situation. He would not age, they would. He could not survive in the daylight. He could only drink blood. And that his family and the town's inhabitants would soon become his personal wine press — he could not bear that thought.

But he kept tabs on them, until his parents died. His mother never got over the fact that her favourite son went missing. He knew they must have suffered tremendously through not knowing what had happened to him and for that he felt guilt. If he had it to do over again, he might have staged his own 'death' and been returned to the village to be buried in the cemetery amidst the extended family. That would have given his parents the chance to grieve and recover.

But he had not been able to think clearly for several years after the change. He had a hard enough time coping with the hunger and finding blood each night without endangering himself. Then there were the crushing effects of impending daylight and the alarming sense of confusion that overwhelmed him before sunrise, sometimes for minutes, sometimes for hours, unpredictably. And the isolation, being completely divorced from human contact. It took him years to come to terms with his new 'self' and to become aware of the scope of his powers. While his parents still lived, he had not been capable of any complicated plans to spare them.

Behind the church lay the cemetery. He walked through the low metal gate and into the graveyard, the stones illuminated by moonlight. These stones were so new! Where were the aging tombstones that should be here? Horrified, confused, he read inscriptions — nothing from the previous century. Where had they taken the dead of his day? The wealthy, and the priests and martyrs were buried in great stone sarcophaguses within the churches or under the floors. But ordinary people had graves. His parents, his siblings had been buried here, in this corner near the woods, but where were they now? Their absence sent a cold shiver through him, one that left him feeling more isolated than he already felt.

With a shock, he suddenly remembered that plots were not forever. The ground was reused, and a hundred years was the usual deadline. The dead disappear, he realised. They disintegrate to dust physically. They only remain as memories in the minds of those who knew them, and when those minds die and disintegrate, the dead are remembered no more. Even the dead die.

"*Guten Abend.* It is a lovely night."

Karl whirled. Behind him stood a priest, robed in black, standing stock still. How had he not heard this mortal's approach?

"It's very quiet here. I often stroll through the churchyard late at night. It lifts my thoughts to a more spiritual realm."

"Yes," Karl stumbled, "I can see how that might be. I'm sorry if I disturbed your meditations."

"Oh no, it is I who have disturbed you. Or perhaps we've disturbed one another, and that might be for a good reason. I... I sense you are troubled. Come into the church where it's warm. We might share some wine."

Karl was still confused. How had he not heard the approach? Perhaps because of that confusion, he found himself passively following the priest into Saint Martin's.

He had not been inside this church since 1844, the year before Antoine forced him into this unholy life. The smells were the same. A building this old, dating back to the 1400s, carried time as a scent. The white walls and pillars were the canvases of the Middle Ages. Here were paintings done directly onto the walls, the artwork fading with time, the colours of the primitive pigments muted to begin with. He remembered these so well: the nativity; the crucifixion; the ascension; St. Martin himself slicing fabric from his cape to clothe an impoverished, disabled man. In Karl's mind he could still hear the litany, smell the incense; the words of a prayer came to him, one requesting peace.

He followed the priest down the centre aisle towards the altar, but then they continued to a door at the side wall. The priest opened the door and led him to a small, sparsely-furnished room. Wooden beams above, leaded casements, heavy dark furniture, a small altar with kneeling bench, and a space where the priest dressed for services — his formal robe on a hanger hung on a clothes tree, and this nod to modern times caused Karl to smile.

The priest motioned and Karl sat on a thick bench at the equally thick table, watching his host pour white wine from a glass decanter into metal goblets with scrollwork that culminated in a cross. Karl wondered whether these were used for official purposes, but doubted it.

As the priest sat down, suddenly Karl realised the man was blind. Under the glare of electricity, it was clear he was a young man in his early thirties. His soft, pale facial skin formed gentle features, as if his handicap had left him elevated rather than merely not bitter. His pale blue eyes stared straight ahead in Karl's direction, with no apparent emotion flickering there.

They sat for a moment in silence, then the priest said, "You have a story to tell. I am a good listener."

That he should talk with a stranger had never occurred to Karl. In all his years walking the earth, he had been nothing if not circumspect. And yet the open face of this man, his genuine interest, and the fact that they were here together, this night, when Karl felt himself sinking by the moment...

In his mortal life, he had been religious. The year before he had been brought over, Karl heard Karl Marx read a paper in which he said religion is the opium of the people. In 1844 those words were heretical and too radical to cause Karl to doubt his religious beliefs — and there was no need to question his faith.

Since Antoine had changed him, though, he'd often questioned the existence of God. That was natural enough. But it had never come to a showdown — his beliefs on the line. He still retained a kernel of respect for theology. How could he not? Theology and philosophy were paternal twins.

"I have a bleak outlook for the future," he said suddenly feeling self-conscious that he had spoken so directly to a stranger and a mortal.

The priest received this with a nod only.

"And my story may sound fantastic," Karl warned, "but I don't know how else to tell it but truthfully."

"Tell it in whatever way suits you," the priest said. "What I cannot read with my eyes I hear with my ears."

This rang of formal divulgence and Karl wondered if times had changed so much that priests now no longer needed confessionals.

"I need your word that what I say will not be repeated."

"Be assured that all you tell me is confidential. No matter how shocking your story or heinous your actions."

"I'm not a murderer."

"I was not suggesting that. And this is not a confession, is it? Simply a discourse."

They were silent again. Karl tried to figure out in his mind the difference between confession and discourse since only one of them was about to bare his soul.

When no further invitation to proceed came from the priest, Karl continued. Even as he spoke, he felt himself scanning the files in his mind, seeing the snapshots of his mortal past. The very air in this church seemed to encourage reflection.

"I was born here, in the village of Oberwesel. A very long time ago. Long before you were born." Again, the priest's nod was the only indication he had heard. There was no look of judgement or scepticism on his face.

"My life was pleasant by most standards. I had a mother, a father, four sisters and four brothers — I was the middle child. Our baby sister died at birth, and two of my brothers — one older, one younger — died before... Both sets of grandparents were alive when I was a boy."

The priest nodded again, and sipped his wine. His pale blue eyes were serious. They had heard many stories before, that was clear.

"My father and mother lived to be grandparents themselves, and went peacefully in their sleep. I discovered that later... after I changed. I'm not living. I'm not dead. I'm something else. Does that frighten you?"

The priest paused a moment. "There are many mysteries in God's universe. What I cannot understand I must accept."

Karl had an urge to sip the wine although he could not digest it. He did. The flavour, the aroma of the white-yellow wine — tart-sweet — all of it swirled like vapours through him, leading a trail home like the bread crumbs Hansel and Gretel dropped.

"My parents loved me as much as one of nine children can expect to be loved. I know I was my mother's favourite. They were not rich but not poor either. My father worked in the fields for the absentee *Schönburgs*. The fields produced many tons of grapes each autumn then, and the grape crushing culminated in a week of celebration."

"This is still the case although, of course, we have other industries now. Tourists," the priest laughed.

Karl looked at the priest. Why did this man not question him? What he was saying was outrageous. Maybe the priest thought he was psychotic and had decided to humour him. "I studied with the priest who was here then, Father Ballard."

This was the first time the mortal before him showed anything but utter calm and acceptance. Karl watched his thoughts turn inward for a moment, as though he was scrolling down a list of the names of the priests of St. Martin's. Finally, he found Father Ballard on the list in the middle of the 19th century. It caused his eyes to flicker.

"Father Ballard felt I possessed an exceptional mind and encouraged my parents to send me to university. This was unusual to say the least, but not completely unheard of — a boy from a small village along the Rhine sent to a large city, destined for the priesthood.

"I studied at the University at Köln. Trust me, father, after sixteen years in this village, living in Köln was an enlightening experience. Before I left for Köln, I had never been further from this village than Bonn. The freedom alone was heady. The sights and sounds and life of a metropolis, my access to and immersion in the writings of the world — within the first year I knew I could never return to live in Oberwesel and I could not enter the priesthood. I found something that engaged me more than religion. The physical sciences, so on the verge of modernisation at that time."

"This must have been a difficult decision for you," the priest said, and poured two more glasses of wine.

"It broke the hearts of my parents. My last visit home told me that. I saw layers of sadness in my mother's eyes. My father avoided me; he simply kept busy. They had hoped I would be the pure one, the ascetic, the one to insure their entrance into heaven. If there is a heaven, father, if there is a god, then I imagine my fate has kept the Pearly Gates locked against them."

"Do you want to confess anything?" the priest asked suddenly, gently.

"I... I don't know."

"You seem inordinately sad. Your past has caught up with you, as it does all of us. But that alone cannot account for what I perceive."

"You are perceptive," Karl acknowledged. He took a deep sigh. "Father, I am what you would call *die vampire*."

This caused the priest to inhale sharply. He blinked. He crossed himself. Karl heard his heart beat faster.

"I won't harm you," he quickly assured the man before him.

The reassurance had the result of a nearly imperceptible slowing of the heartbeat; nothing much worth noting.

"We are not like what the church has written about us," Karl said, desperate to calm the priest. "We are not evil, simply beings who struggle for survival."

"But you have no soul!" the priest cried, crossing himself again, pulling back in his seat.

This put Karl off. Why did they always think so narrowly? "Of course we have souls! Perhaps more so than you mortals. We've suffered death, or a part-death. Think of it as a near-death experience."

"Do you live off the living?"

"Yes."

"Merciful God!" the priest gasped. He began to mumble a prayer as he grasped the large crucifix around his neck and held it before him, shocking Karl.

"I've never killed anyone," Karl explained quickly, "but I did make one like myself. Someone who has now abandoned me. Who holds me responsible for turning her. I'm guilty of creating another like myself."

Now the priest's eyes reflected shock. It had been escalating for minutes and altered a man who had been so open and willing to help. Now he was just another terrified peasant who believed himself seated across from a beast of hell. The son of Satan. Or perhaps the devil himself.

Karl stood, enraged. It had not worked in the past and it did not work now. The religion that had been everything to him as a boy failed to provide him with support again. He moved from the room quickly, letting go of this pathetic human being, foregoing the blood like the Angel of Death flying over a marked doorway. Karl could never drink in anger for he would lose control. But he was tempted, so much so that he fled the church before the unthinkable could occur.

As he hurried back to the castle, he wondered just why he had returned to the place of his birth. What was he hoping to glean here? The memories of his early life were within his grasp for the first time in a long time, but what did they offer him? Only a revival of the disappointment he felt himself to be in the eyes of his family. Going back in time would not help him go forward into the future. With a bitter growl, he cried, "I have no future!"

He had not yet unpacked and it was easy enough to check out. He took the Vietnamese girl up on her offer. She became a willing fountain at which to slake his thirst.

There would be a train eventually, in some direction, and he intended to be on it.

# CHAPTER THIRTEEN

K ARL CAUGHT THE NEXT LOCAL TRAIN TO BONN, and there found accommodation in a good hotel for the day. At sunset, he drank from a lingering chambermaid, then rode the fast-speed European train. Metz sounded good for no particular reason, and he could make it there easily in an hour or so.

He reached the city before midnight, found accommodation in a decent hotel and left the usual instructions with the desk. Alone with his bleak thoughts, eager to escape them, the following night just after sunset he took the train to Nancy — a short distance across the border in France.

The city of Nancy in the province of Lorraine reeked of wealth. Everything revolved around Square Stanislas, named for a former governor, resplendent because of the enormous gilded gates, the two-story classical sculptures in bronze, and the faces carved into the frieze of the Regency-style buildings bounding the square. The Rococo nature of the old part of the city used to appeal to Gerlinde. It was so lavish, so over-the-top, she felt. It inspired her and, she said, reassured her that artistically, the sky was the limit. They had passed through here once, en route to Paris. The memory of that trip made him sad.

Tonight, he left the square to walk the quiet streets, past the faux Gothic church — built in only twenty years in the late 1800s — past *La porte de la Craffe*, the mediaeval tower with the double-barred cross built in 1436, and strolled into a quieter, less well-heeled section of the city. Here he found a tipsy Frenchman who accommodated his thirst readily. The man swayed a bit when Karl stopped him for directions. An alley behind the houses was a step away, and Karl had him down and pierced within moments. Karl left him there to sleep it off and headed towards the train station without knowing why, only feeling that the blood had nourished him, yes, but that was all. He might as well have swallowed a capsule filled with blood.

Nothing inspired him. Nothing filled the expanding void within. He could not return home — he no longer had a home. Not in Montréal with his friends, not in Oberwesel with his ancestors... He did not know what to do but keep moving, aware that it was himself he was attempting to flee from. Knowing the impossibility of that feat did not deter him. The darkness that he sensed massing at the edge of his being terrified him. It felt unbearable, like a weight that would crush him, leaving him smashed to bits and yet still existing. Still in pain. When he stopped to think, it seemed to Karl that the most apt words had been scrawled on a subway wall by some anonymous street poet of the 20th century: "The trouble with life is, nobody gets out alive."

The night was dark with no moon to light the way, although the City of Light held enough illumination that it would never be completely black in Paris.

He walked and walked, past the house Victor Hugo had lived in, beyond the Bastille area, with the tall columned monument the only reminder of the existence of the dreaded prison that housed the poor before the Revolution, and the rich during the Revolution before they were beheaded during the Reign of Terror.

This area of the city had been swamp land at one point earlier, as he recalled, but then so much of Paris had been different in the past.

The tiny streets quivered with life at this hour, and that would be so until close to midnight. He wove through the residential area moving farther away from the right bank, avoiding the avenue Ledru Rollin and Boulevard Voltaire, both lined with shops and brasseries crowded with people. He pursued a course to the north, by intuition, but could not deny to himself where he was headed.

He reached Boulevard de Ménilmontant and scaled the low stone wall easily.

Cimetière du Père-Lachaise at night was a dense necropolis within the larger denser metropolis. But the living had not interested him in a long time, and they did not interest him now, only for the nutrients they could furnish his system. More and more, it was the dead that mattered.

The cemetery spanned forty-four hectares. Over one million people were buried here, and there were at least one hundred thousand monuments. This city of the dead was set up like most cities — tree-lined streets and smaller laneways. Rather than taking the main roads, he moved along the narrow lanes wide enough for one that stretched in front of and behind the crypts. The paths here were dirt, no grass, and the dying leaves crackled underfoot. It would be easy enough to hide between crypts and prey on an unsuspecting stroller. But at night there would be no strollers — only him alone with the dead.

He passed so many lovely structures. Some of the crypts were like mini cathedrals with Gothic and Renaissance spires and crockets along the gabled roofs. The doors alone were works of art, the swirling metal grates culminating in crosses, or rosettes, or romantic designs, and the windows held stained-glass depictions of the Virgin or other religious figures. Some of the coloured glass had shattered over time, but much was still intact. Low fencing and little gates cordoned off tiny gardens here and there, framing the sepulchres, or the sculptures, or the many stone rectangles that imitated coffins. A bronze angel, semi-shrouded face blackened with time, hovered over the form of a newly dead body, both in marble. An angel for company. At least you're not alone, Karl told the effigy, and a sudden pain that he was unprepared for seared him.

The pain had been spreading like a cancer, destined to get the better of him sooner or later. He could not deny to himself that this was so. Whatever purpose to his existence he had envisioned previously seemed to have vanished now. He could see it all as if it were the most obvious pattern: Gerlinde had been his base, his foundation. Without her, he was falling through the universe with nothing to stop him. He could not believe that she had abandoned him, and he could not believe that he had accepted that so readily. But he knew in his heart that whether it was Antoine's control over her or her own decision, Antoine was only partly responsible. He had wronged Gerlinde by bringing her over. Karl felt it to the core of his being and knew he was helpless to alter it, just as he was helpless against Antoine's power. It was as if that first encounter, when Antoine had accosted him so viciously, had set a precedent that he was unable to break with. And no matter how gently he had brought Gerlinde over, the fact remained that he had destroyed her natural life and replaced it with an unnatural one. Because he wanted her. Out of selfishness.

He stopped at one crypt that drew him — a plain grey-white structure with lancet arched roof, Gothic windows and a rosetta glass that reminded him of the *Rosace sud* at Notre-Dame Cathedral. Within, a vaulted ceiling. A kneeling chair rested before the two-level altar. On the top of the altar itself sat an array of crucifixes and candle holders that had oxidised, and a painted ceramic sculpture of the Virgin, her pious face tilted towards heaven, her hands folded in supplication. It was the eyes that got to him, whites only, ghoulish, he thought, then thought further: no, that is how the dead see. How I see. Through eyes that hold no colour.

Many famous dead lay mouldering in this earth. As he wandered the grounds, he passed the resting places of Colette and Rosini, of Charles Nodier the vampire writer — his monument held a marble bust of his likeness —, past the Kardec sculpture at the Oscar Wilde grave, then past the grave of Kardec himself. Gertrude Stein was buried here, and Edith Piaf and her husband. Molière and Maria Callas. Proust and Apollinaire. Modigilani, Chopin and Heloise and Abelard. Jim Morrison had been put to rest at Père-Lachaise, although apparently the Americans wanted to bring him home and the French were not opposed to the idea. His grave was low and modern; a rectangular headstone and a kind of bed-frame stone, both of dark marble. Within the frame lay dried flowers, little messages, stones, even bus tickets, tokens from his fans. The grave would have been unremarkable but for the graffiti spray-painted onto the stones and onto every crypt in the vicinity — "Jim, 3000 miles to see you. It was worth it!" No wonder the French wanted Morrison out.

From Morrison's grave, the ground sloped upward dramatically. Karl climbed the hill between the crypts and graves until he found a secure place to perch and view the valley of the dead below.

It was a remarkable concept, really. These little structures: Gothic telephone booths, altars within, built over the caskets. Metal crosses identified the dead, or their names had been carved above doorways. Many of the crypts lay open; the doors had either never been locked or the locks had broken over decades. Most altars were bare, the contents long-ago removed and sold at flea markets, but some held candles and crucifixes and, occasionally, a photograph of the deceased. He'd seen a pair of high heels in one; in another, a journal and a recorder, the cord hanging down forlornly. He wondered if whoever had put it there was expecting the dead to record a message, or if one had been left by the bereaved.

Rather than an eerie feeling, the silent cemetery gave him peace — the first peace he had felt in... the first peace he had felt since finding Chloe's remains. Since that awful night when his world began crumbling until what remained had clicked into a new, bleak reality that felt eternal.

The view below was a land of cool greys and soft blacks, a city carpeted with decaying leaves and decomposing bones. The structures were half hidden by the oaks and maples, as if the dead, too, wanted privacy. Everywhere in the darkness he saw the outline of crosses, of peaked roofs, of angels, cherubs and, around the edges of one domed crypt, owls. The scent of autumn clogged the air, of life ebbing, perishing, settling in for a long burial beneath frozen ground. A slight rattling of leaves as tree branches moved in the wind. And... nothing.

His world, the world he had known, the existence he had lived was over. If continuing held a point, he could not see what it was. He had been places, done things. He had investigated all the realities he could fathom. Repetition was become reality, and existence had become one large déjà vu. And what was the use of that?

Gerlinde had been everything to him. Everything. He knew when he first met her that he was drowning in loneliness. She said often that he had saved her, given her such a wide palette from which to paint her life. He had given her love. Love she apparently no longer wanted or needed.

But Karl had always been able to face the truth, and the truth was, *he* needed *her*. He always had. She refreshed him. But beyond that, she was home to him, a face that always recognised his, that knew him deeply. A being who made the endless nights not just bearable but invigorating. Without that, without her, he was back where he began. Searching, for what? Another mate? If she could be taken away so easily, he had no reason to think Antoine would allow him anything to sustain him.

A sharp bark broke the silence. A dog. Two, that he could detect with his acute hearing. Guard dogs, he presumed. They would not sense him unless he moved. His odour would not be familiar, or perhaps it would be too familiar, too similar to the bodies that lay just beneath the ground.

The dogs were moving quickly towards the west, the stone fence he had vaulted. At the same time he sensed something to the south. Mortals. Three, no, four of them. They seemed to be coming from inside the cemetery, as if they were already here, but he had not sensed them before. Karl's guard went up.

The dogs were attracted by something, that was clear. He sensed them hovering. Then he caught the scent of blood on the wind. Probably meat, left to entice and distract them.

Meanwhile, the mortals had made their way further into the grounds. Soon he saw them south of Avenue Transversale, not far below him, weaving in and out between the crypts, two males, two females, not yet twenty, each dressed in black.

Layered over their human scent was the heavy smell of petoulie oil — it was as if they had all bathed in it, and washed their clothing in it as well. There was another scent he could not identify because of the strong oil. When they drew closer to where he sat still as one of the statues, he could see a resemblance, if not family, then cultural, or perhaps subcultural. The two females wore long black dresses that brushed the earth and silver crosses at their necks and ears. The males were in black pants, frilly shirts — one wore a velvet coat — and they, too, were wearing crosses. One of the males had an abundance of chains decorating his costume, one hanging over a shoulder, several around his hips, thin silver chain lacing up the outer calves of his pants. Each had long black hair, straight, hanging to shoulder length or below.

They were of the subculture commonly called 'goth'. Gerlinde had had an attraction to the 'gothik' as she spelled it. "After all," she laughed, "they got their start in Germany, didn't they?" referring to the Teutonic peoples of the third to fifth centuries. It was a joke. The barbarians that were the ancestors of he and Gerlinde had little in common with the refined sensibilities of the youth who espoused all things delicate and morbidly romantic.

The little band turned upward, almost in a direct line to where Karl sat. Slowly, he eased himself up and inched backwards into the shadows. One of the females sensed him somehow, and her head lifted. With a slight movement, she signalled the others and they all stopped.

Whatever they were doing here, it was not his business. On the other hand, he did not want to be bothered like this. He felt gloomy, suicidal, and this intrusion into his hard-found peace, dismal as it was, felt like an invasion.

They paused long enough for the dogs to catch their scent. Karl sensed the animals reluctantly finish licking at the remaining blood on the tombstone and sniff in the direction of the humans. Then they started forward, two sturdy beasts, possibly German shepherds, or the new breed of guard dog, the pit bull.

172

The dogs began to bark in the excitement of the chase and the little band of black-clad beings understood the meaning. Wherever these mortals had come from, they were far from that place now, and very far from any of the gates or the fencing.

The taller of the women opened a plastic-sealed pouch and dumped more meat onto the ground. The dogs would find it, but their hunger would be sated for the moment. The human prey were more enticing. And beyond that were the guards — Karl sensed them at the northern gates, on the alert now that the dogs had begun to bark.

The four glanced in all directions, terrified. The dogs were coming, they knew it. Then, suddenly, the tall female turned and looked up directly at Karl, or at where he stood. He knew she could not possibly see him, but something in her face reminded him of Gerlinde as he had first known her. So young, so innocent and trusting.

For no reason he could fathom, he stepped out into what little light existed. The girl gasped, and her companions turned to where she was staring. "*Komm mit mir!*" Karl said automatically in German, then quickly remembered where he was and translated to French. The look of incomprehension on the majority of the faces had him intuitively speak in English — they were bound to speak one of those languages! "Relax. Please. I'll help you. Come up here."

Without thinking, the tall girl hurried up the steps to him. More reluctantly, the other female, then the two males followed, and it was only the sound of the dogs nearing that moved them. Karl waved for them to hurry. He quickly led them further up the hill to the back of a large circular crypt. This crypt stood on a level lower than where they were, but there were windows high up at their level of ground. He slipped his fingers into the holes made by the crisscrossed metalwork and yanked. The window grill pulled out by the frame easily, but the noise alerted the dogs to their exact location.

"Go down first," he told the two males, "and quickly."

One at a time they slipped through the open window and landed on their feet noisily on the stone floor below. The one wearing the chains rattling as well. The drop was a good two and a half meters.

"Come," he said to the taller female, and to the two inside, "You'll need to catch her and help her in. Hurry."

The second he touched the female, her body jerked in cellular awareness. She stared at him. Her eyes widened, her lips parted and a look of shock spread over her features. There was no time to explore her fears though, for the dogs were now howling and Karl heard a vehicle driving through the grounds.

He lifted her through the opening, and the others inside caught her and helped her down. He did the same with the shorter female, then quickly replaced the grating over the window and crouched down against the opening, using his body to block the window — he was not concerned with visuals so much as with keeping the scent of the mortals from wafting towards the canines.

The dogs were now crossing Avenue Transversale. They paused briefly to sniff the new meat but, as Karl guessed, they ignored it. In a few bounds, they reached the steps and were up and then they were before him. And stopped. The larger of the two growled low in her throat.

His kind had always had a strange effect on animals. The more wild ones became subdued. Domestic animals tended to bond, like the cat Julien had owned for a decade. Whether or not he had power over the beasts, as the legends said, Karl did not know. But he knew he could implant into these simple dog minds a message that would send them on their way.

Of the two female shepherds, one was dominant. That one, he locked eyes with. She held the gaze but he could see she was desperate to look away. He could almost watch her mental process, the clicking of signals that culminated in understanding: she turned and trotted back down the hill, the younger, more submissive dog following in confusion. The young one kept looking back at him and forward at the other, as if trying to decipher what had transpired here.

The two dogs reached the bottom of the steps and found the meat. They were still tearing at it when the Renault arrived with the cemetery guard. He got out, looked briefly at the remains they were consuming, probably figured it was a rabbit or a squirrel, and said, "*Merde de chiens, vous avez interrompu mon souper!*"

But he laughed gently, got back into the car, and drove off.

Once the dogs finished the food, they trotted happily downhill, searching for more roadkill.

When the vehicle reached the gates of the main entrance, Karl heard the mortal re-enter the guard building. The dogs were now near the west wall again, on the other side of the cemetery, presumably hoping more food would appear out of nowhere.

Karl turned around and looked through the grating into the blackness. Eight eyes faced him, four on one side of a casket, four on the other, like the eyes of a spider with a rectangular body. "You're safe," he said.

"What are you?" the tall female who had felt him said.

Without answering, he pulled open the grate as silently as he could and motioned to one of the males. "Give me your hand."

The other male helped him up from behind, and then they repeated the process, both women first, and finally the other male until the last of the four was out in the open air.

"You'd better leave as soon as you can," he said. "The dogs will pick up your scent again and the guard will be back." Karl turned to walk away. His job was finished. Whatever they did now was up to them. They could be stupid or smart, it was all the same to him.

"Wait!" the tall female said, touching his arm.

He felt a current go through him, like an electric shock. He turned to stare at her face. She had lovely features, wide-set dark eyes, a wide and full mouth. Her skin was what in former centuries had been called alabaster, it was so pale. But they all had pale skin, and goths were known for their white make-up. The others had dye in their hair, but not her, and he saw under the dim starlight that her natural colour was black. Suddenly, he realised she was Italian. He'd picked up a slight accent from her voice, and now, on seeing her so close, that was confirmed.

"Why did you help us?" she asked.

"Why not?"

"What are you doing here?"

"I could ask you the same thing."

"We," and she gestured to the others, "come here a lot. When the moon waxes and when it wanes."

"Don't tell me you're witches," Karl said, a bit disappointed. He'd thought that went out with the 60s.

"Not exactly," she said. "We're —"

"Don't go telling a stranger!" one of the males snapped, his accent Irish.

"He saved our lives in case you've forgotten," the tall female said sharply. Then to Karl, "Come with us. Please. It's far but you'll like it."

The same male let out a soft groan of disapproval, but the tall girl ignored him.

Whatever made Karl go with them, he did not know. She led the way along the highest part of the hill, going a bit west, and soon they reached a particular crypt which she stopped before. The family named scrawled into the stone at the top read: NOIR. The crypt itself was not black but the usually grey-white stone, with a gabled roof and a metal door with a large 'N' in the centre surrounded by a circular design. The door appeared to be locked, but the tall female had a key, an old one by the looks of it, long, with a circle at one end and two teeth at the other to turn the bolt.

The crypt was the size of all the others, and there was no way that more than two of them could fit inside at once comfortably. Only the tall woman went in. She pushed a heavy-looking crucifix on the altar backwards. A panel at the front of the altar slid aside, accompanied by the sound of stone scraping against stone.

"Give me a candle," she said, and the other female produced one, black, and one of the males lit it with a silver lighter.

The tall female led the way down steps which apparently went under this crypt. The shorter female followed her, then one of the males. The remaining male — the one who had been hostile to Karl's presence — motioned for Karl to go down, which he did. Finally, the male stepped into the crypt behind him and pulled a lever which closed both the altar door, and the door of the crypt itself — Karl heard the outer lock snap.

The stairwell was narrow and dark, the steps steep and of stone, but Karl had the night vision to see that they were worn at the edges. Apparently many feet had travelled here over a long time.

There were no more than twenty steps, and when he reached the bottom he found himself in a small room of sorts, the dirt walls reinforced with wood planks. The tall woman waited there for everyone. When the last male arrived, she took candles from a storage spot in the wall and lit them from hers, handing one to each. Her eyes locked with Karl's, but she said nothing, just, "This way."

They walked through a tunnel that had been carved into the dirt. On each side he could see parts of coffins — the sides, the lids, handles — and sometimes skeletons, where the coffins had collapsed under the weight of sodden earth. The air here felt heavy and moist, with the scent of earth dense and overpowering.

They walked and walked, the candles stealing what oxygen there was from the air, and Karl could feel the change of the air's composition. He was surprised the mortals were not breathing more heavily than they were.

The tunnel curved gently but mostly it was straight enough that he could see fairly far ahead into the blackness with his special vision. At some point, it went from a dirt tunnel — and he presumed they'd left the cemetery — to an old sewer system. He knew the sewers of Paris spanned centuries, and they travelled through the oldest parts, lined with ancient ceramic tiles. The stench here was of things rotting over a long time in a place that was not conducive to transformation. The walls were wet to the touch, and in the rounded tunnel water pooled at the base — soon water had soaked through his shoes.

The sewer tunnel continued endlessly, it seemed. Once it linked up with an old metro station no longer in use, and they walked just a bit more than the length of the platform before turning back into the sewer tunnel. He knew from the slope of the ground they were headed south towards the river.

When the candles had burned half way, they reached a concrete tunnel, more like an aqueduct really, slightly wider than the sewer tunnel. A short walk along this and he realised from the new change of the air pressure that they were deep underwater, and that could only mean the Seine.

Once they had traversed the river, the concrete pipe took a sharp turn to the right; then it gave way to another tunnel of stone and earth, this one without coffins and corpses. Quickly that tunnel altered as well. It was still formed of the same material, but the ceiling became jagged, like the peaks waves make, and there were things embedded in the walls. Bones, he realised, and in a flash he knew they were in the Catacombs. Of course. Paris was a city built on Roman remains, which would explain the tunnels and the aqueduct buried deep under the river. And these portions had been a quarry where fine stones had been extracted. The Catacombs spread beneath the left bank like a giant web. Soon there were more and more bones, one atop the other.

Many millions of skeletons had been interred here. Back in the 1880s, when the above-ground graveyards began overflowing their walls of corpses in various stages of decomposition, and the stench of death and decay ran out through cracks onto the streets poisoning the people, and the impoverished took to digging grottoes in the burial grounds that became their homes, Paris was overrun with disease. The municipal government turned for help to researchers in a budding science, microbiology. It was soon decreed that for sanitary purposes, the remains of the rotting corpses must be cleared out, and future cemeteries built outside what was then the city limits. The *Cimetière des Innocents* was the first to go. The bones of its dead dating back over one hundred years were carted beneath the earth into the old quarries. Somewhere along the way, workmen got the idea of stacking the bones more artistically — this was Paris, after all.

As the little group wove their way through the tunnels of bones, the legacy of Paris' unhygienic dead, the walls became femurs with skulls arranged in the shape of flowers or hearts or crosses. Periodically Karl saw in the distance metal gates, which he'd seen before when he'd visited the Catacombs as a tourist with Gerlinde. But then he'd been on the other side of the gates. They cordoned off the small area that the public saw on tours. The reasoning was that these tunnels were so vast, the city refused to be responsible for missing tourists, and a limited view of the Catacombs was better than nothing. But Karl knew these odd burial tunnels extended over a much greater area than the mile or so that was shown to the tourists. Finally he could see for himself their scope.

Endless rows of large leg and arm bones, the smaller bones stacked behind them, the skulls positioned just so, to make a line, or two leg bones crossed beneath a skull in the classic 'poison' pattern. Concrete pillars joined sections of bone to bone, and it was not long before he became utterly overwhelmed by the sheer numbers. How many millions of human beings were represented? What must it be like to spend eternity crammed in with ones ancestors, and descendants?

They had walked all this time in silence. The tunnels went on and on. The air was humid, dense and filled with the scent of potassium nitrate and lime. And with the sweat-smell of these humans. Why they turned left instead or right, or right and not left, he did not know. Obviously the leader knew her way around down here. The candles were only stumps now and could not last much longer, so he presumed they were nearing their destination.

179

Finally, they reached an area that opened up and led down, down, down a ramp into the bowels of the earth, a very steep incline. How much lower could they go? He felt they were headed to the earth's core. And then, suddenly, they were standing before what could only be the remains of a Roman temple.

From the fragments that had once been an statue, Karl guessed this was a monument to Hecate because he had seen a temple to her in Greece, on the west coast of the mainland, and remembered the distinctive dress and facial features attributed to this goddess. She was a Greek goddess but the Romans had had no qualms about stealing the deities of other cultures. He recalled how the ancient Romans worshipped this goddess of the earth and Hades who had power over sorcery and crossroads.

He stared in awe at the Doric columns, the clean lines of the peaked roof or what remained of it. The temple had deteriorated over two thousand years; much of the pale marble was pockmarked but the basic structure remained intact. Karl knew he was seeing something very special. Something that he suspected only a handful of people on the earth knew existed.

"It's amazing, isn't it?" the tall girl, now standing to his right, said.

"How did you find it?" Karl asked, unable to take his eyes from this astonishing relic of another era.

"My *nonna* told me, and her *nonna* before her."

While they talked, the others set about lighting candles that had been strategically placed. The glow brought the building to life before his eyes.

"Why do you come here? What's the purpose of this trip from Père-Lachaise?"

"Not just from Père-Lachaise. We begin at Cimetière du Montparnasse, and move to Cimetière de Montmarte, and from there to Père-Lachaise, then back to here — Cimetière du Montparnasse is just around the corner."

"All underground?"

"Yes."

"And you go under crypts?"

"Yes."

"Remarkable! You're making a triangle. A trinity. The strongest structure in the universe."

She stared at him. "You're pretty intelligent to know that. But you know the triangle is also the most unstable form —"

"Because it's always in search of a fourth for balance."

"How did you know that?" She looked as awestruck as only youth can. Each one thinks they invented the wheel, he thought. "Anyway," she continued, "three is attractive but always ready to collapse to two, or expand to four, so it can be stable again."

He thought for a moment about the triangle of Antoine, Gerlinde and himself. Yes, unstable was the word at least for him. He had gotten the short end of this, and the form collapsed to two. And one always disintegrates.

"You are more than a sentient being," the girl said, using a word he felt might be too large for her, but she was trying to impress him. There was no need, really — the temple did that. She was also trying to seduce him. Well, he did look no older than twenty five.

"There's poetry in your soul, dark poetry that comes through the grave," she went on dramatically. "What's your name?"

"Karl. And you?"

"Donata."

He paused. "As in donation? A gift?"

"Yes." Again, she looked awed. Mixed with that was a look of captivation, as if she were already enamoured with him.

Fate at work, he thought about her name. If only she could be a means to my end, the muse that helps me create my own demise.

"Karl, what are you?"

The others were clustered at the side of the temple, unrolling pieces of fabric that looked like silk and velvet, stones — mostly crystals — more candles, incense, and other things, obviously for a ritual they intended to conduct. He sat on one of the steps at the front and Donata sat next to him. "I can't tell you what I am, but I'm no longer human. There are words — in your language it's *vampiro*. But they don't really convey my state."

She nodded. A small grain of fear hung at the back of her eyes, but he could see she was not as afraid as most. Now she was even more enthralled.

"I've been this way a long time, and have walked the earth almost two centuries." He hesitated.

"Go on," she said. "You have more to tell me."

"It may be time to finish with this state."

"You mean you want to die."

"That you've said it so plainly, well, it's startling to hear it. But yes, I guess that's what I mean. I don't see the point of continuing."

She placed her warm hand on his cool one. "I think I understand how you feel. I feel the same way."

He turned to her. "You? Why? You've got everything to live for." Before him sat a beautiful girl, no more than a teenager. She possessed style and grace, the energy and enthusiasm of youth, an obvious sensitivity and a wisdom that belied her years. "What on earth could make you think of dying? You don't have the right."

The startled look on her face caused him to reassess that last remark. "I'm sorry. Forgive me. I couldn't possibly know your circumstances. It's just that, from my jaded perspective, well, you seem to have the world at your fingertips, or you could."

"It's all right, *mio amico*. The Americans say, the grass always appears greener, no? And yes, I realise that to most people, I look as though I have everything to live for. My family has a long and illustrious history, and they are incredibly wealthy. I've been told I am not too bad to look at — I've had my share of lovers."

Karl laughed. "I'm sorry. You don't look more than sixteen."

"I'm seventeen, or I soon will be," she said, sounding as insulted as only the young can.

"Well, that's quite young to have had what sounds like quite a few lovers."

"You're German, I'm Italian. My blood is hotter than yours!" She tossed back her hair in a typical Italian movement mixed with a childish stubbornness.

Karl laughed. "Perhaps."

"Tell me," she said, "is being *vampiro* not as wonderful as we are told?"

"I'm not sure what you're been told. We need blood, human preferably. And have an allergy to sunlight which causes us to sleep like the dead during the day. Most of the other mythology doesn't apply — holy water, crosses, garlic, we're immune to those. I don't know if we live eternally. There are drawbacks to age, it seems." He was feeling them now. As if he were an old man who had nothing new to expect from life, nothing to rejuvenate him further.

She was silent for a few moments, then said, "Karl, you're unhappy. Anybody can see that. It involves love. That, too, is clear. Someone you loved, and lost."

He stared at her. "You can tell all that from looking at me?"

"I can see it in your eyes. They're like ancient scrolls and, moment by moment, they reveal more and more of your soul."

Karl sighed. There was no point not talking about it with this girl. His problems were his own. She could not help him, but she could not harm him either. "I lost her to an old one, the one who created me. I think she might be under a spell, but I can't be sure. And it doesn't matter. I only know that she hates me for what I've done to her. And prefers him to me. He's all powerful. I can't fight him. And without her..."

"You cannot go on. I understand."

She had the wisdom of an old woman. Her delivery, though, was so melodramatic. Angst suited her nature, he decided. "You asked me who I am," Karl said. "Now I'll ask you the same thing."

"I told you, I'm called Donata. My parents live in a villa outside Rome. My father owns a couple of factories that make fine leather boots. I have three siblings —"

"That's not what I mean. What I want to know is, how is it you can read so much in my eyes. Why do you know about

183

this?" He waved at the temple behind him. "Why do you dress like this, and have these friends? If I didn't know better, I'd say you were a *strega*."

"I *am* a sorceress. My knowledge comes down to me from generations of women in my family, who passed it one to the next. My special gifts come from living with death. I'm dying of AIDS."

This explained the peculiar smell just hidden by the powerful petoulie scent. Now that she identified it for him, he knew it was true. This young, beautiful girl was dying. He could feel it, see it, smell it.

"Don't feel sorry for me," she snapped, her eyes fiery.

"I don't. I live with death myself. I cannot see it as a negative force. On the contrary, lately I see it in the most alluring way."

"Good!" She crossed her legs and leaned back against a pillar. Her collar bones jutted against the skin. The pallor of her flesh was not make-up like the others, but the fading colour of a rose. He would have asked her how she contracted HIV, but he knew it would be one of a few sources. If she used IV drugs, it hadn't been recently, because he saw no needle marks at her veins. Possibly a blood transfusion. And there was always the obvious — sex. Whatever, he looked at her with some regret. She was so lovely, a bud about to wither on the vine before it could fully bloom. That was always life's greatest sadness, the one least understandable.

"I don't feel sorry for myself," Donata said. "I've come to terms with it. My time's short. Because of that, I refuse to indulge in bullshit. The clarity of a finite future leads one to see the truth, you know."

Something in that larger-than-life statement stunned him. It gave him a jolt, as if the universe had cracked open and something unexpected had seeped out. Something he could not see, touch, taste, smell or hear, and yet he could still sense it. It was unclear to him now but he felt instinctively that it would be revealed.

"I see a lot of despair in you. But Karl, nothing is ever as bad as it seems."

He shifted away from her. "Normally, I would agree with you."

"You have a scientific mind," she said, startling him anew, because he had not yet said anything that would impart that information. "You know about atoms?"

"Of course."

"Their components, protons, neutrons —"

"Yes, but I'm surprised that you know about things like this."

"Because I am female?"

"Because you're so young." He wondered if he'd been too long on the planet, not seeing people clearly, not having been that interested in mortals and their ways for too long a time.

A sudden surge of hunger overtook him. He would need to feed very soon. Already, light must be creeping into the sky. As well, he needed time to return to his hotel on the right bank.

"Karl, you must know, as I do, that there are subatomic particles that do not behave as we expect them to behave."

"If you're talking about the particles that are affected by the observer, yes, I know about them."

"Then you have the answer to your little dilemma."

Frustrated, he stood up. "I don't see it. My 'little dilemma', as you call it, is not really a dilemma. It's a dead-end street. There are no answers. There's nothing I can do about the situation, and I don't think I can continue the way things are."

She held out her arm. "I'm a poor offering, I know, but maybe you can slake your thirst here. I have more to say to you. More you need to know."

Something in her tone irritated him. He felt an urge to lash out, to take her blood, all of it. She was acting like some character in an Anne Rice novel. Mortals are so pompous, he thought. They think everything can be altered. Next she'll be spewing platitudes: go with the flow; life is change. He knew he'd better leave now, before he did her damage.

"I've got to go. The sun is about to rise."

"You can sleep here. No-one comes here but us, and there's no sunlight. We'll do our ritual in honour of Hecate, and then go."

"No. I need to leave. Tell me the quickest way out."

"Of course. I don't want to confine you against your will. You're not a prisoner or anything. There's a turn-off to the right up the tunnel. The second turn to the right. It will take you to a sewer exit — you won't have trouble finding it."

The others had come around from the place where they had sat talking. The shorter female began preparing a circle around the temple, spreading what appeared to be salt from a large bag. The two males were busy creating a type of altar at the top of the steps, using a low table, and the candles and incense and stones Karl had seen them unpacking, presumably to decorate the altar. Whatever their ritual, Karl didn't want to be part of it. And he suspected that if the others discovered he was a vampire, they might try to force him to stay, thinking his presence, maybe even his blood would make it all more powerful. They might even decide they wanted to join him!

He had his own concerns and they involved enough nourishment to get him through the day. And then tomorrow night he would try to think of a way to destroy himself, for he now saw clearly that's what all this wandering had been about. What had led him here. He could not very well die in Germany — whatever sacrifice he would make to Antoine's power, he could not do it on his native soil. Some things were just too humiliating. But Paris... He had always liked Paris. So had Gerlinde.

He began to move away from the small group, towards the tunnel, when Donata's words stopped him: "Karl, if you ever need me, and I think you will, you'll find me. Eventually. Unless I'm dead."

Something in those words chilled him. He could not imagine needing this girl for anything, and yet a part of him stored away the information as if it were vital to the survival of the universe. And that same part thought, *I hope you don't die too soon.*

# CHAPTER FOURTEEN

H OW DOES A VAMPIRE DIE? IT WAS NOT A QUESTION for which there was an easy answer. There were few known deaths in his circles, and Karl went over all the possibilities, based on what he knew would work and what would not. Members of the community had debated means of expiration *ad nauseam*. Death. Always a fascinating subject.

Poison was out — he had yet to hear of any of their kind succumbing to a foreign substance. In fact, their bodies normally extracted anything that it did not consider a nutrient. Having human, animal and plant cells meant there was little that could not be utilised. Any alien substance leftover was expelled through the body's orifices with no damaging effects.

Sunlight was an option. There had been many cases where exposure to the rays did severe damage, and he knew through André that one of their number had actually died from exposure. It had taken several days, true, but at least Karl felt sure it would work — eventually.

Another method was fire. That should do the trick, or he imagined it would, since the effect was similar to sunlight, but the means speedier. There had been one case he'd seen, but the body had already been dismembered. This insult to injury was a guarantee, Julien had said, that the dead stay dead.

Then there was severing of the head or the spinal cord. That had been successful — he'd seen it with his own eyes. Finding a way to sever his own head might be a problem. He could not envision how to do that other than to build a contraption like a guillotine. Possible. Not easily and quickly accomplished. And the thought that he might survive for minutes afterwards — he'd seen death masks from those beheaded during the French Revolution. Some were peaceful like Marie Antoinette's. Others were not. He wondered just when Ms. Antoinette's mask had been cast.

187

Other than that he did not know of a method. Piercing the heart might do it but there were no examples of that. Starvation would be almost impossible — he had a feeling they could live off their bodies for a long long time. Hanging was out — he couldn't imagine that working. He might weigh himself down and dive into water, but again, there were no examples or even near examples, and the thought that he might be stuck underwater and still alive...

He might be in a death phase, but the concept of demise did not just come and go in phases. It lingered, always at the back of the mind. And how could it be otherwise, for beings who kept living and living and did not know when or if they would die?

Death as a concept had fascinated him even before Antoine turned him. His studies as a mortal had led him into the realm of medicine, still in its infancy, still mostly herbal. An outbreak of a new disease, Rubella, occurred just five years before he succumbed to this life, and lasted another five years after. That was one of the reasons he had been in Düsseldorf. The disease — with fever, upper respiratory congestion and the distinctive red rash over the body — was not, in itself, fatal. For most adults, and even children, the symptoms lasted a few days followed by a full recovery. The ones in danger were the unborn — the foetuses in pregnant women. The prognosis was almost always gloomy. Ironically, the disease had given him a golden opportunity to study death.

He had witnessed many deaths from many causes and had seen more than his share of dead bodies. Death had been only a physical occurrence to him in his mortal days. He reasoned quite simply: we are born, we live, we die, then others are born to take our place. That's what generations are for, why people have children. A neat package of thoughts that avoided much of the confusion seers and philosophers, not to mention religious scholars, had struggled with throughout the ages.

His Catholic background had prepared him for a mystical experience. Death was the great unknown; he had learned the catechism. Death was supposed to be the experience which allows the soul to leave its incarnate state — the body is just a shell after all — and begin travelling back to the place from where it had come. The eternal place where it would once again meld with the divine in some manner, be that heaven, or another plane. He had expected to actually see some form of soul-leaving-the-body. But in all the deaths he had witnessed, he had yet to observe anything like that.

Mostly what he saw as a doctor were twisted, distorted forms. Old people, reverting to a catatonic state, their bodies nearly skeletons already; their one desire, if they were capable of expressing it, to be released. Apart from the old, there were the younger ones, victims of disease and accidents, who struggled and fought but succumbed nonetheless. Again, he expected something more than a look of torment or peace on the face, or a rictus grin that *rigor mortis* held in place for a while until the body became supple again.

Where was this subtle body, the spiritual body which he had been taught existed? Where was the white-light tunnel that had become a popular myth within the last part of the twentieth century? The few near-death experiences he had read about sounded so mundane that he could not help but wonder if these were either hallucinations caused in the comatose by the bright lights of hospitals, or if the NDEers had all read one another's books. In fact, the stories sounded suspiciously like alien abduction experiences and he knew some would say that there was a resemblance because we are all the children of aliens. Maybe he had read too much science fiction. Maybe his scientific mind simply made him more sceptical than the average being walking the planet.

What disturbed him most, what he had dwelled on quite a bit, was that there seemed to be no evidence of the spirit. He wanted to believe. It would make existence simpler. And yet he could see nothing concrete to support the idea. His own existence might be the best link to a spirit form. He was, by all definitions, a supernatural creature, outside nature, an aberration. If he could exist in this half-alive, half-dead state, anything was possible. David's poetic view had touched him — the soul trying to leave the body but becoming stuck in a halfway house, as it were. Karl had during most of his existence felt that keenly. He was not alive nor was he dead. He belonged in neither world yet seemed to flow into both. If he were to proceed into whatever place death led to — nothingness as Sartre had postulated — or some holy realm of angels and demons, of heaven and hell and the waiting station of purgatory — he would know. That he would gain knowledge was all that allowed him to even contemplate the unthinkable and overcome his fears and the repugnance of going against his own survival instincts.

He thought that fire was the simplest and the most foolproof solution. He simply had to secure himself in some private place in a way that he could not escape, then set fire to the place, and he would be burned to a crisp within an hour. Quick. Simple. Probably not painless, but exposing himself to sunlight would be far more painful. He could tolerate the notion of watching himself burn — watching himself beheading himself seemed ludicrous and melodramatic. His sensibilities would not tolerate such a preposterous idea, although the notion of a blade scalpel-sharp did appeal to him.

On the outskirts of Paris, near Roissy, he found an abandoned shed. The land was country enough that he did not anticipate interruption.

Chains and handcuffs were easy to obtain, as well as gasoline and matches. It would be a low-cost suicide.

When all was prepared, he felt he owed it to his friends to let them know.

While he placed the call, he thought about David and André especially. Of all that they had been through together. Of how they had met. How close they had become.

It was New York in 1946: not a good time to be German and in the United States. But the general hostility towards the defeated nations had little effect on his nightly lifestyle — he had never been that gregarious when he was mortal and nothing had changed in that regard. Just a year earlier, Karl had celebrated, if that was the word, his hundredth year of being undead. He had been alone the entire century, living always on the fringe of society, and was not looking forward to the two hundred mark. The United States was booming and full of confidence. War is always good for an economy unless you're the loser. In 1918, Germany's loss of the so-called Great War and the reparations imposed to satisfy France sowed the seeds of economic disintegration. That coupled with the Great Depression during the 1920s and 1930s eventually led his country into another war.

Karl could not condone Germany's barbarous actions during that second World War. But he had never been a person who could justify any war and the atrocities that it quite naturally led to. He had always avoided conflicts, both personal and political. Perhaps because of that, he had often found himself more alone than he cared to be.

Until that time he had never met another of his kind, which didn't make sense. Surely he and the beast who had sucked his blood could not be the only such beings in existence! But if there were others, they had not presented themselves. On occasion, he had had what he could only describe as a physical premonition, but nothing had come of those impressions, and he knew he might be reacting to anything: air currents; scents; temperature changes, high frequency sounds — and with the worldwide boom in radio and then television, there were many more frequencies in the air being utilised than ever before.

And when he turned a corner heading east near Central Park and saw two of his kind, blinding in the light they emitted, he stopped dead in his tracks. Jaw gaping. Eyes bulging. Both of them did the same.

That initial shock was quickly replaced by caution. They all felt it — tension sparked the air like currents during an electrical storm. Later, they realised they met at a crossroad. André had turned west. David walked south. But the street heading north was empty. Since then, none of them nor any of the rest of their kind they subsequently met could explain that mystical experience so akin to legend.

After a collective pause, Karl started forward as did the one who looked French. The British one was half way between them and held his ground. I'm nervous, Karl had thought. The other two looked nervous as well. Later they confirmed it.

When they reached one another, they stopped and stared in disbelief.

"We're... we're alike," the one in the middle said.

"Yes." The Frenchman reached out like he was extending a hand to two timid animals. He touched Karl first, then the other, as if to determine that they were both real and this was not some strange dream. Karl knew how he felt.

They talked riveted to the spot, until the sun threatened to rise, as if they had all been storing up words for a long long time. But all too soon they were forced to return to their dwellings — which each kept secret from the other two. But they arranged to meet the following night in Central Park, by the duck pond.

The next night, Karl woke jubilant. This was the first contact he had had with anything but a mortal since 1845! It felt as though an immense burden had been lifted from his shoulders. He ignored the part of him that called for cautious optimism.

When they were all together, the British one named David, said, "This is the oddest feeling — as if we're all fraternal brothers, hatched from the same egg."

"Yes, I feel that too," André confessed.

Karl had a similar feeling. It was like looking at a mirror image. Not that the three looked anything alike. André was tall but not overly so, his build athletic, his eyes dark and hair black with a bit of silver at the temples. He looked to be just under forty, but he told them he had been turned towards the latter part of the nineteenth century. David, tall, lean, British in demeanour, with sandy hair and pale eyes, had died when he was

192

thirty in 1893. That made Karl the oldest and yet he appeared the youngest — they all had a good laugh at that.

It became clear right away that each of them spoke French, English and German — they were each from a time when a classical education was the norm, if you received an education at all. It also became clear that Karl and David had been attacked in a similar manner, probably by the same being. A being who had also attacked André's aunt, now one of their kind and living in France. At least Karl knew there were more than just the three of them in existence — five altogether, if you assumed the mad creature still existed.

Apart from this none of the three knew of any others yet all had had a similar experience, of sensing others but never encountering them.

"I feel," André said it for them, "a strong attraction and an equally strong repulsion towards both of you."

"Yes," David said, "it's as though I'm fearful of being slain in my sleep."

"Or having to fight you both for food," André added. "I feel I need to be on guard. And yet I do not perceive an evil intent from either of you."

"I'm wondering if it's an instinctual reaction," Karl said. "Some animals are like this. They're not herd animals, but not prone to being entirely solitary either. Each of us has been forced into isolation by circumstances."

That made sense to André and David. And over time, their fears proved to be groundless. They were all eager for contact and the association became safe and mutually beneficial.

They soon rented an apartment together in Manhattan where they lived for more than a decade. Over that time they came to discover that although they were extremely different from one another, they shared much. And what they most shared was this experience of being not quite alive, not quite dead. Of being isolated from 'mortals', as they came to call them. Of having no real information as to what they were, the history of their species, their strengths and limitations. And this amalgamation of three minds, hearts and bodies, three different approaches, proved invaluable because they were able to try to construct a template that made sense to them and defined their species. But beyond all of this, it had provided each of them with perhaps what they needed even more — friendship.

The phone was picked up on the other end. Karl was keenly aware that this call to Montréal was not a call for help, but one of farewell.

David and André listened on the extensions as he spoke. There was a pause at their end, then David said, "You're playing into Antoine's hands."

"I know that."

"Antoine wants you dead, as much as he wanted Chloe, Kaellie and the others he destroyed dead. As much as he wants me and Morianna dead. The ones who died succumbed because they wanted to die."

"And I won't be the exception."

"Stop this!" André shouted. Karl knew André could not take it gracefully. It just wasn't in his nature. And he was still reeling from Chloe's death. "You're insane. You don't know what you're doing. Tell me where you are and I'll come to you."

"No," Karl said. "I have to leave this Earth and I have to leave now. You've got to accept that. It has nothing to do with either of you —"

"Of course it does! Do you think we are unaffected by this? Do you think we'll just go on, business as usual? 'Oh, by the way, Karl set himself on fire. Pass me the plasma.'"

Karl had to smile. "Gerlinde's affected you, hasn't she André? Her humour. Her vitality."

"Yes she affected me. All of us. I love her as a sister, but killing yourself because she left you is... insane."

"You're repeating yourself, and to no good end. I've made up my mind."

"You're *out* of your mind!"

"Karl," David said — he'd shifted over the years and become the calmest of the three of them, "we all of us know what it is to want to die. This is not peculiar to our state. Mortals go through it. Even whales beach themselves. Every living thing is in a state of entropy. We're torn between health and sickness, life and death. At times we veer to one side or the other. But we need to fight for life."

"Why?"

"Because it's all we have."

"There may be more. We don't know that. I've always been an agnostic."

"As have I and André. And most of the rest of our kind. We don't presume to know what, if anything, exists on the other side, if there is another side. But we will come to that when we come to it."

"*If* we come to it. We may never reach that stage naturally."

"Of course we will. You can see it in the old ones. They atrophy, in a sense. Antoine is the eldest but only seven hundred years. Why do you think that is? Where are the others, who came before him? He could not be the first."

"All of this is irrelevant, David. I've made up my mind. These are questions I no longer ask myself. I just want the pain of existence to end."

"*Merde!*" André cried. "You are taking the easy way and calling it the difficult path. Trust me, *mon ami*, this is not the answer. It was not for the ones who have died and it is not for you. Come back to us. We can think of a way to help Gerlinde. To help you. Our collective knowledge will make a difference, that I can promise you. It has for me and for David. And you are our friend. We cannot let you pass without making an effort."

The words touched Karl, but their effect did not reach deep enough into his being to alter his course. "Goodbye my friends. I love you both. You know that. Give my love to the others, especially Michel."

They all paused and before another word could be spoken, Karl quoted a few lines from T. S. Eliot's "The Love Song of J. Alfred Prufrock", one of the poems he loved most. The poet began by saying he'd seen his moment of greatness 'flicker'. And ended with the words, 'And in short, I was afraid.' And Karl hung up.

This was not how he wanted to say goodbye. He wanted their blessing, although he knew how unlikely that was. Because they cared about him, they wanted to stay this course. And if their caring alone could make a difference, it would have. One thing he knew: he could have no better friends than André and David.

But their friendship was not enough. He could not convey that. What he had with Gerlinde was a composite relationship: mother/son; sister/brother; daughter/father; lover/lover; and especially friend. They were soulmates. He could not move freely out into the world without that, and he had no hope of duplicating it with someone else. His instincts told him they were like Arctic wolves that mate for life; when one dies, the other never mates again.

He returned to the farmhouse where all was prepared. He simply had to attach the chains hanging from the ceiling to his body, then light a match and toss it onto the gasoline-soaked hay. It would be over in a matter of minutes.

When all was set, when he had affixed himself securely so that he could not escape, he struck the match. And tossed it. Flames sprang up from the moist straw instantly and spread in a circle around him. He felt like a witch at a stake during the Inquisition.

As the flames grew hotter, terror gripped him. He struggled against the chains, but they were too sturdy — he had never been one for halfway measures.

Smoke rose into the air as the flames erupted around him, licking the beams, devouring the roof, the walls. Karl panicked. He could not believe he had done this to himself! He began to scream like any flesh being in danger of extinction. Thoughts of humiliation at being a coward crumbled to ash. He was afraid of dying! He did not want to die!

And then, he turned his head slightly and caught sight of the most hideous thing he had ever seen. Antoine stood outside the window, face pressed to the pane, looking in, laughing, gloating. His enormous fangs clacking against the window pane. It was the same hateful look, the same diabolical laugh Karl knew from those moments when he had struggled for his life before this monster one hundred and fifty years ago, and succumbed.

Antoine had led him here to his end. It was no longer a concept. Reality sunk it. Too late.

# CHAPTER FIFTEEN

KARL HEARD A WAIL. THE LORELEI! THAT STRANGE thought flashed through his burning brain, so inappropriate to the moment. Antoine, he saw, heard the wail too. The grotesque face in the glass twisted even further and became more demonic, more stonelike. But the siren screamed, the malediction, an anathema drawing closer and closer. Karl glanced at the window again, expecting to see the devil himself. But Antoine had disappeared.

Karl heard voices. Words indistinguishable. Could this be the hereafter? The songs of cherubim? Or seraphim? What was he about to enter? What was he soon to face? Panic seized him. This could be hell and his kind had, by legend, been relegated there!

He screamed louder but his throat was raw from smoke, and only a whispered cry emerged. The flames had reached his feet. His shoe leather burned hot, like iron shoes. Fire licked the fabric of his clothing, making the cotton intensely hot; the front of his pants had already caught fire. He danced like a wooden puppet from the Black Forest, struggling to knock the flames from his body.

Above, the beam which held the chains caught fire. Already the metal around his ankles and wrists and waist was hot enough to create third degree burns. He had trapped himself in an inferno and, unlike the commonly held belief, inhaling smoke did not bring him to unconsciousness. Maybe his kind could never find such serenity.

An enormous sound like an explosion — the door burst inward. A being from another realm appeared. A god or a demon? With a weapon!

Karl trembled in pain and terror. But then he realised what was before him — a mortal, a man, bulked out in an orange flame-retardant suit and wearing an oxygen mask. He carried an enormous hose and the edge of a powerful blast of water struck Karl, knocking him backwards towards the flames behind him, but the chains held and kept him from falling. The cooling water wet him instantly, repelling the fire. The water attacked the flames directly. Smoke filled the room, more than before as water doused fire. The smoke became so dense he couldn't see, but he heard the beam above crack. It had weakened and threatened to collapse onto his head.

Firefighters poured into the shed with axes, chopping back the bits of still-burning straw, hacking at the damaged walls to let air in and prohibit injury from falling wood. One slid an oxygen mask over Karl's nose and mouth. Another entered and answered the call of the first — he brought metal-cutters and snapped the chains. Just as they were carrying Karl out, the beam above snapped in two and crashed to the floor. The cindered wood shattered.

Within moments, Karl was lying on the ground out in the cool night air. He heard a further siren and knew an ambulance was about to pull up and take him away.

A fireman was speaking French to him, and although he spoke the language fluently, he decided to feign ignorance and spoke in German — there were questions coming he did not want to answer. Let them think he was a whacked-out tourist.

One of the firefighters knew a little bit of German, but not enough for a conversation. He did manage to say, "You're safe. Help is coming. We'll take you to a hospital."

Karl felt utterly dazed and confused. His lungs and sinuses were clotted with the acrid smoke, although they were already clearing out. Parts of his body had gone numb from the assault of the flames. But his brain still functioned and two thoughts pressed for attention: he could not allow himself to be examined; who had called the fire department?

There was no way he could just get up and walk. He had to wait until they placed him in the ambulance, took him to a hospital. En route he could make an escape.

The ambulance arrived on the scene, a small van with two paramedics. About the same time, others arrived: curious neighbours; people driving by who just stopped their cars to watch the carnage; legitimate reporters; paparazzi — just in case he was a somebody they flashed lights in his face, snapping photos. He still wore chains around his wrists, ankles and waist: that would make a kinky picture! And photos of the remains of the shed. Karl turned his head: the building was gone. The roof and walls had collapsed, the wood, now blackened, lay haphazardly smouldering in the field of wet hay. The sky above held a grey cloud of smoke. The air stank foul from the lingering scent of char and gasoline. Karl trembled and someone said, "*Il est en choc!*"

A metallic stretcher was lowered to ground level. Two paramedics, one male, one female, took positions at his head and feet and, after an *une, deux, trois*, lifted him onto the stretcher. The female attendant pressed the air-lock lever and the stretcher rose to waist height. The male attendant replaced the oxygen mask the firefighter had installed over Karl's nose and mouth with another. This one, Karl knew instantly, was a non-rebreather — he was now getting much purer oxygen, instead of the mix with the outside air the previous mask had provided.

The female checked for his heartbeat, listened to his lungs and the frown on her face made Karl cough loudly to disguise what would be alien sounds to her ears.

The paramedics talked to one another, checked his burns, applied compresses of saline to the worst ones — a temporary measure until a proper doctor could examine the burns and determine if a skin graft was necessary.

Karl began to panic. They were too close to seeing his body regenerate, to discovering that his organs were not exactly as they should be. That Karl was not what he appeared to be.

Quickly, they rolled the stretcher to the back of the ambulance, pushed against it, and the front legs lifted automatically as the gurney was shoved inside. The female jumped into the back with him, closed the door and the male went to the front of the van and started the engine. The mesh partition between the front and back was closed. The driver could see if he turned around, but not otherwise.

The van shifted into gear and headed over the field to the highway at a fast clip, the siren horrifyingly loud in his ears as they sped away. The female had already covered him with a blanket, for shock, and was busy preparing two large-bore IVs — the label on one bag said 'Lactated Ringer' — a fluid volume replacement he'd read about composed of lactose, salt, and various minerals concentrated in plasma, this to restore some of the enormous amount of fluid he'd lost. Or so she thought. There was a better replacement at hand.

She also took a bag of plasma out of a small refrigerator to hook up to the IV. Then she placed a cardiac monitor to his chest, but didn't pay much attention to the results right away — he was still conscious, therefore alive.

He had to make a break soon. Already, she was inserting a needle into the vial to take his blood to determine the type and he could not allow that.

Suddenly, the cardiac monitor made a strange noise, one that drew her attention. She paused to glance at the lines fluctuating violently, then turned to look at Karl.

He sprang at her, catching her offguard, his hand at her throat, pressing at the large nerve running up the front of her neck so that she would lose consciousness temporarily before she could make a sound. She struggled for only a moment, then her eyes closed, but the look of horror in them registered on him — he knew she knew she was seeing something other than a human being.

He glanced around. The driver was busy skirting traffic, not looking into the rear-view to see what was happening in the back. The opportunity presented itself and Karl took it. He needed blood, she had some in her body. He pushed her to the floor just in case the driver did look back — he wouldn't see much. Karl pierced her throat quickly.

The little refrigerator had three more bags of plasma. He grabbed the pouches and then ripped the needles and heart monitor wires from his body.

The ambulance slowed, tilted as it went up a ramp and he knew they had arrived at the emergency entrance when they passed the sign: *Urgence*. Now was the time.

He opened the back door while the driver put the ambulance into park and turned off the ignition.

Within three seconds Karl was out the back and racing faster than sprinter speed across the lawn, onto the highway, beyond it and into the little wood. Overhead, a 747 flew low, and he knew he was close to the airport.

He stopped in the woods only long enough to think — they would not search long for him before calling in the police. He couldn't stay here. He paused temporarily to tear open the plastic bags and drink the plasma. It did not replenish him much and would not accelerate healing. He would need real blood to do that job.

By instinct, he headed towards the airport where he knew he would find people. Blood was a priority, but so was clothing; his had been virtually burnt away.

When he reached the edge of the tarmac, he crouched low to the ground under cover of the darkness of night. Soon he spotted a service worker driving a forklift, hauling away the empty food containers from a recently-landed plane. He took off across the lit tarmac at the speed of light. The coveralls fitted but the shirt was a little tight, and the shoes a full size too small. They would have to do until Karl could find new apparel.

The worker had a wallet with only fifty francs in it. Karl took that, left all the credit cards, and propped the nearly-naked man against the wheel of his forklift to sleep off what would seem like a drunken sleep. He had consumed some alcohol, but not much. Karl drank blood which tasted of traces of wine, red, probably Bordeaux — he knew that region well.

He called AmEx for authorisation to use his credit card without the card. He loved AmEx. They would send over a new card immediately to the airport Hilton. They even called the hotel for him and made a reservation for the night. At an airport shop that sold souvenir T-shirts, sweat shirts, socks and jogging pants with PARIS printed on them, he bought a new outfit. There were no shoes for sale, but he did manage to find a pair in a men's toilet when a size nine walked in. Karl had always thanked human physiology and Mr. Spock for that vein in the neck.

Once he was attired in a way that did not draw unwanted attention, he headed for the hotel and arrived just in time to pick up his temporary credit card. Check-in was quick and he was soon in his room reading the time on the clock radio. 0545 hours. The sun would rise around 0630 and he desperately needed sleep. But first he needed to think.

Death, he now realised, was not the way. Not like this. If he was going to die, then let it be fighting Antoine. To succumb to that monster directly, in a battle, that he could handle. To submit as he had tried to do, having his nemesis watching him expire, gloating in victory — Karl did not have the make-up to handle being on the low end of that type of conquest.

What he had tried to do to himself traumatised him into consciousness. That it could only have been Antoine who called the fire department to come just in time, to rescue Karl, after making certain he saw his hideous face leering... Antoine did that for one purpose only: to increase his suffering. The sadist had driven him to suicide, and then snatched him from the jaws of death simply to watch him sink towards death again — of that Karl was certain. Antoine could do that over and over, for centuries, never letting Karl die, never letting him fully live again because he would keep Gerlinde just out of reach. A cat and mouse game to be sure, with Gerlinde the bait.

Karl wouldn't play it. He just wouldn't. There had to be another way. And if there was, he would find it. He booked the earliest flight after sunset to Montréal.

# CHAPTER SIXTEEN

"IF SHE WANTS TO STAY WITH HIM, I CAN'T SEE there's much we can do about that," André said. "Gerlinde can make her own decisions. It doesn't sound as if she's been either kidnapped or hypnotised."

"You didn't see her," Karl said. "The coldness in her eyes. The things she said to me. She was so unlike herself."

"But David was under a spell and he clearly looked mesmerised. He couldn't even speak."

"It might have been different for me," David said. "Ariel and I had a sexual relationship..." He paused, suddenly realising what he was saying.

André finished the comment for him. "Face it, Antoine is fucking Gerlinde. That's part of it."

He didn't need to spell it out since all three of them knew the power of sexual intimacy that occurred with one of their own. It created a bond that was not easy to sever. And yet, Karl thought, Antoine has managed to come between Gerlinde and me. He's managed to sever *our* bond.

Carol had placed half a dozen glasses of blood before Karl and he drank two of them in a row. He'd already consumed three pints within the first hour of his arrival. At this rate, his body would be healed of the burns by sunrise.

"We've got to focus on protecting you," David said. "And Morianna. And me. We're the three he's after. Gerlinde is a pawn."

"Pawn or not," Karl said, annoyed, "I'm not deserting her. I want her away from him, then she can make a choice that's untainted. And I want him dead. Are you going to help me with this or not? Or were the promises of help empty words?"

"Calm down," André said. "We're just talking. We need to cover all the bases before we can figure out what to do. Antoine is not an easy opponent."

"He is," Morianna said, "an exceptional opponent. One we have little hope of vanquishing."

That dismal pronouncement from the normally enigmatic but optimistic Morianna threw a pall over the room.

Julien sat in one corner, his feet on a footstool. Diabella, his black cat, reclined over most of the foot rest and, to the left of his feet, Jeanette perched on what was left of the ottoman on Julien's right. Claude and Susan were with Michel, by the window.

Carol, Kathy, David and André sat in a row, in that order, on the long couch. Morianna and Wing each had taken an armchair. Several others, including Gertig, who appeared to be in mourning, were scattered about the room.

Without Chloe and Gerlinde at this gathering, the group seemed dismembered to Karl. He was keenly aware that their numbers had diminished. Collectively, they had Antoine outnumbered by almost 20 to 1. And he knew every one of them felt that even combined they were no match for Antoine. The domination he held over other beings was horrifying and it made Karl furious. "Look, he has a larger plan than just our extermination."

"What makes you think that?" André asked.

"Because of what Gerlinde said to me. The power she craves... It's not just being around Antoine. He promised her something I can't give her."

"Which is?"

"Mortality."

"Death?" Carol asked.

"No, being mortal again. Or rather, having the option to be mortal whenever he wants to be. It's what he's always wanted. Julien, you said that yourself."

"It is," Julien said after a pause, "what Antoine longs for, yes. Whether he wants that to the extent he did in the past, I do not know. Certainly his plans must have changed after Ariel."

"His plans," David said, "have changed in that he is now acting alone."

"No, he has Gerlinde," Karl reminded him.

"Yes, but she hasn't the power most of us in this room have. He picked her to lure you —"

"I know that! It's obvious and we've gone over that before. But I sense he wants more. I think he still wants Michel."

"If he wanted my son," Carol said tensely, "then he could have taken him at the cemetery instead of killing Chloe."

"He could have, yes. But Antoine knows Michel can be tracked by you, by André, by others here because so many of us have tasted his blood for just that purpose — to track him so we could protect him after what happened. And Antoine also knows from experience that if he snatched Michel now, none of us would rest until we got him back. We'd come after him *en masse* and find him through Michel."

"Because he's a kid and we care about him," Kathy said it more as a statement of confirmation than as a question. It was a realm with which she was entirely familiar.

Karl nodded and drank the contents of the third glass.

"There's one other aspect to this," he said, picking up another glass.

"Go on," André encouraged him.

"Chloe was in the death phase. I think she was driven by several things. One was paralysis in the presence of Antoine, who took her unawares by masking his scent to throw off her sensing abilities. Also, she was victimised by him before, in much the same way — the precedent we spoke of. But I also think Chloe was trying to protect Michel. I think she thought that if she distracted Antoine, Michel would get away. I don't think she saw the big picture, but she did know that Michel was in danger and she was right."

Everyone in the room thought this over for a few moments. It was André who said, "Thank you."

Karl nodded. He understood. André needed to give Chloe's death a higher meaning. They all did, as did she herself.

Finally, Julien said, and Wing nodded, "I believe I am in tune with your logic. Antoine does not want another major confrontation. He intends to erode within until our forces are too weak to offer much resistance."

"We have discussed this very possibility," Morianna said.

"Then why," Karl demanded, "didn't you let the rest of us know?"

"We needed to be certain. From the additional information you have provided, this now makes perfect sense," Julien said.

"Well, I don't buy it." André stood suddenly, and Karl saw that the tension had increased in his friend. The loss of Chloe, the idea of Antoine wanting Michel... André just could not handle much more.

"What I see," Karl said, trying to put it simply, "is that Antoine wants to get rid of as many of us as he can. He's begun with the ones he created, those of us he can track and who are easier to deal with, since we're automatically intimidated by him and therefore easy prey, perhaps as easy as we were before, when he brought us over. Once we're in the death phase, that's it!"

David nodded. "You've got a good point. With you out of the way, and then presumably Morianna and myself — which would leave Kathy bereaved because of me, André further bereaved because of both you and me, presumably Julien and Wing intimidated because he'd taken out another old one... It goes on and on. The upshot of all this would be far fewer of the strong would remain in our community to contend with, and the community would be beaten down. Fearful. Vulnerable."

"Which means Michel would be more vulnerable," Carol said, "and there would be fewer of us to protect him." The terror present in her voice rang like a bell.

André sat beside her immediately and took her hand. He stared at Karl. "I think I'm agreeing with this, now that I'm hearing it again. It's what any of us would do, if we wanted something badly enough and a community stood in the way."

"Divide and conquer," Julien said. "An ancient military strategy. Antoine has read Machiavelli. He may even have known him — I did. Once Antoine has decimated our community, it would be as nothing to snatch Michel from our grasp. Our efforts at rescuing him would be more difficult. Our troops fewer in numbers, and already emotionally mastered."

"All right," André went on, "we know his plan. Michel, he believes, is the goal to mortality. We need to get that ridiculous idea out of his head."

"We cannot," Wing said. "And for one simple reason."

"Which is?"

"It is the truth."

That stunned everyone, especially Michel who had been seated quietly, listening. The boy jumped to his feet. "What's that mean? Tell me."

Wing turned to Julien, who nodded, then to Morianna, who gave no perceptible sign that she concurred with what he was about to say, yet Wing must have picked up something. He walked to Michel and placed a hand on his shoulder in a paternal way. "Michel, you must be strong now. What I have to tell you is based on an ancient legend, not one from the west, but one from the east. Antoine spent much time in the east. Julien knows." Julien nodded again.

"The story I am about to relate is not one from my own culture, but one of a people who lived in the South Pacific ocean, on a Polynesian island northeast of New Zealand. A small world that time forgot. A world that evolved extremely slowly. So slowly that had a surreptitious atomic explosion not occurred in that region in the middle of the twentieth century, perhaps those people would still exist. But they are no more."

"Sounds like the lost world of Atlantis," Michel said.

"Perhaps in some ways they were a civilisation like Atlantis. These people were called *Anga-ma'a*. They, like every culture on the earth, past and present, had their vampire legends. Theirs was based on a vampire bat that dwelled in their region. This vampire bat was much larger than the South American variety. You can imagine how it must have been for them. On their little isolated island approximately three miles square, a bat the size of a large rat swooped out of the sky at night and frequently attacked not just animals but the natives as well. As we are all aware, the vampire has existed in writing since 2500 BC., referred to in the *Epic of Gilgamesh* as a 'death bringer'. So many variations over the centuries in so many places on the earth. Truly the imagination is humanity's greatest asset.

"To the *Anga-ma'a*, who lived an uncomplicated existence communing with nature in a way that seems idyllic to us: rising with the sun, sleeping as it sets, gathering the fish from the ocean, the fruits from the trees, repopulating their small world, the vampire bat was a fearful monster that brought sickness and death. And yet, this creature was part of their world, and they accepted it as such."

"It is a given," Morianna interrupted, "that the more a society integrates death into its culture, faces it squarely, the more those people will value life and struggle to live.

"We see the opposite all around us, especially in the west. Here, death is hidden. The dead are forgotten even before they die. The old are left to face this passage with strangers who care little for their souls. There is no sense of continuum. And once the body expires, they are burned or buried by people who, rather than following their natural instincts to grieve the loss and wish the departed a safe journey, instead will hold a celebration of the life, as if this were all that matters. And, of course, it is a way to avoid emotions and to increase isolation. We, above all creatures, understand the dangers of isolation."

She paused a moment, looked at Wing, and said, "I did not intend to detract from your discourse."

"On the contrary," he said, "you have offered an ingredient which contributes richness." He bowed slightly. "I am grateful."

Wing sat near the fireplace, facing them all. He picked up his satchel, which had been resting there, and removed from it a narrow, flat case, which might hold a sheaf of paper. The case, as with everything he carried in his bag, was of a quality material, soft leather but still firm enough to hold its shape. The leather was stained blood red, and tied with a black and silver ribbon. He opened the case to reveal what looked to Karl to be a piece of parchment. Wing handled the bottom of the case which held the parchment delicately. It was very old, that was clear. Gently, he placed the parchment still lying on the bottom of the case onto the coffee table.

The others in the room moved closer for a better look, all but Julien and Morianna, who had apparently seen this before.

"This sketch was made nearly two hundred years ago by a woman on the island. It shows the vampire demon they believed to be the father of these dreaded vampire bats. A demon that could rise from the dead and prey off the blood of the living. She drew it with the sharpened tip of a bamboo twig, dipping it into her blood."

The sketch was on a dry, brownish leaf Karl suspected to be from the tapa tree, no larger than six inches long and six inches wide, although the leaf was in no way square or uniform. On it were markings, the colour a fading rust, but even after so much time, unmistakably blood to the eyes and noses of everyone in the room.

The demon depicted was something like a gargoyle, part fish, part tree, and part human. More than anything, it resembled a large rat with wings, and two sharp teeth, both top and bottom. Karl thought it comparable, at least in that way, to demon masks he'd seen from Sri Lanka. This was simple artwork, primitive, the imagination of a native girl drawing from the sources in her environment. The style reminded him of cave paintings he'd seen at Lascaux. What made the work exceptional was how she had painted the eyes of the demon. They bored into the viewer and Karl could almost feel a rumble go through him, as if the earth was quaking. The most astonishing thing was that she had captured perfectly Wing's eyes.

"Powerful," Carol managed to say. "Truly amazing."

Karl glanced around and saw that same look of astonishment on the faces of all in the room. The scent of the blood used for the drawing was intense, more than should be the case after two hundred years.

As if understanding the unasked question, Wing said, "Her blood was exceptional. She was a pure blood, with psychic abilities and, therefore, what we might call a witch or a sorceress. These people had no term for her other than her name, which was the name of her mother, and her mother's mother, and so on back into time. Her name was *Fefine taula-fa'ahikehe*. She knew the past and the future, and predicted the extinction of her race. And she knew me instantly when I came upon the island for what I am."

"Did you... take her?" David asked delicately.

"Yes. Of course. Then, I felt it my right. It was a balance which both she and I understood. I needed her life to survive, and she needed to give hers in exchange for the survival of her people."

"But her people didn't survive," Michel said.

"No, they did not."

"Then that's unfair. You promised her something —"

"I promised her only her fate. I could not save these people, and yet her essence is within me still. She did not die in vain. In fact, she did not die since she speaks through me and all that have come after her time who have encountered me have heard her voice."

The knowledge sobered them. Karl glanced around the room. Most of the beings here had been created within the last two hundred years. Most of them had never killed, or had not killed since they came to find another approach with mortals. The old ones, though — Wing, Julien, Morianna... perhaps Gertig — they had lived in another time with other intentions. Karl had never really thought about it, but each of them must have taken many lives. What that would do, how that would alter one physically, mentally, emotionally, spiritually, he could only guess at. The blood Karl ingested was like the meat mortals purchased in a supermarket, divorced from the source — the carcass of a slaughtered animal from which a portion had been cut out. Karl and the others took their blood from mortals each night, a pint or two, not a sufficient quantity to harm them. And, on rare occasions, from a stock of contaminated blood-bank blood which a dummy corporation they owned purchased for research purposes. The contaminants were not harmful to them and the source was necessary — they never knew when an emergency might develop. It was the blood Karl was drinking at that moment, and he had consumed all but two glasses of it.

He looked at Morianna, so calm, so sophisticated, and at Julien, the just patriarch they all relied on for clarity of thinking, and at Wing, who provided the community with a tie to a part of their spirit from which they had been cut away. These three, above all the others, knew what Antoine was like because they were most like him.

"The girl," Wing said, "drew this on the night of her death. It is a picture of the *fa'ahinga peka 'oku misi toto*. A picture of a vampire. A drawing of me."

"The likeness is clear," Julien said with a small smile, and Wing returned the small conspiratorial smile.

"She drew this after I had drained her."

The room was silent. Finally, Kathy said what they were all thinking. "How?"

"Once I had ingested her, she lived within me, and because of her, I changed. I became human again."

"But how could that be?" David asked. "Even if she was a sorceress, that wouldn't make you mortal."

"Her people had protected her and the women of her line. You see, in her ancestry, lost in time, one of the women had been with an immortal. Perhaps a half mortal, half demon."

"There was another one like me?" Michel said, astonished. "Wow!"

"Like you, I do not know. I do not know if her forbear's encounter was with one like us. From this depiction, I think not, but I can't be certain. I am only certain that her blood transformed me, temporarily. And for a brief time I reverted to my mortal state. In order for that to occur, she had to die."

The room was silent for a time, until Wing added, "What I did, I could not help but do. We feed, and we live. We attain a perspective which enables us to be selective, to have the veneer of control over our passions. But this is a façade. Underneath, we are predators. Whatever prey enriches us in any way is desirable. And none here could have done differently than I did."

"Why didn't we know this before?" André said softly. "How can we safeguard Michel if we don't know everything?"

"We were endeavouring to protect Michel," Morianna said. "And now you know the truth. You must never forget, André, we are all predators, including you."

"If you're saying André or I could prey on our son...," Carol said, standing suddenly, her body tense, unconsciously shaking her head. "That is just not possible."

"Perhaps," Morianna told her. "But perhaps not. When the death phase occurs, one is not... how shall I put it, for it is not a question of a right or wrong mind —"

"One is not one's usual self," Wing offered.

"Yes. One is not one's usual self. The universe makes sense with a different set of parameters, a different band of logic. What is unthinkable becomes desirable, for reasons that make sense. The possible becomes probable."

Everyone started talking at once and the volume in the room rose by the second.

David said to Wing, "How do you know this change would come into effect by drinking Michel's blood? Your experience was not the same. This sorceress was a pure blood of a long line, and we don't know what type of entity her ancestor mated with. Michel is a halfway being in our world and his blood might not alter the balance?"

"We do not know," Wing said. "I related to you a legend, one of hundreds mortals have woven to explain what is unexplainable. There are other legends which talk about how the vampire may become mortal."

Karl thought about some of the vampire legends. Gypsies of the Moslem faith, and some Serbs and Albanians believed that if a vampire can survive thirty years, he or she will become mortal again. A tale from the Ukraine tells of a boy who rescued an icon of St. Michel and then travelled abroad with his merchant uncles. In another empire, the Czar's daughter had gone to the river to bathe and did not cross herself before entering the water. This allowed an unclean spirit to take possession of her. She fell ill and died. The Czar required that everyone read prayers over her to exorcise the evil spirit, and whoever delivered her would have half his kingdom. Each evening, one of the villagers went into the village church to read prayers and every morning the caretaker swept a pile of human bones out the door. The czar then decreed that all foreigners were to read prayers as well so that the locals wouldn't all be destroyed. Each of the boy's uncles persuaded him to go in their place to read the prayers, and each time St. Michel advised the boy how to keep the vampire girl from biting him: the first night he scattered a basket of fruits again and again, which kept her busy picking them up; the second night he used a basket of nuts; the third night he joined her in her coffin before she could emerge from it. St. Michel went into the coffin as well. She awoke, and the boy would not let her out until she called him, "My consort." She resisted, with much pleading, but when the cock crowed at sunrise, finally she called him her consort. They were found together praying in the sunlight, after which she was rebaptised since the unclean spirit had departed.

Despite these and other myths that seemed very childlike and were obviously simple metaphors for hopes and fears, Karl felt there was something different about the legend from the South Pacific. He could not put his finger on it at first, but suddenly, when Michel said, "Well, I guess I'd better not cut myself. You never know when somebody will be in a death phase and want to lap up my blood so they can change into a bat or something," it all snapped into place. It was as though metal parts dovetailed and now he could see the entire machine.

"I've got it!" he blurted out.

The others, who had been discussing the story Wing related and other things, stopped talking and looked at him.

He felt suddenly elated, lighter, filled with hope for a good outcome. The answer was simple and had been staring them in the face for some time.

"It's in the cells!"

"Elaborate," David said.

"All right. Listen." Karl drank down the last two glasses of blood. "Mortals carry within them preprogrammed cells, cells which have a specific life span and then die. But we're immortal, or at least we are until the death phase hits, when there's a chance, and it looks like a good chance, that we will succumb. Which might mean that we too have preprogrammed cells."

"That's a stretch," David said.

"No, it isn't. Remember when I analysed Chloe's and Kaellie's blood? Both samples had one red blood cell with a nucleus. As I mentioned before, in a mortal mature red blood cells expel the nucleus and, if they don't, it indicates disease. A disease from such an aberrant cell is serious and can lead to death. That cell in Chloe and Kaellie was aberrant and would lead to death, just like a mortal cell with a nucleus. It's just that in our kind, it's less obvious —"

"Because our cells are already odd," Michel said. "So we don't know what can and can't be there."

"Exactly! We are, by our nature, already a mutation, an aberration. We're freaks. And because we have such an odd blending of cells — human, animal, plant and other cells we can't yet classify — a mutation in one of our cells may not be stable because the molecules that bonded to create that cell can also bond with *other* molecules and re-alter the cell."

"Can you make this simpler?" Kathy said.

"Okay. Michel is a pure blood. He's never hunted, never pierced a vein and taken blood directly from a mortal, but only drunk it indirectly. His blood is so pure that it may affect a mutant red cell with a nucleus by bonding with it, causing it to expel the nucleus. In other words, his blood will reinvigorate the cell structure and force the elimination of the death phase nucleus. And that is what that cell with the nucleus is all about. It's a cell destined to die — a death phase cell."

"Are you saying the cell causes the death phase?" David asked.

"I don't think there's a way of determining whether the cell causes the phase or the phase alters the cell. It's a little like the chicken or the egg, which came first. And in the end, it doesn't really matter."

"So his blood can 'cure', if you will, the death phase cell?"

"I'm guessing his blood can do more than that. I think it will do what the sorceress's blood did for Wing. It will reverse the movement towards death we all made when we were brought over, and I think it will be permanent."

"But what do you base that on?" David asked.

"Mendel. And his peas. Basic genetics. Dominant and recessive traits in genes that determine heredity. My God, but Mendel was doing his research the year Antoine brought me over, in 1845! I even read his paper "Experiments in Plant Hybridisation" twenty years later."

"This is all fascinating, Karl," André said, "but it's irrelevant."

"It's not. Listen, if I can become mortal, I can fight Antoine!"

After a heartbeat's pause, André said. "If you can become mortal. Have you entirely lost it?"

"I hate to remind you of this," David added, "but none of us know how to become mortal again, even if we wanted to."

"Don't you see, Wing's story makes sense," Karl said. "It's the answer. Michel's blood is special. He can go either way, mortal or immortal, and anyone who drinks his blood can go in those same directions. But his mortal blood cells are dominant when it comes to our immortal cells, including any aberrant cells with a nucleus — the cells that correlate with the death phase. Antoine must know that on some level. He's undoubtedly heard all the legends, and probably he's put it together. He's been on the right track all along. Michel is the key to transformation back to mortality, during the death phase."

David sighed heavily. "Karl, these are legends. They are symbolism at most, simple folk tales at least. How can you, a scientist, believe such rubbish?"

"I believe it because it makes sense."

"We've each tasted Michel's blood. I, for one, do not feel more mortal."

"We probably didn't have any blood cells with a nucleus when we drank it, since none of us were apparently in a death phase."

"I *was* in a death phase, if you'll recall."

"Yes, but you only *tasted* Michel's blood for the purpose of tracking him. A few drops wouldn't do it. That's not the same as taking equal numbers of his blood cells to replace, or dominate your distorted cells. Remember, there was one red cell with a nucleus in one sample of blood from Chloe and one from Kaellie. Each sample might contain two hundred red blood cells altogether. There would be maybe twenty-five thousand cells with a nucleus in an entire body, or more, and each would need to be dominated by a biopholic cell. It would take *all* of Michel's blood to do the job. For instance, I'm in a death phase —"

"How do you know that?"

"I checked my blood under a microscope and found a cell with a nucleus."

That gave everyone pause. Karl knew it was like a mortal hearing a friend say he or she tested positive for HIV.

"Anyway, I can take a sample of Michel's blood and match it with an equal sample of mine. That will show concretely what will happen if I replaced the blood in my veins with Michel's blood —"

"Where's the empirical evidence that this would do anything at all to change your state of being and not just your body chemistry?" David asked.

Karl knew he could see light and was trying to explain it to blind beings who saw only darkness. He felt a bit benevolent and humbled by the truth. He smiled a little, which seemed to put David off, but he wasn't feeling superior. "Look, don't get defensive on me. I'm just trying to show you how it makes perfect sense. I ingest Michel's blood — better yet, his should replace mine intravenously rather than through the stomach which is an indirect infusion, so his blood will start in the veins where it will be most effective — and I undergo the change back to mortal, temporarily or permanently, we don't know. If I approach Antoine as a mortal, he will not be able to track me — I think so anyway, since I won't be one of his creations — and he will not be wary of me when I approach him. He'll react the way we all react to mortals — they are potential food, but certainly not a threat. I'll have him undefended and be able to kill him by one of the tried and true methods. The empirical evidence that this works will be in the outcome."

"It will not be in the outcome because there will be no outcome!" André said, standing, his tone angry. "Michel will not be donating his blood to anybody's cause."

"Dad," the boy began, "Karl's right. I know it. You guys are always telling me how special I am, and how intuitive, and I think you understand this... well, as Chloe would have said, on a cellular level. That he's right. I mean, if I can give him my blood, he can get close to Antoine, kill him and get Gerlinde back —"

"We know how close you've been to Gerlinde," Carol said, her own voice very tight. "We all love her and want her back safe with us. But not this way, Michel. It's dangerous for you."

Karl was deep in thought, almost oblivious to the drama playing out before him. "I imagine the most effective means would be to siphon out all of my blood first, to avoid contamination. Then transfer Michel's blood into my veins. Once he's empty, new blood can be fed into him —"

"So I won't die. At least not permanently," Michel said. "But I'll get to experience death, just like everybody else."

André stalked across the room and grabbed Michel by the arm. "You won't die because you won't participate in this."

The boy shrugged him off. "I have a right to make my own decisions."

"Not while you're still a child."

"I'm not a child. I'll be sixteen in four months. I'm an adult."

"You *think* you're an adult. I have the wisdom of more than one lifetime at my disposal and I'm telling you this is a crazy scheme that is dangerous for you, whether or not you see that danger."

"It's not dangerous. Karl said —"

"Michel, I don't want to hear it. It's already settled. *Tu ne feras pas sela!*"

They argued more, and soon Michel yelled, "Stop telling me what I am and what I'm not! You're not me, so just leave me alone!" He raced out of the room, slamming the door behind him. André and Carol glanced at each other and left as well, presumably to try to calm Michel.

Those remaining stayed silent. Karl felt sobered. Finally, he murmured to no-one in particular, "It wasn't my intention to upset everyone."

David said gently, "I wouldn't worry. It will pass."

"I think I'm right," Karl said.

No-one responded to that.

He felt demoralised suddenly. Hope had been snatched from his grasp. Was he insane? How could he even consider exposing Michel to any danger. Even if the two samples proved his point, they did not know the outcome of taking all of the boy's blood. Of course André and Carol were livid — any sane being who cared about the boy would be angry. If Karl was thinking correctly, he would see this path was not an option. Still, he looked at Julien, then at Wing, and finally Morianna. "What do you three think? Does anything I said make sense, or am I a raving lunatic?"

Julien spoke for the triumvirate. "Your hypothesis resonates. If you could become mortal — and Michel's blood would likely accomplish that transformation — Antoine would be offguard. Perhaps, if you were lucky, you could turn the situation to your advantage." He looked at Wing and then at Morianna. "It might be your only hope."

"Is there any other way to become mortal?" Karl asked, but even as he asked this, he knew the answer. It was Michel or nothing, and he also knew it would be nothing. André and Carol, not to mention the others in the community, would not allow it. In his more lucid moments, he knew they were right.

And despite knowing that, he also knew that each one of them realised that a Pandora's box had been opened here tonight. Michel's status had increased dramatically. As Wing had said, they were all predators and, given the right circumstances, none of them would think twice about taking the boy's blood. Karl had just proved that.

He stood. "I'm going to Germany to get Gerlinde. I know it's not the best way, but I don't think there are any alternatives. If there are, I'd like to hear them now."

The room went mute. Karl turned and walked to the door. "Remember," Morianna said quietly, "in the death phase, the logic of demise always makes sense."

His back still to them, Karl said, "There's nothing I can do about that."

Julien said, "We understand."

# Part III

"It is easy to go down into Hell; night and day, the gates of dark Death stand wide; but to climb back again, to retrace one's steps to the upper air — there's the rub, the task."

Virgil

# CHAPTER SEVENTEEN

KARL FLEW TO LONDON BY THE OVERNIGHT, and the following night caught a flight to Hanover. He'd done a bit of tracking before he left Montréal: Gerlinde was still there, and, he assumed, so was Antoine.

His plans were shattered but he did not blame his friends. They had every right to protect Michel. The boy was unusual — the only one of his kind. That Karl could even consider putting him through a procedure where the outcome was dubious showed how irrational he had become. But irrational or not, one thing he knew: he loved Gerlinde, had loved her from the moment they met. He had come to rely on her, to depend on her and he could not, would not, exist without her. And he could not let her exist under the power of Antoine without at least one more attempt to make her aware of the ramifications of that alliance. She might be under Antoine's control, or not. She might still choose Antoine over him. But regardless, he knew he had to do his best to get her back. And if he couldn't, he would find a way to extinguish himself that would be more sane, less the result of volatile emotions. A way that was his own and not him acting as a player in a drama Antoine had written and was directing. He would not die with that fiend laughing at him!

Hanover was an old city, devastated during two world wars, but still standing. The roughly half a million inhabitants were typically German — serious, work-oriented and wholly in love with their beer. The architecture of the old section of the city that had remained standing after the bombs dated back to the Middle Ages.

Karl had been here once, just after Antoine turned him. This was where it dawned on Karl that he could never go home again. When he realised he had nowhere else to go either. North seemed as good as south. Hanover, why not?

But he had not enjoyed the city and had stayed there just a week. The climate was not as pleasant as along the lower Rhine. The people seemed more tense, generally, and it did not surprise him that Hanover had become so thoroughly industrialised — the nature of the populace suited industry rather than agriculture.

It amused Karl in a macabre way that Hanover, like Düsseldorf, had boasted a vampire. Fritz Haarmann, a pederast, had stalked the train station for young boys following World War I, when refugees flooded the city. Haarmann, along with a prostitute named Hans Grans who became his lover, slaughtered their victims. Haarmann and Grans were enterprising. They black-marketed the clothing and the flesh, calling the latter 'horse meat'. The bones they tossed into the Leine River.

Haarmann was finally brought to trial and convicted of twenty seven murders, although it's estimated his victims totalled closer to fifty. At his request, he was beheaded in the square of the city's marketplace. Goettingen University received his brain for study, and Karl had often thought he would like to examine it.

What made Haarmann a vampire was the way he assaulted his victims. He overpowered the boys and attacked the throat with his teeth, chewing until the head had almost separated from the body. He claimed to love the blood.

It was well after midnight as Karl wandered along the Leine River bank on cobbled stones that millions of feet had walked smooth. The feet of Haarmann and Grans had trod here as well, as they carried the deconstructed skeletons to toss into the chilly waters.

In this place of death, Karl felt Gerlinde's vibrations as ripples along the inside of his body, between the skin and muscles. She was close. Presumably so was Antoine. Karl did not feel at all surprised when they stepped out of the shadows like black ghosts.

Antoine had his arm around Gerlinde's shoulders possessively, an unnecessary action, it seemed to Karl. Primitive. Obvious. Still, he felt a jolt of jealousy, even though he knew that was the intended effect. He also felt horrified. Antoine wore Chloe's amulet around his throat!

"So, *liebkin*, you're back," Gerlinde said. "Well, nothing's changed. I'm staying with Tony, as you can see. I'm surprised you're still alive."

That cut him. That she knew he'd almost died, and it didn't seem to matter to her. He tried to keep hold of his emotions which were threatening to drive him out of control. "I've come back because there are some things you need to know."

Antoine laughed. The sound travelled through the air like some hideous demon cry cutting through the night as smoothly as a cleaver severing bone from muscle. Briefly, Karl wondered what mortals heard. No doubt the sensible ones would be checking the bolts of their doors tonight.

"Antoine is crazy," Karl said, ignoring his creator, treating him as a nonentity by talking about him in the third person. Treating Antoine as Antoine treated him. "His vision of world domination is not feasible. Whatever he's promised you can't happen."

"You mean Michel?" Gerlinde said.

It was so blatant a question that he felt set back by it. Perhaps that made him sound unconfident. "The boy's blood will not alter anyone."

"You were never a good liar, Karl. You haven't done any tests on Michel's blood. You're saying that to sway me, but you can't sway me. My mind is made up."

"Perhaps. Perhaps not. But I'm telling you that Michel, even if you could get to him, is not the answer. And you did care about him once."

For a moment, he thought he saw emotion flicker in her eyes, but it might just have been light from the street lamp.

"I care about his blood and that's it. He's the answer to our prayers. He can be our the passageway to mortality and back. That's why he was created, to serve us. He's an evolutionary marvel, and we'd be stupid to ignore what that's about because of sentimentality."

These were words he knew she had heard Antoine say. This was not how she thought. Gerlinde had never been excessively sentimental and never concerned with evolution. But she did possess strong feelings. And she had been as protective of Michel as a mother with an infant.

"What's made you so callous?" Karl asked. "You were sweet, loving. Michel was like a son to you. A son you would protect with your life. And now you're talking about using him as if he were a lab rat."

"You should be able to relate to that, Karl. You're the scientist here. You've done your share of experiments. Now I'm doing mine."

"I've experimented, yes. But not on my friends."

"Because you didn't have the backbone. Well, Antoine does. He can see the bigger picture and act on it. And I'm tired of existence in a cramped space. I want to experience more. I want the option of mortality."

"For instance?"

"Motherhood. I want a child."

Karl was startled to silence. All he could say was something so cold he did not recognise himself. "You're dreaming."

"And you're boring. Why didn't you die in Paris? Just go away!"

He'd been prepared for this and the words only stung a bit. It was useless to talk with her. Whatever change had come over Gerlinde, he did not understand it. But he knew it was pointless to keep this circular discussion going.

"Antoine," he said, pushing within himself against the resistance he felt towards addressing his creator, "you have a plan. It's obvious to me. Kill the ones you've created and ravage the community to get to Michel. The others know your plan. They're on guard."

Antoine only laughed again, the sound black thunder, splitting the stratosphere. A laugh that said Karl was a simpleton, and Antoine was the new Thor, god of the universe.

"You could have been part of our world," Karl went on. "Not alone —"

"What makes you think I have ever wished to be part of your little world? You are all like ants to me, inferior creatures I watch when I want to be amused, and step on when it suits me. You offer me nothing but the pleasure of seeing you wither, longing in your hopelessness for death, yet having it always out of reach because I keep it from you. And believe me, I shall not let *you* die. Not you."

Karl ignored the warning voice in his head, the voice that screamed at him to run, as fast and as far as he could. "Chloe, Kaellie, the others, they were in a death phase. You took advantage of that."

"What do you mean by 'death phase'?" Gerlinde said.

She looked at Antoine, but he ignored the question. "They capitulated," he said, "because they were weak and I am stronger, just as you are weak and easy to crush."

"I'm surprised Antoine didn't tell you about the death phase," Karl said to Gerlinde, feeling he'd gained a slight edge with her. "We all go through it at some point, maybe more than once. It's a little like an intense suicidal fantasy that leads to action, a grapple with death. When others are in the midst of it, Antoine uses it to his advantage. He turns the potential suicide into murder."

Gerlinde glanced at Antoine again, a look of fear on her face.

"It's a natural phase for us," Karl went on. "You're in one now, Gerlinde. That's why you've moved away from me, from the others. You're seeing a large movie on your personal VCR, and you're the star. Tell me you haven't seen some sort of role for yourself as a kind of pregnant virgin sacrifice that will bring us all back to mortality and save us from this bleak night existence?"

The look on her face said he had touched a cord. It was so obvious. "Antoine," he said, "uses the death phase. If he wants to destroy one of us, he waits until we enter the phase. Or, in my case, he took you as you entered your phase, to draw me out. To annihilate me. You're just a pawn."

Antoine left his godlike responses behind and simply snarled like a rabid animal. "You think you have some knowledge, but I have half a millennium of time over your brief span. You are pathetic. Less than a worm, crawling on its belly."

"I may be a worm, but I have never destroyed. You have never created."

"Fool! I created you."

"Only because I allowed it. It was my own strength that permitted me to survive the ordeal, as it was with Chloe, Kaellie, David, and all the others you created so violently. There are two sides to every creation, the creator and the created, but you wouldn't know about that."

Gerlinde looked startled, as if something was becoming clear to her. The look on her face showed vulnerability and helplessness.

"Let her go," Karl said. "You don't love her —"

Antoine laughed again, his power fully restored by Karl's plea, and Karl realised he had said the wrong thing. The sound of that diabolical laugh cut the dark air with something blacker, more dense, more permanent. It was the absence of all light from the universe, a black hole of entropy that spiralled towards an oblivion that could never be reached, but the process could never be halted either.

A chill settled in Karl's lower spine. This mad entity did think he was a god, omnipotent, with the powers of the almighty. Karl felt helpless before him. Antoine would never change. He could not be swayed. It was clear he would not release Gerlinde, even if she wanted to go, and the look on her face told Karl that the same thought had occurred to her. What Karl knew had been confirmed — Antoine would dangle death before him like a carrot but always out of reach. There was nothing to do but react.

Karl's fury surged, propelling him forward, faster than he had ever moved before. He reached Antoine in a split second, his body already altering, ready for battle: muscles iron; nails talons; teeth fangs. His fangs snapped at flesh but bit air. In a split second Karl hurtled through space, into the night, as if he were a toy tossed by a giant. A toy that landed unceremoniously into the Leine River with a splash.

He sank fast and deep into the dark water. Water that held the memory of human bones, the reality of bones not yet found. Bones that sang to his bones — 'Join the underwater boneyard!'

Karl struggled to go up, not down, unable to change direction. Finally, his descent slowed. A moment's pause. He began to rise. He moved up slower than he had gone down. But eventually his head broke the surface. And when he collected himself and glanced around, he saw at once that the waterfront was empty. Antoine and Gerlinde were gone. Even Gerlinde's vibrations were dim, as if the two of them had transformed into birds of the night that had taken flight instantly and were now many miles away.

Karl climbed to the bank, shaking, the adrenaline still pumping through his system. Water would not kill him. His body would float before it would sink. The plant cells in his blood would consume the liquid. Death by drowning was not in the picture. Antoine had only tossed him into the water to show power, not for any other reason. And as Karl crawled to a bench, feeling defeated, he felt that power oppressing him, like the weight of the ages.

He truly was helpless. It was not a state he ever believed possible, but now he felt it to the core of his being. What could he do to get Gerlinde back, to destroy Antoine? Nothing. And there was likely nothing he could do to destroy himself until the day Antoine allowed him to die, if that day ever came. It was a lose-lose situation. How do I carry on knowing that? he wondered.

Sunrise approached. The eastern sky had lightened, the western sky was still dark. Karl still sat on the same bench by the water, facing east. He did not know if he could bring himself to just wait here for light to emerge and incinerate him. Light that would, if not annihilate him immediately, at least cause him great harm.

It was a stupid plan, he knew. Not a plan at all. More, he felt unable to proceed, even back to his hotel. He imagined that

Antoine would not bother rescuing him, since he would not die from sun exposure. He would simply fry. He did not know the extent of the burns, but imagined they would be severe, third degree. Of course, mortals would find him. And take him to a hospital. That would be even more stupid, and certainly he was not thinking of his friends who he would be exposing to danger simply because mortals would now have proof of the existence of beings other than themselves. Beings with peculiar organs, and blood components that they had never seen the like of.

He would be hospitalised, where he would be treated in a burn trauma unit. How ridiculous! He would be surrounded by mortals and, once he had the strength, probably attack one or more of them for the blood, out of starvation. And to what end? So that he could revive and recover and continue with this mad game of Antoine's?

But knowing the probable outcome could not rouse him. He felt depleted of will and that kept him stuck to the bench, staring at the horizon, waiting for the sun. Hoping against hope that he would die, knowing he would not.

"You're on a suicide mission, aren't you?"

He turned at the familiar voice. Donata walked towards him. A vision in black velvet, with death-white skin and a slash of red at her mouth. The girl-woman glided like the spectre she resembled, as if she had already entered another more spiritual realm. Maybe, he thought, she isn't even here. Maybe she's died already and this is her ghost.

As if reading his thoughts, she said, "I'm still alive. More or less. Enough that I could come here."

Nothing surprised him now. All his questions were simply the curiosity of a mind devoid of emotional complexity. "How did you know I was here?"

"I've been following you."

"Since when?"

"Since you left the underground temple in Paris. Since you left me."

He did not want to hear any sort of mortal love angst. If that was her game, he would have to drag himself away from this bench and, now that he knew she was on his trail, find a way to vanish. With a great effort, he pulled himself to his feet with that intent. What was the use of more words?

"Don't go," she said, "touching his arm. I didn't mean it the way it sounded. It's just that there's something between us. I feel it. I know you do. Or did. I know I can help you. Like I did in Roissy."

It dawned on him. "*You* called the ambulance and the fire department."

"Yes."

He sighed heavily, annoyed, frustrated. Antoine didn't need to do much with all these unwitting 'helpers' around. "I wish you hadn't. I was trying to die, which isn't easy for me. You just put me in a bad position with my enemy."

"I know. I was there, at the scene. I saw him. He's like Satan. Or some demon. He hates you and loves the power he holds over you —"

"Look, you're not telling me anything I don't know. In fact, you're irritating me. What do you want?"

"I'm here to help."

"Stop helping me. You're hurting me. Go back to your little temple in the sewers of Paris and worship the ancient gods. You and your group do it so well."

He was being cruel to her. It was that or sucking the blood from her veins. He considered that, but she probably wanted it, and it would only bring him more alive, more appreciative of his agony. Maybe he should just toss her in the river and drown her in memory of Fritz Haarmann. That he could even think this way showed him that the monster Antoine was had infiltrated his defences. In the likeness of my father! he thought with horror. But what could he do about that, or anything else?

"Karl, I don't know how to help you, but I know I'm supposed to help you. I've been ordered to. By a higher power."

He shook his head and started to walk away. He had no patience for airy-fairy new-age nonsense.

"I've got Michel with me."

Karl stopped dead in his tracks.

"When I followed you to Montréal, I met him. We left right after you did. We took a day flight. I knew what he was, of course."

"I suppose you astral travelled into the house in Montréal," he said snidely.

"I didn't have to. I was across the street and Michel came running out the front door. I caught up with him, told him who I was, how I knew you and he wanted to help. We decided to follow you here. I think you need both of us."

"Come," Karl said, more than irritated. "Take me to Michel."

They arrived at the hotel before sunrise, but not by much. She led him to room 23, and he just stared at the number, knowing it should mean something to him, but not knowing what.

Donata took his stunned state for interest in the occult. "Two and three together make five," she said, pulling out her key card. "Very positive. Lots of pentagrams."

Half the time he thought she was a flake, the rest of the time that she had the goods to be a sorceress.

His energy was low. Sleep pressed against his body like a weight. He could not stay awake much longer. He hoped this wasn't a trick, because he was not in the mood, and he didn't have the will to deal with much.

Michel sat on the bed reading *Hex Files — the goth bible.* The curtains had been drawn.

"Michel, what are you doing here? Your parents will be crazy. Come on, I'm putting you on a plane for home."

"I'm not going home. I want to help destroy Antoine. And rescue Gerlinde."

"Absolutely not!"

"Well, I'm not going back."

"You are." Karl picked up the phone and began to dial the house in Montréal direct.

"If you call my parents, they'll come here to get me. It's midnight in Montréal. They won't arrive here tonight. You have to sleep soon, but I don't. I'll run away with Donata. And if I run away, Antoine will find me and take my blood and I'll be dead so none of this will matter."

Karl slammed down the phone. "When did you become such a rebel?"

"I'm a teenager. I have to rebel," Michel said, and smiled with exaggerated sweetness.

"Look, Michel, I appreciate what you're thinking, I really do. And I know Gerlinde does as well. But I can't let you do this. And she wouldn't want it either. We don't know if it would work, and it's far too dangerous for you."

"What's dangerous about it? You take my blood, you become mortal, then you feed me Donata's blood and I come back from the dead. Isn't that the way it works?"

Karl sighed. "First of all, if you take Donata's blood, she dies."

"I'm dying anyway," she said. "I don't mind giving my life for a good cause."

"Everybody is ready to sacrifice for a good cause," Karl snapped. "We should form a euthanasia society for would-be martyrs."

"I'm not being a martyr. It's my purpose on earth to help, to find a greater cause, for the continuum —"

"Stop!" Karl held up a hand. He was growing exhausted. The sun pressed against the walls of the building and he could almost feel it sinking past those walls and pushing him down. "Please."

Michel said, "Well, you could turn her before we do this, that way she'll come back as one of us."

Frustrated, Karl just shook his head. Everything was easy and simple to youth. "I doubt I could do it. I don't feel intensely enough to accomplish that with her."

The girl looked a little hurt.

232

"Well," Michel said, "maybe somebody else could do it."

"Look, Michel, all of this is just speculation to start with. We don't know if your blood contains transformative qualities in the way we're talking about. I might not become mortal. And we don't know how you will react to being drained. You're not completely like the rest of us. It might be you can't survive a total depletion because the part of you that's mortal would be severely affected."

Karl felt he was repeating himself. His brain was close to a shutdown. His body weighed a ton, metal instead of flesh, blood and bone.

"Are you all right?" Donata said.

"He needs sleep," Michel said. "Use the bathroom. We'll stay out."

Karl wanted to argue further, at least his mind did, but his body was incapable of sustaining, and he could no longer articulate his thoughts.

He turned towards the open bathroom door, and the long bathtub which would be his bed for the night. "Put the 'Do Not Disturb' sign on the door," he said, his words slurring from exhaustion. "And Michel, I need your word you'll be here when I wake up."

The boy hesitated. "I'll give you my word if you give me yours — don't call my parents. Not yet."

Karl felt boxed into a corner. There was nothing to do but nod assent.

The bathroom door locked, he shoved towels into the crack at the bottom of the door to block out light. His face in the mirror was a horror to behold. He looked wild, hair askew, skin pallid, eyelids droopy, irises a flat colour. In short, he looked like a depressed man on a week-long drunk.

He snapped off the light, climbed into the bathtub and pulled the shower curtain around him, just for a bit of added protection.

Sleep opened like a trap door beneath him. Almost the second his prone body touched the enamel of the tub, he fell through that door into oblivion.

# CHAPTER EIGHTEEN

D ONATA DROPPED ONTO THE BED NEXT TO
Michel. He'd never been this close to a girl in such an
intimate situation before. Well, they'd sat next to one another on
the plane. But he'd been just a little stunned at that point.

She'd appeared out of nowhere as he ran out the door and
jumped into the Fiat to get away from his parents — God, but
he'd needed some air! He just wanted to drive somewhere and
clear his head. And there she was, tapping on the window on the
driver's side, saying "Hi!" Something about her face made him
roll down the window. According to all the myths and everything,
he was the one who was supposed to appear at windows and ask
to come in.

After she was seated in the passenger's seat, she introduced
herself, then she reached over and touched his arm. That was too
much. He shifted the car into gear and hit the gas. And while he
drove, thinking about that touch, he listened to her wacky story.

Or it seemed wacky at first. But she knew so much about
Karl and Gerlinde, and what was what, and she'd been there
when Karl was trying to kill himself — all the things Karl had
told them about before he left again. She knew it all.

"How do I know Antoine didn't send you?" he asked her.

"Well, you don't. But you can taste my blood if you want
to. I mean, can't you tell if I'm telling the truth that way?"

He'd been tempted, but it was far too intimate an act for
the first five minutes. Not to mention the fact that he'd never
taken it from a vein before. Besides, in the confinement of the
car, he could smell her blood and knew she was sick.

He listened to everything she said. And while she talked, and
while he thought about Karl and Gerlinde, and Chloe's and Kaellie's
death, and all the misery that Antoine had caused, mostly because
of him, Michel figured that regardless of what his parents said, and

how much he knew he would hurt them, he had to do something to make it all okay. And he was the only one who could. But he didn't delude himself completely. He also knew he wanted something out of this. Something very personal. He wanted to be like everybody else, like every organism on Earth. He wanted to taste death. And he wanted to come back. And he told Donata this.

"I'd like that too," she said. "I'm not afraid to die — I mean, I'm already dead in a way, just like you."

"How's that?"

"Well, our bodies are dead on the outside. Our skin is dead cells, and our hair is dead, and our eyelashes."

He'd never thought of things that way before. He looked at her with new eyes. "But dying, I mean, I don't want it to be the end."

"Maybe there's a way," he told her, and together they'd hatched the plan. He tracked Karl to Hanover and they flew out in the day time.

Michel had only flown in the daylight twice before. The sunglasses helped — the light was excessively bright. He was glad he had the foresight to book seats in the middle of the plane far from the windows, and was really happy that the woman by the left window, the one he was closest to, had the shade down most of the flight. It was a good thing Donata had two sets of earphones for her portable CD player. If he'd had time to think about it, he could have brought some CDs along. But she had some good ones, like *Terror Against Terror*, *Qntal*, and *Trisome 21*.

Because Antoine would sense him in the vicinity, Michel suggested to Donata that she go and fetch Karl, once he'd been tracked to a specific street. But he warned her that she had to hang back. "Antoine's a real killer," he told her. "If he smells your blood, he'll come after you. I mean, it's midnight. There won't be too many people wandering around where Karl is. You gotta be careful."

Well, she'd gotten to Karl okay and they came back without being spotted, or at least he thought so. He'd tracked Gerlinde and she wasn't near the hotel, so he figured Antoine wasn't either, or at least he hoped he wasn't.

And now Gerlinde and Antoine were sleeping. Just as Karl was sleeping. And he and Donata were sitting together on a bed in a hotel room and he was very aware of her body, of her scent, of everything about her. He felt his own body responding and it wasn't to her blood either. It was to her as a female. The response felt powerful, almost uncontrollable, but fantastic at the same time. He didn't know what to do about it. He didn't know if she felt anything like what he felt. She was two years older — well, a year and a half, since he'd be sixteen in a few months, and he'd asked and she said she'd be eighteen next June, which made her seventeen now, and June made her a Cancer. He didn't know if Capricorn and Cancer were compatible signs, but she brought it up and said they were. Well, that was one down. Maybe they had more in common. Maybe it didn't matter.

"What do you think death's like?" she asked.

"I don't know. I haven't thought a lot about that part of it. More like I just want to do it and see."

"I think it's like going into a liquid room, and you kind of meld with the furniture so you become part of everything."

"I think it's more like you pass through something invisible and come out the other side somewhere else," he said.

"Maybe," she conceded. "I just think it's a place where you end up staying, and it's not so bad there. At least you're safe."

It suddenly occurred to him that she didn't feel safe. "Safe from what?" he asked, hoping being so direct didn't scare her away.

"Well, nobody can hurt you there."

"You mean physically?"

"No, more like your feelings. Nobody can love you and then tell you they don't love you anymore."

He paused. "Did somebody do that to you?"

She shifted away from him a bit and picked up the room service menu. "Want to get something to eat?"

"Um, maybe later. But you can now, if you want something."

"I'll wait." She put the menu back down on the night table. Suddenly, she went from a seated position to a horizontal one. The quickness of the change startled him. Now he felt really awkward. Here was this really cute girl lying next to him in a bed and he was sitting up, kind of towering over her and all, and he didn't know if he should lie down too — maybe she'd get scared, or maybe laugh at him and tell him he was stupid for even thinking she might be interested, or maybe she'd just get up and leave and be disgusted by him...

Well, all these worries were a waste of time. He decided to half lie down, so he propped up his head with his hand, elbow digging into the pillow, one leg bent at the knee, so it didn't look like he was actually lying next to her, even though he was.

She turned her head and stared at him with those large, almond-shaped dark eyes. So dark, he couldn't see any light in them at first, since she had her back to the window and the bits of light coming from below the heavy curtain didn't connect. Her lips were pretty, so long and full. He really wanted to kiss her, and they were only about a half a meter apart, but he couldn't tell if she wanted that.

God, but he hated this! How did people ever get together? Obviously she found him attractive — he could read that much in her eyes. But all mortals found his kind attractive, so it might be only that. She might not be interested in *him*, but just the immortal part of him. And from what she said, she'd almost slept with Karl! Wow, that was weird. But then she didn't know Karl was a hundred and fifty plus.

Maybe it wasn't important that she knew Karl and had wanted to sleep with him. Maybe they could get to know each other first. Yeah, that made sense. They could spend a little time together, maybe go to some concerts, and...

Donata reached over, pulled his head towards hers and kissed him full on the lips. He was stunned for a moment, but just a moment.

237

Her eyes were closed, but she opened them, just a nose away from his eyes. His hands found her body, his lips found hers, and none of what he'd been thinking mattered at all. Not any of it. Not anymore.

# CHAPTER NINETEEN

KARL'S EYES SNAPPED OPEN TO DARKNESS. THE scent of bleach assaulted his nostrils, and human waste, both in minor quantities but enough to annoy him. He knew precisely where he was and the time. The sun had just a moment ago dropped below the horizon — he felt that in every cell, on a molecular level, as if the liquid content had been under pressure and that pressure was finally released.

He climbed out of the bathtub, unlocked the door and immediately perceived a peculiar energy as he entered the hotel room.

Donata and Michel sat on the bed together, between them a room service tray littered with the remains of french fries, sausages and sauerkraut, and cans of Coke. *Masochistic Religion* blared from the portable CD player, something about 'Absinthe and Death's Desire'. They were fully dressed, but they might as well have been naked.

Both of them looked up as he came into the room. Their eyes sparkled. Donata looked shy. Michel turned red instantly and busied himself with tidying the mess on the tray. Both of them seemed happier than he had ever seen either one. He didn't bother to address the issue — obviously they had made love, or came damn close. To his finely-tuned olfactory nerve, the scent of secretions wafted through the air.

Oddly, this affected Karl in two ways. He felt slightly repulsed. But when he examined that feeling, he realised it was a thin mask for the sadness overwhelming him from the loss of Gerlinde. He did not know if he would ever be with her again, ever take her in his arms, taste her flesh, feel her bring herself to him and open.

"Something wrong?" Michel asked. "You look mad."

"It's nothing," he told the boy. "Nothing to do with you two. Look, I've got to go out and nourish myself —"

239

"Take what you need from me," Donata said, pulling her high lace collar down to expose her jugular. "It's okay."

This could be a ploy, so that he would become connected to her and agree to bring her over, but somehow the way she said it didn't imply that. It was more someone who had a plate of food they were willing to share out of generosity, not for any ulterior motive.

Michel, in the possessive and instant-gratification mode of youth, said, "Go ahead. I mean, it doesn't mean anything anyway, and we've got to get started." He took Donata's hand, just to make that clear.

The scene before him made Karl want to laugh. "I think I'll make a quick trip to the streets," he said. "I need some air anyway. I won't be long."

It had rained that day and although the rain had stopped, the grey stone streets were wet and the sky looked threatening. He found a small park near the hotel and sat for a few minutes on a wrought iron bench covered with raindrops. No-one else was in the park, of course. Not many people on the streets. Those who were scurried, hoping to make it home or wherever they were going before the next cloud burst.

Gerlinde was still in the city. He didn't need to track her to know that. Her vibrations were everywhere but not close, that was clear. Wherever she and Antoine were sequestered, it was not in the core of Hanover. Assuming Antoine was still with her. Karl knew he couldn't really assume anything about Antoine.

He saw a street vendor with a cart. How little things have changed in one hundred and fifty years, he thought. The old square had been a shopping area in his day. Most of the traditional squares in Europe had been used for this purpose because hundreds of years ago these cities were not nearly as large as they were today. There was the church, the town hall, a few shops, and the sellers with wheeled carts selling everything from food to clothing to blinkers for your horse — now sunglasses in a seemingly endless assortment of shapes and colours.

The vendor stopped pushing his cart and set it down at the entrance to a narrow alleyway. He moved down the alley a few paces to urinate. This might be as good as it gets, Karl thought. It wasn't perfect food but it was fast.

He came up behind the man who turned, startled, and then collapsed from the pressure applied to his throat. Karl pierced him quickly, using the bulky body to block the view from the street. He left the man slumped over a water grate. He might be out for an hour or less. Hopefully his cart of wares would still be there.

Karl passed it as he emerged into the street. The cart was closed up but the sign said he sold watches. Cheap versions of designer watches, from the stickers. Karl opened the lid of the cart. The Rolex on his wrist looked just about the same as the one in the tray, which only confirmed to him that a value could not be placed on time. He exchanged his one-of-a-kind for the knock-off. Someone, somewhere, would soon be buying a very expensive watch for very little money.

Karl returned to the hotel quickly. As he arrived at the door, he saw the food tray in the hallway waiting for pick-up. Donata was in the bathroom and Michel at the desk with a pen and paper, working out a schedule, it seemed. He looked up.

"I figure we can both track Gerlinde, get her precise coordinates. Then you can take my blood — we already bought the IV stuff you'll need. Just before I'm empty, I can drink from Donata and change her. You can head out in the daytime. Antoine won't be able to track you then."

Karl sat down and stared at the boy. "Michel, I've racked my brain trying to find another route, but I don't see it. The only way that makes sense for me to fight him is to approach him as a mortal during the daytime. The only way I can see to become mortal is through you. But I can't risk what might happen to you."

"It's already decided, Karl. I mean, I can't go back now. I've got to do this. Not just for you. I've got to know what it's like to die and come back. I can't be the only one like me. It's too lonely."

Karl had never really considered life from Michel's perspective, but he could easily see now how it was for the boy. To always feel apart from both mortal and immortal. He was too different. Too alone.

"And what I said before is true too. Antoine wants my blood. And I hate him. For what he did to Chloe and Kaellie, and the others. For taking Gerlinde. For the way he brought you guys over. For just being evil. You said it yourself, and so has everybody else. I sure don't want him to get my blood, and he will. There's no way you guys can protect me twenty-four hours a day, and he'll never give up; we all know that. If I'm going to die and not come back, I'd rather give you my blood so you can kill the bastard. At least that makes it all worthwhile."

Karl had no words to reply to this. Everything Michel said made sense. And it left Karl a bit stunned. Finally he said, "There's one thing. You must phone your parents. I can't guarantee the outcome of this. No-one can. Not for you, not for me, not for Gerlinde. I feel guilty enough that you're here, but not letting them know is cruel."

"Yeah, I've thought about that too. I already phoned. I left a message on the machine — you know how you can do it without the phone ringing? I didn't leave a number, though. They'll trace the call to here, phone the hotel for sure, and they'll come. But by the time they arrive it will be two nights from now and things will be different."

An understatement, Karl thought. It's just that he didn't know exactly *how* they would be different. And at this point, he could not really allow himself the luxury of speculation. There were so many danger points, not the least of which was that if Antoine killed him, he would take his blood. And then he would likely be able to track Michel. If Michel survived this. Hell, if Antoine took his blood, he would *have* Michel's blood.

Fortunately Michel handed him the blood pump and IV equipment, which Karl set up immediately so that he could concentrate on something besides the worst prognostication.

"This procedure will take a few hours," Karl said as he worked. "You've got about five litres of blood in you. We could take it in half an hour, but I suspect the human side of you would go into shock. So, we'll do it as safely as possible. I'll be transferring your blood into my veins. I think for maximum effect, I should be as empty as possible, but I don't think it's good for you to drink from me. Your blood will be purer if it's not mixed with mine or anyone else's." He paused, avoiding stating the obvious. "We'll get started after we've done the tracking."

Donata was back in the room. She sat in a corner, wearing not just the cross she always wore around her neck, but a stone that looked like rose quartz. She confirmed this when Karl asked about it, adding, "It has to do with love. Michel gave it to me."

Karl said nothing. It was not his business. In fact, the less he knew about their relationship, the better. The less guilt he would feel, because there was absolutely no guarantee that Michel could change Donata. None whatsoever. He didn't tell Michel this and felt some guilt over that. But he knew *he* couldn't change her — he just was not motivated emotionally, and the change required some strong emotion. If not love, then hate. But something that could force one of their kind to allow his or her blood to be siphoned off by another being. Michel could only undergo this process himself, of giving up his blood because, Karl now realised, the boy had a passionate desire to experience death the way his parents and everyone he knew who lived in the night had experienced it. And because he hated Antoine.

He and Michel sat down with a detailed map of the city and its environs and proceeded to move inward, drawing on the Gerlinde that they kept inside of them always. When they both returned to the room, they compared notes. Michel's tracking abilities seemed sharper than any of the others of their kind. It might be because of his youth or that he was pure, untainted by so many mortals passing through his system in liquid form. Or because he had yet to actually hunt a mortal and take the blood directly.

Or maybe it was just that he was special — that alone accounted for so many differences. Karl wondered how Michel would be after all this, and if he would welcome the changes or not. And the thought crossed his mind more than once that Michel might not even survive, but he couldn't let himself think about that.

Gerlinde seemed to be at the outskirts of Hanover. It was the direction in which Karl sensed the remnants of her energy when he was sitting by the water, after she and Antoine departed so abruptly. Michel was able to narrow it down to a particular street, even, and Karl marvelled at the boy's fine-tuning abilities. Through her eyes, Michel could see what Karl saw and more: Gerlinde was in darkness, below ground, likely a basement. What neither of them said to the other, and which was painfully apparent to Karl was that Gerlinde was not alone. She was engaged in some activity that absorbed her emotionally and brought those emotions to the fore. Karl figured she was having sex with Antoine. He looked at Michel with new eyes, grateful that the boy had not brought this up.

Once the tracking was accomplished, Michel explained to Donata what was about to take place.

"But why don't you bring me over first?" she asked him.

"His blood needs to be as pure as possible," Karl said. "We can't risk it being tainted with anything at this point, particularly the HIV virus. His pure blood, hopefully, will alter me back to mortal. If I'm infected with an advanced case of the virus, that's going to hamper my abilities to deal with Antoine. I'll be weaker than I need be."

"Well, you could bring me over first," she said to Karl. "You said that your body will expel the tainted part of the blood quickly."

"Quickly, yes, but not instantly. It would take hours. And we don't have hours for that to occur and then more hours to do the transfusion. You'll have to wait until after we've done the transference." He did not want to tell her any more. It was out of his hands.

"Well, I'll take my chances," she said, smiling at Michel. But Karl could read her thoughts — there was nothing wrong with her ESP. She knew her change would not be either easy or likely.

He and Michel lay down, the boy on the double bed, Karl on the floor beside him, each with a needle stuck into a vein in the inner elbow. A small blood pump extracted the blood from Michel rhythmically, like a metronome attuned to his heartbeat. An anticoagulant kept it liquified and moving down through the feeding tubing to a triangular clamp that opened and closed with regularity. Then the blood proceeded further along the tube, down, and moved directly into Karl's vein.

He could feel the boy entering him. Feel him moving through his veins and expanding out, feel the blood flowing towards his heart, washing his heart, then through the arteries, filling out the little capillaries, moving out into his body, pumping like no mortal blood pumped. Michel *was* pure. His essence uncomplicated, natural.

Karl also felt his own blood draining out of him through another tube inserted into a vein inside his other elbow, the vein held open with small surgical clamps. Michel's blood replaced his, but there were uncomfortable gaps, places where for a moment there was no blood. That created pain, a kind of physical loss.

He thought he could feel the changes in his body on a cellular level. It was the way he heard some mortals talk about the sun, and how the ozone depletion left them experiencing the rays penetrating below the surface layer of epidermis down into the corium, and moving down below that into the muscle. He felt something similar. It was as if the cells of his body were... reshaping... that was the only way he could understand it. Michel's blood, which Karl had examined many times beneath a microscope, held mostly human cells, very few animal cells, and no plant cells, which made it different from the rest of their kind. The lack of hard-edged plant cells filled with chlorophyll alone was evidence of Michel's strong tie to mortality, which precluded much regeneration.

Michel's blood cells and plasma saturated Karl's body and he felt a change coming over him, one that left him exhausted in a way he had not experienced for almost two hundred years. Like any mortal being having his blood removed and undergoing an infusion of the blood of another. As an afterthought, it occurred to him that his formerly mortal blood type might not match up with Michel's. He knew he had been O Positive, the most common type, but he'd never thought to check Michel's for type. If that mattered, it was far too late now.

Donata read aloud to Michel from a book of vampire stories called "Endorphins". They listened to her portable CD player — now it was a German goth band, *Umbra et Imago*. She sat beside Michel and they talked a bit, and she held his hand.

Karl distanced himself on purpose. The procedure was painful to him. Even though he was receiving new blood, the sensation of having his extracted was not something he could ignore by talking or listening to music.

And it was clear Michel was fading. Over the hours of this procedure his voice had gone from buoyant to dull, from louder to softer. Every once in a while Karl asked him, "Do you want to continue?"

Michel, to his credit, always answered, "Of course."

Finally, about four am., the transfer was complete. Karl did not know if he was mortal, but he knew his body was different.

Donata was asleep in the chair she'd pulled up next to the bed. Michel's hand had slipped from hers and hung limply over the edge of the bed. Karl removed the IV needles from his arm and from Michel's inert form.

The boy looked dead. Not a part of his body moved, neither eyelid fluttered, not a finger twitched.

Donata opened her eyes. She looked at Michel and her face registered worry. "Is he.. is he okay?" She sounded tense.

Karl didn't know. He lifted Michel's eyelid. His pupil was dilated. He listened and did not find a heartbeat. The flesh was cold, not especially pliant, and held a bluish tinge.

Panic seized Karl. What had he done! He had killed this boy, like many of his kind had done over the centuries, draining a mortal for their blood, leaving the body behind, an empty carcass! But Michel was not a mortal. He was a unique being who might have been the salvation of their kind.

"I... I have to go," Karl said, terrified to dwell on it. Knowing that if he did, he would stay here trying to resuscitate Michel, losing precious daylight hours. And there was nothing he could do right now for Michel. If Michel was still alive, he would be alive later. If the boy was dead, Karl could not bring him back to life like Dr. Frankenstein reviving a corpse.

"I've got to get to the area where we tracked them, so I'll be there just after the sun rises. I don't know yet whether or not I'll be able to tolerate the sun, but I won't have much time to find them and then, once I enter the place where they are, I have to act quickly."

He was babbling in avoidance, just like a mortal! And what he didn't say was that he had no idea if Antoine could tolerate daylight. Presumably he could, indoors. Julien could. That alone might be a big problem.

"But what about Michel?"

She asked what he was trying to forget for now. He didn't know about Michel. Maybe, when all this was over, he could think about Michel's state, whatever that was. Not now. The end might or might not justify the means. But he could not do anything now! And it was getting late.

"Stay with him," he told Donata, because he knew she needed to do something. "He probably won't be awake during daylight. He's too depleted. Keep the room as dark as you can. Talk to him. Touch him. But before the sun rises, from time to time, just moisten his lips with a little blood." He didn't have to spell it out for her — the blood would come from her veins. And if Michel did revive, Karl knew there was an excellent chance he would attack her. But he couldn't think about that either. He just could not.

He left while the sky was still dark. As it began to lighten, as he moved out of the city and towards the suburbs, he was keenly aware that he did not feel the pressure he normally felt as the sun rose and darkness faded. Oddly, something in him welcomed the sun. He was not used to that sensation.

By the time he reached the street where he and Michel had tracked Gerlinde, the sun was ready to break the horizon. This area was heavily industrial, huge metallic buildings and sheds with company logos for all sorts of goods, and smoke stacks spewing greater or lesser quantities of contaminated smoke into the air. One of the factories was a twenty-four hour production house — he saw workers sitting on ledges eating bratwurst sandwiches and drinking coffee from thermos containers.

Karl stood in the middle of Eisenbergerstrasse, between buildings. The street ran east-west and he faced east. If he was going to incinerate, he might as well know it now. This might not be working. But he *felt* different.

And then sun, the glorious sun, the first he'd seen since 1845, rose like a royal entity, brilliant in its golden red majesty. This ball of fire that lifted higher and higher as the earth spun to allow its emergence was a deity. He could appreciate how the ancients had seen it, what had always been true. The sun was the source of life.

Karl stared at the sight and soon realised his face was moist with tears. No wonder so many of his kind yearned for mortality again! No wonder Antoine would kill them all for this. How did they survive only at night? Only half-lives. Distorted. Fragmented. And here, before him, the symbol of the other half. The light side. The part of the day, the part of life that supported growth and expansion.

His skin tingled but not in a dangerous way. Sunlight spread over him, nurturing, warming him, encouraging him, and everything mortal in him responded with open arms to this radiance that was the foundation of existence for lifeforms on this planet.

But time, he knew, was of the essence. He could stand here all day, and wanted to, but he must not. He checked his watch, which previously he had only checked in front of mortals as a ruse since he had marked time by instinct. Today, though, he needed to see the numbers. It was six am. Gerlinde was here, somewhere in one of a dozen factories along this road. Below ground, he remembered. And then he remembered Michel and a sob racked him, causing a mild spasm in his chest. About where his heart was. The boy might have given his life for this. To save Gerlinde. To kill Antoine. Karl knew it was the mortal part of Michel that encouraged such sacrifice, not the death phase of his immortal soul.

Again, he felt touched to the core of his being. How very capable these mortals are, *we* mortals are, he corrected himself. Of ethics. Of love. Of heroic deeds.

# CHAPTER TWENTY

E ISENBERGERSTRASSE WAS A STREET COMPOSED of one dozen industrial buildings, six on one side of the street, six on the other. Orderly. German.

Karl had no extraordinary senses to guide him. He was mortal now with five simple senses, none of which could alert him as to which building hid Gerlinde and, hopefully, Antoine from the sunlight. If he possessed a sixth sense it wasn't functioning. He would need to check each building thoroughly, particularly the floors below ground level. The two of them could be anywhere, as long as it was a secure dark space large enough for a body or two.

There was nothing to do but begin at the beginning. The building to his left was a factory with two stories above ground and, as he entered, he saw a deep basement with more machines. It looked like a thread plant and he marvelled at how they now made thread, so different from the way it was made in his day when women carded wool by hand and then spun it on wheels with a foot pedal. Of course, this was synthetic material as well, better adapted to being worked by machinery.

The giant thread processors were at a standstill. Apparently modern threadmaking was not a twenty-four hour a day endeavour. Just as well. He needed all the luck he could get.

He found a pair of coveralls with the company logo on the chest and donned them. The thread factory took some time to search. The basement contained many storage rooms and closets. It would definitely be handy to have preternatural senses — smell in particular would be good. But if he still possessed the sense of smell in that way, he would not be walking around in daylight now.

Workers began entering the building about eight am., and Karl tried to will himself to blend in. Still, people stopped to talk with him and he said he was new to the job, directed by a supervisor to have a look at the layout of the building and to see what was what. Everyone pointed out the important points — the lunchroom, the washrooms, the time clock — and directed him back to the office where he promised to head.

Karl's new awareness startled him: he did not see these mortals in the same way he had seen them before last night. They were no longer pulsing, pumping food sources. And in their eyes he could read how they saw him, and it was quite different. He was a young man, new to them. They were both open and distrustful at the same time. None seemed to find him inordinately attractive. Nor were they afraid of him. He was just another stranger who might or might not become a friend.

He discarded the overalls as he left the building and headed across the street to a one-story structure, small relative to the others — an industrial office building rather than a factory. It did not appear to be operational yet, although Karl expected to run into early morning workers.

Just inside the door, he encountered a small reception/secretarial desk and, around the corner, he found a washroom which doubled as a locker room. Karl pulled open one of the locker doors. Nothing useful. Nothing but the full-length mirror he stared into. He saw a pleasant-enough looking man, no more than twenty-five years of age with ordinary features and a slight build, wearing a nondescript suit and tie. This is what mortals saw — another mortal. Not only had he lost the personal magnetism and the sharpened senses of his former state, but he no longer possessed the inordinate physical strength of his former condition. He simply had the normal strength of one his size and age, perhaps slightly weaker because of the transfusion and exsanguination.

A bit horrified, Karl realised he would need to rely on wits alone because the supernatural, which he had grown so accustomed to relying on, had vanished.

He had no trouble making his way around the building which was no more than fifty meters by fifty meters. He walked quickly through the main floor space divided into offices with low-level fabric dividers. Each space had a desk, chair, small filing cabinet, computer and telephone. As he passed these 'rooms', he automatically glanced at the IN and OUT trays: invoices, letters, government forms to be filled out... What a horrible way to spend precious time, he thought.

Finally he found a door that led down to the basement.

Below ground was one large space with walls, ceiling and floor of concrete. From the number of boxes, this was a storage area — inside were plastic name card holders, cards with company symbols on them and plain cards together with rolls of plastic for lamination — all of it the type of thing people wore at conventions or as the badges they wore pinned to clothing to confirm their identity as workers at such and such a place and which would gain them admittance to secure buildings.

He walked the periphery of the basement first, ascertaining there were no closets and that the only doors led to washrooms. A quick move through the maze of boxes that crowded the room itself let him know there were no serious hiding places here, and no boxes large enough to house a body unless it was curled into a foetal position. He could not envision either Gerlinde or Antoine sleeping that way when they had a choice and he knew Antoine would never inconvenience himself.

Two down, he thought, and ten to go.

As he stepped to a window, he checked his watch, having no sense of time. Nine am. It had taken him two hours to check two buildings and one of them was very small. And they were both relatively empty, at least when he entered. From the number of people on the street, it was clear these factories were now operational. Ten buildings in operation would take, at this rate, ten hours. He did not have ten hours until sunset. He did not want to encounter Antoine after the sun had gone down.

There was nothing to do but speed up his search somehow. What he regretted most was the inability to sense a vampiric presence. But this was but one of so many drawbacks to being mortal, things he had forgotten about but which were now obvious.

Karl had thought carefully about how to dress and was glad he had chosen a suit and tie — they were always the best defence. On impulse, he turned into one of the back cubicles far from the front of this office — he heard the sound of phones ringing and being answered and smelled coffee being brewed.

Quickly, he shuffled through the papers in the tray and snatched one up. The scanner, printer and computer were all on. Fortunately he was up on the most sophisticated computer equipment. It was easy enough to scan the government letterhead and snap a photo of himself using the little camera on top of the monitor. There was probably a form for the card he could use already in the computer, but he didn't have the time to search for it. Using a drawing program, he created a reasonable facsimile of an identification card, moved the government logo and his photo onto it, and then printed it out.

A lamination machine in the hallway coated the badge which identified him as Karl Sterblich, a building inspector for the City of Hanover. If he flashed it fast enough and took the authoritarian tone of a civil servant, he could probably bluff his way into each of the buildings remaining and get some help from the staff. He hoped the ten minutes he spent here would add up to a considerable saving of time overall.

He left the office building while the receptionist was in an alcove pouring coffee for herself. Outdoors, the sun blazed stronger now and, fortunately, he felt no ill effects. Something gnawed at his stomach though, and he wondered what was going on. Maybe he was having an adverse reaction to the transfusion. He hoped it wouldn't grow worse.

At the next building where production was round the clock, he flashed his badge and was ushered in to see a supervisor. Karl said he needed to check the basement for possible bombs. The supervisor looked startled, and Karl smiled reassuringly. "This is confidential," he said. "There are no bomb threats against this factory, of course, but you know the city and prevention *is* worth a pound of cure," and yes it was a disgraceful waste of resources and taxpayers' money, but wasn't it better to be safe than sorry? And on and on in the German way, a circular conversation filled with platitudes that said little, but was absolutely necessary before any action could be taken. It annoyed Karl how much time this took. Formerly, he would have simply looked into this man's eyes and that would have been that.

The supervisor, a man on whom words were slow-dawning, finally said, "*Vorsicht ist besser alf nachsicht,*" repeating the cliché as if he had invented it. He showed Karl down to a massive space nearly half a city block square, crammed with clanking machinery and populated by men and women in coveralls tending to it.

"I need to look at every area which can hold a body," Karl said officiously, shrugging his shoulders in resignation.

The supervisor shook his head in sympathy with Karl's plight, but said, "*Ja, natürlich,*" and led him to closets, a couple of large storage bins, one room that held a generator, and another smaller one where the power box was kept.

Karl thanked the man, refused the offer of coffee and made his way to the next building. His stomach still bothered him. To ignore it, he checked his watch en route — forty-five minutes had passed. It was not much faster but minutes might make a difference. If only he had some sense of Antoine and Gerlinde! But he did not.

Time passed and soon it was afternoon, the sun in the western sky. As he came out of the ninth building, he checked his watch to find it was closing in on four o'clock and there were still three buildings to go.

He hurried through number ten, a tool and dye maker, his stomach killing him. At points he almost doubled over with pain. Why this hit in the stomach, he did not know. The tool and dye plant was straightforward, with no hidden areas and he was out in thirty minutes.

Building number eleven, though, was the opposite, with many closets and small rooms below ground. "*Was ist das?*" Karl asked, about a plank on the floor with a metal bar that looked like a handle.

The white-haired man who appeared to be long past retirement age said it was storage. "*Einen untergeschoss.*"

"A subbasement?"

"*Ja.*"

Karl made him open the door and, as they descended the steps, he worried that he should have asked all the others if there were subbasements. Still, he had not noticed any horizontal doors in the floor with handles. He knew he would just have to trust that there had been nothing crucial he'd missed.

An open area lay at the bottom of the steps. Why it was so cool and dry here he did not know, but the bricks seemed to be the answer — the walls, floor and curved ceiling were built of them. The area became a tunnel which went on for a long time, but the supervisor's powerful flashlight sent a beam of light ahead of them and Karl finally saw the tunnel open up into a room. This was a bit similar to the tunnels he'd travelled under in Paris, but surely no ancient Romans had built sewers here! Obviously, this was just a simple subbasement.

That thought crumbled to ashes abruptly when they reached where the tunnel opened up. Much to Karl's horror, it was like the body of an brick octopus, with tentacles stretching out in every direction. He turned to look at the supervisor, and asked the man where all these corridors went to.

"*Hier und dort,*" the man said evasively.

Karl probed for more information and learned that the 'here and there' went under the other eleven buildings on this street! How had he been so lax? His mortal brain could not hold as many possibilities as his immortal brain had.

"Why didn't the other supervisors identify these tunnels?" he asked in German.

"Because they're all a dead end. They go maybe sixty feet under each building and are walled up. Look here!" He went

255

down one corridor, shining the light ahead of him, and Karl followed. Eventually, they came to a wall of bricks. "Each is like this, the wall bricked up about sixty feet from both ends."

These tunnels were strange. Karl guessed that the infrastructures above had been built after World War II. Why was there a need for tunnels? These seemed designed to survive attacks.

"What was here before the factories were built?" Karl asked.

"*Ich weiss es nicht.*"

But Karl felt this senior citizen either did know or had his suspicions, and Karl certainly had his. This area might have housed munitions factories, the arms stored underground by the Nazis to prevent destruction if the factories were bombed by the Allied forces.

"Why is only this tunnel under your building not walled up?"

"It's not the only one. There's one other, and the two are connected still."

"Which other building?"

"The one next door."

"At the end of the street?"

"*Ja.*"

The man was being evasive and answering just what he had to, nothing more. "Why these two?" Karl asked.

"Why? Because we're the same company and the owners found that storing the finished product underground was safer."

Safer? Karl thought for a moment, then remembered the sign outside — *FEUERWERKS*. This factory manufactured fireworks.

"What does the other factory produce?"

The supervisor hesitated. His voice hardened with suspicion that had been building. "*Sprengstoffs.*"

Explosives.

"You're the building inspector and you don't know that? And surely you've examined the building plans for these two buildings, so you should know about the tunnels. I'd like to see your credentials again."

Karl panicked. He grabbed the man by the throat. The man struggled. The flashlight dropped to the brick floor. "Which tunnel leads to the other building?"

The man fought with him and, although Karl did not have the physical strength he once possessed, it did not take a preternatural to bring this old fellow down. Pressure to the throat resulted in the usual unconsciousness and soon the heavy man joined the flashlight on the floor.

Karl picked up the light. The man had passed out before he could say which tunnel was not blocked, and down here it was difficult to get a sense of the direction above ground. Karl glanced at his watch — it was already five thirty. He did not know what time the sun set, but it had risen around six am., which meant it set around six pm. How would he find out which tunnel led next door quickly? Calm down, he told himself, something he would not have had to tell himself in his former state. But then he had been almost invincible before.

There were twelve tunnels, one for each building. He was in one that was bricked up and had been in the one that led to the fireworks building. That left ten he would need to check out, fast.

He ran back to the belly of the beast and proceeded down the tunnel to the right at a quick clip. The second the light illuminated a brick wall, he turned on his heels and retraced his steps.

Tunnel after tunnel, each ending abruptly with a brick wall and then, finally, as he started down the next to the last one, he discovered what seemed like a narrow train track with small flatbeds on it holding crates.

Sixty feet led to one hundred and twenty and, along the way, he flashed the light onto the wooden crates and saw the word *Feuerwerks* stencilled on their sides. The track was crammed with crates from one end of this portion of the tunnel to the other end, which he finally reached. Another open area — this one without a shorter tunnel, but it was crammed with crates. There were a few steps up and a door leading, no doubt, to the last building on the street.

Where were they? They should be down here? Could it be that they were in the subbasement of the building above him? Maybe he should check that final corridor that led off from the previous building.

A quick look at his watch told him it was 6:10. If the sun had not set, it would any second.

Karl pushed on the heavy door, but it would not budge. Although it was dry and cool, his body was covered with sweat, his mind frantic. What could he do? Even if he could get out of here and up to the actual basement level, it might be too late.

And then he felt it. His mortal sixth sense kicked in and the result caused the hairs at the back of his neck to stand straight up. A cold, dull fear crawled from his legs, snaking through his backbone. Something was in the tunnel with him. Something dangerous to his health. Without knowing why, without questioning, he understood that it was stalking him, moving forward at a fast pace.

Every molecule in his body, every atom that composed those molecules, every particle that composed those atoms, all of him knew the danger for what it was: Antoine. His body had been ravaged before by the onslaught of this diabolic being. It would forever quiver in fear in the presence of that fiend.

Karl pounded on the door and screamed. He heard a scream and thought it was his own, then realised it was the man he'd left in the tunnel. A man who was now dead, drained of his blood. As dead as Karl would soon be unless someone let him out of here!

He pounded on the door as if his life depended on it being opened. Some angel must be watching over me, he thought, in a split second realising he was thinking the way mortals think, because, magically, the door opened.

"Quickly, evacuate the building!" Karl ordered the startled worker. He flashed his badge. "I'm the building inspector. There's a bomb in the tunnel!"

The man Karl addressed wasted no time but sent out a call and, in moments, workers were scurrying through the basement, up the ladders and steps to the main floor, shouting as they went.

Karl caught one of them. "Get the next building evacuated as well. The fireworks factory. And the other buildings on the street."

The man nodded and turned to run, but Karl held his arm. "Give me your lighter." The man handed over his lighter without question. The fear on his face precluded anything but action.

Once the man had turned and run from the building with his co-workers, Karl lit whatever he could find — fabric, paper, anything and everything used to make the shell of fireworks. A warning siren blared, insistent, continuous. Karl ignored it. When he had a good blaze going, maybe six feet by six feet, one that threatened to spread out of control, he got a grip on his fear and opened the door.

Darkness met him, a darkness that the fire illuminated. It was an intangible, rather than a tangible darkness, something black and loathsome. He had time while kicking the fire down the steps to think: Is this how mortals have always perceived me?

The fire toppled over itself as it fell. Karl kicked at it and knocked the burning debris with a piece of metal pipe, extremely careful because of his recent encounter with fire. He wasn't trying to burn down the building or even explode the tunnels — both Gerlinde and Antoine could tolerate smoke and probably even such a low-grade explosion. What he hoped to do was ignite some of the firecrackers. It wasn't the magnesium he cared about, it was the gunpowder. If he could get a chain reaction going down there, it would drive Antoine and Gerlinde to the surface. Once they were on street level, he did not have a clue what he would do. He just knew he couldn't let them stay down here.

With the door open, the malevolent presence felt fearsome, overbearing. Every moment it swelled closer, stronger in its influence. Once the fire had caught on the steps and flames were playing on a few of the crates, Karl slammed the door shut and slid the one flimsy bolt into place. It would not stop Antoine. Not in a million years.

He turned and raced up the steps to join the others out on the street which was a mass of people, a quagmire of confusion.

The darkening sky annihilated the question of whether or not the sun had set — that had occurred at least half an hour ago. Fortunately, most of the workers had already left for home, although some plants worked overtime shifts.

Those who recognised him from his trek through the other buildings and the man whose lighter he had borrowed, approached him for information. "Get away from here!" he yelled. "Move back, into the fields. There's going to be an explosion. *Die bombe!*"

The word 'bomb' sent them scurrying. It wasn't long before loud popping and whistling sounds filled the air, sounds that grew louder as the chain reaction he'd hoped to create occurred.

It lasted almost an hour. And when it was over, when the fire department and the police arrived, when parts of one factory were smouldering, Antoine and Gerlinde had still not appeared.

Karl had been thinking the entire time: they probably demolished one of the brick walls blocking a tunnel and run out another building. Why that hadn't occurred to him, he did not know. His lack of a larger view frightened him and caused him to feel vulnerable. The way mortals felt.

Now, of course, he had an additional problem. He made an excuse and managed to extricate himself from the crowded area as soon as he could. The authorities had questions for him, questions he couldn't, wouldn't answer. Stealing a car and leaving the scene of the crime was the best he could manage.

On the drive back downtown, Karl felt dismal. He had failed dreadfully. Not only had Antoine and Gerlinde escaped, but he was headed back to the hotel where he might find a dead body. The body of Michel. The only one besides himself who could track Gerlinde. And now that Karl was mortal again, he could no longer track her. And even if Michel were alive, he might be in an altered state and unable to track her as well. Which meant they would not find Gerlinde. Ever.

Karl parked the car six blocks from the hotel. He buried his suit jacket and his tie in a trash bin under a mound of fast food wrappers and empty cigarette packages, aware that the collectors were already coming up this street.

With heavy steps, he returned to the hotel, hoping for the best. Expecting the worst.

# CHAPTER TWENTY ONE

"*WILLKOMMEN, ALT LIEBHABER!*" WE THOUGHT you'd never get here."

The scene that greeted Karl was one that filled him with dread. Gerlinde had opened the door, smiling, fangs showing. Even from here, the scent of gunpowder and magnesium clung to her clothing, enough that a mortal like him could pick it up. Through the doorway, Karl saw Michel lying on the bed as he had left him, pale, corpse-like, but possibly not dead. His lips were stained with what looked like more than a few drops of blood. Donata must have been feeding him all last night.

Antoine stood by the window holding Donata in front of him like a doll. He gripped her by the shoulders, her long hair caught in one of his fists so that her head tilted, for dramatic effect, no doubt. Presumably so Karl could easily see the two large raw puncture wounds at the throat. Blood, a fair amount of it, had run down her neck and soaked the front of her dress. The vein in her neck pulsed wildly and her face — paler than usual — looked masklike. Karl assessed the situation quickly — it was Michel who had bitten her, that was clear. The blood was dry and, also, Antoine had none on his lips.

"Karl!" the girl sobbed, betraying the fear the mask concealed, "Help me!"

But, of course, he could not. Not as a mortal. Even if he were still immortal, he couldn't help her. The human part of him wanted to shout at Antoine in disgust, "Unclean Thing!" Wouldn't that sound as if they were all actors in a Werner Herzog movie? But this was not a movie. And where would such theatrics get him?

Karl closed the door and stepped into the room, never taking his eyes off Antoine.

"So," Gerlinde said, "you're mortal again. With his blood." She nodded at Michel's prone form. "I thought you said it wouldn't work."

"No-one knew if it would work."

"Well, it did, and now you're vulnerable."

He glanced at Gerlinde. The impact was startling. The woman he had loved was no more. What happened to her? He did not need to ask too many questions of himself — it was obvious. The change had begun long before Antoine took her away. It was Karl who had made her into a gorgeous fiend. He looked deep into her hypnotic eyes and said simply, "Gerlinde, I'm so sorry."

She blinked once. Understanding lit her eyes. She seemed stunned. Then touched.

And then Antoine's cold laughter filled the room, destroying everything alive in its path. "Yes, you made her a monster, I made you a monster, and now you'll both free me. But first, a snack."

Without warning, he tore the dress from Donata's body. The girl began a scream that he cut short by pressing against the pulsing in her throat. A direct, understandable message came with that action and, from the look on Donata's face, she realised her life was on the line. Clearly, she had no thoughts of suicide now.

"I'll make a deal with you," Karl said. "Take my blood. It's Michel's. What you've wanted all along. Let Gerlinde go and the girl go, and you can have me."

Antoine sneered. "I'll have your blood anyway. As I did before. It's my right."

"Don't worry about me," Donata said. "I don't care if I die and come back. I told you that."

"Who said anything about you coming back?" Antoine told her. He laughed again. Karl was amazed that such a sound could exist in the universe outside of hell. Suddenly, Antoine reared his head back like a snake and snapped it forward, biting viciously into Donata's neck.

She screamed but his hand over her mouth muffled the sound.

Taking Donata's blood would occupy him for only a minute or two or three, depending on how fast he took it. Karl tried to think. His brain felt as if he had attention deficit disorder.

"You look tasty," Gerlinde said, licking her lips. He could see, though, that her heart was not entirely in the words and he took that tiny offering as a good omen.

He scanned the room for a weapon and picked up a chair. Gerlinde knocked it out of his hands. So much for omens.

"Take me," a voice said. A weak but familiar voice. One that reached Antoine's ears.

Antoine let go of Donata and she dropped to the floor like a rag doll. Michel struggled to sit up in the bed, skin pale, eyes glazed. "Drink my blood. You want it bad. You want to be mortal."

"Such submission," Antoine said, obviously pleased with this turn of events.

"Michel, don't do it," Karl said. "It won't help. Save yourself."

But the boy shook his head a little, which seemed to make him dizzy. When he levelled again, he said, "Now I know what everybody else knows. What it's like to love somebody. What it's like to lose them. What it's like to die..." He turned to Antoine. "You can't remember any of that, can you? I feel sorry for you."

The stillness that lasted roughly two seconds felt to Karl like the eye of a hurricane. When it broke, Antoine was all over Michel, sucking his blood in a fury, growling like a deranged beast.

Karl started towards the window, hoping to pull open the curtains, hoping sunrise had happened. He got halfway there when Gerlinde caught him. The demonic look in her eyes seemed unholy. If he didn't know better, he would have thought a crucifix would repel her.

"You took mine, now I get to take yours," she said. She held him tightly, so he could not move.

"Don't worry, lover, tit for tat. I'll be gentle. And after all, I want this to last."

He saw her incisors glisten with saliva, then her head moved closer until he lost sight of the teeth. But he felt them. Suddenly, pain flared in his throat. The sharpness turned to a burning that grew hotter and hotter. Her teeth went beyond skin into muscle, and she held his neck firmly so the vein would not move around and she'd miss it.

Those teeth were serrated razors. Despite the restraint of her steely embrace, he struggled and the vein slipped away from her, back and forth, a game of dodge, one he knew only because he had been on both sides of this game before. But it could not last and the points of her eye teeth tore up enough muscle that he began to groan. And with the pain came numbing and he could no longer feel the muscles to move them. He did feel it, though, when she sliced into the vein. The blood leaving his heart flowed out — he was surprised to be so aware of it physically. It was the first time; when Antoine took him it was so quick he felt nothing. Now he knew what had been going on in all of his victims. They were not just asleep or dazed or numbed. He shuddered.

While she sucked, he listened to the slurping sounds her lips made, listened to the guttural sounds coming out of Antoine. Karl thought, uselessly, If only I could open the drapes! But it was not possible. He could not move. They were all doomed He had become weaker in the last seconds. So very very tired. As if the energy in his body were a solid being lifted out of him, leaving behind ephemeral gas. Michel, at least, would be in shock from such a quick extraction. He would feel little. He might even be unconscious already.

Gerlinde took her time, but alternated between fast and slow as well. Her strength ebbed with the sunrise, but it still outclassed Karl's. Both she and Antoine knew the sun was near the horizon. Whatever benefits Michel's blood would have — directly from the boy and indirectly from Karl — probably would not have an instant effect on them any more than drinking Michel's blood had had on Karl.

Karl lost awareness of his body. All the new-found human sensations disappeared. He seemed to ascend up and away from his body for safety reasons, and saw himself hovering near the ceiling in a kind of white-light form. He became that form, looking down on himself in Gerlinde's arms, at Antoine over Michel in the bed and at Donata struggling to pull herself up. Everything seemed calm and peaceful. Right. He was near fainting — he knew that.

Abruptly, the scene became brighter. A floodlight washed out details, bathing him, bathing everything. So intense, it penetrated his skin and sensation began to return to his arms and legs and face...

Gerlinde screamed. Antoine roared like a demon. Karl's awareness snapped into focus. The light no longer within his mind but outside, illuminating the room.

Donata lay on the floor, drapes piled on top of her; her hand still clutched the fabric. Sunlight cracked the horizon and seeped in through the long picture window.

Antoine dove for the bathroom. En route, Karl noticed patches of blackened skin, where the sunbeams had scorched him. His face was creased in a furious terror. Once he'd made it to safety, Karl saw the door slam shut and heard it locked from within.

Gerlinde had the same idea, but when she managed to stagger to the door, pounding, screaming, Antoine would not open to her.

She cried hysterically, clawing and scratching at the wood. Smoke rose from her skin. "This way," Karl said. But she couldn't move. The paralysis that comes with daylight had locked on to her.

"Don't help her!" Donata cried. "Let her die!"

Karl grabbed Gerlinde around the waist and pulled her backwards a few feet to the closet door. All the while she tried to claw at him, and did manage to tear the skin of his face. "In here," he said. "You'll be safe." She didn't seem to hear anything he said.

Adrenaline surged and Karl knew that if it wasn't for those human glands that could produce superhuman strength on occasion, he would never have been able to shove Gerlinde into the closet and shut the door.

He leaned his back against it.

"Why did you do it?" Donata gasped from the floor.

Karl just shook his head. How could he convey forty years and the debt he felt he owed Gerlinde for what he had done to her, even if she had wanted it. And even if she tried to kill him. No mortal could want this change. They did not have the least idea of its effect, of what they would have to give up or how they would have to exist. And he knew now she could never accept that she would not bear a child. He had not had the right —

"We've got to get out of here," Donata cried. "Michel. Michel!"

Karl looked to where she stared in horror. Michel lay sprawled across the bed, the spread saturated with his blood. The right side of the boy's throat had all but been torn out and the carotid artery still gushed.

"My god!" Karl whispered. He hurried to Michel. The jugular and the vein had both been severed. The vein was the least of his worries. "Hand me those two surgical clamps," he said.

"Where?"

"On the dresser. With the IV equipment." He'd used them to keep his vein open as he'd drained his own blood out. Now they would keep blood in. A clamp to each side of the sliced artery stemmed the blood flow. Hopefully the artery on the other side of Michel's neck would keep blood pumping into his brain. "We've got to get him to a hospital!"

The risk was great, but he saw no alternative at this point. Michel had never had the plant cells in his blood like the others, and his body could not regenerate as quickly or easily. If the boy could be saved, he would need a human surgeon.

"He can't be found in this room. If it were just Antoine," Karl said, "I wouldn't hesitate for a moment. But I don't want Gerlinde discovered."

Karl wrapped Michel in the bedspread. "Call emergency. I hope they can't trace it to a specific room."

Donata leaned heavily on the desk and dialled the number. She stared at Karl and said in a weak voice, "I wish somebody loved me as much as you love her."

He was aware that she was not in good condition. But Michel was in worse shape and the boy had to be Karl's first priority.

Karl carried Michel out of the room, up the emergency stairs to the third floor and left him by the elevator. Outside, the siren sound drew near.

"Come on," Karl said, and led Donata who trailed behind him back down the hallway to the end near the stairwell.

The chambermaid had left several doors of vacated rooms open on three. They ducked into the last room and washed up in the bathroom. Donata's wounds were clean since it was Michel who had made them, but Antoine's larger teeth had opened them further, causing greater damage. But she would live; she only needed rest. She had no strength and had to sit on the edge of the tub while he cleaned her up.

Karl felt his own neck. The puncture wounds were very very sore. In the mirror he saw a man with two raw holes in his throat. He wished there was some sort of medical kit around — both of them could use bandages to stop the blood flow, if not to disguise the wounds, and maybe antiseptic. An anticoagulant in the saliva of his kind — what had formerly been his kind — kept the blood from clotting. They were like vampire bats in that way. Eventually, the anticoagulant would dissolve and the seeping would cease. In the meantime, he handed Donata a wash cloth and took one for himself. "Use this as a compress and apply as much pressure at your throat as you can." Leaving her for a moment, he surveyed the room.

"Can you fold these so we can carry them?" he said, unhooking the drapes from the rod. He removed the bedding, then filled an ice bucket with water, grabbed a couple of towels and the drapes, and motioned for Donata to come as quickly as possible. He was loaded down. She carried the bottled water but even that seemed to be a burden.

He pushed open the stairwell door and moved her inside first. Then he followed. Just as the door closed behind him, he heard a scream, letting them know Michel had been found.

Back on two, he stripped the spread and sheets from the bed in their room, gathered up the drapes from the floor — Donata's bloody finger prints were at the hems but there was nothing they could do about that. Slowly, she removed her black dress — she was exhausted, but he had so much to do, he couldn't really help her. He took off his shirt and added it and her dress to the pile. While Donata removed another dress from her overnight bag and pulled it over her head — he was happy to see it had a neckline high enough to hide her throat — and while Karl packed everything together tightly for disposal, they heard a loud siren cut off just outside the hotel.

"Thank God," Donata said, as she peered out the window.

Fortunately, the bar refrigerator also had bottled water and he used that and what was in the ice bucket to clean up as much as they could. Karl stuffed the bloody towels into the bundle. He hung the drapes and made the bed in a rumpled way that looked like it had been slept in.

"The floor has some blood spots, but I think we can move the bed over it," he said.

He struggled with the heavy frame until it moved the four inches needed. Unfortunately, impressions where the legs had been were left in the carpet. Only the ones at the foot of the bed mattered, and Karl tried to fluff them up with his fingers but didn't have much success.

"This is so if the maid or the cops come in, they'll see things are normal, right?" Donata said.

"More than that. They'll think the bloody fabric came from that other room. It's on the same floor where they'll find Michel. Hopefully it will keep them at bay for a while. Did Michel go out at all after you checked in?"

"Uh, no, I don't think so."

"What about room service?"

"I took the food. I don't think the waiter saw Michel."

"Well, that still leaves the desk clerk —"

"Not really. Michel waited by the elevator while I checked in."

"What name did you sign?"

"Mr. and Mrs. Michel Blak."

Karl lifted an eyebrow. The girl loved theatrics.

He opened the door and went into the hallway cautiously, like a cat. They had not started to clean this floor yet, but the maid would be here soon, and possibly the police would want to check the entire building. Two and three were only a floor apart. Suddenly, he remembered the *I CHING* and the hexagram Wing had thrown — 23. What was the ending of that hexagram? He'd be damned if he could remember now.

He moved down the hallway silently, trying room doors gently on the west side of the floor opposite their room, but they were all locked.

"I can get in," said a voice behind him and he whirled to see Donata dragging herself along the corridor.

"I told you to stay in the room," he whispered.

Donata, leaning against the wall for support, held up one of the plastic key cards.

"How did you get this?"

"I found it on the third floor where we left Michel."

"But it won't fit this room."

"Yes it will." She slid the key card into the lock and the green light flickered. Donata looked up at him. "The chambermaid left it in the room we washed up in."

Quickly they returned to their room. Karl hoisted the bundle of bloody fabric onto his shoulder. Now would be a good time to possess a bit of immortal strength, he thought. "This time, wait here."

He took the bundle to the open room and shoved it out the window. It landed with a soft plop in the courtyard below. It would be found soon, below the window of the only room without drapes, he imagined.

"Do you think Michel will be all right?" she asked as he re-entered their room.

"I don't know," he said truthfully. Nobody could know that. And Karl could not bear to think too much about it right now. "We need to make an appearance at the desk," he said. "Can you do it?"

She nodded and he had to help her stand up. He picked up her black velvet scarf hanging over the back of a chair and tied it around his throat. In the full-length mirror it looked strange, but his face, with the scratches, looked stranger.

"I can fix those," she said, and pulled out her make-up bag. His face was pale enough from blood loss that the liquid foundation blended in.

They left the room with a 'Do Not Disturb' sign on the door. He had to almost carry her down, his arm around her waist. In his ear, her breathing was laboured.

They entered a lobby in a state of turmoil. The police had already arrived. Just as Karl and Donata crossed it to the front desk, several attendants emerged from an elevator pushing a stretcher on which Michel lay pale, comatose.

Donata gripped Karl's arm and a gasp escaped her lips.

They'd bundled Michel to the neck with blankets and IV tubes had been hooked up to his exposed arm. He did not look good, but he did not look dead. Karl knew that his condition was critical and could deteriorate rapidly. That kind of damage and blood loss would kill most people.

They stood with everyone else, watching the stretcher being rolled out the door rapidly. Once the ambulance drew away, and people around them had made comments on the situation, Karl turned Donata towards the desk. She looked pale, her eyes large and as if she was about to cry.

"I'm Herr Blak," he said in German. "Are there any messages for myself or my wife?"

The clerk looked through the message box. "I'm afraid not."

"We're in..." Karl looked at the paper pocket with his key card inside, although he knew the number quite well, "room 23. Would you mind ringing my room when something arrives? I'm expecting a note from my sister."

"Of course, sir. That's not a problem at all."

"I think we'd better take breakfast in our room," he said to Donata. "Is that all right with you, my dear?"

"Yes, of course."

"May we order here, and have room service bring it up?"

"Of course," the clerk said again.

Karl ordered one American breakfast and one continental, with a pot of coffee. "Please charge it to the room," he said.

They had started back towards the elevator when Karl turned and, as an after thought, or so he made it appear, said, "Do you think you could send the maid right up to clean our room?"

The clerk smiled, "Right away."

As he and Donata entered the elevator, she said, "I can't eat. I feel sick."

He looked at the girl. She was paler than normal, moving slowly, gasping with each step. She seemed incredibly weak. In her condition, her body having to contend with the AIDS virus, all that had happened would be very damaging to her.

"You need rest," he told her as they entered the room. "We'll stay in here. I wanted it impressed in the clerk's mind that I'm Mr. Blak and that everything is normal. Is he the one who was on duty when you checked in?"

"Yes, I think so."

"All right. When room service brings the food, I'll get him to bring it in so he will see both of us. But when the maid arrives, hide under the bed."

"Why?"

A knock came on the door and Karl asked, "*Wer gehen?*"

"*Der zhimmermadhen.*"

The maid appeared almost instantly, and Donata barely managed to get under the bed. The woman made up the bed under which Donata lay, straightened things in the room, opening the drapes. He'd been engaging her in conversation the whole time, acting like a tourist, wondering where would be a good place to go for dinner, but maybe his sister would have some ideas when he heard from her. No, she wasn't from Hanover, but lived in London now. Her husband was playing with the philharmonic in town, and Karl and Donata were vacationing and wasn't it fortunate he and his sister could meet up? When the chambermaid tried to go into the bathroom, Karl said, "My wife is having a bath. I'll just take the clean towels."

Breakfast arrived about ten minutes after the maid left. The server brought the food into the room, saw Karl, saw Donata seated at the table where he placed the tray, and then Karl tipped him generously and he left.

"Is he the one who came before?" Karl asked Donata.

"No. There was an older man before."

"All right, it doesn't matter. He didn't see Michel. This one saw me."

The smell of the food hit him full blast. Karl suddenly realised that not only was he exhausted and depleted, but he was also hungry. Now he knew why his stomach had been bothering him on Eisenbergerstrasse — the last meal of solid food he'd eaten had been in 1845. He was starving! He'd forgotten that mortal bodies needed fuel too, and regularly.

He sat down and devoured the American breakfast. Donata wanted only coffee, but he insisted she eat part of a croissant from the Continental, and Karl polished off the other one and the two Danish pastries. She had one cup of coffee, he had the rest.

The smells and taste overwhelmed to him. Everything was distinct. Delicious. Delightful! Some of these items he was eating for the first time. The coffee had an instantly rejuvenating effect and he felt a burst of energy.

Donata, overcome, lay down on the bed and curled into a foetal position. "I hope Michel will be all right. How can we find out?"

"I expect we'll see something on the TV news." He switched on the TV to the German news channel and used the remote to lower the volume.

The girl was both sick and grief-stricken. He could see that. He didn't know what to do for her or what to tell her. He didn't know much of anything. He checked the clock radio beside the bed — eleven in the morning.

A maniac vampire slept in their bathtub, and another one — his former love — was curled on the closet floor. Both of them would revive at sunset. And he didn't have a plan.

"Why are we staying here?" Donata said in a small voice. "We should go. Before they wake up."

Karl could hardly stand to look at her. He opened his arms and she crawled into them like a child — the child that she was — desperate for reassurance.

"I've been thinking about that much. *You* should go. You need to be in a safe place, and that's not here. We'll get a couple of hours sleep — I'll set the alarm — then I want you out of here."

"What about you?"

"I've got to stay here. Face this. It's got to end here, one way or another."

"What's your plan?"

He shook his head dully. "I wish I had one."

He switched on the alarm on the bedside clock, and set it for three o'clock. That would give them four hours sleep. Not nearly enough to recover. But it was better than nothing.

# CHAPTER TWENTY TWO

H E WOKE DISORIENTED. NO SENSE OF TIME OR place. His head turned left. The drapes were open. Outside the window, light had faded from the sky.

Then he saw the clock radio and the red numbers 1900. He had some thought of having set it. Had he slept through it?

He turned his head right to find Donata lying next to him very still. He reached over and shook her. Her arm was icy cold, and rigid.

"She's dead," a voice said from a dark corner of the room. A voice he recognised.

Gerlinde stood and walked to the end of the bed. "I guess the blood loss was too much for her."

"She had AIDS. The blood loss put her over the edge."

He felt different. He couldn't identify it at first, because he also felt the same. And then he realised what was going on — his body was already reverting. He was not immortal yet, but the signs were there, internally. Subtle but unmistakable.

Karl sat up. And instantly he saw something entirely unexpected — Gerlinde, as he had known her when they first met. The girl she had been. I'm dreaming, he thought. This cannot be.

But it was. The blood she had consumed from him last night, Michel's blood, had made her mortal again.

She touched the post at the foot of the bed. "I... I can't believe it," she said. "I never thought this could happen. I'm alive again, the way I was —"

Karl heard a noise. He snapped his head towards the bathroom. The door was still closed.

"He's in there," Gerlinde said, her voice bitter. Karl got to his feet. He moved around the bed, and she grabbed his arm as he passed. He paused long enough to look at her, to listen to some of what she said. "I... I don't know what happened to me."

"He controlled you," he said, words they both wanted to hear, wanted to believe.

She shook her head. "No. It was me. I'm responsible for my decisions. Karl, I don't know if you can ever forgive me..."

He looked at her as if she were a stranger and that look silenced her. She *was* a stranger to him They both felt it. The woman he'd known when she was mortal, the one he brought over, the one who had been with him for so many nights over so many decades, with whom he had shared so much, that woman was no more.

He felt cold towards her, that was the only way he could describe it to himself. All that she had meant to him had vanished. In her place stood a betrayer. Someone he not only could no longer trust, but a woman who had shattered his ability to trust.

He pulled away and walked to the bathroom door. Karl tried the knob but it was still locked from the inside. He used foot power and, after a dozen kicks, knocked the door off its hinges.

The shower curtain still surrounded the tub. Karl didn't know what he would find, but prepared for an attack. He stepped a bit back from the tub and in one quick sweep, shoved the plastic aside.

What lay in the bathtub shocked him, yet it was so clear. Antoine had become mortal all right — Michel's blood accomplished that. But so did Donata's blood.

This one who had been larger than life, who always seemed nine feet tall, capable of the impossible, lay pale and shrivelled. Small like a child. Dry skin and white lips, his body covered with lesions. Eyes glazed, dull, childlike, sunken into his skull-like head. Only a hole for a mouth, the rest of the flesh rotting already. A collapsed, withered face. Hands already of the dead. He gasped and wheezed, unable to breathe easily.

Clearly, Antoine had contracted Donata's disease. Michel's blood in one of their own would change the cells back to mortal.

But the infected blood had been in Antoine's body at the same time. Michel's blood probably attacked the vampiric aberrant cells first. But the AIDS virus must have been working at the same moments to infect Antoine's newly mortal blood cells. Michel had been able to ingest HIV tainted blood with no ill effects. But when Antoine took that blood and the complicated biochemical process of transforming vampiric blood back to normal began, the HIV virus ran riot.

As Karl looked down on Antoine, hardly believing what he saw, terrified this was some trick, that Antoine would spring up any second and destroy him. He thought: both of them will revert to immortal in a couple of days or less, just like me. But Antoine, he knew, would not live a couple of days. He would not live the night.

Karl heard a commotion in the room, voices, and left the bathroom. André, David, Morianna and Wing had arrived. Gerlinde stood pressed against the wall in the corner, looking frightened.

"You're... you're mortal!" André said, glancing from Karl to Gerlinde and back. "Who's this?" he asked, nodding at Donata's body.

"A pure blood," Wing said before Karl could answer.

"I can explain everything later," Karl said. "But we've got to get to Michel —"

"We got him. He's with the others. He's safe. He'll recover."

"In... in what state."

"We don't know yet. They're giving him blood."

Guilt washed over Karl. He had almost killed André's son. That was something he could not expect his friend to ever forgive him for. André stepped towards him, as if reading his thoughts. Of course, he could. He was immortal, and Karl was not.

André placed a hand on his arm. "We'll talk about it all later. When we're safely away from here. Let's go."

Karl nodded. He glanced at Gerlinde who looked at all of them with horror on her face. Morianna had approached her, but he could see Gerlinde felt boxed into the corner. These beings were predators to her now. And, more than that — they had not so long ago been her friends. Before she sided with their enemy.

"Come here first," Karl said, specifically to David and Morianna. "There's something you need to witness."

He led them into the bathroom. The others followed and crowded in the doorway.

"I don't believe this," David said quietly.

Morianna said nothing but the look on her face was one Karl had never seen before. She wanted nothing more than to tear Antoine limb from limb.

"Let's kill him," André said. "Destroy the bastard."

"We don't need to," Karl said. "He's dying of AIDS. Will likely die tonight. He's mortal — as you can all see. From his breathing, his colour, his skin, I'd say it's a question of just a few hours."

"The three of us should take his blood," David said, his voice hard. He glanced at Morianna and Karl. "Drain him dry, the way he drained us."

"I can't," Karl said. "The HIV would infect me. And with you and Morianna, I'm not sure what would happen — Michel's blood is in Antoine, as is Donata's — the girl. You might end up becoming like him — mortal and infected."

"He doesn't deserve this easy death," André said.

Karl watched Antoine's face as all this was being discussed. Despite his decrepit state, Antoine had not lost his smug, superior look. Impending death did not humble him. The others saw this better than Karl did.

"Why?" Morianna snapped.

Karl looked at her. She stared directly into Antoine's eyes, unafraid. She was asking him why he had been so violent. Why he had forced the change of them, specifically. Why he could not adapt and learn a modicum of co-operation. She was asking him why he was evil.

278

But if Karl had learned one thing, it was this: there are no reasons for evil, no answers, no excuses. Evil simply exists. In the past, he could not have just accepted that. But now he could. He'd been through too much. Through the death phase. He'd sacrificed almost everything.

Despite Antoine's deteriorating state and how close true death hovered, he did not deign to answer. Instead, he laughed. A laugh Karl had heard so often in his dreams, in his mind, in reality. The sound conveyed everything: 'I am unrepentant! I will always be unrepentant!' It conveyed nothing.

In the blink of an eye, Morianna crouched low. Her claws slashed at his wrists, his throat, everywhere and anywhere she could find a vein, severing them, avoiding the arteries — clearly she wanted to drain him, but she wanted this to last. "If not for myself, then for David and Karl. For Michel. And the ones you murdered. But especially for Chloe and Kaellie. Die!"

Blood flowed from Antoine's mortal body in all directions. It soon painted his body, dyed the clothing he wore, stained the enamel of the tub crimson. The veins had no reason to stay open and, whenever they began to close, Morianna slashed them again.

More than anything, Karl knew that the only humiliation Antoine might experience, if he did experience any, was having to die with all of them watching and gloating over his demise. That gave Karl no small pleasure.

It took an hour for the lungs to give up the struggle for air, for the heart to weary of beating, for the blood to cease its flow out of the openings and wash down the drain. His dull eyes stared straight up, like some distorted demonic angel calling on heaven to remember him. But heaven had forgotten Antoine long ago.

"We need to make sure he's dead," David said.

"He's mortal. He's dead. He can't come back," Karl assured him.

"I agree," Morianna added. "It is clear to all of us that the life energy has departed."

They left him there, left the room and, as they moved to the elevator, Karl said, "Where's Gerlinde?"

"She left when we moved to the bathroom," Wing said. "I did not think it wise to stop her."

"No," Karl said, resigned, "it's good you let her go. I don't know if this is what she wanted or not. I know the change isn't permanent. I'm already reverting. And she took Michel's blood indirectly, through me — I imagine the mortal state won't last as long for her as it has for me. And it wasn't very long at all."

She was gone. Antoine was gone. He felt so little about that. How could it be? To love someone so long and so well, and to hate another to the core of your being, and then to have them disappear from your world... It was as though neither had ever existed. As if both had been just dreams, dreams he needed. Ones he would, from time to time, resurrect in his memory. One of the two he would miss very much.

Wing and Morianna went down the stairs, but André and David took the elevator with Karl. As they waited, André suddenly turned to Karl and asked, "What was it like? Being mortal again?"

It was so unlike André to ask a question, so peculiar that when the elevator door opened, Karl did not move to get on. He looked at André and David, his brothers in blood. Everything changes, all the time, but not all changes are for the worst.

Karl thought for a moment. "Being mortal was... how can I put it... supernatural."